Susan Sallis is one of the most popular writers of women's fiction today. Her Rising family sequence of novels has now become an established classic saga, and *Summer Visitors, By Sun and Candlelight, An Ordinary Woman, Daughters of the Moon, Sweeter than Wine, Water under the Bridge, Touched by Angels, Choices, Come Rain or Shine, The Keys to the Garden, The Apple Barrel* and *Sea of Dreams* are well-loved bestsellers.

www.booksattransworld.co.uk

TOUCHED
BY ANGELS

Susan Sallis

CORGI BOOKS

TOUCHED BY ANGELS
A CORGI BOOK : 9780552144667

Originally published in Great Britain by Bantam Press,
a division of Transworld Publishers

PRINTING HISTORY
Bantam Press edition published 1996
Corgi edition published 1996

9 10

Set in 10/11pt New Baskerville by
Hewer Text Composition Services, Edinburgh.

Corgi Books are published by Transworld Publishers,
61–63 Uxbridge Road, London W5 5SA,
A Random House Group Company.

Addresses for Random House Group Ltd companies outside the UK
can be found at: www.randomhouse.co.uk
The Random House Group Ltd Reg. No. 954009.

Printed and bound in Great Britain by
Cox & Wyman Ltd, Reading, Berkshire.

The Random House Group Limited supports The Forest Stewardship
Council (FSC), the leading international forest certification organisation.
All our titles that are printed on Greenpeace approved FSC certified paper
carry the FSC logo. Our paper procurement policy can be found at:
www.rbooks.co.uk/environment.

To Jane and Mike

CHAPTER ONE

1941

The Bluebell School for Girls, which occupied seventeenth-century buildings above Bristol, was evacuated to Gallenwick House on Exmoor in January of 1941. Already the centre of the city had suffered severe bombing and the recently appointed headmistress of the school, Dr Wilkie, made her decision during the Christmas holiday with unqualified support from staff and parents alike.

Most of the fifth-formers, rising seventeen and coming up to their matriculation, were day-girls and vociferously against what they saw as banishment. They quickly discovered that there was no cinema within fifteen miles of Gallenwick House and any male company was likely to come from Lyn Abbey, a turreted monastery built on a finger of land pointing out to sea; even that was ten miles away.

Mrs Maitland, school secretary for as long as anyone could remember and therefore very much in the know, was besieged by three of the girls on the first day of that winter term. She looked at them humorously over the top of her three-bank Oliver typewriter; she knew how they felt. She wasn't all that keen on the thought of the coming isolation. Nevertheless she spoke rallyingly.

'As Bluebells, you should know where your duty lies, girls. You want to make your parents proud of you, surely?'

'How can they be proud of us when we're a million miles away?' Vallery McKinley said, opening her enormous blue eyes and spreading her hands palms upwards.

'Exaggeration, Vallery,' Mrs Maitland pointed out.

'Hyperbole, even,' Morag Heyward added for good measure and because she was trying to lighten the awfulness of leaving home and parents just at this time.

Vallery made a hideous face to stop herself from blubbing. 'I shall miss Teddy's birthday. He will be twenty-one. That's important.'

Mrs Maitland said sternly, 'More important to keep you safe, girls. Your brother will have other birthdays, Vallery. You must see this thing in perspective.'

'But he'll be posted soon! He's bound to be! They won't keep him here much longer. And if he's sent abroad – Africa or somewhere – he might never have another birthday!'

Morag said quickly, 'Knowing your Teddy, he'll wangle a car and petrol and come to see us.' She grinned at Mrs Maitland. 'I suppose we'll be allowed visitors, Mrs Maitie? Even prisoners are allowed visitors!'

Janice Mears, silently petulant till now, said suddenly, 'You're right, Morrie. That's what we are – prisoners! Dr Wilkie thinks we don't work hard enough so she's in-interring us in this gallows place to make sure we never have any fun – just work, work, work!'

Morag said, 'I think you mean incarcerate, Jannie. Interring means burying people.'

'Well, that's what I meant – so you need not try to be clever, Morrie! We'll be buried alive in that ghastly hole! I'd just like to know why it's called Gallowick. Was it where they hung people, Maitie?'

Mrs Maitland looked at the pile of correspondence still to be done. 'Gallenwick, dear. It's called Gallenwick. And Dr Wilkie stayed there as a girl – about your age I imagine – just after the Great War. She loved it. When she heard it was empty she thought you would love it too.'

For a moment the girls were silent. They had been

brought up to dislike ungraciousness and suddenly it seemed they were all being ungracious.

Mrs Maitland saw her opportunity and went on, 'Her main goal is your safety. Obviously. Bristol is a danger zone as you well know.'

Vallery said in a small voice, 'But I actually live in Clevedon, Maitie. And lots of people have actually been evacuated there from London. Actually.'

Jannie said, 'It's only that it'll be like a nunnery. No male company for ten miles then just a houseful of monks!'

Morag said very quietly indeed, 'If anything is going to happen to my parents, I'd prefer to be with them.'

Mrs Maitland dealt with only one of those statements. 'Really Janice, I am afraid you are becoming a very shallow person!' And she rolled a fresh piece of paper into the Oliver and turned a shoulder on the girls. But she was going to miss Bristol too, for a variety of reasons. She began to type fiercely and automatically and let her mind range over the possibilities of Hitler being assassinated. Tomorrow at the latest.

They had Saturday at home. A special coach was being attached to the Cornishman the next day. It would be slipped off into the sidings at Exeter and coupled to the Barnstaple service. There they would unload and transfer into local buses which would run specially that Sunday to transport them directly to Gallenwick. The whole journey would take six hours.

'It's practically the whole day,' Vallery mourned to her mother as they sat over tea and toast in the large Georgian house on the outskirts of Clevedon. 'Not a hope in hell of coming home for a weekend or anything!'

Margaret McKinley shook her head gently. 'If Dr Wilkie could hear you . . .' she murmured. But her heart wasn't in it. Vallery at seventeen was Margaret's best friend. They looked alike; their riotously curly hair and round girlish faces, dominated by big blue eyes, often gave an impression of feminine helplessness. They were not helpless, though they were both capable of exploiting their Shirley Temple looks at times. But more than the physical resemblance, they thought alike. They liked people; they were outgoing; they were very loving. For Margaret the little town of Clevedon clinging to the Bristol Channel bubbled when Val was in it. Together they could take walks, pay calls, attend the local dramatic society – it was all fun. Without her, life would seem dull. The house, even the town, would be silent, cut off, claustrophobic. Margaret fought a stupid wave of panic which, after all, was only the menopause, and said bravely, 'It's a wonderful thing she's doing, actually, Val. Taking her girls into safety. The school has definitely improved since she took over. No doubt about it.'

Vallery looked at the toast on the end of her fork and replaced it next to a red cavern in the fire. She allowed her eyes to fill with tears now; she knew her mother would cry too and then they would both feel better.

'We're not her girls though! At least, I'm not. I'm your girl. Yours and Daddy's and Teddy's! And you're already forgetting that! When I come home there won't be room for me any more! You'll have the house full of evacuees and they'll all love you because everyone does and you'll be taking them to the Saturday matinée at the Curzon and picking up shells on the beach for them in the summer— '

Margaret cast her toasting fork into the fender and buried her face in her hands.

'Oh Val, how could you! As if – as if— '

And Val threw down her fork as well and they dissolved into each other's arms. Eric McKinley, returning from the golf club early because the nights were drawing in, opened the door, saw the wailing women and closed it gently again. It was cold in the hall, but he would give them five minutes. He frowned wondering what would happen once Val and Teddy had gone. The house would either be requisitioned or filled with evacuees. He thought he would prefer the former. He had other property in Clevedon; a cottage up on the hill with good sea views. They could move there.

Engine sounds came from outside and he opened the front door. A Royal Air Force transport lorry was at the gate, just disgorging Teddy.

'Hello, Dad!' Teddy had also inherited his mother's curly hair and blue eyes, but he was taller than any of them. He pumped his father's hand looking down at him humorously. 'Had the chance of a lift and a twenty-four-hour pass. Couldn't let the kid disappear without saying goodbye, could I?'

Eric McKinley clapped his son on the shoulder and thanked God for his family. If only they could get through this blasted war. That was all he asked.

The drawing room door burst open and Val flew through into Teddy's arms.

'I knew you'd come! Oh Teddy, isn't it just awful? I'll miss your birthday – and mine as well of course! And we won't be able to go out picking mushrooms this spring . . . oh Teddy!'

'Steady on old girl. Keep the hair in place. There is a war on, you know!'

'But why can't we be together? I could face Hitler, Goebbels, Goering – even that nasty little Himmler – if we were together! But being so far away . . . and I bet you a million pounds I'll have to share with Jannie Mears instead of Morrie!'

'You like Jannie!' He was laughing, holding her away, moving her shoulders gently in remonstrance.

'She's shallow. Dear Mrs Maitland said she was. And Maitie never says anything horrid.'

'Then I'll telephone Dr Wilkie and make sure you room with Morag Heyward,' Margaret said firmly. 'That is one small thing we can do.'

11

'Mummy, don't you dare! Dr Wilkie will think I'm a spoiled brat and put me in a dungeon or something! And if Jannie ever heard of it— '

'Yes, I see your point. All right, darling. You'll have to take pot luck. We'll all keep our fingers crossed.'

'It won't be that bad either, Val,' Teddy said, slinging his kitbag at the foot of the stairs and making for the fire and the toasting forks. 'Rather like those ghastly boarding school books you always loved. You know, midnight feasts and pillow fights.'

Vallery picked up a cushion and hurled it at him. 'Like this, you mean? That's my toast and you've just put a whole week's butter ration on it!'

Eric McKinley watched and smiled and prayed that nothing would happen to any of them. He looked at his wife. She too was watching the children and smiling. But the smile was tight and the large blue eyes were dark with fear.

Eric said sharply, 'Settle down children! Let your mother sit there, Teddy. Margaret, drink some tea. Lean back. Relax.' He settled her with a cushion behind her back. 'The rector was in the club house. He asked after you.'

Margaret smiled and felt the panic die down.

'How kind,' she said.

Henry Heyward had two operations scheduled for that Saturday and left the house as usual at nine o'clock to walk along Park Row to the infirmary. Morag, wrapped in her mother's old dressing-gown, sat in the oriel window which overhung the top of Park Street and watched him as he strode past the university and dropped out of sight down the hill past Red Lodge. Since she was old enough to treasure various routines, she had made a point of watching her father come and go from the infirmary. Her mother had told her how, as a small baby, she had first spotted him from this very window and leapt with excitement. Morag knew what pleasure that would

12

have given him; she continued it deliberately whenever she could.

He was a distinguished figure in his morning suit and top hat. She smiled, unembarrassed now that he wore such old-fashioned clothes. 'When I was training in Edinburgh, all the surgeons wore formal dress and top hats,' he had told her when she asked, at the tender age of nine, why he dressed up to cut people open. 'I promised myself I would do the same.' He smiled. 'It's one of my idiosyncrasies.' She had reduced her mother to tears of laughter when she was overheard telling Vallery McKinley that her father dressed in his 'hideous crinklies' when he went to work. The joke was now part of their family vocabulary and only Aunt Harriet, matron of a private hospital in Edinburgh, disapproved.

Morag got on to her knees on the window-seat and leaned out of the window knowing her father would turn just before he disappeared from view. He did, stopping long enough to remove his top hat and salute her gravely. She waved back, clutching the neck of the dressing-gown close. It was one of the coldest days of that year so far.

Behind her, Lucy Heyward said, 'Close that window immediately, Morrie! You'll not only catch your death of cold but you are exposing my dressing-gown – bought in 1929 I'll have you know – to the vulgar gaze of anyone who happens to look up!'

Lucy had the happy knack of clothing a reprimand or instruction in a swab of humour. Morag closed the window, smiling in spite of herself. Even so her mother knew.

'You were thinking that that is the last time for ages you will watch your father walk to work,' she said matter-of-factly, setting a breakfast tray on the table and clattering tea cups unnecessarily. 'You were seeing yourself as Sister Anne, waiting at the window. Wondering how he will manage when Sister Anne is no longer there!'

'Mummy!' Morag remonstrated though smiling help-lessly. 'You really are awful! I'm not as melodramatic as you make out!' She met her mother's mild grey gaze; her smile developed unwillingly. 'All right. I was thinking all that stuff. But . . . it's true, isn't it? It'll be Easter before I'm home. That's three months. It is . . . rather a long time.'

'Not in the context of our lives.' Lucy poured tea thankful that her hand was steady. 'I hope you can be cheerful for Val and Jannie. It will hit them hard.'

'Why should it be worse for them?' Morag asked, aggrieved. 'I think you and me and Daddy are closer than Val and her lot. And as for Jannie— '

'It's not a competition, darling.' Lucy placed tea cup and toast rack within easy reach and sat back. 'You'll all feel the parting badly. Of course. But you are stronger than they are, Morrie.' Her gaze was as steady as her hand; they could have been discussing plans for a morning's shopping. 'You can make it worse or better. That's the sort of strength you have.'

Morag remembered the conversation yesterday in Mrs Maitland's office. She had been conscious even then of trying to help Val and Jannie – and even Mrs Maitland herself.

She said in a low voice, 'I don't think I want to have that sort of strength, Mummy. In a way it's easier to weep and wail like Val, or go looking for boys like Jannie.'

'Of course.' Her mother smiled gently and took a piece of toast. If Morag had hoped for some qualifying crumb of comfort, she was disappointed. Her mother changed the subject and said briskly, 'Daddy has a treat for you this morning, Morrie. If you can be outside the operating theatre at midday – prompt, mind – he'll let you scrub up and watch a really nice straightforward appendectomy. How's that?'

Morag was delighted. She wasn't quite sure whether she wanted to be a doctor or a nurse, but she certainly wanted to be associated with surgery.

'Oh!' She clasped her hands and grinned at her mother across the table. 'It's the glare of the lights and the smell of the ether, don't you know!'

Lucy laughed and began to butter another piece of toast.

'That's my girl,' she said approvingly.

Henry Heyward emerged into Park Row at three o'clock that afternoon, his daughter on his arm, to find an inch of snow making even the smokescreen canisters into objects of beauty. He pushed his top hat firmly down to his ears; his 'hideous crinklies' were in any case enveloped in an enormous Burberry. He tucked Morag's arm into his and advised her to watch her footing.

'Yes, I know it's all too exquisite for words, my dear.' He clutched at a lamppost as his leather soles slipped uncertainly beneath him. 'But we don't really want you laid up and unable to go tomorrow.'

'I say, what a splendid idea!' Morag said in a deliberately jovial voice. Then, more seriously, 'Perhaps we won't go actually, Daddy. The train might not get through.'

'The train will be all right. It's the bus trip from Barnstaple that worries me. They get a lot of snow up on Exmoor.'

Morag felt some of the weight of her 'strength' momentarily lifted. 'Dr Wilkie won't take any chances,' she said.

'Especially as the weather will keep the German air force at home,' Henry agreed. They looked at each other conspiratorially. 'It would be rather nice to have one of our usual Sundays, wouldn't it?'

Morag said, 'We could take the sledge on the Downs!'

'There are some chestnuts left from Christmas. We could roast them,' Henry said. 'Meanwhile, we'll wait here for the bus, child. I refuse to shuffle the length of Park Row.'

He watched his daughter as they huddled under the

15

awning of Brown's Bootmakers. He was, he knew it, overweeningly proud of her. She had the dark good looks of the Heyward women combined with Lucy's strength of character. He had no doubt she would be able to deal with anything life meted out to her; he could only hope it would include a lot of happiness.

He said, 'Morrie, why don't you tuck your plait inside your raincoat? It's fraying out and each little hair is supporting a snowflake. The weight of it might pull your head off quite soon.'

She complied, shivering as its coldness struck through her cardigan, blouse, liberty bodice and vest. She said, 'I don't know why you won't let me cut my hair! It really is such a nuisance hanging down like a cat's tail all the time!'

'Don't be selfish, dear. It's one of my great pleasures.'

Morag laughed. 'Oh well, in that case . . .'

She recalled the last two hours and her father's deft movements above the supine figure on the operating table. She loved watching him work, loved the feeling of excitement he generated in his team. He had told her once that surgery was like exploring. 'There's so much we don't know yet,' he expounded. 'The spleen for instance. We really do not understand the spleen. But we will do. One day. The appendix on the other hand is rather like the dodo and has probably outlived its usefulness. But who knows? We must keep an open mind.'

Today it had been familiar ground and he had guided one of the students through it as much for Morag's sake as the student's. 'Incision just there, Mr Buckley, if you please.' Then, 'One day we might reduce the length of the incision even more. Less knife, more life. As it is, we know what we are doing here. Just two inches . . . pressure here and here, Mr Buckley, and the offending vermiform will surely reveal itself.'

The blind-ended tube emerged rather like a solid boil.

It was distended beyond belief and seemed on the point of rupture.

'Plenty of time,' her father said reassuringly. 'Now let us see how neatly we can manage this, Mr Buckley.' And later, 'Splendid, Mr Buckley! Simply splendid!' He glinted at the young man. 'Just think, if you had gone in for pediatrics the baby would doubtless be named for you!'

There had been muffled chuckles all around. All the students liked Mr Heyward.

Morag looked up the road; the tram was emerging through the fog of snow.

'Thank you, Daddy. I enjoyed this afternoon very much.'

'I thought you might.' Henry hugged her shoulders suddenly. 'Remember, my dear, that when things get you down, it helps to work.'

'Yes.'

She did not doubt it. As she clambered onto the platform of the tram she thought, I must remember this day for ever; photograph it on my brain; watching Daddy from the oriel window; breakfast with Mummy, her pale English face and canny eyes; snow, muffled sounds; the satisfaction of helping someone; Daddy and me . . . together . . . going to see Mummy.

Janice Mears lived with her mother in a red brick villa overlooking Durdham Down. The house had been built in 1936 and was designed to make the least possible work. Which could have been why it was so uninteresting and characterless. Jannie watched the snow drift across the observatory and thought about her father who was in Africa under General Wavell. The war was going well out there. His last letter had been heavily blue-pencilled, but she knew from the Pathé News at the cinema that the Italians were not only being pushed right back into Libya, they were surrendering in their hundreds. There had been newsreel of our Tommies, cigarettes in mouths,

17

stripped to the waists, giving Mr Churchill's victory sign to the cameras, grinning for all they were worth. Jannie had narrowed her eyes fiercely, trying to pick out her father. He could have been an officer of course, but he had wanted to join the P.B.I. – the Poor Bloody Infantry – and actually do some fighting. Her mother had said it was only because he was frightened of responsibility. But Jannie knew better. She understood his loneliness; understood that her mother made the loneliness worse; understood his need for popularity which he could only find in public houses. It was like that for her with Morag and Vallery, she knew she was the odd one out and they only let her make a threesome because they were sorry for her. She was the plain one of the three, she knew that. Morag looked like a Red Indian princess and Vallery was everybody's favourite little girl. Jannie had straw-coloured hair that somehow missed being golden, and pale blue eyes that reminded her of marbles. Her nose was not snub and pretty like Val's nor classic like Morag's. It was just a nose stuck in the middle of a small, pinched-looking face with cheek-bones that somehow pushed the marble-eyes upwards, half closing them somehow. She looked as if she had a perpetual cold. She hated her face. She hated her thinness. She had no breasts and no hips. She hungered for admiration and knew she could only get it from men. Certain men. Her father thought she was all right. He'd called her a pocket Venus once. She liked that. A couple of the boys from the grammar school had trailed her home one day from hockey and called after her, 'Hey, Blondie! You with the legs!' And she had smiled sideways at them as she scuttled into the house. And there had been one or two 'uncles' . . . maybe the present one. Marius. She wasn't sure. She knew her mother sometimes liked to include her when she was with one of the 'uncles' but that was probably because Jannie's paleness made her own looks even more vivid.

She frowned through the window at the snow and

wondered about the monks of Lyn Abbey. What sort of men were they?

Her mother's voice called from upstairs.

'Jan! How many sets of underwear was it?'

'Six!' She turned to go upstairs and check her case. She was willing to bet that Mrs Heyward and Mrs McKinley did not have to ask questions like that. Eve was hopeless. She stood now in the middle of Jannie's bedroom staring irritably at the open case on the bed and tapping her bottom teeth with the mother-of-pearl cigarette holder Marius had given her last night.

'Darling, you simply have not got six sets of anything any more!' Eve Mears looked at her daughter and frowned, wishing she would brush her hair more often and try to smile. 'I don't quite know where your Dr Wilkie gets her clothing coupons, but you haven't got any left!'

'Oh, Eve. You know very well you pinched my coupons for that evening dress! Let me have some of your camis, for goodness' sake. Marius will get some black market coupons and you can buy some new ones.'

Eve giggled delightedly. 'Camiknicks! That will shock Doc Wilkie! Righty-ho, my darling.' She disappeared into her room and came back with a huge bundle of glamorous underwear. 'Might as well go the whole hog!' She stuffed them anyhow into the case. 'Curse about this snow, baby, isn't it? Hope to goodness Marius can get through.'

Jannie made a face. 'Oh he's not coming tonight, is he? It's my last night home!'

'Oh darling, you don't mind, surely? He's heard of this most marvellous nightclub. Somewhere underground, would you believe. It sounds so exciting. He'll have some petrol – we could drop you off at Morrie's if you like.'

'Eve! She'll want her parents to herself, I can't go barging in like that.' Jannie drooped over to the window and looked down the garden. What on earth could she do with herself all evening? 'Wish Pops was here,' she said unthinkingly.

'Darling, are you deliberately trying to upset me? And

19

why do you call him Pops? His name is Ronald. You manage to call me Eve, surely you could— '

'Sorry.'

'It's all right, baby.' Eve Mears hesitated. 'Why don't you come with us? Marius will dance with you.' She smiled and Jannie knew she had been right. Eve used her as a foil. Something else too, only Jannie couldn't think of a word for it. Titivation?

'Do come, Jannie. It's our last evening together for God knows how long— '

'Easter, Ma.'

'Jannie – don't call me Ma! If you so much as breathe that dreadful word, I shall send you home in a taxi! I mean it!'

'Sorry, Eve. In any case Marius won't be keen.'

Eve lowered her lashes and looked at Jannie meaningfully. 'Marius does what Eve tells him, darling. That is how it should be. And that is a better lesson than anything your Dr Wilkie – or Willie or whatever your ghastly friends call her – will teach you!'

Jannie suddenly hated Marius and hated her mother being friends with him when Pops was in Africa. But at the same time, wondering whether he might be one of those uncles who told her she wasn't 'half bad', the whole scenario became exciting though she did not know why.

'All right,' she said ungraciously. 'If I can borrow your red dress.'

'*Certainement, chérie!*' Eve whirled into her own room and fetched the dress; she had discovered long ago it drained her face of any colour. 'Take it to Exmoor with you, sweetheart. You're bound to have socials and things. You can wear it down there.'

Jannie felt another pang of excitement.

Marius – surprisingly – offered no objections to taking Jannie with them. The club was in one of the old wine cellars by the docks and was quite safe from raids.

However, the snow kept the Germans at bay that particular night and seemed to intensify the party atmosphere into near hysteria. Eve danced a great deal with one of the Free French officers who were based in Bristol and Marius took Jannie onto the floor and tried to ignore her ineptness at the foxtrot.

'Stand on my feet,' he said briefly after her third 'Sorry'. She did so and suddenly he seemed to be enjoying it, holding her waist low down and pressing their thighs together quite painfully. She felt a sense of power but was still glad when Eve insisted tipsily on going home.

'The kid's got a long journey tomorrow,' she said to Marius, staring at him angrily as he lounged in his chair, his arm across Jannie's shoulders. 'She's only sixteen!'

'Seventeen next month,' Jannie reminded her.

Marius looked down at her. 'Seventeen, eh? She's like a waif. Something about her. She'll be old enough to get married next month then?'

'With my permission!' Eve snapped.

Jannie hated it when they talked about her as if she wasn't there. She reached for her school coat which was over the chair and shouldered into it clumsily. And, still bickering about everything, Marius and Eve followed her to the cellar steps.

Marius had never been so ardent. Eve tried to protest at one point and he said fiercely, 'It's your fault for bringing the kid! All your fault!' And she gasped and surrendered herself to him.

On the other side of the wall, Jannie pressed her ear to one of the tumblers from the bathroom and listened. Then she got into bed shivering convulsively. It was the coldest night of the year. She prayed that it wouldn't stop them leaving tomorrow for the gallows place on Exmoor. And she prayed that they would stay there for ever and she need not see Eve or Marius again. Because, perhaps then, she could also stop hating herself.

CHAPTER TWO

1941

Exmoor proved to be as the girls had expected. The thin layer of snow that had covered Bristol became head-high drifts as the Barnstaple train climbed from Exeter through deserted landscape to the lonely heights of the moor. The total lack of form to the outside view robbed it of its prettiness and made it into a Siberian waste. There were glad cries when smoke arose from one of the dunes, heralding a farmhouse, only to change to wails when a ploughed area revealed a group of wild ponies, heads down, being fed by hand. Dr Wilkie walked down the coach pointing out fox trails and the hardly perceptible paw prints from rabbits or badgers.

'Your powers of observation are vital in the countryside, girls,' she announced to the huddled fifth-formers. 'This whole area is like a book to be read.' She glanced at Juliet Mortimer and Caroline Prosser both sniffing loudly and using soggy handkerchiefs on their streaming eyes. 'For those who have eyes to see, of course,' she added without much hope.

Jennifer Tewson, who was the unacknowledged leader of the inner group who were doing Greek and were therefore swots, said piously, 'My father says that the Bluebell School encourages our powers of observation.'

Dr Wilkie nodded briskly and went on down the corridor. The other four girls in the Greek set claimed loudly that they had just spotted a deer. Caroline Prosser sniffed and suggested Father Christmas might be stationed somewhere near. No-one smiled. Vallery said out of the blue, 'I don't know why anyone wants to do Greek. Or Latin for that matter.'

Jennifer explained, 'We're interested in theology. I've told you before, Vallery McKinley. Sometimes I think you try to be stupid.' She glanced at her friends. 'Not that you would have to try very hard,' she added.

Vallery said hotly, 'Well the only reason for doing theology is to become a priest. And I don't suppose even you lot think that lady vicars are a possibility!'

Morag crossed her eyes and spoke with an exaggerated lisp. 'The outfits, my dear, who would want to be seen dead in a dog-collar!'

Jannie leaned forward and pointed to a line of footprints as the train slowed for Barnstaple station. 'Those are the kind of things I like to read,' she said. 'Nice big boot prints. Size eleven I would say. Made by someone well over six feet tall. Young. Rugged.'

Vallery managed a giggle though she had thought her heart would break the further they travelled from Clevedon. The Bristol train had roared through Yatton which was only four miles from Clevedon and there, waving on the platform, had been her parents. They must have driven straight back from Bristol and waited on the freezing station for the express to go through. Val had had to retire to the toilet and sob into the tiny triangular wash-basin until they were well past Weston-super-Mare.

She said now, 'You are awful, Jannie.'

Morag was delighted to see Val smile at last. She egged Jannie on.

'How can you tell he is young and rugged – that's wishful thinking!'

But Jannie shook her head pedantically and looked so like Dr Wilkie her audience laughed together.

'You're not going to get many older chaps – sorry – gentlemen – out in this weather, girls. Are you? And whoever does turn out is bound to be rugged to put up with it! I rest my case.'

Mrs Maitland opened the door of their compartment. 'All ready, girls? Bring your satchels and shoebags into the corridor and wait in an orderly file. The juniors are to be taken off first.'

It was colder still in the corridor. They pulled their velours down over their ears and stuck their noses inside their scarves. Morag wiped the condensation from the window with her gloved hand and they peered out. The juniors, about sixty of them, were scrunching their way across the swept but icy platform to the booking hall. Everything seemed to be steaming, the train itself, the platform canopy and, vaguely through the windows of the booking hall, a line of buses, their exhausts panting like dragons. The staff walked gingerly alongside the girls, holding some of them up, stumbling themselves. The French mademoiselle could be heard exclaiming, 'It is so beautiful with the sun on it fully!' and the stationmaster, all done up in gold braid for the occasion, said, 'A beautiful part of the country, ladies! Welcome to Devon!' And the girls giggled and clumped past him, their minds on the high tea which was promised as soon as they arrived at Gallenwick.

The two dozen fifth-formers filed silently into the last but one bus and piled their satchels on the overhead nets. The bus was old but clean. The engine had been kept running for some time and it shook rhythmically to the count of five, then hiccoughed, shuddered and started again. The driver was about the same, too old to be called up, a face as shiny as an apple and a beaming grin that was not unsympathetic as he looked around at the girls huddling themselves behind him. They started off with some difficulty, the unchained wheels skidding desperately until they gripped the cinders put down earlier, then they chugged along in bottom gear at about ten miles an hour, enveloped in a cloud of exhaust. 'Keep the windows clear, my dears!' the driver called back. 'Don't want any of 'ee to miss the view!' As the road out of Barnstaple was cut between two

24

six-foot-high walls of snow, Morag assumed his remark was ironic and she smiled politely. But Jennifer Tewson muttered, 'Some view!'

The driver did not take offence. 'We shall get clear of this when we gets to the tops. But try not to breathe young ladies! Otherwise we'll be steamed up afore we starts and we won't see nothing when there's something. If you gets my drift!'

A ripple of polite laughter greeted this. Jannie, sitting just behind him, leaned forward.

'How are we going to get through? If it's like this here, it'll surely get worse away from the town?'

'It will that, m'dear. But we got the Reids' big tractor out this morning. Put a couple of plough shares on 'e, and you've got a snow plough.'

'Reids'?' Jannie probed.

'Reid's farm is your nearest. 'Bout two mile from Gallenwick I reckon. Will Reid bought the place back in the twenties. Gennelman farmer he was.' The bus hiccoughed more loudly as it stuck in an icy rut and swayed to and fro in waltz time. The driver changed into first gear and revved furiously. Caroline Prosser and Juliet Mortimer screamed in unison. The wheels bit into the edge of the rut and they were off again.

The driver went on in a loud voice, obviously trying to take their thoughts away from the journey, 'Din't do no good at farming. 'E were good at making clay models. But there weren't much call for clay models, 'specially the sort he made.' He changed gear and the bus settled into a grinding ten miles an hour again.

Jannie leaned forward again.

'So. They just live at the farm, do they? I mean they've got enough money to—' Morag and Vallery pulled her back unceremoniously.

'Doc Willie would have a blue fit if she could hear you!' Val hissed furiously.

The driver raised his voice higher still. 'They nearly went bust, little lady. That's what would have happened.

25

Only 'e died, did Will Reid. An' 'is missis and 'er ma pulled the place up, worked their fingers to the bone. Brought the boys back from their posh boarding school to 'elp 'em – no money for that no more anyway.' The wheels on the bus began to skid helplessly in a dip and the driver changed back down hastily and revved the engine so that the bus skittered freakishly sideways before gripping at some fresh snow. Morag and Val clutched each other.

'So . . .' The driver had forgotten where he'd got to and leaned forward to wipe the inside of the windscreen with his sleeve.

Jannie said avidly, 'So there are some boys on the farm? And it's quite near to Gallow-thing?'

'Ah. It's not that far off. An' it's called Gallenwick, little lady. It were a nunnery long time ago. But the monks found it distracting, so it were closed.'

Morag and Val exchanged glances which gave Jannie a chance to continue her interrogation.

'How many sons did the Reids have?'

'Three. Named for Will Reid's family. Durston, Fitzhugh and Berwick. Bit of a mouthful, eh? We calls 'em Dusty, Hugh and Berry.' The driver forgot himself for a moment. 'Bluggy good workers all three of 'em. Praps Dusty could do with a mite more energy but Hugh and Berry— '

Juliet Mortimer said in her high and aristocratic voice, 'Exactly what does bluggy mean, driver?'

'Naught for you to worry about, missie.' The driver obviously objected to the question and made sure the bus slid perilously close to the icy wall on the left. Juliet gasped and was silent.

Jannie avoided Morag's censorious gaze and went on, 'And the Reid boys run the farm, do they? Of course, farming is a reserved occupation.'

'It might be for others, m'dear. Not for the Reids. Hugh and Durston have been in the Navy for over a year now. And young Berry is waiting for his papers.'

Jannie sat back at last. 'So he's eighteen,' she said

happily. 'I expect they were his footprints outside the station. He's probably driving the tractor and clearing the way for the buses.'

The driver glanced round, grinning broadly. 'You're almost spot-on there, m'dear. Except that he's twenty, is our Berry. He got deferred until last harvest. Now he's awaiting his ship being fitted down at Devonport.'

'Twenty?' Jannie murmured. 'Even better.'

Gallenwick was guarded by an enormous arched stone gateway. 'Almost a lych-gate,' Vallery said grimly. 'Except there's nowhere in the middle to put the coffin.'

'I expect they took that away when the nuns were sacked,' Morag said, rolling her eyes humorously. 'Poor old loves. Hounded from their home by a load of amorous monks— '

Jannie exploded appreciatively.

Val said, 'Sorry, Mo. I find I can't laugh.'

'Well, I know it wasn't that funny,' Morag began, mock apologetically.

'I can't laugh at anything,' Val put in. 'I think you're wonderful to talk about Cresta Runs and Siberian wastes and sacked nuns. But in the end, that's what it's like. Siberian wastes. Two hours we've been in this bus— '

The driver, who had not spoken since they cleared the walled drifts and he could point out the sweeping tracts of land which apparently pitched into the sea from enormous cliffs, said suddenly, 'Less than an hour in the summer, m'dear. And Barnstaple's a mighty pretty town. As for Lynton and Lynmouth— '

'How often do the buses run?' Val asked grimly.

'There's one on a Wednesday and two on a Saturday,' the driver said proudly.

The girls said nothing. They were chugging between an avenue of elms which curved around a large area of what might be lawn, bounded by a mysterious ribbon of darkness.

'What is that?' Jannie asked.

'The Gall. 'Tis no more than a brook really. It girdles the house. We drove over it just now. The gateway is a bridge. Very pretty it is too. When you can see it.'

Jannie said, 'Is that the only bridge?'

'I don't think so. The gardeners have put down planks here and there. Saves 'em walking all the way round to their cottages.'

'So it's like a moat,' Jannie continued.

'Kept people away from the nuns in the old days.' The driver turned the wheel a little too firmly and the rear of the bus slid sideways. Screams drowned his next words. And then screams were forgotten. The house had come into view. Dr Wilkie was right. It was beautiful. Outlined in snow it was fantastic. The typical E-shape of an Elizabethan manor with mullioned windows, a steep roof and a crenellated abutment on the end.

'That there's the chapel,' said their helpful driver. 'And that's the front door. We goes into the stable yard.' They made for the side of the building. The first three buses were emerging empty. To one side of what seemed to be a stable block, a tractor was parked. A young man stood behind its wheel waving them in. He wore a knitted balaclava and an ancient greatcoat. But his eyes were big and black and full of laughter and as the bus jiggled its way over the ruts past him, he leaned forward to peer through the windows and wave to the girls.

Jannie said with quiet satisfaction, 'Well. That must be Berry Reid.'

The driver brought the bus to rest by a snow-covered edifice just recognizable as a pump.

'Aye. That was young Berry. 'E's done a good job today.'

The girls were all standing up to reach for their satchels. Jannie moved to the driver and said confidentially, 'I think you should come inside for a cup of tea before you start back. And bring Mr Reid with you.'

'Can't do that, young miss. We've got to get back to the depot before the snow starts again – which it

28

will tonight. If it weren't for the snow it'd be dark already.'

Morag grinned at Val. 'What a shame,' she said.

Val could not manage to smile in return.

It all seemed to get steadily worse that term. In an effort to 'keep things in perspective' as she put it, Morag made a list of every small good happening. Some days it was simply 'jam for tea' or 'letters arrived'. One never-to-be-forgotten entry read, 'Maitie's bloomers descended very gently while she was conducting the recorder group and were visible up to the pocket by the time they had finished "All Through the Night".'

That first evening it was most definitely the fact that the fifth- and sixth-formers were dormitoried in the stable block – converted lofts completely separate from the house. They had their own kitchenette on the ground floor, next to a nice sitting room complete with wireless and gramophone; the main stables had been converted into the school library which was open to the other girls between ten a.m. and six p.m. After that the whole block was theirs, watched over very leniently by Mrs Maitland.

'It's like having our own flat,' Morag pointed out to a very disconsolate Vallery after their trunks had been unceremoniously deposited just inside the door, barely leaving room to move around the beds. 'And it's marvellous that the three of us are together. I should have hated it if we'd been split up.'

Jannie smiled brilliantly and was momentarily transformed from plainness to beauty. Val was not cheered. She had hoped to have Morag to herself. For one thing, she knew she was going to cry for her mother once she got to bed and Morag would have climbed in beside her and rocked her to sleep. And for another, she had evolved a wonderful plan for after-the-war. Morag would marry Teddy and come to live in Redley Lodge. It was a dream that slightly consoled her for the awfulness of homesickness. Jannie knew nothing of homesickness; Jannie was so hard and unfeeling. And, of course, shallow.

High tea turned out to be scrambled reconstituted egg on enormous doorsteps of toast with a particularly delicious chutney to spread over the top. It was served on plates that were almost red-hot; even so Dr Wilkie said a very short grace so that nothing got cold and announced above the rattle of cutlery that the chutney had been supplied – all ten jars – by Mrs Peggy Reid from Reid's farm. Jannie's eyes gleamed. Morag whispered, 'See, Val? We're not deserted and friendless as you so pathetically put it!'

Jannie hissed, 'For God's sake cheer up, Val! It's going to be great here. The Gallow Girls – that's who we'll be! I bet there are ghosts here – I bet one of the nuns was pregnant by a monk and they walled her up and she walks at nights. Especially snowy nights. Especially the stable block where they used to meet clandestinely!'

Val looked at her with blue lacklustre eyes. 'I hate you, Jannie Mears,' she said.

Long after Jannie was asleep that night, Morag said quietly into the freezing darkness, 'Don't cry any more, Val. You'll be ill and that will make it worse than ever.'

'I'm ill now,' Val sobbed, glad to admit her grief. 'My pillow is soaking and I'm cold and feel sick!'

Morag said, 'Come into my bed.' She tented the bedclothes while Val settled herself on the hard mattress, then she propped herself on an elbow and wiped Val's face with a clean handkerchief.

'You'll be all right now,' she comforted as she imagined Val's mother might.

'Close your eyes and go to sleep.'

'Oh Morrie . . . I wish Jannie wasn't here. She doesn't understand. She doesn't— '

As if summoned from the deep, Jannie's voice cut clearly through the room. It was high and tense, like a violin note.

'Leave her alone, Marius! She's my mother! I'll tell Pops – I will – I will . . .'

It trembled and faded; there was a small hiccoughing sob and then silence.

Morag wrapped her arms tighter around Val and held onto her. And Val stared into the night, her eyes dry and tearless at last.

So their grumbling became a way of life; they thought of new words to describe it. They were not only fed up and browned off, they were de-right-to-the-bottom-jected. When the snow melted and they went for cross-country runs and Sunday walks, they stopped feeling as flat as a pancake and became flatter than a cow-pat. Val and Morag were sustained by daily letters from home. Jannie heard once a week. Morag said, 'Your mother must trust you a lot more than ours trust us, Jan!' Val said heartily, 'You've always been more mature than we have, I suppose.' Jannie said nothing. Her hobby was encountering Berwick Reid when he brought anything from the farm. He drove a horse and trap on these occasions and clattered into the stable yard as if he were driving a stagecoach, pulling his horse up so that it whinnied and shouting at it unmercifully. Jannie usually managed to be crossing from dormitory to school at these times and would dimple up at him. Sometimes he noticed her, sometimes he did not. She seemed to have become even more nondescript since arriving at Gallenwick.

In March there came a few bright days and, of course, more daylight. On the first clear evening the air raid warden from Galford cycled frantically along the drive to inform them that the siren had sounded in Lynmouth. Almost immediately the drone of aeroplanes could be heard overhead and the girls congregated in the stable yard to watch the silhouettes of the German bombers follow the sea to where it narrowed into the Bristol Channel. The next morning Dr Wilkie suggested they form a queue outside Mrs Maitland's office to telephone their parents. During morning prayers she informed them that hard work helped alleviate anxiety. Morag already knew this; her revision papers for matriculation were gaining 100 per cent, she could do no more. Jannie and Val cribbed from her books each evening and still did poorly. As the raids increased, they too applied themselves rigorously to their books and longed for the morning telephone calls.

Then news came from one of the maids that Berwick Reid's call-up had again been deferred so that he could help with planting the potatoes at Easter and getting in the hay during June.

''E don't like it,' Bessie informed Jannie as she dished out the Sunday morning porridge. 'But it be part of the war effort an' 'e's got to knuckle under like the rest of us!'

'So he should,' Jannie replied righteously. 'He can't expect his mother and grandmother to do it all.' She barely waited for Bessie to move away before she made her suggestion.

'Let's skip matins, girls, and go for a really decent walk. How about it?'

Morag nodded. 'We could do the Doone Valley. Or the rocks. Or go towards Lyn Abbey.'

Val shivered. 'I don't want to go anywhere near those creepy monks. I wouldn't be at all surprised if Jannie was right about them. Getting the nuns into trouble, I mean.'

'I think we should call on our neighbours,' Jannie said, still very righteous. 'Mrs Reid sends over such a lot of stuff – that damson jam – the chutney. We should go and thank her.'

The others stared at her suspiciously. She grinned. 'Didn't you hear? Bessie says Berwick Reid is still at home.'

Morag said definitely, 'Then we're not going calling! I can just imagine you – you really are impossible, Jan!'

Vallery said superstitiously, 'I don't want to miss matins

anyway. Something might happen to them at home if we don't go to church.'

'Oh all right.' Jannie knew she had lost that one. 'But let's walk up to the tops after lunch. Please, girls. At least we can look down on the farm from there. We've never even seen it and we've been here almost three months!'

It was during the morning service that Dr Wilkie dropped her bombshell.

'I know this will upset all of you and I am very sorry. Believe me I would not have suggested it if the raids had lessened. But your parents are all in agreement and I think it best if . . .'

Val turned and looked at Morag, her blue eyes enormous.

'It will be a wonderful opportunity for those of you who are sitting exams to do some intensive revision. And for others who are less busy, the staff and I are organizing working parties to engage in important war work.'

Val whispered incredulously, 'We're not going home for Easter!'

Jannie said, 'I have to. I need to check . . . on someone.'

Morag swallowed. She thought of the oriel window, the tall figure walking along Park Row, her mother's dressing-gown . . .

She said, 'We'll go for that walk. We'll talk about it.'

They tramped over the bridge and took the lane that would eventually join the Barnstaple road, then they struck across the fields.

Underfoot it was still squelchy but already on the drained banks primroses were appearing and the trees were all in young leaf. They saw none of it. If they had thought they were miserable before, they knew they were more miserable now. Morag could find no words of comfort for the other two and after expounding at great length on the unfairness of it all, they too fell silent.

They came to one of the many streams which drained

the tops. It was full and rushing down to join the Lyn at some point. Along its banks, clumps of willow and alder leaned over as if to protect it. The girls stood and surveyed it without appreciation.

Morag said dully, 'I suppose this might be John Ridd's river. You know, where he clambered up the water slide.'

'Could be any of 'em,' Jannie said indifferently. 'They're all the same.'

A voice from the willow made them literally leap in unison.

'They're not the same at all! Each and every one of the moor streams has its own character.'

The willow shook convulsively as someone swung out of its cupped centre and dropped to the ground. Jannie, who had immediately hoped to see Berwick Reid, pouted with disappointment. The man who came up the bank towards them had none of the Reid's dark good looks. His whole aura was one of mildness; from grey eyes and brown hair, to gently curving mouth, he was the typical Englishman.

'Hello.' He smiled at them all. His voice was low and husky. They had all heard Berry shouting at his horses when he delivered his mother's goodies; it was hard to imagine this man shouting at anything.

'My name is Hugh Reid. I come from the farm. I understand you all know my brother. And you'll know my mother and grandmother quite soon too.'

The girls made assenting sounds and shuffled about in a very unladylike manner. As Jannie said after, 'It was because he looked like Leslie Howard. I just wanted to lie down and die!'

Hugh Reid's smile widened slightly. 'I couldn't help overhearing you. Of course, I've grown up with the moor streams. They've got moods and personalities. You'll get to know them too. They're quite fascinating characters.'

Morag said, 'Is this John Ridd's stream?'

'No. That's further over. It leads now to the Doone Arms. Berry has climbed it just like John Ridd.'

Jannie found her voice. 'Have you climbed it too? Will you show us?'

'No, I've never tried it. I'm much too lazy. But I will certainly show you where it is. When you come to the farm to work.'

'To work?' Jannie's eyes appeared to bulge.

'Sorry. Am I putting my foot in it again? I thought your headmistress would have mentioned it by now. She came to see us. Apparently you are not going home for Easter and she wondered whether you could help us to plant the seed potatoes. Your war effort, don't you know!'

Val spoke at last. 'That would make all the difference.'

'It would. My ship will be refitting for the next three or four weeks, so I can lend a hand too.' He smiled again, already turning away. 'In fact I've used up my free time, so I had better leave you. Perhaps – next week—'

He waved and moved down the bank, swung himself back into the willow and quite suddenly was gone. One of the trees on the opposite bank dipped further into the stream as he obviously crossed over and that was all.

'The Scarlet Pimpernel,' Val breathed.

'Working on the farm. With him,' Jannie said.

Morag thought of the oriel window again. Perhaps she could postpone it a little longer.

CHAPTER THREE

Easter 1941

The potato field was on the side of the valley. It had recently been ploughed in accordance with the Dig for Victory campaign and the turned soil still smelled of the sheep who had grazed it for centuries. It faced south and the watery April sun shone on the backs of the girls as they plodded up the hill treading in a potato at every stride, then beamed into their faces when they moved to their left and down. All twenty-five fifth-formers were deployed on the field; the sixth-formers were engaged in helping to spring clean the house and the juniors were Knitting for Yugoslavia. They all hated knitting but Mademoiselle had painted a picture of the partisans taking to the mountains; all of them handsome, all of them with frostbitten fingers. The older girls secreted little notes in the long cuffs of their gloves. Marjorie White, thirteen and very precocious, wrote, 'If you come to England, my parents would be delighted to offer you tea.'

Meanwhile Jannie, Vallery and Morag worked with less than their original enthusiasm. Hugh Reid had been recalled two days before the planting began.

'It's not fair,' Jannie said, sitting on the edge of her bed to darn her stockings for church the next day. 'The one bright spot on the horizon suddenly gone! I do think God is hard on us!'

Morag considered protesting, but then was silent. She too had been looking forward to meeting Hugh Reid again. His quiet grey eyes and slightly smiling mouth had stayed in her mind's eye for the past ten days. She hated to think she shared Jannie's avid interest in men, but she missed talking to her father and Val's father and Val's brother.

Val said disconsolately, 'It wouldn't have made much difference, anyway, Jan. Mrs Maitie was telling me how it works. We'll be lucky if we can talk to each other let alone anyone else.'

'I'd have found a way,' Jannie maintained, breaking off her wool and stretching the darn over her hand for inspection. 'And he wanted to talk to us. You could tell.'

'Oh, Jannie. We exchanged a few words, that was all. He was going back to do that wretched convoy work— '

'How do you know that? Did he tell you?' Jannie asked, eyes wide, stocking forgotten.

'Of course not. But he was home during the Cape Matapan battle so he couldn't be in a destroyer or cruiser or anything, and Maitie said both the Reid sons were in the same kind of work and Berry hoped to join them. And he said all he was going to do was nannying.' She smiled at Jannie's expression. 'It means looking after other ships. More important ships.'

'When did he tell you that?' Jannie asked, still wide-eyed.

'He didn't tell me, idiot! He told Maitie when she was asking him who would be superintending our work on the farm.'

'So all three sons will be together?' Vallery showed some interest for the first time. 'I suppose that will mean something. I mean, the family will be split into two camps as it were. At home and in the Navy. Not like us, scattered to the winds!' She thought about it then added mournfully, 'Poor Mrs Reid. If one goes all three go.'

Morag exploded. 'Honestly, Val! Talk about Job's comforter! They could be in the same convoy but on different ships!' She started to get out her own darning kit. 'And anyway, Jannie, you're just the littlest bit fickle, aren't you? I thought it was Berry Reid you were so interested in!'

Jannie rubbed her new darn across her cheek and looked into space. 'He'll never notice me,' she said looking more like a waif than ever. 'But Hugh . . . Hugh would take care to notice people. Anyone. D'you know what I mean?'

And the others answered almost in unison, 'Yes.'

Contrarily, because the three of them had decided to have a 'thing' about the elusive Hugh Reid, they all found it very much easier to get along with Berry. The first day on the potato field was incredibly hard; the wagon, stacked high with seed potatoes, waited for them at the top. It meant that on the way down they half emptied their sacks and carried only half the weight back up. Even so, after two hours they found it difficult to set their feet in their own particular furrow and spent more and more time at the top, panting and refilling their sacks. Berry Reid was at least half a dozen furrows ahead of them and at last waited for them at the top yelling encouragement and derision in equal parts.

'Come along there, girls! Caroline, shake your feet for Pete's sake! You're bringing half the field up here on your boots! Morag – not such big strides. You – the little fair one – push the spud right in – don't be frightened of it!'

Jannie looked mortified and Vallery, used to dealing with bossy young men, spoke to him as if he were Teddy.

'Why don't you shut up and get on with it? Fill some sacks for us instead of standing there shouting at us like Hitler!'

Berry looked at her and gave a shout of laughter.

'OK, Miss Curly-top! What's your name, pray?'

'None of your business. Not so silly as yours though.'

The three of them arrived at the top of the field and

gathered around him, panting desperately, leaning over their depleted sacks of seed potatoes.

He said, 'One more double row and we'll knock off for dinner.' He began to replenish their sacks from the wagon, grinning at Vallery over his shoulder. 'Nothing silly about a family name, Curly. My great uncle was an artist of some repute and I intend to follow in his footsteps!'

Vallery looked at him scornfully. 'You an artist? You haven't got the vision of a worm!'

He laughed again, thoroughly enjoying what he considered to be a flirtation.

'I've got vision. I notice things. Like Morag's legs and Caroline's . . . figure. And now, your hair and mouth.'

Caroline, arriving at that moment, blushed deeply and hunched her shoulders over her breasts. Morag turned her back and surveyed the view. The undulations of the moor were blanketed in mist.

Vallery gave a snicker of disgust. 'And we've noticed your mouth too. It loves to hear itself, doesn't it?' She hitched her sack over one arm and took out three potatoes. 'I'm off. Come on, Mo.'

They swung down the slope, treading in their potatoes with a firmness lacking before. Berry Reid grinned, well satisfied. Behind him a small voice said, 'My name is Janice. I'm called Jannie.'

He looked around at the sliver of girl who seemed too frail for this work.

'Do your best then, Jannie,' he said encouragingly and immediately turned to Caroline. 'D'you dance?' he asked directly.

'Dance?' She looked at him as if he had spoken Chinese.

'There's a hop in Lynmouth next Saturday. Church hall. In aid of the Free French. Like to come?'

Caroline grabbed some potatoes and thrust them into her sack as she mumbled something inaudible.

'Sorry?'

She took a pace, dropped a potato, stamped on it fiercely and said over her shoulder, 'We're not allowed.'

Berry grinned again and again the small voice said, 'I'll come. I'm very good at dancing.'

He looked down at . . . what was her name? Jannie.

'We'll see, shall we? When you're a bit older.'

He moved on to the rest of the class before she could tell him angrily that she was in fact older than Caroline.

That night, exhausted but better fed than they'd been since they arrived, the three girls voiced their similar opinions of Berwick Reid.

'Reminds me of Teddy. Wants taking down several pegs,' Vallery said.

'Well, don't try it,' Morag advised. 'He's not like Teddy. Not really. And he's quite different from his brother. He – he's sort of . . . dangerous.'

'He thinks I'm younger than everyone else!' fumed Jannie. 'I'll show him! I'll have him eating out of my hand before I've finished with him!'

'Oh Jannie, be careful,' Morag said, knowing she sounded like her Aunt Harriet from Edinburgh.

Val pooh-poohed her. 'Dangerous my foot! He was goading us – just so that we'd do another couple of rows before dinner! That's all that was about! I tell you, he's like Teddy!'

Jannie said gloomily, 'He asked Caro to go to a dance with him.'

'He what?' Val exploded.

'She said no. I offered to go but he wouldn't take me.' She went to the small mirror over the chest of drawers. 'Perhaps if I put some hankies inside my slip tomorrow . . . oh damn! Trouble with Ma's satin stuff it's all so slippery!'

Morag said impatiently, 'For goodness' sake, Jannie! You're not funny, you know! In fact, you sound cheap!'

Jannie's face flamed.

'It's all right for you, Morag Heyward! He'd noticed your legs so he'd found out your name! And Val – he thought Val was an almighty scream! He hardly saw me!' She registered Morag's withdrawal from the discussion and turned to her, hands held out. 'Mo – it's not just him! He – he's just an example! Nobody notices me – not Ma – not you and Val . . . no-one! Only some . . . men. Well, two boys from the Cathedral school. And . . . someone else. An older man.' She drooped. 'So I thought perhaps men might . . . you know. Like me. But it doesn't work. Look at my face.' She thrust it upwards. 'There's at least three pimples and another on the way. It's a big grease-spot! I hate it! I hate me!'

Morag and Vallery were vociferous with reassurance. But that night they were both awake when Jannie started again and this time it was worse. 'Ma! Don't let him – please! I don't want to kiss him – I don't want him to touch me – I'll tell Pops – I will, I will . . .'

Val's hand reached out and scrabbled on Morag's eiderdown and Morag took it and held it tightly. Val whispered, 'I'm glad I want to be an old maid, Mo. If you marry Teddy, I'll come and keep house for you!'

But neither of them laughed. They lay awake and wondered about Eve Mears.

Mrs Reid was small but she had shoulders like an ox, a voice like the crack of a whip and a delicate hand with pastry. She made meat pies of gargantuan proportions, six of them at a time in enamel washing-up bowls. She stabbed the pastry tops at regular intervals to let out the steam and they sat on the enormous deal table simmering like active volcanoes and emitting a smell that made Morag want to drool. All the vegetables were contained with the meat beneath the pastry so dishing up took only minutes. Granny Thomas, small, wizened but as persistent as a digging mole, made fresh bread each day and several loaves sat on bread boards at regular intervals down the table ready to be hacked up and spread with the deep yellow butter. Between half-past twelve and half-past one was dinner-time on the farm; the girls called it gorge-time. If Jannie dreamed of adultery and rejection, the others fell asleep to thoughts of food. And the best of it was Mrs Reid absolved them from the deadly sin of gluttony by pointing out it was their wages.

'That doctor-woman – I don't hold with lady doctors myself but she seems a sensible sort – she says you're not to be paid for this work. It's voluntary war work, is what she says. So I reckon if my land has given you a good appetite, then my land can repay you with a good meal. There's apple pie to follow so leave a corner.' She stopped by Jannie and looked at her closely. 'You could do with some feeding, I reckon. But don't overdo it. I can put a cover over the plate and you can take the pie back with you. You boarding school girls like midnight feasts, so I understand!' She smiled at everyone. She looked like Berry and was as blunt and bossy as he was too.

Berry spoke to Morag recognizing she was the natural leader.

'Come on then, Mo. Time to put the boots back on. We'll stop at half-past three and you can have a slice of cake. After all you are the tallest here. Apart from me of course.'

She looked at her plate and realized she had eaten two slices of apple pie. She was mortified. Mrs Maitland had said last year that her height would probably entitle her to extra clothing coupons. Her mother had understood only too well when Morag begged to be let off the humiliation of public measuring.

And Berry had called her Mo. He was laughing now, pulling her up to compare her with his small and busy mother.

'For the good Lord's sake, son!' Mrs Reid scolded, rattling cutlery into a bowl like a machine-gunner. 'Stop embarrassing the girl. She probably plants more spuds than anyone else with those long legs of hers.'

'Doesn't work like that, Ma, as you very well know.'
But Berry was fired with a new idea. 'How about a
competition, girls?' They were all in the porch, pushing
newly warm feet into heavy wellington boots, groaning
aloud. 'The one who plants most potatoes in this session
gets a cake from Ma. All to herself!'

There was an uproar of banter. Mrs Reid wanted to
know who said so. Jannie insisted loudly that she would
win hands down. Val warned, 'Come off it, girls! He'll
get the cake. He's been doing this job for years.' Berry
ruffled her curls in a very Teddy-like way and she lunged
at him and received a sharp slap on the backside. Caroline
said nothing and Morag wondered whether she intended
going to the dance in Lynmouth on Saturday. Berry said,
'I'm not taking part. I'm adjudicating. How's that?'

Morag admired his tactics. Everyone had been flagging
after their dinner; now suddenly they were anxious to
get started. She pushed unwilling feet into unwelcoming
boots and watched them running over the yard and
through the five-barred gate like a flock of sheep. And
Berwick Reid was the sheep dog, chivvying, watching,
waiting. Guarding.

It was amazing what the week of potato planting did
for all of them. Vallery slept all through the nights and
never once reached for Morag's hand. Jannie focused
her random thoughts about the male sex on to Berwick
Reid. Her determination to have him 'eating out of her
hand' increased with his continuing indifference. But in
Mrs Reid she had found someone to love properly. Jannie
was Mrs Reid's idea of what a little girl should be; tiny and
rather plain and obviously in need of mothering. Jannie
was the daughter she had never had. She bought a jar of
Virol and insisted Jannie have some every time she set foot
over the door. When term began again, she continued
to send Berry over with 'treats' and usually there was
a separate parcel for Jannie containing greengage jam,
six fresh goose eggs, and always – not so welcome –

cod-liver oil. By Whitsun, Jannie was indeed taking on a new bloom. Her hair, the colour and texture of straw, fell over her shoulders in waves and became soft and shining. She learned to droop her eyelids so that her pale blue eyes, so unfortunately like marbles – took on an almond shape. Vallery called them 'bedroom eyes' and accused her of trying 'to do a Veronica Lake'. But Morag knew – because she still lay wakeful at nights – that Jannie no longer talked in her sleep.

Morag realized that she herself had changed. She did not like it. Before, she had not slept because she was homesick; now . . . she forced herself to admit – she was lovesick. She, Morag Heyward, the most sensible girl in the fifth form, who believed that logical thought could control 75 per cent of emotions, lay awake thinking of Berry Reid. And when she slept she dreamed of Berry Reid. And when she was at the farm she was conscious – terribly terribly conscious – the whole time of Berry Reid.

She despised herself for this ridiculous obsession. He had as good as called her a giantess; he had the cheek to use her pet name Mo, and only Jannie and Val were allowed to do that outside the family. He was a bully and the tactics he used to keep them hard at work were both devious and – and devious. But when his dark eyes met her equally dark ones, something happened to her. She felt at once warm and shiveringly cold. She felt . . . melting. And she hated it because it was putting her in the power of someone she did not like. In fact she would probably hate him if it weren't that she loved him.

The awful, the really terrible thing was, she was practically certain Jannie felt the same. Not only Jannie; Caroline Prosser admitted she was 'smitten' and if only she had a bit more nerve she would go dancing with him every Saturday night. In fact most of the girls responded to Berry Reid as if he were Errol Flynn. Except Val. Dear Val, used to her cheeky brother, managed to stay immune. Morag was deeply thankful for Val. In

44

the gathering gloom of each dawn she would turn on her side and look at Val's humped shape beneath the honeycomb counterpane and make up her mind that she would emulate Val's attitude. She too would give Berry as good as he gave them. She would tell him off for being a slave driver and bribing them with food. She might even go one further and tell him it would be good riddance when he got his call-up papers. But just the thought of that made her heart ache so much she dismissed it. She hardly ever let herself think of Berry on the deck of an E boat, soaked to the skin by the huge Atlantic rollers, waiting, watching, depth-charges at the ready, as the asdic bleeped below and any piece of flotsam could be a German periscope. No, she fought against conjuring up that picture, and when it happened unbidden, she squeezed her eyes shut as if she could push it out of her head physically.

Meanwhile Berry might come to Gallenwick tomorrow with a load of wood for next winter. Or maybe when they went for one of their cross-country runs they might see him at the head of one of the big shire horses as he scythed the hay, and he would take off his hat and wave it in the air as they gallumped past, and doubtless think to himself that they looked like a skein of suet puddings bouncing over his moor. Because it was his moor. He knew it so intimately and when he was – very occasionally – serious during their midday meals, he had told them where to find the deer; when they would be rutting; how the moorland ponies found the fresh young shoots beneath the burned bracken and lifted their lips so delicately to nibble at them. And the girls were seeing all these things for themselves as they explored further into their isolated haven. Because of Berry Reid they were growing to love this place; to want to claim it for their own. It pleased Dr Wilkie; this was what she had hoped for her girls. She smiled and congratulated them on each new find. She had no idea they were looking and discovering because of the brash

45

young gypsy-like man at Reid's farm. Though when she made her announcement two weeks after Whitsun, she may well have got an idea of how her fifth-formers were feeling.

She knocked on the sitting room door one evening, waited two seconds and then went in. She was carrying the large red book which was a register of all the girls in the school. She wore her gown but not her cap, and Morag noticed that her hair was much greyer than it had been when she joined the school two years previously.

She waited while Juliet Mortimer vacated the one armchair and ushered her into it, then she sat down and crossed her legs at the ankles.

'Girls . . . this is an informal visit. I decided when we moved into Gallenwick that I would wait for an invitation to your sitting room – I wanted you to feel it was strictly your own domain. However, as you usually congregate here after supper, and as I have something to say to you exclusively, I am presuming . . .' A chorus of welcome interrupted her and she smiled at them almost fondly.

'You are indeed developing into a fifth form of which I am proud,' she pontificated, smiling particularly at Jannie who had decided that very morning to be a nun and had scraped her hair back severely revealing fine, high cheek-bones and emphasizing a well-moulded chin.

'The way you accepted the loss of your Easter holiday and buckled to work at the farm – it was an example to our juniors . . . and indeed to the sixth-form girls.' She smiled again, this time at Morag who was almost the only girl in the school who did not appear to be benefiting from the country air. 'And now, of course, your matriculation examinations are in sight. I know your parents are going to rejoice at the results . . .' there was just a hint of menace in her tone now, '. . . and to that end I am singling out some of you for special tuition.' The faces around her became still and slightly wary. She swept on, 'Timetabling will be suspended for the rest of this month and the following girls will meet me

46

in my study at nine o'clock sharp where special work will be planned carefully and carried out under my personal supervision.' Somebody dared to groan and Dr Wilkie's eyes widened slightly. 'I assure you, girls, that my role will be one of tutoress. I am here to help, and my criticisms will be constructive, never destructive.' She paused long enough to meet each young gaze with her own; it seemed an eternity. Then she opened the book on her knees and read out a list of names in a slightly higher voice that brooked no questions, certainly no interruptions. The list included Val, Jannie, and at least another dozen girls. There was a blank silence.

She said, 'This is a privilege, girls. Not a punishment in any sense of the word. Do you understand that?'

'Yes, Dr Wilkie.' They had not chorused a reply in that way since the upper thirds and looked down at their knees in some embarrassment.

Dr Wilkie laughed. 'I see. You cannot accept my assurance, obviously. I can only reiterate it, girls. This will be precious time for you.' She swept them again with that penetrating gaze and added, 'And for me too.'

She did not stand up. So there was something else. She closed the book gently and looked directly at Morag and Juliet Mortimer who was next to her.

'There are eight names still left on the register.' She smiled slightly. 'Caroline. Morag. Juliet. And the five girls in the Greek set.' Morag looked over her shoulder. The Janson twins, Margaret Downend, Sibyl Porter and Jennifer Tewson smiled smugly. They were the elite of the fifth and were insufferable about it.

Dr Wilkie took a breath. 'I intended my tutorials to include all of you. But I was approached yesterday by Mrs Reid from the farm.' It was as if a current of electricity had passed through the sitting room. The girls sat a little straighter. 'As you may have heard,' Dr Wilkie nodded towards the wireless set in the corner, 'the weather forecast is excellent for the next two weeks. And then rain is forecast. Haymaking has just started on the farm and they are desperate to have it finished while they can. Mrs Reid particularly asked for you girls because you had worked so well during the potato planting. I explained the position and of course she understood. We cannot spare any of our sixth-form girls because of the State Scholarship. And I am afraid Mrs Reid considers the juniors are not strong enough to tackle the work. However, it is work of national importance and I found myself unable to turn her down out of hand. I have picked the eight of you because I believe you are well able to manage all of your examinations without extra tuition.' There were subdued sniggers from the Greek set. 'And I have complete faith in your ability to revise during your spare time.' She fixed the five of them with a severe gaze, then looked back at Morag. 'I explained to Mrs Reid that the decision would be yours, and I apologize for giving you such a responsibility. Perhaps . . .' here she gathered up her book, smoothed the skirt of her gown and prepared to rise, '. . . perhaps you would like to think about it, talk it over among yourselves and let me have your decision tomorrow. I assure you if you decide to take advantage of the tutorials, no-one will blame you. In any way whatsoever.'

Caroline said quickly, 'I want to help them, Doctor. If you think I can get the matric. all right, then I want to do some war work.'

Jannie muttered, 'I bet you do!'

Jennifer Tewson said, 'I feel the same, Dr Wilkie. I'm quite confident about the matric.— '

The Janson twins spoke in unison. 'So are we.'

Sibyl Porter said righteously, 'Our duty is obviously to the Reids. They have been very kind to us— '

'Hear, hear!' said the others.

'Like a Greek chorus,' Jannie hissed.

Dr Wilkie said quickly, 'I think you had better sleep on it. You need not feel in the least unpatriotic if you decide against it.'

Morag swallowed her embarrassment and said clearly, 'I think we would all like to do it, Dr Wilkie. It is no sacrifice.' She bared her soul completely. 'We enjoyed working for the Reids.'

Jannie cast discretion to the winds and said in an American accent, 'And how!'

There was a pause. Then Dr Wilkie said, 'I see.' She stood up at last. 'Very well. I will inform Mrs Reid tonight by telephone. And on Monday morning you will wait by the river gate for your transport. Seven o'clock sharp.'

She went to the door; her manner was less friendly now and not at all conciliatory.

'I expect the highest standards of behaviour out of school as well as in it. As you well know. This work is certainly of great national importance, but it is not a licence for any kind of foolishness whatsoever.'

She closed the door behind her with a decided snap and Jannie turned bitterly to Morag.

'Why didn't you just tell her we all want to have babies by Berry Reid!'

Val was more shocked than anyone. She spluttered helplessly before she exploded with, 'Jannie Mears! You are – you are – outrageous!'

But then the twins began to snigger and Juliet gave a screech of helpless mirth and soon even Val was trying not to laugh. Morag tried to join in, then thankfully noticed the time.

'Nine o'clock, girls! Silence for Alvar Liddell!'

And she switched on the news. And when they heard his sonorous voice announcing that Nazi Germany had attacked Russia, they all stopped laughing.

CHAPTER FOUR

June 1941

It was only two months since the potato planting, but everything about the moor and Reid's farm had changed in that time. Then the predominant colours had been grey and brown; grey skies, mud-brown fields. Now the early morning sun picked out every drop of dew on every blade of grass so that the eye was forced to seek out individual form and colour.

As the eight fifth-formers congregated by the bridge-gate that first morning, they all experienced a sense of euphoria at this sudden chance to 'commune with Nature' as Jennifer put it. Juliet said, 'When I think of the others – poor devils – swotting away under Willie's eagle eye, it makes me realize that we must have been touched by angels!'

Morag exploded. '"Touched by angels"? Are you reading Ethel M. Dell again, Ju?'

Juliet flushed slightly. 'As a matter of fact it's what my mother always said when I was a little girl.' She assumed a falsetto voice to show she was being funny. '"You're so beautiful, little Juliet – you must have been touched by angels!"'

The Janson twins sniggered their disparagement. Caroline half closed her eyes and took a deep breath. 'I'd rather be touched by Berry Reid,' she said.

There were some sounds of disgust from the Greek set. Morag did not laugh; she looked quickly at Caroline, then away.

The wagon hove into sight down the lane and the girls

50

ran towards it, hoping Berry would be driving, but it was their bus driver from last winter walking just under the chin of one of the shire horses.

'Take care, young ladies. I'll 'ave to back him round. Wait where he can see you – I've told him you're coming to help.'

Juliet said, 'How perfectly sweet! We'll introduce ourselves, shall we?' She pointed to the top button of her school blouse. 'I'm Juliet!' she announced solemnly. 'And this is Morag. And Caro. And Sibyl— '

'If you could just move over a bit, young lady, while I gets him around.'

'Sorry – sorry. You can call me Juliet, Mr . . .'

'And you can call me Cyril. Right my beauty, let's get our young ladies inside the wagon then we'll walk on.'

Morag wished so much that Val was there. They would have looked at each other, relished this exchange to the full. Juliet's tweeness had been so gracefully accepted by Cyril. And the very name, Cyril, would have been treasured.

They clambered over the tailgate of the wagon and disposed themselves on its dusty, hay-strewn floor. Something moved in the corner; Caroline screeched and the Janson twins clutched each other in terror.

Morag crawled forward and put her hand over a tiny shivering mouse.

'It's a harvest mouse!' she exclaimed in delight. 'Look.' She cupped the creature gently to show the others. 'Don't be frightened, girls, it's so pretty. And it came to escort us to the farm. Just like the horse and – and . . .' she giggled, 'Cyril.'

'Chuck it over the side, m'dear,' that gentleman called from in front. 'I know you young ladies don't like nothing like that.'

'Oh I do!' Morag settled back on her haunches, the mouse carefully held between her palms. 'It would die out there. I'll put it back in the stubble.'

'It'll die there too,' called Cyril. 'Kinder to put it out of its misery now.'

But Morag could not throw the mouse into the road not even when Caroline begged her. 'It's vermin, Mo! And it gives me the absolute creeps!'

Juliet was won over by the bulbous eyes and twitching whiskers. 'It should have a name. Mrs Tiggy-Winkle . . . But if Granny or Mrs Reid see you . . . well, I saw Granny wring the neck of a chicken at Easter. She's got no pity.'

Morag put the mouse inside the pocket of her dress and pleated it closed with a safety pin.

'Busy Lizzie,' she said, deciding to be as twee as Juliet. 'That's her name. Poor little Busy Lizzie. I'll make sure she's all right.'

They breasted the long rise of their own small valley and began the descent into the next. All the valleys on the moor were drained by shallow streams and Cyril clambered into the wagon to ford this one. The enormous shire horse plodded through the ankle-deep water and the cart tottered after him while the girls shouted excitedly and hung onto the sides as if they expected the squat cart to overturn. And then they were descending the last of the hills and the farm lay quietly in its folds, a thin spiral of smoke coming from the chimney, geese forming themselves into a hasty platoon and squawking as they came to meet the new arrivals.

Granny swotted them away with her apron while Mrs Reid let down the tailgate and held out her hands to each one of them.

'We're lucky to have you,' she beamed. 'But where's the little one? Jannie?'

'She's having to revise for the exams, Mrs Reid.' Morag kept her hand over her pocket. 'Vallery too.'

'Ah. So you are the clever girls. The ones who do not need to revise.' Mrs Reid smiled. 'I knew you were clever,' she nodded towards the Greek five, then smiled at Morag. 'But we thought you were the tomboy of the school! And Berry decided that you are too pretty to be clever, Caro. And you – Juliet is it? You are too silly!'

There was a chorus of protest. Then everyone laughed, simply because Mrs Reid was laughing and even Granny was showing her gums and it was such a beautiful morning. And anyway only Juliet and Morag felt wronged. Juliet considered herself sensitive rather than silly, and Morag, though she was good at games, had never thought of herself as a tomboy. And all of them registered that Berry thought Caroline was pretty. They all glanced at her covertly as they walked towards the fields. She was golden rather than blond; creamy skin and red lips like a cherry. And those enormous breasts . . .

The haywain was drawn up by the first of the ricks. Berry Reid and another man who could have been Cyril's twin were tossing and spreading the hay with pitchforks. The air was full of flying dust and seeds and bits of hay. Sybil sneezed.

Berry did not stop work. 'You'll get used to the dust, girls! Take a pitchfork each and emulate your elders and betters!' He pirouetted, his fork held high. 'Pretend it's a ballet class! The object of the exercise is to get the air in the stuff, then lay it out to dry. After that we pack it onto the rick. Got it?'

Cyril handed pitchforks around and began working himself, his movements economical but just as effective. For the first hour the girls were like dervishes, unloading the wain, scattering and tossing the hay. By ten o'clock their energy had evaporated with the sun and they were thankful to creep beneath the wagon bed and pass a bottle of cold tea around. Berry and the two men sprawled outside. Sybil propped herself against one of the wagon wheels and looked miserable.

Berry said, 'Listen, kid. If it's too much for you, you can go and lie down in the farmhouse. We can't spare the wagon to take you back yet, but you don't have to stay out here.'

'I'm all right,' Sybil said huskily, eyes streaming.

'Don't be ridiculous, Sibbie.' Morag poured some of the tea onto her handkerchief and held it out. 'Here. Press this against your eyes. Tannin is good for them. And then I'll walk back to the farm with you.'

Berry laughed. 'Good old Morag! You can take back the empty bottles and bring some fresh ones. And tell Ma we'll break at midday.'

Somehow Morag resented all of this: the bossiness, the jolly voice; as if she were vice-captain to his captain. She walked alongside the streaming Sibyl, her arms full of empty bottles and knew that he would never have spoken to Caroline like that.

Mrs Reid was not delighted to see them and settled Sibyl on a hard *chaise longue* in a gaunt parlour obviously kept for visitors. 'Not always the clever ones who are the best workers,' she commented as she closed the curtains. 'But you'd have had to come for some more tea, so we've only wasted one pair of hands.' She bustled around the kitchen swilling the bottles and refilling them. Granny sat in the porch plucking a chicken. Morag was glad she had not seen its neck wrung. With sudden horror she remembered the harvest mouse in her pocket.

'Busy Lizzie!' she exclaimed, terrified the creature had died already.

'That's right,' Mrs Reid said. 'Grows wild round here – no stopping it.' She grinned at Morag. 'Bit like you, m'dear. Strong and cheerful!' She put the half a dozen bottles in a sack and handed it to Morag, already ushering her to the door. 'Got to get on with the dinner. We'll see you at midday.'

Morag eased the heavy sack past Granny.

The old lady said unexpectedly, 'Cheap. Not strong. Cheap.'

Morag turned and looked at her. She was like something out of a children's story-book. The archetypal old crone.

'Sorry?'

' 'Tidn't strong and cheerful, like our Peggy just said. It's cheap and cheerful. And that's what busy lizzies is. Cheap and cheerful.'

The full implication of this was not lost on Morag. She should have laughed. But Granny had not intended to crack a joke. So she said, 'Oh,' and marched off across the farmyard, slinging the bottles over one shoulder with difficulty, thinking that as far as labour went they were all cheap; and they jolly well had to be strong unless they wanted to be like Sibyl.

She waited until she was out of sight of the back door, then put the sack of bottles carefully at the side of the track and cut across the stubble to where the land dipped into a natural hollow leading to the next stream. She crouched down and undid the safety pin with great care. Immediately the tiny mouse-head popped up and the bulbous eyes met hers, wildly questioning.

'Poor little Busy Lizzie.' Morag laughed her relief. 'You must be half suffocated! You were so still I forgot all about you!'

The mouse-whiskers twitched as if in response and the creature made no attempt to struggle out of the gingham pocket. It was so touching Morag wondered if there was any possibility of keeping it as a pet. Then she thought of the reaction from Val and Jannie and shook her head. 'Sorry, Lizzie. We've simply got to part company. It's just trying to find the best place to leave you.'

And Berry's voice said, 'Not there anyway. The first storm of rain and it will drown. High land.'

She managed to control her shock; it seemed important to show Berry Reid that his presence had no effect on her at all. She put a hand over the mouse-head and stood up gingerly. 'All right then. High ground.' She did not so much as look into his face and he too appeared to make a point of being matter-of-fact and simply turned and led the way out of the dell and then crouched and parted the stubble, looking down on to the baked earth as if searching for something.

'Here,' he said at last when she had started to feel the silence between them was unbearable. 'See? There are droppings. Just two . . . so tiny . . .' He held the stubble and moved to one side. 'Can you see? Mice have been here before. Maybe still are.'

She recalled Dr Wilkie's words last January about reading the moor like a book. Berry had seemed to be reading as he peered into the ground. She crouched too and stared down but could not distinguish anything in the packed earth.

'You're making fun of the whole thing,' she said making her voice light, furious with him.

But he protested. 'No. Seriously, Mo. I know it's an absolute mass of bits and pieces down there, but see . . .' his head touched hers as he leaned down, '. . . on that yellow stalk . . . can't you see?'

A speck of dust could have been adhering to the stalk. She was so conscious of his thatch of black gypsy-hair pressing against her centre parting that it was difficult to see anything. It was simply vital to put space between them.

'Then Lizzie can go down here,' she said, straightening and reaching into her pocket.

'You know their life-span is very short?' He sat back on his haunches and watched as she placed the mouse into the stubble.

'Hardly worth all this fuss?' She made the mistake of smiling up at him and saw that for once his dark eyes were very serious.

'Life is worth any amount of fuss.' He smiled at last. Almost apologetically. 'I mean, isn't she a symbol of what we're fighting for?'

'Lizzie?' Morag was astonished. Was this still Berry Reid?

'It's the sort of thing Hugh would do . . . rescue a mouse.' He was still apologetic. 'My brother, Hugh. He's very like you.'

She recalled Hugh Reid. Gentle and very English.

Hadn't someone likened him to Leslie Howard? Not a bit like Morag Heyward.

Berry cleared his throat. 'Sorry. Perhaps we'd better get back to the others.'

'Yes. I left the tea bottles back there.' She made a movement of her head.

'I saw them. That's how I found you.'

'You were looking for me?'

'Yes. No. Not really looking. I thought I'd walk back with you.'

'Oh.'

He stood up and held out his hands. She took them because the Bluebell girls were never ungracious; but she dropped them very quickly. They began to walk back to the track.

He laughed, sounding more like the Berry Reid who teased and bossed and was generally insufferable.

'D'you know they call you the nuns?'

'The nuns?'

'Yes. You must have heard that Gallenwick was a nunnery a hundred years ago.'

'Someone did say. Cyril, I think.' She cleared her throat. 'Who calls us that?'

'People around here.'

'But there's no-one. Not until Lynmouth.'

'We're not the only farm.'

'But everything is so scattered. How do you know that is what people call us?'

'We have social evenings. Young Farmers' dances. We see each other in the Doone Arms.'

'Oh . . . I didn't realize . . .'

'Surely you must have realized that the arrival of a girls' school in a place like this was certain to cause a lot of talk. Speculation.'

'How do you mean . . . speculation?'

He laughed again, this time uncomfortably. 'Well . . . about what you are all . . . like.'

There was a long pause. They came to the sack

containing the bottles but neither of them bent to pick it up.

She said at last. 'You have taken it upon yourself to find out?'

'No! Not like that. That sounds . . . you know . . . caddish.' He laughed again at his own choice of words. Then, in the face of her silence he blurted, 'I've always said that one day I'll live in the abbey. It's got the most perfect light – some of those turrets are just made for an artist. You should go and see it. Though I suppose it's forbidden ground after what happened before.'

She risked looking right at him. His boyish enthusiasm was somehow endearing and she permitted herself a small smile. 'What did happen before? And when?'

Encouraged, he grinned. 'I'm not sure. Some scandal. One of the nuns made an ass of herself.'

She was instantly nettled. 'Are you sure it wasn't one of the monks doing that?'

'Possibly. Possibly. Though as a general rule . . .' He saw her face and went on quickly. 'They can't get any more postulants, you know. Young men want to go to war, they don't want to sit and think about it! In another ten years time it will be up for sale. You'll see.'

'And you'll buy it?'

'If I can.'

'And meanwhile the people around here who call us nuns, call you a monk?'

He knew she was goading him and flushed slightly. 'The analogy was silly in the first place. Sorry, Mo. It's just that . . . well . . . as I come to Gallenwick with supplies and things . . . they think I ought to be finding out all about you girls.'

She studied him, enjoying his discomfiture but angry at all the implications behind this. The school was obviously considered some kind of freak show. It was disgusting. She stared him right in the eyes and noticed their apparent lack of pupil; registered that his nose was definitely Roman and his mouth long and his teeth very white and his chin prominent.

He fidgeted like a small boy and blurted, 'For instance, you are the Indian princess.'

She was startled. 'The what?'

'Black hair, parted in the middle, single plait always fraying out. Perfectly oval face and long arms and legs— '

'And Caroline?' she said sharply.

'The milkmaid. Dimpled. Shy— '

'I think you are being insulting!' Her voice was so haughty she could practically hear it in her nostrils. 'And actually, I find the local gossip-mongerers incredibly boring. Do pass on that we are not in the least interested in them or their . . . messenger!'

She was so glad she had got that in before it was too late. She marched up the track and left the heavy sack to him. She was simply fuming. When she reached the haywain, the girls were working slowly and without enthusiasm under Cyril's direction. At the sight of Berry Reid they became instantly alert and threw the hay around like maniacs.

Morag despised them all.

She was not quite certain whether Berry kept his distance from her or she from him during the rest of the haymaking. When they began to make the ricks, either she was below him, tossing the hay up, or she was with Cyril on top of the rick catching the flying bundles and tamping them down to Cyril's gentle instructions. At 'gorge-times' he took his food outside and ate with the other two men; they kept an eye on the weather and argued with Granny Thomas about various signs and portents. But there was no sign of rain and every early morning was a repeat of that first one and every evening the sun would stain the sky with glowing streaks over the invisible sea.

Meanwhile Val and Jannie were doing most of their

revision sitting under the line of elms that bordered the lawns, and though they envied Morag her time with Berry Reid, when the eight girls returned each evening, red as lobsters and scratching frantically at their midge bites, they decided piously they were doing the right thing. 'We've got to do well in matric.,' Val said, almost apologetically as she dabbed witch-hazel on Morag's back. 'The extra boarding fees and all . . .'

Jannie, sitting at the top of the bed trying to brush burrs from Morag's long hair, murmured, 'Yes . . . certainly,' though she was quite sure Marius would pay twice the fees to get her out of the house.

'It's not as bad as it looks,' Morag said, her voice muffled by her pillow. 'It's pure Thomas Hardy what with little Busy Lizzie and Granny Thomas and everything. I mean, if it weren't for that self-satisfied chump of a son, it would be utterly delightful.'

Val and Jannie exchanged glances. Jannie said, 'You've had a row with Berry Reid?'

'Not really. He's not worth rowing with.' Morag shifted her face so that she could breathe. 'It's simply the way he . . . manipulates all of us. Labels us. Oh, I don't know! He seems to think we're all like the old nuns used to be. Sex-starved or something.'

'Well . . .' Val had tried several times to reason with Morag about Berry Reid; she was bored by him. 'At least tomorrow is your last day.'

But Morag, very uncharacteristically, was not to be comforted. 'And then it's the start of the matric.! And I won't have a chance to revise! And I bet I won't get it so I won't be able to sit the Higher or take a State Scholarship . . . my life will be ruined!'

Val sighed. Obviously Morag was about to have her period. Not that Doc Willie believed in people getting tetchy before their periods.

She said peaceably, 'Let's go and have supper and walk down the avenue in time for the nightjars.'

The girls had made a routine of walking in the avenue

60

as the sun went down. It had become a superstition. Just before the air raid warden arrived and the intermittent hum of the engines warned them that the German bombers were again flying up the Severn estuary, they would go and listen to the nightjars. Mrs Maitland had first introduced them to the unusual nocturnal churring sound. 'It's not a song like the nightingales, certainly, but it's rather special,' she had said. 'And the nuns thought of them as guardians warning off intruders.'

Val had seized on this.

'They'll warn the bombers off too,' she had said determinedly. 'So long as they keep churring away, we're all safe!'

That evening it was almost dark beneath the elms and the heat seemed to have been trapped beneath the umbrella of foliage so that the air was difficult to breathe. The three friends half sat, half lay on the slope of the lawn watching the tiny birds flitting through the branches like bats after the insects.

Jannie said, 'Do you realize that it is exactly six months since we arrived here?'

The other two digested this and Val said slowly, 'It's the longest time I've ever been away from home.'

Morag said, 'But it's been good, hasn't it? On the whole, I mean.'

'It's been the best time of my life,' Jannie said.

'Not for me.' Val was very definite.

Morag persisted. 'It's been good for us, Val. No, seriously. We know now that we can manage on our own. That's pretty good, isn't it?'

Val was astonished. 'Who wants to manage on their own? I certainly do not!'

'Well, not on our own exactly. But we've got each other.'

Jannie said happily, 'Yes. We've got each other. We'll always have each other whatever happens.'

'Oh I know that. Of course.' Val did not want to hurt anyone's feelings. 'But . . . oh my Lord, I think

I'd die if anything happened to Mother and Dad. Or Teddy.'

Morag persisted. 'But you wouldn't. That's the trouble, Val. You have to go on living. And these past six months have shown you that you could.'

Val was almost angry. 'Are you saying you can manage without your parents?'

For an instant Morag had a vision of the oriel window at home; her mother's face, alight with interest as she brought the toast rack to the breakfast table; her father's tall figure walking along Park Row. But still she said slowly, 'I suppose that's what I am saying.'

Jannie put in eagerly, 'I know what you mean, Mo. It's a feeling of independence. Of-of-self-reliance— '

Val made a sound of disgusted disbelief and from further down the avenue Mrs Maitland's voice called them.

'Girls, are you there? Vallery – Morag?'

'Here, Maitie,' Morag called back, thankful to put an end to the conversation.

Mrs Maitland appeared. 'Thought I'd come and find you with some good news. Vallery, apparently your brother has managed to get a job driving an officer to Exeter tomorrow— '

Val gave a glad cry. 'Don't tell me! I can go in to Exeter and meet him!'

Mrs Maitland laughed. 'Better than that. He's got permission to bring your mother with him, Morag. And after they've delivered their wing commander, they're going to be allowed to drive home via Gallenwick!'

Morag leapt high in the air, midge bites and Berry Reid forgotten.

'How wonderful! When will they come – how long – oh Maitie, I'll have to wriggle out of the haymaking somehow!'

'No need. They won't be here until supper-time. Dr Wilkie has suggested that the four of you have sandwiches and cocoa in your sitting room. I imagine they'll want to start back before it's completely dark. But you should have a couple of hours at least.'

Val said, 'Oh, Maitie, I love you!'

'Nothing to do with me. But I am very happy for you. And I think you'd better come back to the house now. It's almost dark and you've frightened the nightjars half to death with your screeching.'

Val said, 'We need them . . . here comes the air raid warden.'

And even as he came pedalling up the drive bent low over his handlebars, the bombers began droning across the sky like a swarm of hornets. The girls hurried up the drive, Mrs Maitland holding Jannie's arm comfortingly. Mrs Mears could have had a lift with Mrs Heyward and Teddy McKinley, but apparently she had been too busy.

The girls no longer filed into the cellars; Dr Wilkie had decided that with the examinations coming up, rest was the first priority. They might not sleep but they could learn to relax. 'Mind over matter, girls,' she had exhorted them during evening prayers. 'By relaxing we gain a small victory over the Hun.' Dr Wilkie had been at school herself during the Great War and they had called the Germans Huns then.

As Mrs Maitland ran her across the stable yard and past the pump, Jannie laughed suddenly and said, 'Here comes the Horrid Hun, zooming from the setting sun!'

Mrs Maitland squeezed her arm. 'Steady the Buffs!'

They paused breathlessly inside the old stables. Morag and Val opened the door to the sitting room where the others were clustered around the unblacked-out windows in the twilight, trying to spot the enemy armada.

Jannie laughed again. 'Hun. Such an ugly word. Hun. Hun. Hun. Hun.'

'For God's sake, Jannie!' protested Val.

Mrs Maitland said conversationally, 'Actually it rhymes with fun, doesn't it?'

Jannie hung back for a moment and watched her friends join the others in the window. She said quietly, 'But it's not fun, is it? It reminds me of someone I know. He rapes and pillages too. And calls it fun.'

She turned suddenly and planted a kiss on Mrs Maitland's forehead. 'It's all right, I don't mind. Honestly.' And she moved swiftly across the room like a shadow and joined the other shadows by the window.

The next day the prospect of seeing her mother that evening made Morag feel incandescent with happiness. The hard work, the midge bites, the prickly heat, the awful consciousness of being in the same area as Berry Reid, all took second place. She was her old self, jollying the others along, pitching and tossing the hay long after they had retired beneath the wain for their cold tea.

At gorge-time there was pickled mackerel with as much green salad as the girls could eat.

'This is a treat as it's your last day,' Mrs Reid said, beaming with pleasure at their enthusiasm. 'Our Hugh came home last night with a crate of 'em! So I set to and pickled them all! I want you to take some back with you and make sure that little Jannie gets her share!'

Morag grinned hugely. She would present the fish as a present from Hugh. The three of them were the only ones who had actually seen Hugh Reid and Jannie had thought he looked like Leslie Howard.

Juliet said, 'Hugh is your middle son, Mrs Reid?'

'Aye. The gentlest and the kindest.' Mrs Reid spoke matter-of-factly. 'Durston is the one who gets things done. Ambitious is Durston. And Berry— ' She glinted at her youngest who had just brought in three empty plates from the 'street café' as he called it. 'Berry takes after his father. Berry is going to live in the abbey and paint pictures. Aren't you, Berry?'

For the first time since she had met him, Morag saw the dark gypsy skin flush red.

'Ma . . .' he protested.

Caroline said eagerly, 'Are you a painter, Berry? You never told me!'

'See what you've done, Ma?'

Juliet said, 'Shall we meet Hugh, Mrs Reid?'

'I dare say he'll give a hand this afternoon. He's on a forty-eight pass.'

They were silent knowing what that meant. Hugh's ship would be taking out another convoy the day after tomorrow.

Sibyl, supposedly disinterested in 'local gossip' said, 'Is your oldest son not home, Mrs Reid? I understood they were in the same crew?'

Mrs Reid looked at Berry who rolled his eyes.

'Dusty has other fish to fry,' he told Sibyl. Then, glancing at his reloaded plates, he added as humorously as he could, 'Or to pickle, of course.' He aimed a kiss at Mrs Reid's nose. 'Nothing like fresh pickled mackerel, Ma.'

She darted to the sink. 'I suppose that means thank you very much for my nice dinner,' she commented dryly, shaking soda onto a pile of plates and going for the kettle.

The girls chorused their own thanks and watched Granny as she came to the table with an enormous bowl of stewed gooseberries.

'I thought it was boys who was always hungry,' commented the old lady as they ladled fruit with a will.

Morag looked directly at Berry. 'Well, these girls are doing men's work,' she said.

He met her gaze. His eyes were as black as coals. He said, 'And doing it better than most men.'

She swallowed. She was certain he said it just to make sure she worked harder than ever that afternoon but still she wondered if she would ever be as happy as at this precise moment.

Sure enough, before the afternoon was halfway over, Hugh Reid appeared in old grey flannels and a cricket shirt open at the neck. Standing next to Berry, laughing, slapping each other's backs, he looked slight, almost insubstantial. But when he picked up a fork and joined Morag and Juliet beneath their rick, she could see the knotted muscles in his forearms and neck.

He smiled at Morag. 'We've met, I believe. In the rain. Do you remember?'

Juliet was pop-eyed. He might not be a swashbuckler like Berry but as if anyone would forget meeting this man.

Morag smiled back. 'Of course I remember.' It was so easy to be natural with Hugh. 'It was just before we all came to the farm for the potato planting.'

He twirled his fork as if loading it with spaghetti and sent a knot of hay whirling up to Cyril and the Janson twins.

'That's right. I was going to help, wasn't I? And then I was recalled.' He turned his nice smile on Juliet. 'And you are— '

'This is Juliet Mortimer.' Morag introduced her formally.

He paused long enough to shake Juliet's hand. She giggled foolishly.

'There were two other girls with you that day.' He tossed the hay expertly as he looked from Juliet to Morag. 'One like a water sprite, the other like Bubbles.'

Morag laughed. How the others would be flattered by this vivid memory. He was so sweet . . . so different from his brother.

'Yes. They can't come this time. Revising for the exams.' She tried to toss as much hay as he did and was out of breath. 'The exams are next week.' He made a sympathetic face and she suddenly had to tell him how happy she was. 'But Val's brother and my mother are coming to see us this evening!' She had wanted to tell someone else all day and he was the perfect recipient.

'How top-hole!' He rested momentarily on his fork

and gave her his undivided attention. 'Of course you did not see them at Easter, did you?'

She shook her head and he smiled sympathetically then turned to Juliet who, after all, had no visitors that evening. 'Only another four or five weeks and you'll be home for the summer,' he consoled her.

'Yes.' Juliet smiled back adoringly. 'Rather.'

Cyril shouted from above, 'Send it up, boy!'

But from across the field Berry yelled, 'A hand needed here! Someone's fallen by the wayside!'

Morag glanced at Juliet who was still staring adoringly at Hugh.

'All right. I'll go.'

She felt completely selfless as she ran across the stubble. She was letting Juliet have Hugh entirely to herself and she was showing fate that she didn't care whether she breathed the same air as Berry Reid or not. But when she arrived at his rick and discovered that it was Caro who was being supported to the shade of the cart, she wasn't so sure of herself. Because Caro's place was on top of the rick with Berry.

'Hello there!' Berry grinned as he hauled her up by his side. 'You can't get away from me this time – and I'm almost certain you're not the sort who will faint away in the midday sun!'

She reminded herself of this evening's visit; told herself she did not care about the obnoxious Berry Reid and his universal, domineering, utterly repulsive charm. She caught the flying hay, pushed it into the rick, packed it with her feet, did not let any visions come between her and her work . . . especially not of Berry in a painting smock, standing by a window overlooking the sea.

He said, 'Don't put quite so much into it, Mo. You'll exhaust yourself.' He steadied her, his hand warm on her upper arm. 'Look. Just press with the instep . . . use your own weight to tamp it down— '

'Are you trying to tell me I am fat?' she asked, her voice high and unreasonable.

'Oh stop it!' He pulled her round to face him. 'You're acting like – like – Caroline Prosser!'

That was probably the worst insult he could have inflicted in that context. She stared at him, wanting quite desperately to whack him across the head and knowing that it was probably what he would enjoy most.

He said, 'Mo, you really are very beautiful. Your plait is all over the place and your face is the colour of mellow brick. But you're still beautiful.'

And quite suddenly his words defused all her feelings of anger. She held her breath, caught in a moment of sheer magic. Everything slowed down; it was as if she were hovering somewhere, maybe she had become one of the molecules of sunlit air, part of the universe, yet able to observe, to see, to understand. She and Berry were isolated on top of this mound of packed hay and there were the others below them, tossing and twirling flying strands. Everything seemed suspended in the thick density of the dust motes, the still, hot, golden glow of the sun. She saw it all, like a scene from a play, separate from herself, yet including her as a someone with a part to play. And Berry saw it too. That was the marvellous thing. Their perceptions flowed together. Slowly, inevitably, they leaned in towards each other. Their mouths touched and held. He dropped his pitchfork and gripped her shoulders. For what seemed eternity and was no more than a second, they were an entity. She had been kissed often before: her parents, her aunt, once by Teddy McKinley under the mistletoe. This kiss was not like any of those.

Caroline sat huddled in the corner of the haywain, looking sick. Juliet walked with the shire alongside Hugh Reid. The Greek set were sharing some private intellectual joke.

Morag, wondering if any of this afternoon had really happened, said, 'If it's any consolation I felt the sun up there too.'

Caroline began to cry quietly.

'Whatever is it? Come on, Caro. You know you'll feel better after a lie-down in the dorm.'

Caroline said something inaudible and Morag, suddenly anxious, crouched by her trying to get an arm around her.

'I can't hear you . . . do you want to be sick?'

'No – yes! Oh God, Morrie . . . I've made such a fool of myself! He told me to pull myself together! He said just because he – he took me dancing didn't mean he wanted to marry me!' She groaned and lowered her head to her knees. 'Oh, Morrie, I actually thought – I asked him if we were engaged! Oh, Morrie, I wish I could die!'

Morag stared at the weeping girl for some time. She did not doubt Caroline was talking about Berry Reid. Then she knelt, putting her back between Caroline and the Janson twins. She said in a low, urgent voice, 'It's all right. Honestly. He makes fools of all of us. It's his way of getting us to work like the Trojan women. But we've finished here now and he'll be called up and you need never see him again.'

Caroline looked up, her face drowning in tears. 'It was my own fault, Morrie! I – I'm no better than a – a Jezebel! I – I offered myself to him, Morrie! I put his hand here,' she touched her rounded breast. 'I knew, you see – he's looked at me there so often. So I asked him to feel my heart beating and put his hand . . .' Her face contracted and she groaned again and lowered her head almost to the dusty floor of the wagon. Morag stared at the exposed nape of her neck. Its creamy vulnerability made her want to weep. She rubbed the top of Caroline's spine and saw the scene on the top of the haywain through distorting spectacles. What a fool she had been. The same as Caroline; exactly the same as Caroline. How he must be laughing. Right now.

Caroline wept quietly for a while then lifted her head and looked at Morag with a new expression of determination.

'I'm going to forget all this. You're right, it's our last day and the heat . . . he said it would break tomorrow and we'd just finished in time. He said . . .' Her face began to crumple and she straightened it with difficulty. 'He said they'd never have done it without us. That we were an inspiration . . .'

Morag said drily, 'He says those kind of things to get that extra effort out of us. He's very clever like that.'

'Yes. I was a fool to take it personally. It was just that . . . he always looked at me. And he asked me to go dancing with him. Ages ago. And I went. I'm no good at dancing but it was . . . he held me very close . . . I can't tell you.'

'I know,' Morag said woodenly.

'And I thought he must like me . . . really like me . . . because he kept asking me . . . And afterwards he would kiss me— '

'He kissed you too?' Morag asked.

'Yes. It was . . . you know, what Jannie calls a French kiss. It was as if he came right into my body and took over.'

Morag said, 'Yes.'

Caroline was breathing quickly. 'I shouldn't have let him, Mo. I knew it was wrong.'

Morag said scornfully, 'It doesn't mean anything. Just a kiss.'

Caroline groaned and sank her head to her knees again.

'It was . . . more than that. But it was my fault. I put his hand . . .' She sobbed again and Morag held her close and tried not to think of Berry Reid kissing Caroline Prosser and then putting his hand on her breast.

After a while, Caroline stopped sobbing and then she said in her high little-girl voice, 'Men are different from us, Morrie. They don't feel things like we do.'

Morag looked over the edge of the wagon at Juliet walking alongside Hugh Reid and visibly falling in love with him.

'No,' she agreed.

CHAPTER FIVE

Her mother looked older than Morag remembered; her hair had been flattened by her linen hat, and the long day had worn away her usual discreet make-up so that the lines around her eyes were plainly etched. But when she laughed it was all right again, and she laughed more often than usual, almost as if she were nervous.

'Daddy is all right?' Morag asked for the second time as they were ushered into the sitting room by a delighted Mrs Maitland bearing tea and sponge cakes.

'Of course, my darling.' Lucy Heyward smiled reassuringly and sat by the window where she could watch the sun setting. 'He's working too hard, of course, but so is everyone else.' She glanced at her watch. 'He misses you. We both miss you.'

'Oh, Mummy.' Morag wished she could tell her mother about Berry; about the kiss. There was not time. If there had been she would still have kept silent.

'Now, darling, we mustn't be sad, we've only got an hour. Teddy and I want to be home before the siren goes.' Lucy laughed again, then hugged Morag. 'I'm so pleased to see you, dear girl. And looking well too. You all look well. I couldn't believe it when I set eyes on Jannie – she's positively blooming!'

Teddy passed tea, nodding agreement. 'Val's put on so much weight – at least you've kept a decent figure, Mo!'

Val hit him perfunctorily and turned to Lucy Heyward to enquire after her own mother.

Teddy said humorously to Morag, 'She doesn't believe me – told her the parents are fine.' His blue eyes narrowed. 'Actually, old girl, you are looking a bit

71

pinched. Sure you're OK? Getting your share of all these eggs, butter and whatnot from the farm?'

'Yes.' Morag smiled. Teddy was so nice. 'I simply work harder than anyone else!' She too became serious. 'Mummy looks as if she could do with some of our extras. I bet she gives her rations to Daddy.'

'It's not lack of food.' Teddy looked gloomy. 'It's lack of sleep. And your father is working all hours. Casualties, you know.' He saw Morag's expression. 'I shouldn't tell you this – I'm such a damned fool! Look, old girl, nothing to be done about it, so no point in worrying.'

Lucy caught the remark and said, 'Who is worrying? Not you two, I hope. We don't want any of that!' She picked up Morag's and Val's hands and held them tightly. 'We've come to wish you luck with the matric. next week – not to worry you!'

Val groaned theatrically but Morag persisted.

'That's all very well, but what about the holidays? Shall we have to stay here again?'

Val groaned louder and with very real horror.

Lucy swung their hands in hers. 'Some of you will be staying here, yes. But Val's mother has offered to have Mo and Jannie at Clevedon. Don't you think that is great news?' She squeezed Morag's fingers as she spoke and looked at her directly.

Morag swallowed. 'Yes. That really is most kind— '

Val whooped her approbation. 'We can camp out in Norton's Woods!' she said. 'D'you remember, Teddy? We used to take Daddy's old scout tent and go on survival courses!'

Teddy said, 'Lugging a trolley behind us absolutely piled high with provisions!'

'Except,' Val added defensively, 'that Mummy forgot to put the tin opener in!'

Morag said quietly, 'Could I come home in the daytime, Mother? It might be useful to watch Daddy do an op now and then.'

'Of course, Mo!' Lucy pulled on her hat and opened

her bag to find her gloves. 'And Mrs McKinley says I can come out at any time. It's only fifteen miles and there are still plenty of trains.'

'That will be . . . good,' Morag said. And Teddy added, 'Gooder than good. Let's say rather superb! I might have some embark. leave then so we'll have four for tennis!'

Val looked at him, her blue eyes enormous.

'You've got a posting?' she said.

'Yes. And don't ask where because I have to be like Dad and keep Mum!' He grinned and ruffled her curls. 'Come on now, sis. There is a war on, you know!'

Lucy stood up. 'I rather think we must go. We shall be thinking of you on Monday. French oral, isn't it?' She took Val's arm. 'Walk with me as far as the gate, will you, Val? It's so beautiful along that avenue. Mo can go with Teddy in the car.'

Morag thought it was her mother's way of easing the parting; she let Teddy lead the way to the pump in the stable yard where the car was parked, its gasbag undulating gently in the heat. He opened the passenger door and bowed as she sat in and she laughed dutifully and wished she did not feel so – so dislocated. The inside of the car smelled of warm leather and cigarettes and when Teddy rounded the bonnet and got in beside her, his smell added to the general maleness. For so long she had been mostly in the company of women. Now there were Berry, Hugh, Teddy, all of them jostling into her consciousness.

He started the engine with some difficulty – 'Damned gas . . . the engines don't like it, you know,' – and bounced sedately out of the yard and onto the gravel sweep in front of the house. The avenue was still empty; the girls were all at supper. Far ahead of them they could see Val and Lucy standing beneath a tree obviously listening for an early nightjar.

'They won't come yet,' Morag said. 'Too early.'

Teddy misunderstood. 'They like to find the Bristol Channel before dark. Gives them the perfect landfall.'

73

Morag realized he meant the Heinkel bombers. She bit her lip.

Teddy pulled in to the side of the avenue and sat back, eyes closed, letting the engine run.

'I asked your mother to try to give us a few minutes alone,' he said, his voice suddenly much deeper than usual. 'It won't take a moment.'

Morag looked at him sharply. 'She's ill, isn't she? Or is it my father?'

'Neither. They're fine. I just wanted to tell you. About my posting. It's Africa.'

'I see.' Morag stared at his closed eyes. His lashes were blond; the sun glinted on a dusting of hairs over his cheeks. He was older than Berry yet looked much younger.

She said, 'I suppose you want me to keep an eye on Val. But should you tell me?'

He opened his eyes; they were intensely blue, like Val's. 'I want you to know. I'll write, of course. But I want you to know about it so that – well, you'll understand why I am asking you to marry me.'

She opened her own eyes. 'Marry you? I don't understand. How can I marry you? I'm at school – there's matric. Then Higher— '

'Not yet. Of course not yet. But I want to know – when I'm away – that you're thinking it over. Just thinking it over. That's all.' He turned and looked through the windscreen. Skeins of gnats were everywhere. 'I've never been away from home before.'

'Oh . . . Teddy. Oh, how awful. I'm so selfish – I didn't realize— ' She could have broken down then. Teddy McKinley, always laughing, always teasing, and now, homesick.

She said, 'It'll be all right, Teddy. I thought, like you, that I couldn't survive without Mother and Dad. We were only talking about it last evening . . .'

He said woodenly, 'You and Val and Jannie. You're together.'

'You'll make friends too, Teddy. Of course you will!'

'But you see, old girl, if I had something to hang on to – a future – can you understand?'

'I think so. Oh I do think so, Teddy. But I really . . . I mean, you've always been like the brother I didn't have – I simply cannot – cannot— '

'Adjust. That's what you have to do. Adjust. And I thought if I put it into your head now, when you come to Redley Lodge in the summer, you'd be able to – to see me in a different way. And you'll be able to tell me whether there's any hope at all or whether . . . well, you know.'

'Oh, Teddy, of course.' She looked at him earnestly. 'I promise I'll do that. I won't let you down.'

'It's not a question of letting me down, old girl. It's finding out how you feel about me. I would want you to be quite honest – you mustn't be sorry for me or anything.'

'All right. I won't be. Oh, Teddy!'

'I say, look here, you mustn't be upset, Mo. I didn't want you to be upset!' He was all concern.

She wiped furiously at her cheek. 'Does Mother know about this?'

'Yes. I told her after we'd dropped the wingco. On our way here from Exeter.'

'Is she for it?'

'I think so. Well, I suppose both our families . . . I mean . . . you know.'

'Yes. Oh, Teddy.'

'Morag, I'm sorry. Maybe I shouldn't have said anything yet. But later – in August – we'll be together then and— '

'Yes, Teddy, all right. Yes.'

'Do you mean— ?'

'No. I mean in August I'll – we'll talk about it – perhaps— '

'Yes. That was what I meant.' He forced a sudden laugh. 'I say, we're getting mixed up, aren't we? But at the end of it all, we do understand each other, don't we, Mo? I mean, I understand about you wanting to be a doctor and I'll help you – I will, I promise. And you understand that I just want to go into the business and help Pa. I mean, I'm not ambitious or anything. Would that worry you?'

'No. Not a bit. When I've come to some of the sales with Val . . . I've loved it.'

He said quietly, 'Auctioneering is all about . . . homes.'

Morag stopped looking at him; she knew he was almost crying.

Far down the avenue at the arched gateway, Val and Lucy waved. Teddy put the car into gear and they chugged slowly between the elms.

During the two weeks that followed, Morag concentrated her whole attention on her work. She would not let herself think of Berry Reid or of her mother; even Jannie and Val became shadowy. The only person she could relate to was Caroline Prosser and even she seemed a pale shadow of her former buxom self.

After the English paper Caroline said wanly, 'I didn't bother much. I described the farm all à la Hardy and left it at that.'

Morag had wanted to write about the haymaking; instead she had described Gallenwick and its old associations with Lyn Abbey. She had aimed at a satirical Gothic pastiche; it was easy now to be cutting and cynical about . . . everything.

Val and Jannie were very pleasantly surprised that they were able to deal with most of the papers.

'The revision paid off!' Jannie said, imitating James Cagney without success. 'Good job we didn't go to the farm that week, Val. Old Willie was right after all.'

'Yes.' Val narrowed her blue eyes at Morag. 'It seems those who helped with the haymaking are all a bit Keatsy and Lady of Shallottish now.'

'How?' Jannie asked blankly.

'"Alone and palely loitering",' Val explained watching Morag and Caroline languishing against the pump down in the stable yard.

Jannie looked out of the window. 'They're only going to listen to the nightjars,' she said.

'At tea-time?' Val watched the two girls walk slowly across the yard. 'And together?'

Jannie said, 'It's that Hugh Reid. Juliet's the worst. I'm not really surprised. Did Mo tell you what he called me? A water sprite!' Her small face flushed with the thought of it. 'A water sprite indeed!'

'We must have looked pretty watery that day. It was raining buckets.'

'Yes, but a sprite!'

'Oh for goodness' sake!' Val picked up an armful of books and made for the door. 'I'm going down for tea in the sitting room. And I think I'll sit by bloody Sibyl Porter! At least she can talk about something other than the bloody Reids!'

Jannie grinned. 'Language, Vallery dear. And just because he called you Bubbles instead of a sprite!'

She sat on her bed and listened to Val clattering down the stairs to the sitting room. The threatened rain had not yet come but the sky was steely grey and the heat prickly. She wondered what her mother was doing right now. She wondered whether Marius still called round regularly at the ugly modern house looking out on to the observatory tower. Whether he went up to her mother's bedroom some nights and made her cry out as he had done that snowy night last January. And why her mother had never cried out like that when her father went to bed with her. She thought of Hugh Reid who looked as gentle as Leslie Howard the film star. He would never make anyone cry out. Maybe she was like her mother and that would not be enough. Maybe she needed someone else . . . someone like Berry Reid. Yes, Berry Reid would make her cry out.

Slowly she lay back on the bed and slipped her hand inside the wide leg of her mother's camiknickers. And afterwards she wept with guilt and shame and whispered, 'Mummy, why didn't you come to see me? There was room in the damned and bloody car, after all!'

The Fateful Fortnight, as Val called it, wound itself to a close at last. The Greek set were still involved in their special papers, but they were escorted to Oxford by train for those; the sixth had long finished their Highers and State Scholarships; the school returned to normal. The juniors, practically locked up for the past two weeks, burst onto the lawns and danced like dervishes. The sixth were sent home to do their bit for the war, their education deferred for 'the duration'. There was a special dinner for them and Dr Wilkie made a speech that reduced the girls to tears.

They walked down the avenue and listened dutifully to the nightjars.

'Well . . .' Val flung herself onto the grass and stared through the dense foliage at the sky. It had been overcast and showery since that last day of haymaking. 'Well, what now?'

Jannie said, 'Ten days before we break up. They've let the sixth go home. D'you think we could go early?'

'What a wonderful idea.' Val propped herself on an elbow. 'Mo . . . you're well in with Doc Willie. Go and ask her if we can pack up tomorrow and get the train.' She stared at Morag's back and said loudly, 'Morrie! Are you listening? I just said— '

'Yes, I know. I heard. I suppose it's a good idea.'

'Well, don't have hysterics about it, please.' Val's face tightened. 'You're not the only one who has moods, you know! Jannie and I have had to put up with you like this for over a fortnight— '

'Seventeen days, actually.'

'Oh, you admit you've been absolutely insufferable?'

'Sorry.' Morag turned with one of her rare smiles. 'Sorry, girls. What between the matric. and— '

'And what?' Jannie asked curiously.

'And the fact that I think I caught the sun that last day . . . Anyway, of course I'll see Doc Willie. But if she sticks her toes in, I've just thought of something we can do.'

'Which is?' Val asked suspiciously.

'Investigate the mystery of Lyn Abbey!' Morag said triumphantly.

Val was unimpressed. 'How exciting,' she said flatly.

Jannie said, 'Hang on, Val. If we're going to be stuck here for the next week and a bit, that would be a good idea. All those men, practically eunuchs . . . voluntary eunuchs too . . . I think we ought to find out a bit more about them!'

Val groaned. Morag said briskly, 'We're not interested in the present, Jannie, just the past. Something happened there. Something concerning Gallenwick . . . and therefore, in a way, concerning us!'

Val said prosaically, 'It's probably common knowledge in the village. Let's ask Mrs Reid.'

'Yes!' Jannie jumped up and down. 'Let's go to the farm and ask Mrs Reid.'

'I'm never going to Reid's farm again,' Morag said definitely.

'Why not? The boys have gone if that's what's worrying you,' Val said.

'Don't be silly! There will be no mystery if we ask Mrs Reid and she tells us!' Morag rolled her eyes despairingly. 'Don't you see? She might know the facts. We have to find out more than facts!'

Jannie said, 'I don't get it.'

Morag sighed. 'We need to feel the – the ambience of the place itself! How it affected one of our nuns. The kind of journey she had to make to get there . . .'

Jannie said, 'I can tell you the story now without asking a soul. She fell for one of the monks. She got pregnant. They excommunicated her.'

Val and Morag tore up grass and pelted Jannie, laughing helplessly. Then they escorted Morag to the door of Dr Wilkie's office and made sure she went inside to ask permission for an early return home.

The answer, as they had expected, was no.

The next morning they informed Mrs Maitland that they were going to do an all-day ramble.

'Very well. But you must be back in time for tea, girls. Well before dark. Otherwise it will be the dreaded search party!'

Two of the juniors had gone missing once before and the local defence volunteers had discovered them camping in a shepherd's hut and had threatened them with the police if it ever happened again. 'Taking us away from our important war duties,' one of the men had said.

'Oh it won't take us that long,' Morag assured her. 'We'll see you in the sitting room at four.'

'Why don't you go towards the abbey?' Mrs Maitland said innocently. 'It's well worth a view.'

Morag smiled but said later to the others, 'There's more to Maitie than meets the eye!'

The walk was, as usual, delightful. They took the Lynmouth road and then struck off across country, following one of the sheep tracks which would leave Lynmouth to their right. They were familiar with a wide area around Gallenwick because of their running and had learned to identify various landmarks. They knew they were heading for the sea and hoped that the tower of the abbey would then be visible.

By ten o'clock the sea filled the horizon but because the land was so high any shoreline was hidden from view.

'We're going to be grease-spots by the time we get there!' Jannie complained. 'My Lord, the weather would have to improve the very day we needed an overcast sky!'

'There's a road down here,' Morag discovered. 'This has got to lead somewhere!'

'Yes, but for all we know we've gone past the abbey.

We're not going to find it. And if we've got to be back by four, we must start back by one at the latest!'

'Oh doomy gloomy!' Val scoffed. 'Come on, let's enjoy it! Perhaps we'll get a lift back or something!'

'Oh yes. In a Rolls-Royce, I dare say.'

'For Pete's sake, come on!'

They tramped down the narrow lane for another hour and then quite suddenly, came upon a track leading to the sea.

'This must be it. Where's a sign – surely there would be a sign?'

'They'll have taken it down in case a German parachutist should land here and know where he is— '

'Anyway, who cares whether it's going to the abbey or not?' Val swung off down the path. 'It's going to the sea! We can have a swim. A glorious dip! We'll be the three mermaids – the sirens of North Devon! Come on!'

They followed her, energies renewed, half running down the stony track and then just as suddenly stopping as the land fell away and they saw what lay ahead. A narrow headland stretched a finger of rock into the sea and from it a stone-built house seemed to grow quite naturally. It wasn't massive, three storeys with a tower at the seaward end: a primitive lighthouse. The front door was set inside a deep porch facing the cliff and the many latticed windows shone in the morning sun so that the house seemed almost crystalline. The house was constructed of mellow grey-gold stone and the rocks from which it sprang were a riot of heather and fern and clumps of rhododendron.

They were seeing it from above, not so much diminished as made compact and magical; the path twisted down the almost vertical cliff in a series of hairpin bends. Certainly no motor vehicle could negotiate it. How stone had been brought and fashioned into this good-looking and strangely simple house was hard to imagine.

Val breathed, 'Good Lord! Is it real?'

Jannie, refusing to be awestruck, said, 'No wonder they couldn't keep the nuns away!'

Morag said nothing. It was Berry Reid's house. There was no doubt in her mind that one day he would live here and paint. He would be famous. People would walk along this track especially to see where he worked. She narrowed her eyes to limit her frame of vision so that she could imprint this first view of the abbey on her brain. It was added to the pictures of the oriel window above Park Street at home, her mother holding a toast rack, her father in his 'hideous crinklies' turning to salute her on the corner of Park Row. Then she spoke.

'Girls. We have to see inside. Let's do the polite, knock on the door and ask if we can see around.'

'Have we got time?' Jannie, the instigator of the whole outing, was unexpectedly reluctant to go further. 'It'll take ages to get down this path and I doubt if they will let us in – they're probably Trappist or something dreadful and won't even be able to speak to us— '

Val exploded. 'For goodness' sake, Jannie! We've got to try! This is the most marvellous place – to think we've been here for seven months and this is the first time we've seen it! Come on!' She led the way at a brisk pace further down the path and the others followed her, Morag with enthusiasm, Jannie less so. Suddenly the idea of a houseful of men was not so exciting. She had a horrid feeling they might be imbued with second sight and know full well that she was a sinner. She must remember not to smile or lower her eyelashes in her Veronica Lake imitation.

They arrived at the deep porch to find the doors inside wide open. They could see halfway down a large hall, obviously used as a refectory as its centre was taken up with an enormous table edged with chairs. There seemed to be no windows in the hall, the only light coming from the open doors at the front and several others opening into rooms to the right and the left. It was deserted yet did not seem empty; a golden silence cushioned it comfortably. Yet Val's knock on the oak panel was thin and her voice as she called out 'Hello! Is anyone at home?' seemed instantly swallowed by the inner space.

Then a voice spoke behind them.

'Can I help you young ladies?' And they turned in unison to confront an elderly man in the brown habit and sandals expected of all monks. The funny thing was, he sounded like Cyril the bus driver, and his amiable expression was similar too.

Morag was the first to recover some composure.

'We're sorry to intrude. We're from Gallenwick. The Bluebell School, you know. And we're walking and suddenly . . . found this place. It's so beautiful— '

Val blurted, 'Where is everyone? Are you by yourself? The doors are open— '

The elderly monk smiled. 'We don't get many visitors and certainly no-one who would be unwelcome! Our doors stay open unless the wind and rain are in the wrong direction!' He held out his hand and one by one the girls shook it awkwardly.

He said, 'My brothers are working the land as usual. We're almost entirely self-supporting here, you see. I'm on kitchen duty this morning and have come outside to pick peas.'

Val smiled back at him. 'May we help? We're quite good with vegetables. We worked at Reid's farm last Easter. And Morag helped with the haymaking too.'

The benevolent smile widened. 'How very kind. Follow me.'

The track split into three in front of the abbey; the way they had just come and a coastal path going to the right and to the left. The monk led them almost along the shoreline until the brush which clothed the cliff like hedgehog quills fell back and several patches of land were revealed as terraced garden plots. Brown habits could be seen, here and there. No-one looked up at their appearance.

'I am Brother Michael,' the monk told them as he left the path and edged his way through a forest of pea sticks. He gestured higher up the field. 'That is Brother Andrew. I would introduce you to the abbot, but he is in Barnstaple on businesss today.'

'Business,' repeated Val. 'How strange.'

Brother Michael pulled an enormous basket through the narrow terraces towards them. It was half full of peas. 'Even monks have to live in a secular world,' he said.

The girls set to and in half an hour the basket was overflowing. Meanwhile Brother Michael told them about the Order.

'We're Franciscans, so we're not a closed Order. But our situation does cut us off from the routine of the world. We pray a great deal. We often pray outside.'

'I say. That must be very . . . moving,' Val commented.

'All prayer is moving.' He straightened his back and looked around. 'This kind of work – with the land – is our speciality. We have to cut out our fields where we can. Shelter from the west is essential – that is where the prevailing winds come from. Sunshine. Soil. A lot of the cliff is eroded almost to the rock. That is no good, of course.'

He went on to show them the other cultivated spots and Morag was reminded of Berry Reid. This man knew his land just as Berry knew his. She closed her eyes momentarily to blot out the thought and conjured up a picture of Teddy McKinley instead.

'Is there any chance of seeing over the abbey?' Val asked as they picked up the basket of peas between them and started back. 'We understand Gallenwick was a nunnery and there was a lot of coming and going between the two places— '

Brother Michael interrupted. 'No. There never was any coming and going as you put it. Not until the last war. The nunnery was actually a convent and took pupils. One of the pupils came to see us for harpsichord lessons.'

He sighed. 'We have a very fine instrument here. And at that time we also had a young man – a layman – staying with us before his call-up. He could play the harpsichord very well. Beautifully. He gave her lessons. That was the only time there was any contact between us.'

There was a silence.

Morag said, 'So. It was one of the pupils. Not a nun. That is why the local people are intrigued by us. They think history might repeat itself, perhaps.'

The girls laughed; Brother Michael did not. Then Val stumbled on a stone and put down her side of the basket.

'Did something awful happen? Was he killed? The man who played the harpsichord?'

'Yes.' Brother Michael picked up the basket and swung it onto the porch. 'He was eventually called up and went to France. He was killed before the end of summer.'

The three girls stood in front of him feeling suddenly small and very insignificant. And inquisitive.

Brother Michael smiled wryly. 'It happened so often, my children. It is still happening. You see, history – part of it – does repeat itself.' He turned. 'I must take the vegetables down to the kitchens. Will you excuse me?'

Val blurted, 'We wondered . . . we hoped we might be able to see inside.'

He paused. 'I do not think that is a good idea. No-one from Gallenwick has been inside the abbey since . . . then.'

Jannie broke her silence. 'So there is a mystery!' she said triumphantly. 'I bet the girl – the schoolgirl from the convent – I bet she was pregnant! And there was a real stink. And it was all hushed up and no-one will talk about it!'

Morag said, 'Jannie! Shut up!'

Brother Michael turned back to them. They stood stock-still just as they stood in front of Dr Wilkie when they were waiting to be reprimanded.

He said slowly, 'You are right. It was hushed up. And

probably should not have been.' He looked past them at the cliff. 'I do not think she was pregnant. Though perhaps . . . They were in love. She was seventeen. He was twenty-one. They would have been married if . . . but of course he was killed.' He looked at them; Jannie was sure he was looking at her. She felt her face flame. His voice became sonorous. 'It happened here so, of course, we all felt responsible. That is why . . . you must be content with seeing the gardens only.'

'What happened to her?' Morag asked hoarsely. She knew how that girl had felt. She was seventeen . . . Berry Reid was twenty-one. She knew exactly how it had been.

Brother Michael said quietly, 'She was so unhappy. Wildly unhappy. She came here one afternoon – the sun was out – it was like this.' He swept his hand around the cloudless horizon. 'There was no reason to think . . . we hoped she would gain comfort from the house itself. She went to the music room as she had done in the past. And we gave her privacy in which to grieve. And then someone saw her at the window. But, of course, by then it was too late. She was killed instantly. Before we could reach her body, the sea took it. We never saw it again.' Brother Michael looked up. 'There. That is the mystery. Not a mystery any longer. But perhaps a lesson for you to learn.'

Val said, 'You mean, it is a warning not to fall in love?'

Morag said, 'You were the one? You saw it happen?'

'Yes. I saw her at the window. I have never forgotten.'

'What was her name?' Morag persisted.

'Winifred. We knew her only as Winifred.'

Jannie shivered violently. 'How awful. I wouldn't want to see inside now.'

The monk inclined his head as if taking punishment. And then, without another word, he turned, picked up the basket of peas and went into the dimness of the refectory.

The girls began the long trudge up the angular path back to the road. They had no breath to discuss what they had learned, but when they reached the top and stood holding their sides and breathing deeply, Val said, 'What a story! Can you believe all that happened? It's like a novel!'

Jannie said, 'I can imagine it though, can't you? After last winter when we were interred – sorry, Mo – incarcerated at Gallenwick, it's easy to understand how someone would become deeply – really deeply – depressed.'

'Well, you would understand!' Val commented rolling her eyes. 'The way you went on and on about Berry Reid!'

Jannie touched her toes and came up breathing deeply. 'Yes, but don't you see, I'd never get stuck with one person. When Berry Reid was no good, I transferred my pash to Hugh Reid!'

Val laughed. 'You – you are incorrigible, Jannie Mears!' She glanced at Morag. 'D'you hear that, Morrie?'

Morag was gazing across the water at the hazy hump of Lundy Island. She said nothing for a moment, then took a quick breath and turned to the others.

'Jannie's got the right idea, of course. We must not ever put ourselves into that girl's situation. When one person becomes so important that life is worthless without them.'

'That's what I meant,' Jannie agreed, nodding. 'Val thinks I'm just being shallow again. But that is exactly what I meant!'

Val said, 'Well it's not likely to happen to us, is it? We've got each other. Obviously that poor girl – Winifred – my Lord, what a name – had no friends.'

'We don't know that.' Morag straightened her shoulders. 'Anyway, we're going to have to pace ourselves pretty strictly to get back for tea. So come on, girls! Best foot forward!'

They began to goose-step ridiculously along the dusty

road. And when they had stopped laughing and began to walk in earnest, Morag suddenly and completely uncharacteristically, linked the three of them with her long arms and swung them along in step with her.

Jannie, flushed and very happy, sang out, 'One for all and all for one!'

Val, glancing anxiously up at her tall friend, merely said, 'Oh do shut up, Jannie!' and they all laughed and tramped on their way.

That night they went to bed immediately after supper, tired and footsore and wanting to lie for a while in the twilight thinking their own thoughts. Before they could marshal anything coherent they were all three asleep and did not hear the familiar drone of the Heinkels as they made their landfall at the wide estuary of the channel and continued to follow the shining silver ribbon of water to Bristol.

CHAPTER SIX

When Dr Wilkie told her the next morning that the house in Park Street had received a direct hit and that both her parents had been in it at the time, she knew that fate or God or whoever controlled destinies, was punishing her for being so certain of her own independence. She made a small whimpering sound and slid forward in the visitor's chair until her knees touched Dr Wilkie's desk and her arms splayed across the surface.

Dr Wilkie who had been standing, ready for such a reaction, gathered her up and held her against the padded seat.

'They knew nothing, my dear. And they haven't gone, not really. You know that. They are more with you now than they were before. In your heart – in your head. Feel them there, Morag. Know that they are with you.'

She stood behind Morag, pressing her shoulders back so that she was bolt upright. 'Be proud, Morag. That they were your parents. Be thankful that there was no knowledge, no suffering. Let them comfort you – fill your being—' Morag felt a dampness on her cheek and assumed she was weeping because people always wept when they learned of such bereavements. She put up a hand and scrubbed her eyes. The tear was not hers. Dr Wilkie was weeping for her. She whimpered again.

Dr Wilkie crouched and cupped her head awkwardly. Her plait was caught in the chair. The older woman's voice was rough, uncontrolled.

'Morag, if you want to cry – or scream – or anything – it is all right to do so.'

It was suddenly clear to Morag that Dr Wilkie was about to break down completely and that was unthinkable.

She said very clearly, 'I am all right, Doctor. I think I had better go home and-and-and-see to things.'

'Mrs Maitland is telephoning your aunt at this moment, my dear. And then she will bring in some tea.'

'Thank you. That will be nice,' Morag said politely.

Dr Wilkie seemed at a loss. She continued to cup Morag's head and pull her plait quite painfully, unable to abandon the pose, not knowing what to do next. It was a relief when there was a tap on the door and she could immediately straighten and go to the window.

'Come in, Mrs Maitland,' she called, fiddling with a handkerchief. 'Ah. Tea. The cup that . . . put it here, if you would.' She moved the telephone and uncovered the yellow slip of the telegram which must have brought the news. 'Morag is being very brave. Very brave indeed. I think . . . the shock you know.' She gave up being discreet with the handkerchief and blew her nose.

Mrs Maitland came to Morag and put a hand on her shoulder.

'I can't tell you how sorry I am, Morag. You know you've got all of us here . . . your family. You're not alone, my darling.'

It was the endearment that did it. Morag turned, put her hands around Mrs Maitland's waist and let out a desperate cry of terror and anguish. The oriel window was gone for ever.

Dr Willie sent for Val and Jannie and the three of them were left alone in the study while vital phone calls were made. Val's face was so white it was nearly blue; yet her eyes, normally azure, were pale grey. She knelt in front of the visitor's chair and took Morag's hands in a crushing grip.

'Oh, Mo – I can't bear it – I can't bear it for me as well as for you! Mo – come back to us – please— '

Jannie stood back, leaning on Dr Wilkie's desk, staring, staring.

Morag forced a voice through her sore throat. The outburst into Maitie's waistband had not really helped.

'It'll be all right. Don't cry, Val. Jannie, come here.' Val had her head on Morag's gingham skirt, already Morag could feel the hot wetness of her tears. Jannie knelt by her, drooping eyelids forgotten, eyes like marbles.

Morag said, 'One for all . . . don't you remember?' She frowned trying to recall when Jannie had given the clarion call of the Three Musketeers. Had it really been only yesterday? 'We've got each other,' she concluded lamely and looked around the room, noting the fresh flowers in the cut-glass vase, Dr Wilkie's gown and mortarboard behind the door. These things had been there always, part of a pattern; now they stood out individually and there was no pattern. She had to make a new pattern, note everything and put it into place. It would stop her thinking of the oriel window.

'It's such a pretty room, isn't it?' she said conversationally. 'We're usually in here to get a wigging or something. But when you look at it properly, it's an Elizabethan withdrawing room.'

Val groaned and pushed her head harder into the gingham. Jannie whispered, 'Mo . . . don't. Please don't.'

Morag looked at her. 'Cheer up, Jannie. I'm no worse off than you, am I? In fact I think I'm luckier than you. I think I'm luckier than anyone else I know. They – they loved me completely, you see. And now . . . even if I fail the exams or do something dreadful, that can't change, can it? They've sort of rolled up all that love and given it to me for ever.'

Val bunched up the skirt and tried to stuff it into her mouth. Even so her wails were heard through the door and Dr Wilkie returned at a gallop.

'Girls . . . I think perhaps Morag had better lie down now. Mrs Maitland has suggested that she should use her room. There's a telephone in there and she can ring her aunt . . .' She swept Val and Jannie to one side and lifted Morag almost bodily. 'We have spoken to Miss Heyward, Morag. She is catching a train later this morning and will be in Bristol this evening. I have suggested to her that the Royal Hotel . . . Mrs Maitland is booking a double room at this moment. Let me . . .'

Morag smiled gently at her. 'I know the way. Would anyone mind if I spent a little while on my own?'

They fell away from her; she went through Maitie's little office and avoided the outstretched hand. There was the main hall with the oak stair going up to the Long Gallery. She went along the passage past the dining room, through a cloakroom and emerged in the stable yard. The pump was a smother of nasturtiums and she thought how cruel they were to continue blooming so flagrantly. A sliver of glass glinted in the brazen sunshine and she bent and picked it up in case the juniors ran across in bare feet and were cut. They did that sometimes. They were so thoughtless; so carefree. She had been like that yesterday. Going off to Lyn Abbey to solve some schoolgirl mystery. Her parents had been alive then. Her father had doubtless worked most of the day in the theatre and they had eaten supper together as the sun set and the sirens wailed. She remembered her mother's nervousness when she had called in two weeks ago. Teddy had said it was because of the sleepless nights. Perhaps they had both known that one of those nights would be their last. Perhaps . . . perhaps . . . She took the narrow stairs to the stable loft and walked down the passage to Maitie's room at the end. It had windows on three sides, green curtains and bedspread, an old-fashioned pyjama case in the shape of a sleeping cat. Morag let herself fall face downwards on to the bed. She put the pyjama case over her head and closed her eyes and prayed for oblivion.

The next week passed somehow. Teddy McKinley came to drive her to Bristol. It was another heartless, halcyon day and they barely spoke a word during the three hour drive. Morag wound down the window and closed her eyes, concentrating on identifying smells, the dry sheep smell of the uplands gradually changing to something more earthy as they went through the dairy farms of lowland Somerset. She opened her eyes and noted the apple orchards already being harvested; the thin white spirals of vapour trails from the fighters constantly circling above them.

As they crossed the river and took the narrow Hotwells Road to the docks, she sat up very straight and kept her eyes ahead refusing to glance towards Park Street. The smells here were rankly hot; sometimes of rubber, sometimes metal, always sulphurous. The skyline had changed and a haze of dust hovered over the city like a pall.

Teddy cleared his throat and said, 'Your aunt is waiting for you, Mo. You'll be all right, won't you?'

'Of course.' She glanced at him, remembering the last time they had spoken. 'And what about you? Will you be all right?'

He smiled briefly as they edged past a convoy of army trucks. 'I'll be fine once the holidays begin and you are at Redley Lodge.'

She made up her mind suddenly. 'Teddy ... I'm going to stay in school this summer. Try to understand. I really do need to be by myself a great deal.' She saw his expression and put a hand on his arm. 'You must keep Jannie and Val happy, Teddy. That is what I want you to do.'

'But – but ...' He bit his lip and frowned fiercely through the windscreen. 'I suppose after ... everything ... you cannot even think of – of what I suggested.'

She smiled. 'I've thought of it a great deal. It's kept me sane, Teddy. I know I should spend your embarkation leave with you, but I am going to be selfish and ask you to understand and let me stay at Gallenwick.'

'Oh Morrie ... of course ... anything.' His frown had gone. 'But does that mean ... what does that mean? Exactly?'

'It means that you are my lifebelt.'

His Adam's apple moved convulsively in his throat. 'Morrie ... I want to be that. Always.'

'Thank you.'

'Does that mean . . . are we engaged, Morrie?'

She thought about it as they rounded Neptune's monument and made for the steps of the hotel.

'I suppose so.' His whooop of joy was alarming. 'Secretly. We must keep it secret, Teddy. In the circumstances.'

'Oh yes. All right. Though I want to tell everyone!' He pulled up outside the hotel. Already the upright figure of Aunt Harriet was hurrying down the steps to meet them. He said swiftly before she arrived, 'Morrie, I love you. I will make it all right for you. You'll be happy again.'

She managed another smile before she got out of the car to be enfolded in Aunt Harriet's long and blessedly familiar arms.

She hardly remembered the 'business talks' which Aunt Harriet assured her later they had had. The funeral too was a blur. She recalled vividly the day afterwards when she had searched the rubble of the house for anything that might be left and found a shred of her mother's dressing-gown. And that was all. The oriel window, without glass, but otherwise intact, lay on its side like a half-lantern. She touched it fleetingly as she stumbled past the huge crater and looked out to the river. It did not matter after all; she had the photographs in her head always.

Then she was back at Gallenwick in time to help Jannie and Val pack their trunks. Both of them were determined to respect her wish to remain behind, but for Val it was hard.

'I've never wished a holiday away before,' she said, clinging desperately to Morrie as the bus drew up in the stable yard.

'Don't, Val.' Morag suddenly wished quite desperately that she was going to Clevedon after all. 'When you get back, I'll be myself again.'

Jannie tried to be cheerful. 'You could hike out to

that abbey again, Mo. Take Maitie and her sister. There's loads of places to explore.'

'I'll do it all,' Morag promised. And stood waving at the bus until it went through the arched gateway and disappeared into the lane. She shivered and then braced her shoulders. This was how it was going to be from now on. She had to get used to it.

For a week she made the most of the enormous spaces of Gallenwick. True most of the juniors were still in residence, but Mrs Maitland and her sister took them out and about every day and the gardens belonged entirely to Morag. She did not leave the grounds at all; here and there willow trees leaned over the little River Gall, and she found one that was easily climbed and sat in its cup as Hugh Reid must have sat last Easter. She felt safe there; no-one could find her to ask if she was all right or would like a walk or a glass of lemonade. She watched Maitie and her sister chivvy half a dozen fourteen-year-olds through the lych-gate for the bus to Lynmouth. Then Dr Wilkie in her brogues and sun-hat set out for a walk. No-one else came along the lane; the postman had been and it was too early for the air raid warden. Morag tried to read, then she thought of Teddy and wept.

The second week the weather broke and she stayed in the sitting room watching the rain stream down the windows. Dr Wilkie brought in some coffee and stayed to discuss the various merits of Oxford, Cambridge and Edinburgh.

'You would of course be close to your aunt in Edinburgh,' she pointed out. 'Perhaps that would be an advantage?'

Morag looked at the rain then into her coffee cup. The girls never drank coffee; this was a privilege.

She said, 'Actually, I thought I might start nursing training. Now I'm seventeen I should be able . . . I'm sure my aunt could . . .'

Dr Wilkie said incredulously, 'You mean you wouldn't go to university?'

Morag said, 'I was going to go to university if I decided to be a doctor. But I think I would prefer . . . my aunt and I talked about it.' She frowned. She could not remember what they had discussed.

Dr Wilkie said slowly, 'I see. I have to confess to a certain disappointment, Morag. You are one of our most promising girls. I would have liked you to continue your education.'

'Nursing is a continuing . . .' Morag stopped; she knew full well what Dr Wilkie meant.

'We'll talk about it again. Before Christmas perhaps.' The older woman stood up. 'I have some paper work to do, Morag. Would you like to help me with it?'

Morag hesitated a moment too long and Dr Wilkie smiled, 'All right. But if you think something more vigorous would help, Mrs Maitland is doing country dancing in the hall.'

'Thank you.'

Morag picked up both coffee cups and headed for the kitchen. They both knew she would return to the sitting room for the rest of the day. Dr Wilkie sighed and shook her head as she put up an umbrella to cross the stable yard.

The rain continued unremittingly for the next two days. On the third day when it eased off slightly, Morag put on her Oxfords, belted her raincoat tightly around her waist and crossed a plank footbridge used by the gardeners. She felt her loneliness tangibly now, it encased her, insulating her from everyone and everything. Even the turf seemed to squelch around another pair of feet not quite hers; the mist which shifted softly around all the familiar folds of the moor increased her loneliness. If there was anyone else out here they would not see her and she would not see them. She told herself this was what she wanted; but a small irrepressible voice somewhere in her head wondered whether she would ever be able to break out of this isolation.

She walked in no particular direction; except that she was moving upwards all the time she could have been going in circles. Twice she came to a stream, found a shallow crossing and splashed through it to the other side. She could feel the mist as rain on her face and lifted her head to let it run over her eyes and cheeks and into her mouth. It had a strangely disturbing effect on her; it was sensual, not entirely unpleasant; but it was all pervasive and she could feel it trickling down her neck and back.

She reached a plateau of the high moor and kept going until her feet felt so heavy it was a conscious effort to take the next step; then she looked at her watch. It was three o'clock and she had left Gallenwick soon after nine. If she was covering only two miles each hour she was twelve miles from school; so far she had not come across any roads or even tracks and she had absolutely no idea where she was. The last thing she wanted was to have any kind of search party coming for her; the kind of cocoon she had made for herself would not tolerate the sheer publicity of a search party. She stood still for a long moment, then turned slowly on the spot, looking and listening for all she was worth. All she could see were the swirling molecules of mist, all she could hear was her own heart pumping all over her body. That made her realize her own exhaustion and she sank onto her heels, clutched her knees and stayed very still for as long as it took to quieten her heartbeat to approximate normality. And then, very faintly, smothered by the mist, she heard what she had dreaded; her name being called.

She squeezed her eyes shut. 'Damn!' she whispered. 'Damn and double damn!'

'Morag!' The voice was away to her right. 'Morag, where are you?'

'I'm here!' She stood up wearily. After all, there

97

would be a road near the voice and perhaps transport of a kind.

'Don't move!' Already the voice was nearer. 'Stay where you are. Keep calling. Keep calling.'

She sighed and raised her own voice. 'Here! Over here!'

It was when the unknown rescuer said 'Good girl,' that she knew who it was. She blurted loudly, 'I thought you'd joined your ship ages ago!'

And there he was, materializing before her, bulky in the greatcoat he had worn last winter when he had carved a way for them through the snow to Gallenwick.

'I did. I'm home on embark.'

She continued to stare at him stupidly. Embarkation leave meant going away for a long time; it meant danger.

He said, 'Ma told me. About your parents. I – we – thought you'd be with your friends.'

'I wanted to stay on my own for a bit. And – and this place is a sort of home now.'

'Yes. I would always come here to be healed. Of anything.' He came a step nearer. She could just make out his face; it was very tanned, his black brows beaded with moisture. He said, 'You should go to Lyn. Just sit in one of the rooms overlooking the sea. It's a marvellous place.'

'We went. They wouldn't let us in. Some old trouble with pupils from the school – when it was a convent or something. I don't know.'

'I'd get you in. Only . . . I'm due on board tomorrow.'

'Tomorrow?' She was unexpectedly aghast. If he could have taken her to Lyn . . . if they could have sat together maybe in the music room . . . she was certain it would have made everything all right.

'I've been home for nine days. If only I'd known you were here.'

'It's all right.' He was so close now that the bulk of

him came between her and everything else. She had a glimpse of what it would be like to be protected by this man ... this boy ... this human being. She said, 'Actually, it isn't all right. I don't know what to feel any more ... or how to feel.'

He said unexpectedly, shockingly, 'May I kiss you again, Mo?'

He waited, his face right there had she wanted to lift hers slightly. She considered the question carefully, remembering the sudden invasion of her physical being. Was that what she wanted?

She said, 'I don't think so. Not after Caroline.'

He was still for a moment, then snorted a laugh. 'Ah. She told you, did she? I wondered where you were when I brought the eggs. You hid.'

'Not really. We had our matric. papers for two weeks ...'

'I was gone after that.' He sighed audibly. 'I can't apologize, Mo. You were all so beautiful ... I think I fell in love with everyone. Should I be sorry for that?'

She had never had such an honest discussion before. 'No,' she admitted. 'I think we were all the same. You ... Hugh ... the farm itself ... everything.'

'Oh, Morag.' He reached out at last and took her hands. 'It's gone for you, hasn't it? Gone into the past ... tucked away like old photographs.'

He was so exactly right that she almost cried out. But then he said, 'Your hands are warm enough. Do you want my coat?'

'No. I'm just wet.'

'You are.' His thumbs were massaging her knuckles; he seemed to be thinking. Then he said, 'Listen. I've got Hugh's old car at the Doone Arms. It's quite a trek up country and this damned fog is misleading. Could you manage the Ridd water slide? If I helped you?'

Something stirred in her mind; a little worm of excitement. 'John Ridd's steps in the river, d'you mean? The ones he climbed in *Lorna Doone*?'

'I'm not sure. I expect lots of the moor streams descend in steps of one sort or another. But this one from the inn, I've done it several times and it's easier going up. It'll take about half an hour instead of two. And as you're wet already . . . what do you say?'

Suddenly she knew this was what she wanted. She was almost exhausted, but to push herself physically by the side of Berry Reid – match her strength to his as they had done so often before – battle with one of the moor's famous rushing streams . . . was exactly right.

She nodded once and he turned immediately and led her the way he had come, and within five minutes the sound of rushing water echoed eerily through the fog and they began to scramble down a rocky gorge. He released her hand and slid from rock to rock, turning each time to steady her as she joined him. She became used to the feel of his hands on her shoulders, on her waist. When they reached the bank of the river he waded, waist-deep, to a flat stone around which the water swirled and eddied and she did not hesitate to lean forward and give herself to his outstretched arms. They stood like one form on the shelf of rock; the banks invisible in the fog, the water rushing around their ankles. She felt no fear at all, but this was not the numbness of the past four weeks because sheer excitement surmounted fear; or even became part of it.

The sound of the river was too loud for conversation. Silently he undid the belt of his greatcoat, then the belt of her gaberdine. He tied them together and fastened an end to her wrist, another to his. Then put his mouth to her ear and said very clearly, 'This is the first step. Between each one the water is deep. Sometimes the steps shelve and it is difficult to keep a footing. Do not leave a step until I pull on the belt.'

She had not realized it would be so difficult. Perhaps on a summer's day when rain had not swelled the stream high up its banks and they had not been hampered with heavy waterlogged clothing, it would have been easy. Shrouded in mist and struggling against so many odds, there were times when the fierce scramble between 'steps' needed superhuman effort. She knew that Berry would not let her drown, but he respected her enough to let her make her own way while she could. Each time he left her she felt bereft; he almost disappeared into the fog and she would hold out her arm and stare down at the navy blue belt on her wrist, waiting for the tug to reunite them, ridiculously frightened that it would not come, that she had lost him. When he leaned down and drew her onto the next rock shelf, she clung to him for a moment, pushing her head into his sodden shoulder, thankful that he was still there. For just a few hours, he would still be there.

It took them twice as long as he had said. When the lip of the cascade was within hand's reach, she had almost forgotten there was another place beyond this watery one of constant effort and sudden gasping drenchings. They stood just below the edge; Berry held one of the rocks which rose like teeth from the water, and grasped her close to him with his free arm. Already the roar of the water receded behind them.

'This is the hardest bit,' he panted. 'You must get a good handhold here while I haul myself up. Then I can lift you clear.'

She realized that the exposed teeth of rock were at such an angle they created a barrier. He fitted her arm around one of them, pushing it emphatically into place, then untied his side of the belt and wrapped it around the rock. When he released her she felt immediately the terrific drag of the water. He looked at her, grinned, and taking a fresh handhold swung himself out, free of the water, and continued swinging until he could hook one of his legs around another rock. It was a desperate manoeuvre and she realized why he had disconnected the belts. If he had fallen he would surely have taken her with him.

But he did not fall. He straddled his rock as if it

were one of his shire horses, reached down for her and lifted her up easily and for perhaps three seconds they sat together, the water moving smoothly around their waists, triumph and relief making them laugh foolishly, wetly, helplessly. When he kissed her, it was at first just a meeting of mouths, an extension of the relief. When the triumph took over, it became something joyous; they still laughed, snorting like horses, Morag splashing the surface of the water with outspread palms.

He got to his feet with difficulty, water pouring from his greatcoat. They stumbled into the quiet shallows of the river and up the bank. They seemed to be in a field. He led her, still snorting, to where the blacked-out Doone Arms was suddenly solid in the mist. Then into a barn where he lit a storm lantern and revealed an ancient Morris.

'Oh, Hugh's car!' she exclaimed. 'I remember you said it was here. Ages ago . . .'

He hung the lantern and turned to her and they began to kiss again.

'Get this wet stuff off,' he mumbled, pulling at his greatcoat. She kissed him again as she unbuttoned her gaberdine. 'I love you,' she said. 'I love you, I love you, I love you, I . . .' He cupped her face and kissed her and she was still and unresisting at first, and then suddenly passionate. It was as if the dead weeks since the death of her parents had been a fallow time during which amazing fires were building. The explosion was intense. Her perceptions, carefully and unemotionally cultivated for so long, were at their height. And her whole universe was suddenly concentrated in Berry Reid. The smell, taste and sight of him, and especially the touch, filled her being and became her being.

When at last they were quiet she moved her fingers across the planes of his face, so that her 'photograph' would be entirely three dimensional. She murmured again and again, 'I love you.' And he stared at her with tears in his dark eyes whispering back, 'Oh my God . . . I love you too, Mo . . . I love you so much.'

The sound of a door opening in the pub brought them back to reality. He stood up and extinguished the lantern and then gathered her to him and held her while someone shouted, 'Berry! That you?'

When the door closed again, she would have drawn him back to her, but he was anxious.

'Darling girl, they will be sending out the troops soon— '

'Oh, Berry . . .' she laughed at such flippancy.

'Seriously, Mo. Your Dr Wilkie rang Ma and asked if I would look for you at this end of the moor. They'll give me three – perhaps four hours, then . . . besides, my love, they will be so worried. We can't do that to them.'

'No. They must be happy too.'

She drew his face to hers and said sadly, 'If only . . . oh, Berry, if only . . .'

'I'll be home before you know it. The war will be over. We'll get married and have ten kids who will do all the work and I'll paint and you'll be beautiful . . . oh, Morag, you are so beautiful.'

They held each other and she whispered, 'Please be careful. You will be careful, won't you?'

'Of course. And you . . . how will you be?'

'I shall be so full of feelings I might burst.' She tried to laugh then stopped. 'My father told me that hard work was the answer to problems. I shall leave school, Berry. And begin training to be a nurse.'

He drew back. 'I wanted to think of you at Gallenwick. And on the moor.'

'I'll stay till Christmas.'

He tried to focus on her eyes. At last he said, 'All right. All right. But when I come home . . . you will be with me, won't you?'

'Yes.'

They both knew it was a solemn promise. They kissed again and stood up.

* * *

A month later, Aunt Harriet came to stay with her at Gallenwick for the final week of the long summer vacation. Morag had been anxious for a while that she might be pregnant, but by then she was certain she was not and her well-being surprised and delighted her staid aunt. Together they walked – even paddled in the streams. She took Aunt Harriet to visit the farm and was delighted when Mrs Reid and Granny Thomas welcomed them both and put on a cream tea. Mrs Reid was as busy as ever. There was no news of the boys and Cyril and his brothers were only part-time, so the winter promised to be hard with lambing starting at the end of January.

'Hope I can rely on you girls for help with the potatoes?' she said smilingly. 'I know you only came to see Berry— '

Morag flushed bright red.

Aunt Harriet said, 'Why not? They're like nuns secluded in that big house.'

Morag smiled at her gratefully. Mrs Reid's teasing was without subtlety.

They took the Woolacombe bus which dropped them a few miles from Lyn, but this time it was raining and the doors were shut against an eddying wind.

Aunt Harriet said, 'I can well imagine anyone throwing themselves into the sea here.'

Then at the end of her week's holiday they made a picnic and decided to go swimming. Cyril had taken to driving the local bus right into the stable yard to pick up anyone who wanted to go to Lynmouth and he leapt out with his usual courtesy to help Aunt Harriet up the two steep steps and into her seat.

'It's a lovely day again, Miss Heyward,' he said. 'Reckon we've had enough rain and fog to last us through till Christmas.'

He smiled sadly at Morag as he took his place behind the wheel again. 'Glad you're going out and about, missie. No good sitting in and brooding about it.'

'I'm all right now, Cyril,' Morag reassured him. She wished she could tell everyone about Berry so that they would not worry about her any more. Perhaps when Val came back to school she might tell her. No-one else.

It was Aunt Harriet who said anxiously, 'Has anything happened, Mr Miller?'

Morag remembered afterwards that she wondered how Aunt Harriet had discovered Cyril's name. But then Cyril said, 'Haven't you heard, ladies? Poor Mrs Reid had a telegram just yesterday. All three of them gone. All three. Can't believe it. They was all . . . I dunno . . . so alive. So very alive.'

Morag registered Aunt Harriet's gasp and realized she was already halfway out of her seat.

'We must cancel our outing, Mr Miller. We must call on Mrs Reid. Will you pull up by the lych-gate, please?'

Morag stared through the windscreen and refused to let the truth go further than her ears. She wouldn't believe it. She simply would not.

She said, 'I think I'll stay here. If you don't mind, Aunt. I'm sure Mrs Reid would prefer to see you alone.'

Aunt Harriet looked at her wondering whether she should mention words like duty and responsibility. Then she said, 'Very well, Morag. Perhaps it would be best.'

They separated at the lych-gate, Aunt Harriet to take the lane towards the farm and Morag to walk back between the elms carrying the picnic and remembering the night she did not listen for the nightjars.

CHAPTER SEVEN

1945

Vallery heard of the sale of Lyn Abbey the day after VJ day. She was sitting at her desk overlooking Clevedon's Bellevue Road, drinking her mid-afternoon cup of tea and wishing her mother would call in and suggest shutting up shop early for once, and for want of anything better to do she picked up her father's copy of *Auctioneers' Weekly* and skimmed the list of forthcoming sales.

She was feeling most definitely the worse for wear. Last night there had been a Victory Dance at Clevedon Hall and as usual on these kind of occasions she had gone with Teddy's old school friend, Leonard Oates. Leonard had always been called Titus at school and in an ongoing effort to win Val's love as well as her friendship, he was vainly trying to change that to Leo. Her reaction to the suggestion was uncontrolled mirth; he had not been one bit pleased and had grabbed her hard and kissed her full on the mouth in just the way she disliked. She had pushed him off unceremoniously and told him not to be an idiot and he had sulked for the remainder of the evening.

She sighed deeply. Nothing had been the same since Teddy was killed in November of 1941 during the offensive against Rommel. It had finished Morag completely. She had seemed so much better when the autumn term began that year; still sad and very quiet, but definitely back in the land of the living. When the news of Teddy's death came through, she announced immediately that she was leaving school and starting her training at the

Bristol Royal Infirmary where her father had worked for so many years. She actually left school the day the Japanese bombed Pearl Harbor. Vallery and Jannie had stayed on until after their Higher Certificates, but neither of them wanted to go to university. Val had come back to Clevedon to help her father run the auctioneering business. Jannie had gone to London where she was secretary to someone called Marius Copping. She came down for Val's and Morag's joint twenty-first party; her hair was like slipper satin and hung almost to her waist. It was so eye-catching that nobody noticed the still plain face beneath it; she played with the hair a great deal, drawing it over one shoulder then tossing it back. Morag, dabbling in psychiatry in her spare time, thought she might be on the verge of a breakdown. But Val watched Jannie vamp Eve Mears' naval officer right under her mother's nose, and thought otherwise.

She smiled as she sipped her tea. Jannie was what her mother called an 'incorrigible case'. Val was not quite sure what kind of 'case' Jannie was, but she was certainly incorrigible, and she had come a very long way since the nights she would call out for her mother.

And then Val stopped smiling and concentrated on the column of small print before her. 'Early nineteenth-century house, Lyn Abbey, until recently a Franciscan monastery, to be sold by auction unless an offer is received above reserve.' There were other details, a map reference, the date of the auction. She stared at it disbelievingly. Lyn Abbey. Where they had walked that suddenly hot day in late June and heard the story of the lovelorn pupil from Gallenwick. What romantics they had been, each one of them identifying with the girl, none of them able to imagine the man.

Val sipped again and stared through the window wondering whether it had been just herself who had been unable to imagine the harpsichordist who had been killed in the Great War. Maybe Jannie had thought of Hugh Reid. Jannie had seen Hugh for that brief moment in February and had had a thing about him afterwards. But Val herself had always had her feet firmly on the ground; there had never been anyone for her. Only Teddy. And as for Morag . . . well, they had teased her about Berry Reid, but of course there had never been anything in that. Morag might well have loved Teddy; she had grieved for him terribly. It had been Val's dream to see them marry and live in Clevedon. She screwed up her eyes against ridiculous tears: after all, Teddy had been dead for almost four years now and would hate to think she was still crying for him.

She gulped down the rest of her tea and looked outside again. The road was still empty; probably her mother was resting in the garden. She rested a great deal lately.

Val lifted the telephone and dialled the number of Morag's flat. She never could remember Morag's duty times but there was an outside chance she would be home now. She was. The ringing stopped and Morag's crisp voice came on the line.

'Morag Heyward. Who is calling, please?'

'Me. I've just opened Daddy's boring old paper and seen something absolutely amazing. You'll never guess in a thousand years.'

Morag said, 'I don't intend to try when I know very well you're going to tell me.'

'Oh . . . you! Well, all right then. Lyn Abbey. D'you remember it?'

There was a moment of silence, then Morag said, 'Of course. Just about four years ago, isn't it?'

'In June or July. I'm not sure. Anyway, dear heart, it's up for sale! Can you believe it? That wonderful place – we never saw inside it, did we?'

Another pause. Then Morag said a slow, 'No.'

'Listen, Mo. How about driving down there on Sunday? Having a look round?'

'Can't. Have to swot. Exams soon.'

Val emitted an explosive sigh. 'God, then you really

will be insufferable. Sister Heyward! I shall feel sorry for your probationers.'

'I'm very kind to them actually! When I think of my first sister . . .'

'What about the following week? I could have a day off any time.'

'You are completely spoiled, Vallery McKinley!'

'So? Say you'll come! It would be such fun to visit the old place again! I can get a car and some juice. We could lunch at the Doone Arms and go to see Mrs Reid— '

'No!' Morag's voice sharpened suddenly. 'Sorry, old girl, but no. I never want to see Exmoor again.'

Val was shocked. 'Mo . . . I didn't realize . . . but you never did come back, did you? We used to spend time here during the hols but . . . Oh, Mo, I didn't realize you hated it so much.'

'I didn't. But such awful things happened while we were there, Val. I don't want to go back.'

'You know . . . I might go down by myself.'

'Well, why not? Take Titus with you – give him a treat.'

'We've had a row. Party thing last night. I don't care if I never see him again.'

It was Morag's turn to be shocked. 'Val – he adores you. Don't be unkind.'

Val hesitated then blurted quickly, 'Actually, Mo, I hate it when anyone . . . sort of . . . tries anything. You know. I think I might be a bit . . . sort of . . . odd. Frigid.'

Morag's laughter rang down the wires. 'Not you, Val! Not our Bubbles!'

Val laughed too. 'That was what Hugh Reid called me, wasn't it? Bubbles. What a name! Well, I don't know what that has got to do with it. But actually, Mo, if I never get married, I won't care. Not a jot.'

Morag laughed again then sobered and said, 'Neither will I. I mean, I definitely won't get married, and I definitely do not care a jot!'

*   *   *

Val drove herself to Exmoor. She had talked to her father and suggested to him that the abbey might well be worth an inspection and she was the one to do it, so she had the car and the petrol allowance and a picnic carefully wrapped in clean tea towels on the back seat. She had wanted to take her mother for the ride, but Margaret turned down the offer.

'I'm happier at home in this hot weather, darling. You know how it is.'

Val had no idea how it was. She had an abundance of energy and wondered sometimes what to do with it. But Margaret's tiredness had crept up on them so gradually Val hardly noticed it now.

She took the longer route, turning off the main road at Bridgwater and keeping to the coast past Dunster and Minehead. The steep ascent up the toll road at Porlock was dramatically sudden; within a few minutes the car had left the cosy civilization of the coastal resorts with their ice-cream parlours and donkeys and reached the untamed plateau of Exmoor. Almost immediately her well-trained eye saw evidence of wild ponies; she found herself surveying the landscape for signs of deer, heath fires, habitation. She sat forward over the wheel, excited, feeling that something was going to happen. She felt different here; as if she belonged; she who had been so terribly homesick when they were evacuated, suddenly felt as if she were coming home. She belonged to this place, and it belonged to her too.

She had stopped to spend some of her precious petrol coupons at Minehead, now at the top of Countisbury Hill she pulled over again to let the engine cool off after its frantic work on the Porlock road. The view was fantastic, enormous cliffs leaping into the sea which creamed lazily on red sandy coves and beaches. Far below a small family group were setting up deckchairs and an umbrella; the children screamed as they ran into the water.

Val smiled, then she let the car coast down to Lynmouth and engaged the engine noisily to drive up through the valley to Lynton and then on along the narrow coastal lane that would bring her to the turning for the abbey.

She pulled onto the grass, reached into the back for her picnic and got out stiffly. She would look around the house, make notes of anything worth buying and then eat her lunch outside in one of the garden plots cultivated by the monks. She set out down the zigzag path carved into the cliff face; this was the best thing that had happened to her since Teddy died . . . the very best thing.

The house was exactly as she recalled it, the doors open to the sunshine, the interior still taken up darkly by the refectory table and chairs. The sense of emptiness had been illusory then; now it was probably real, though there must be a caretaker somewhere. However, no-one was in evidence, so Val strolled into shadowy hall, noted the lot number stuck to the edge of the table and wrote in her notebook, 'tbl, poss.oak, 20/24 placings; 16 ladder-back chairs, rush seats'. She had made a start. There were dim pictures on the walls between the doors but she ignored them and began looking into the other rooms. There was a kitchen, but no utensils of any kind, just a range and an enormous stone sink. Three more small rooms adjoined, perhaps serveries or store rooms. One of them contained an enormous dumb waiter which could obviously contain a man as well as a trolley of food. She peered doubtfully at the ropes, wondering whether to try it. Then shook her head. She moved on. There was a pantry with stone slabs and slatted windows. They were all bare. She crossed the hall and opened two doors. One led into a kind of sitting room with leaded windows on two sides looking out to sea. It was a marvellous room, hugely dignified in its emptiness. She pirouetted across the polished wooden boards and sat down suddenly on one of the window-seats. It occurred to her that this might be the fateful music room; there was no telling. She peered through the window; there was a small rose garden outside. No-one would do much damage by throwing

111

themselves out of this window. The same applied to the room behind, which might well have been used as a chapel by the brothers as there was a window facing the east and a plain bench beneath it which could have been an altar. Val heaved a sigh of relief and went to the back of the hall where a staircase wound out of view.

Upstairs were a series of partitioned cubicles, obviously the monks' cells. She carried on to the second floor and went into the first room at the top of the stairs, then stopped and took a deep breath. This was it. It was like the prow of a ship, windows on three sides overhanging the other floors; there was no sign of the harpsichord but in the corner was a clutch of music stands. Val said aloud, 'Yes. This is the music room all right. Oh, Mo, you should have come with me. You would know exactly how that girl felt. And when I tell you about it, it will sound . . . silly.'

Even so, she made copious notes so that she could tell Morag accurately what the room looked like. 'Enormous . . .' she murmured as she paced it out. 'And so light – no morning sun but it looks north, south and west . . . golly, what a room!' She found slight dents in the boards where the harpsichord must have stood; she stood in them and half closed her eyes. 'I wonder what they said to each other . . .' She went to the window and looked down. It was a long drop; a ghastly way for anyone to go to their death. 'But of course,' she murmured, 'she didn't see it like that. She was joining him.' She took a pace back and stared through the glass, surprised at herself. She was not by nature imaginative and had always thought Morag's imagination was a curse. But here . . . she could imagine that girl so clearly. So . . . so enviously.

She breathed a little laugh and shook her shoulders as she turned to leave. There was obviously nothing at all left in the house except the table and that had probably been made *in situ* and would never be moved out. She ran down the stairs and into the sunshine again, then walked along the coast footpath to where the first garden plot had been made, and there, as if he never had been anywhere else, was Brother . . . what was his name? Brother Michael.

Her exclamation made him turn around, surprised. Of course he did not recognize her. She went to meet him with outstretched hand.

'We have met before. Ages ago when I was at school here.'

He stared at her, ignoring the hand. 'At school?' His eyes were enormous. 'Winifred? You cannot be Winifred?'

She laughed uncomfortably. He had obviously gone gaga.

'My name is Vallery McKinley. I came here exploring back in 1941. With two other friends.'

He very obviously relaxed.

'Of course. I do remember. One beautiful afternoon rather like this. You would have liked to see inside the abbey and I was stuffy enough to keep you out!' He smiled. 'You must forgive me. My sight is not what it was.'

She put her hand into the pocket of her cardigan; she could see the cataracts over his eyes now; he was almost totally blind.

'I'm terribly sorry. Are you here alone?'

'No. There are three of us. We act as caretakers. We show people around. You are our first customer.'

She laughed. 'I've already looked around. I work for my father who is an auctioneer near Bristol. We were hoping to find some artefacts . . . you have of course moved everything to your next . . . er . . . place.'

'Yes. It is simply the house that is for sale now.'

'We may well attend the auction. I am not certain of the reserve price. But it would be interesting anyway.'

'We rented it as I expect you know. It belongs to a family who live away . . . I rather think it will be left to fall into ruin.'

'Oh. That's dreadful. Perhaps not . . . an eccentric recluse . . .'

'Or someone who was connected with Winifred.'

'Winifred?'

'The pupil from Gallenwick . . .' Brother Michael frowned. 'You did say you are from Gallenwick?'

'Yes.' Val swallowed. So he was gaga after all.

'Then you will know about Winifred Wilkie. I believe her sister is now your headmistress.'

'I've left now . . . they've all left and gone back to Bristol.' Val gazed at him, her blue eyes very dark. 'I did not realize that Dr Wilkie's sister was the girl who – who— '

'Died for love,' Brother Michael supplied. 'Yes. Winifred's sister, Amelia, was also a pupil at the convent. It was hard for her. But I think she accepted it in the end. She came to see us, you know. Not long after your visit. She said that she understood how privileged Winifred had been to love so deeply, so intensely.'

'Oh my dear Lord,' Val breathed.

'Yes. He is always there to help,' Brother Michael said simply.

There was a pause. Val fought an impulse to burst into tears or to scream or simply to fall to the sandy ground.

Brother Michael said, 'May I offer you some food? We are living in a flat made from the cellars. There is soup today with bread.'

Val found her voice somehow. 'No. Thank you. I must leave. I want to call at the farm before I . . . I must go now.'

The monk held out his hand. 'It was good to meet you again. And who knows, perhaps you will live here one day.'

'Me? No. Not me,' Val said. 'I don't think I will ever love anyone like that.'

She knew she was not making sense. She shook the dry, earthy hand quickly and almost ran back down the path and up the zigzag to the car. She was sweating horribly when she got there. She flung herself on the grass and began to unwrap her sandwiches, trying to ignore the fact that she was weeping profusely and her heart was pumping fit to burst and she was shaking all over.

She tried to chew the stale bread and then suddenly gave up and bowed over her knees in a paroxysm of grief.

'What's the matter with you?' she asked herself furiously as the first flood abated. 'You don't *want* to love anyone like that! You don't *mind* being like Doc Willie – she's happy and fulfilled and . . . all right! Whoever would want to be driven mad by love like her poor sister! Pull yourself together this instant, Vallery McKinley, and eat your lunch!' And after another senseless bout of weeping, she managed to do that.

It was mid-afternoon when she drew up at Gallenwick's lych-gate. The gates were open as usual but it was obvious the school was closed, not even a lone boarder left to walk down the avenue of elms and listen to the nightjars. She drove very slowly to the stable yard and circled the pump; the years rushed away and she remembered how awful it had been when Morag left and she and Jannie soldiered on as sixth-formers together. The agony of losing Teddy had been doubled without Morag. Jannie had grated on her; she had been worried about her parents, especially her mother. It had been such a relief when she muddled through her Higher Certificate the following summer and went home. She hadn't wanted to do any war work; when her father asked if she would like to do Teddy's clerical work in the firm, she had jumped at the chance.

She looked up at the window of their room and shook her head slowly; Morag had been right, she should not have come back. She drove down to the lane again and almost decided against visiting Mrs Reid but then she turned right automatically. The poor woman had run the farm alone now for four years; it would be heartless not to visit her when she was so near. She and Jannie had gone to offer their condolences at the beginning of that Christmas term; and then again after Morag had left, to show the new fifth-formers how to plant seed potatoes. It had been a melancholy time but Mrs Reid had still produced huge pies in enamel bowls and Granny had still wrung the necks of fowls and poured neat iodine onto any cuts or abrasions she could find.

Val stopped the car at the five-barred gate and climbed over. Geese formed a hasty line and came to meet her, honking horribly just like that first time. Suddenly she dreaded seeing Mrs Reid; what might the years have done to her? Would Granny still be alive? Would they even be here at all? Perhaps they had had to sell up and move to some awful flat in Barnstaple . . . She rounded the cowshed wall and there, sitting at the open back door, plucking a limp-necked fowl, was Granny Thomas.

Val rushed forward, so glad to see her she forgot any embarrassment. And, incredibly, Granny recognized her.

'Well, I'll be blessed! If it isn't one of them first girls . . .' She allowed herself to be embraced, feathers and all. 'The one who kept our Berry in his place, I'll be bound! And still got all her curls!'

Val was laughing with relief. 'Did you expect them all to drop out?' she asked, already beating feathers from the front of her blouse. 'Oh, I am glad to see you, Granny! Everything seemed . . . dead. The abbey and Gallenwick! And here you are, just the same!'

'Nay, you can't bury me just yet,' the old lady said grinning wickedly. 'Can't bury any of us seemingly!' She looked over her shoulder as her daughter appeared, drying her hands on the usual voluminous apron. 'It's that little Curly-top,' Granny crowed. 'Thinking we be all dead and buried at the farm!'

'Oh Mrs Reid!' Val tried to scoop up the small figure, forgetting Mrs Reid's big shoulders and stolid frame. 'Oh it really is good to see you! I nearly didn't come –

thought you'd be all sad and – maybe not even here! And everything seems the same!' She drew back and surveyed the dark face. 'You look younger if anything!'

Mrs Reid said, 'Stop all that blithering and come and sit down. Have you got little Jannie with you? Or the tall one – Maureen was it?'

'Morag. No. Nor Jannie. We're all working girls now, Mrs Reid.'

Val followed the stocky figure into the well-remembered kitchen and sat at the huge table. The sun glinted on pots and pans and glowed warmly on the bread crocks. She said simply, 'This is . . . good. You're both wonderful!'

Granny joined them, the denuded chicken dangling from one hand.

'We couldna done it without the school. That doctor of yours turned up trumps, she did. We had all the help we needed whenever we needed it.' She went into the pantry and called back, 'But you first lot . . . we never forgot you 'cos you worked with our Berry.'

Val swallowed, looking at Mrs Reid. That lady was pouring boiling water into a brown enamel teapot and did not falter.

Val said, 'It was such a terrible blow . . . all three boys . . . I can't tell you how sorry we were. And almost straight afterwards my brother was killed in Africa. It was an awful time.'

'Aye.' Mrs Reid glanced up, her dark eyes warm with sympathy. 'I remember you coming here that spring to do the potatoes. You were like a lost soul then. We were all lost souls. Together. But then, o' course, the year after – you'd gone then – we heard our boys had been picked up . . . prisoners of course and a terrible time they had in Singapore. But— '

She was interrupted by Val's glad cry. 'What? We never knew! They are all safe? Oh my dear Lord – wait till Mo and Jannie hear this! Where are they?'

Mrs Reid laughed delightedly. 'You didn't know then?

I thought you might've kept in touch with your doctor lady up at Gallenwick. She's been very good to us, hasn't she, Mother?'

Granny nodded lugubriously. 'Knows a few in high places, she does.'

Mrs Reid brought the tea to the enormous table and for once sat down herself.

'We knew they were alive but in a sorry state. In a camp just outside Singapore. Seems Hugh and Dusty were able to walk . . . they're being brought back by sea. But it was Berry . . . he was hurt in the leg, it seems. They were ten days on a life-raft and it went green on him.' Her face screwed up involuntarily. 'Had to be taken off by the camp doctor when they were picked up.' She forced a smile. 'They're alive, that's all that matters.'

Val's expression of shock and pleasure had graduated downwards to equally shocked sobriety. She remembered the schoolboy exuberance of Berry Reid. She remembered how he had reminded her of Teddy. He had bullied the girls into working hard; but not Val. She remembered punching him and having her backside slapped. She said, 'Oh . . . poor Berry.'

Mrs Reid said bracingly, 'He's been flown home. To a hospital where they fit artificial legs . . . you know the sort of place. Rehab . . . something.'

'Rehabilitation unit,' Val said, primed by Morag when she had done her war-injuries course.

'That's right. In Dorset.' Mrs Reid glanced at her briefly. 'He won't see us. Not yet.'

'Oh . . .' Again Val remembered some of Morag's training. 'That's not unusual, I believe.' She looked around the big kitchen. There were steps into the stuffy front parlour and a step out onto the porch. 'Will he be able to manage here, d'you think?' she asked.

'I don't see why not. It's his home.'

'But he won't be able to . . .' Val wanted to say that he would not be able to pull his weight; that perhaps

118

a job in an office – like her father's – might be more suited to his capabilities now.

Mrs Reid said quietly, 'He'll need to live on the moor. It's a part of him . . . he belongs to Exmoor does our Berry.'

Val nodded. That was true.

She left the farm in the early evening and drove slowly across the moor and down to Taunton through Simonsbath. Her mind was so full of impressions, information, ideas, that her head gently ached. She felt on the brink of something new. Something positive. A direction that her life might well be able to take. She drew into a farm gate on the other side of Taunton and chewed an aspirin fiercely, making faces at the ghastly taste. She remembered bossing Berry Reid, telling him he was a little Hitler. Insulting him buoyantly, just as she insulted her brother, Teddy. Berry had reminded her of Teddy, an overgrown schoolboy, wanting only to live and work at home. Hadn't Berry Reid inherited his father's artistic talent? Hadn't he wanted to be a painter? Hadn't he wanted to live in the abbey?

She arrived in Clevedon just as the sun was drowning in the sea. Her mother was ensconced in the big chair in the sitting room, her prescribed glass of stout at her side.

'Isn't it wonderful to know that the sirens won't be wailing at any moment?' she said as Val leaned down to hug her. 'How did you get on, darling?'

'I drove down the avenue of elms,' Val told her. 'But it was too early for the nightjars.'

She went on to describe the abbey. She would tell Margaret about the Reid boys . . . but not yet. She would tell Morag too. But not until she had slept and made more plans.

Her father was horrified; though even then Vallery knew that Margaret understood.

Eric said, 'Darling girl! You cannot possibly buy that

awful old place for a man you hardly know who is
suffering war injuries— '

Val said eagerly, 'There's a sort of dumb waiter
thing. Huge. Could take two wheelchairs. I could get
it seen to— '

Eric said, 'It'll be damp, next to the sea like that.
Absolutely unsuitable. It's ridiculous, Val. Absolutely
ridiculous.'

'The monks managed pretty well. And the music room
– the old music room where Doc Willie's sister hurled
herself onto the rocks, would make the most wonderful
studio you have ever seen. I did tell you he is an artist,
didn't I?'

Margaret smiled. 'You did mention it. And that he
somehow reminds you of Teddy.' She glanced at Eric.
'That is why you want to do this thing, Val. Isn't it? For
Teddy's sake.'

Val paused. She hadn't stopped talking for a long
time, but she still had not discovered her true motives
for this crazy plan. Maybe this was it.

'He's not like Teddy. Not really. Teddy was gentle
and shy. Berry was . . . boisterous. And not a bit shy.'
She remembered how all the girls had fallen for him;
even the austere Greek set. Even reserved Morag. She
grinned. 'No. Not a bit like Teddy. And yet – and yet . . .'
She shook her head, baffled. 'I treated him just as I
treated Teddy. And he liked it!'

Margaret said steadily, 'And you can't do anything
now for Teddy. But for this other boy, who felt like
another brother . . . you think you can patch up his
injuries, compensate in some way— '

Val exploded apologetically. 'Oh darling, you make
me sound positively pi! But listen . . . we've got oodles
of cash – all right, we don't talk about it and we live quite
modestly . . . but we've got it, haven't we? And the Reids
haven't got much except land and stock which Berry
can't work any more. But there's this other side to him.
The artist side. The side that wanted to live in the abbey

120

and paint. And the abbey is for sale. And . . .' she spread her hands helplessly and repeated, 'we've got oodles of cash . . .'

Margaret laughed but Eric said seriously, 'That's not the issue, sweetheart. What is the issue is that you are proposing to make a complete ass of yourself! You want to visit this chap – remember he's just got back from some hell-hole in the Far East – and inform him you are setting him up . . .' He lifted his shoulders helplessly as Val started to protest. 'Can't you see, Val? It's a bloody cheek!'

Margaret raised her brows at him, but said practically, 'There would have to be a trained nurse, Val. You must see it is completely impracticable.'

Val opened her mouth to explain that she would look after Berry. And then closed it. Perhaps her mother was right. But she couldn't give up on the scheme just yet. It had come to her out of the blue. It was meant.

She took a deep breath.

'All right. Maybe it's silly. Put it aside for the time being. But I have to go and see him. His brothers are still in Singapore. He refuses to see his mother. I must go and see him.'

Eric sat down at last and began the long process of filling his pipe.

'What makes you think he will see you?'

'Well . . . because he felt the same about me as I felt about him. Brotherly. Yet without any real ties.' She too subsided into a chair, knowing she had as good as won this round. 'He'll see me,' she said confidently.

Margaret looked at them both and said peaceably, 'I know. Ask Morag's advice.'

Val wrinkled her nose. 'She'd think I was mad. We teased her about Berry but I don't think she liked him very much, so if I told her he reminded me of Teddy she wouldn't understand.' She sighed. 'Anyway, she's swotting for exams.'

Eric said, 'Oh well, that's out. Morag is so ... single-minded.'

Margaret said, 'I don't like to think of you going to Dorset on your own. It's a cross-country journey by train. It'll take hours. You don't even know where this place is.'

Eric said heavily, 'I'll make some enquiries. Dorset you say? I suppose it's a Royal Naval hospital?'

'Oh, Daddy –' Val cast herself onto her knees before him. He moved his pipe judiciously.

'Well, the sooner you get these crazy ideas out of your head, the better. And the quickest way of doing that is to see this young man and let him tell you just what he thinks of your would-be philanthropy.'

The appalling thing was that when she got there, after five hours in trains that were dirty and hot and always late, her parents were right. He refused to see her. She had been so certain that she could break through his barrier that she was completely thrown. Why on earth had she been so – so arrogant? She shook her head and pain shot from eye to eye as if her brain were loose. She felt suddenly lonely and bereft and wished her father were there to take her into the nearby village and give her a good lunch at an hotel. She knew she was spoiled; until she had had to go to Gallenwick and then Teddy had been taken away, she had had everything she wanted. She was trying very hard now to do something good for someone else and it wasn't working. The taxi had dropped her outside the Victorian hospital and she had walked in so confidently expecting to be met by wheelchairs, all ready to smile optimistically and receive smiles in return. But she had been received by a harassed nurse who had led her down a deserted corridor to the sister's office and had not had time for any conversation.

Vallery had said breathlessly, 'Where are all the patients?'

And she had replied, 'They're in the main block,' as if they were animals to be kept away from the general public. It had made Vallery more determined than ever to get Berry out of there and look after him properly. A thought had suddenly come into her head. She would dedicate her life to him. Yes, if need be, that was what she was prepared to do. Just as she would if Teddy had come home terribly injured . . . as she would have been glad to do.

So when the sister arrived and said apologetically that Able Seaman Reid was not seeing visitors at all, Val was at a complete loss.

She bit her lip and stared at the sister helplessly.

'I've come so far,' she said, hating her bleating tone. She cleared her throat. 'Is he too ill for visitors, d'you mean?'

'Not physically. He is learning to walk with his new leg. Making excellent progress.'

'But,' prompted Vallery.

The sister shook her head. 'He has refused visitors up till now. When his brothers arrive – we hope in a week or so – he has said he will see them. And then things might. . . they have had experiences in the prison camps which are – are – unshareable!' She smiled helplessly. 'Once he can see them, share those things again, without explanations – without words at all – I think he will begin to live again.' She looked at Vallery. 'Are you a relative?'

'Oh no. Just . . . a friend.' Had they been friends? They had barely known each other. Val straightened wondering what on earth she was doing here.

The sister hesitated. 'If you could come back later this afternoon, he will be in the garden. You could see him from this window. It might . . . help?'

Vallery bit her lip again. She had acted as usual like an impulsive child. How could she hope to help Berry Reid who had seen and suffered unimaginable things.

She said, 'I'm not sure. I feel . . . rather small.'

The nurse said, 'I understand. I feel like that all the time.' She moved to the door. 'I have to go. If you decide to come back this afternoon, you are welcome to sit here in my office. I'll look in on you at some time.'

'Thank you.'

Vallery walked down the white corridor slowly, glad now that she could not go through to the wards and see . . . whatever there was to be seen. She would no longer be able to smile and call a greeting. How could she – for one moment – have thought that she, Vallery McKinley, might brighten the lives of these men?

Nevertheless, after catching a bus into Weymouth and eating a very greasy piece of fish in the Royal William Hotel, she did go back to the hospital. For one thing the train service she had so carefully worked out did not leave until after tea, and for another, she felt she could not go home without having set eyes on Berry Reid.

She went straight to the sister's office and drew a chair to the window. The weather was not as good as it had been last week in Devon. The sky had a metallic edge to it that threatened thunder. She stared across a rather scruffy lawn at a line of trees which must bound the hospital grounds; it was a far cry from the farm and Gallenwick and the swooping hills of the moor. She could easily have melted into a bathos of maudin tears, but then some wheelchairs appeared from further down the building; half a dozen of them trundled over the bumpy grass towards the shade of the trees. She spotted Berry immediately. He was the one propelling himself, bent almost double over the wheels, outstripping the nurses as if trying to escape. She drew a breath. It was impossible to see his face, but his hair was still black, his shoulders powerful. He was not emaciated as she had feared. He was not grey. He looked like any young man of twenty-four who happened to be sitting in a wheelchair.

He went to the far end of the lawn then whirled his chair and faced the building. With some difficulty he turned and removed two crutches from a clip at the back of the chair. He leaned down and applied a brake somewhere then he pushed aside the footrest and with some difficulty he stood up.

Val gave a little cry and stood up too, involuntarily. When he began to walk using the crutches but apparently on two legs, she found her hands clenching as if helping him to make the effort. She said aloud, 'You fool, Vallery McKinley! You can hardly bear this! How on earth do you think you could help him?'

He stumped along with a kind of grim determination to divorce himself from his and the other wheelchairs. Val watched as one of the nurses detached herself and began to stroll ever so casually after him. It was the sister she had seen earlier. She lifted an arm towards the window in salutation. Val lifted one back uncertainly.

The sister fell into step with Berry and they began to stroll around the perimeter of the lawn in what looked like companionable silence. Then the sister turned her head and obviously said something to Berry. He stopped, said something vehement and turned to go back to his chair.

She put out a hand and detained him, then pointed to the window. Val forced herself to stay where she was; she felt her face suffuse with heat.

Berry paused. Had he seen her through the glass? And if he had, did he recognize her? Whether he had or not did not matter, he was returning to his chair, falling back into it awkwardly as he waved away any help, replacing the crutches and leaning to move the footplate into position again. And then he said something and the sister moved away.

When she came into the office and told Val that he would see her, Val felt only terror. She looked at the pleasant-faced girl – not much older than Morag – her own face wide open.

The sister smiled. 'Well, you did come all this way.' She went to the door. 'Come on. He won't bite and if he's rude, then you can surely forgive him?'

'Of course ... I'm sorry ...' Val was stammering helplessly, wondering what to say, what to do.

But Berry was not going to be rude. He grinned and although she could now see the ravages of the last four years, it was still as if time rolled back and she was in that potato field again and he was exhorting her to look lively.

'I didn't realize it was you, Curly-top,' he said, holding out a hand. 'My God, you haven't changed, have you? Barging in where angels fear to tread and all that sort of stuff! Trust you!'

'Oh, Berry!' She knew the one thing she must not do was cry. Even so her eyes filled and she hung her head, ashamed. He did not release her hand, just pressed it hard.

'Stop it, Curly. Otherwise, I leave. OK?'

She forced a smile. 'You haven't changed either. Bossy as ever!'

'Oh, I've changed.' He made a face at his trousered knees neatly pressed together. 'I've changed quite a bit.' He grinned at her expression. 'Come on, Curly-top! You're not going to pretend you don't know, are you?'

'No, of course not. I'm sorry, Berry. I came here full of ... ideas. Stupid ideas. I am ... stupid.'

'Hey, that's some admission from you. But it's good to see you, stupid or not. I couldn't bear it if Ma turned up, or even Gran. And when Sister said something about a visitor from Bristol I was terrified it might be ... someone else.'

'Who?' She was feeling easier now. She kept his hand and squatted by the chair in a pose that hid her legs. She felt suddenly as if she were flaunting them.

'Oh ... no-one.' He gave her hand a little shake that was not unfriendly and released it. 'So tell me everything that has happened to the three of you since ... then.'

She said awkwardly, 'Well, nothing much. Morag is a nurse. Jannie is a secretary. I suppose I'm a secretary too. I work for Daddy at the auctioneer's office. In Clevedon.'

'Sounds good.'

'It is. Yet, it isn't. I mean . . . it's not exactly a life's-work. Like Morag's nursing.'

There was a small silence then he said, 'How is she?'

'Morag? All right. She doesn't talk a lot. You know she and Teddy were sort of engaged? She hasn't been the same since he was killed.'

'No, I didn't know that. I'm sorry.'

She thought back. 'No, of course you wouldn't. It happened just after you and your brothers were . . . well . . . missing. It was funny that year, wasn't it? We arrived in Gallenwick in January and by December our lives had all been turned upside down. Morag had left school – the one person who we all thought would stay on. Hitler attacked Russia and America came into the war. Everything seemed to happen in 1941.'

He looked down at his knees. 'Yes,' he said.

She followed his gaze and said suddenly, 'Berry . . . it need not be the end for you. You do know that, surely?'

He looked at her and grinned. 'Val the Valiant?' The grin became rueful. 'I suppose I know it in one way. We've had talks from psychiatrist chappies . . . seen films of men with no legs . . . dancing, playing tennis. What they never mention is the pain.' His grin returned and became mocking. 'Sorry, Val. I'm no hero, am I? There's a sort of unwritten law that the word pain or agony is never mentioned. We talk of "some discomfort".' He barked a laugh. 'And it sure is – some discomfort!'

She was contrite. 'Oh, Berry . . . I didn't mean . . . I'm so dreadfully sorry.'

'Don't be. It's good to be able to say things straight out. I remember now. You were good at that, weren't you?'

Her voice was small. 'Is it good? I'm not sure. Teddy and me . . . we always told each other . . . everything. He told me how he asked Morag to marry him and how he cried because he was so homesick – before he'd even left home!' She too began to cry quietly, head bent so that he would not see. 'I miss that. I tell Morag everything still, but she doesn't come back at me in the same way.'

'No . . . she wouldn't.'

'Is it better to button it all up, Berry?'

He put his hand down and covered her head. 'I'm not sure.'

'Berry . . . I've got to tell you. You can laugh if you like – in fact, please do. It might make me feel that the whole idea had some good points!' His hand began to massage her scalp. She found it the most reassuring sensation in the world. She blurted, 'When I went to the farm last week – I'll tell you about that later – and heard that you were alive and here and injured and everything . . . I couldn't get you out of my mind! I remembered every little thing about you – I wanted to help so much. I was sort of obsessed – with the idea of you . . .' She stopped and waited for the laughter. His hand paused, then his fingers combed gently through her curls again. 'I know it sounds stupid. But you see, I felt I had another chance. Teddy was taken away from us. But you were sent back. And we would have been . . . oh, so glad to look after Teddy. And I felt . . .' She was weeping freely and he continued to stroke her hair silently. She knew that for Berry Reid to remain silent must mean something. '. . . I felt I wanted to look after you. Make a life for you. Stay with you and look after you. Oh, I must have been mad. Stupid. I thought I could come down here and simply whisk you back home and Daddy would buy the abbey and you could paint in that lovely upstairs room and I would look after you and – and— ' She stopped on a sob of pure humiliation and put her head on her knees.

He was still for a long time, his fingers just touching her curls. And then he gave her a sort of pat and removed his hand.

He said very quietly, 'Thank you, Val. I'll always remember that you wanted to look after me. Thank you.'

She looked up. Her face was streaked with tears.

'I'm sorry, Berry. I did not mean to be so – so – patronizing.'

He grinned. 'I don't feel patronized. I feel honoured. Not many pretty girls are going to make me an offer like that now, are they?'

She gave a damp and faltering smile and his grin widened. 'You look terrible. You shouldn't wear mascara. Your eyes don't need emphasizing.'

She snuffled a laugh and scrabbled into the sleeve of her cardigan for a handkerchief. It came away from her face black and smudged and she laughed again.

He said, 'Let's change the subject. Tell me all the news. Tell me about the farm . . . Ma and Gran. Are the geese still there? Tell me more about Morag . . . how does she look in uniform . . . and Jannie. The little one always on the verge of a nervous breakdown— '

Val was suitably diverted.

'Jannie? A nervous breakdown? I never thought . . . although . . . anyway, I think she's got what she wanted. She's not just anyone's secretary. Her boss is her mother's old flame. I think she's done it to spite Eve – that's her mother— ' She stopped and looked at him. 'You could be right. She was always very . . . mixed up. How did you know?'

He shrugged. 'She brought out the protective in Ma. That's always a bad sign.'

He laughed and after a moment so did Val. She went on to tell him about her recent day on Exmoor. The farm and Gallenwick and the abbey, Brother Michael, Dr Wilkie's sister.

'My God,' he said, awestruck. 'All that drama . . . no wonder the place has got atmosphere.'

'It's so beautiful, Berry!' Val's enthusiasm rekindled as she told him about it. 'And whatever Daddy says it would be ideal for you. There's a funny old-fashioned lift that could be modernized and all that space and light and the sea . . .' She stopped speaking and was apologetic again. 'Sorry. Sorry. My tongue runs away with itself at times.'

'I remember that.' He grinned, unoffended. She knew suddenly that no-one else would be able to talk like this to him and get away with it. So there was something special between them. He said thoughtfully, 'And it's for sale, is it?'

'Yes.' She took a breath. 'Berry, is it so ridiculous, my idea? Is it? I know it's frightful taste to talk about money . . . but I'd so love to buy it for you. And I'd look after you – I'm a good cook, you know, and Morag would teach me how to nurse you properly— '

'Be quiet, Val!' For an instant he looked thunderous and she thought he would wheel himself away from her and leave her crouching on the grass. But then he softened. 'It's OK. Don't look like that. It's just . . . you'll realize later on what a narrow escape you've had. You'll get married and have a brood of babies and be the perfect mother. If I let you make a fool of yourself about this— '

'I'll never marry, Berry!' she said passionately. 'I can tell you – I've told Mo but she won't take me seriously. I'm not . . . like that. I wasn't at school and I'm not now. When the girls were all going gaga over you and Hugh, I was irritated. Completely outside it all. I'm still like that. I think Teddy was the only man in my life. I – I'm frigid!'

He stared at her, his black eyes unfathomable. But he didn't laugh. After a long while he sighed deeply and said, 'Well. That makes two of us. I'm never going to marry either.'

She wasn't really surprised. After all he was a proud man and would never be able to support a wife and children. In Val's personal experience that was what husbands did. Still she said for the sake of that pride, 'Why ever not?'

His dark gaze shifted and he looked beyond her and into himself. He said slowly, 'Because I'm impotent. That's why, Val. What between that and being a cripple and in pain . . . I don't think I'm the catch of the year.'

He refocused on her and grinned. 'The one unselfish thing I've done in my life, Val. Don't forget that!'

She stared at him, her eyes so wide they ached. She knew now that all this was written in the stars in some way. She did not 'like' men. Berry no longer 'liked' women. She wanted – needed – a brother. And it seemed as if Berry could well do with a sister.

She picked up his hand and felt it was shaking with weariness.

'Listen, my dear. You're tired. We'll continue this conversation tomorrow. I have to go and get a bed somewhere in the village.'

He said exhaustedly, 'Val, go home. Find a nice young man who will make you forget about— '

'I don't like nice young men. I like crotchety ones.' She was smiling and standing up. 'Let me push you back to the house, Berry. I know you want to show off and beat me to it – perhaps tomorrow though.'

He looked up at her, frowning slightly.

'I don't think I understand you, Val.'

She shrugged slightly. 'What do you see?' she stood back and lifted her arms slightly.

He said slowly, 'I see a girl. A very attractive girl. About five-five, maybe eight or nine stone. She looks younger than she is because of her mop of curls. Her eyes are blue. Very big.' He held out his thumb and screwed up his eyes. 'She is in perfect proportion. A pocket Venus.'

She moved to the chair and began to push it back to the hospital. 'That is all there is. You understand me very well,' she said contentedly.

They just got inside before the first large drops of rain began to fall. And then, while they watched through a window, the heavens opened and the storm began.

He said, 'What an omen!' But suddenly his dark eyes were shining.

CHAPTER EIGHT

Val breakfasted early the next morning and left the hotel at nine o'clock, booking a second night there as she passed the desk. The storm of the previous day had washed everything clean and the little seaside town gleamed under the mid-August sunshine. She walked purposefully through the streets noting where various shops were situated. The men's outfitters were advertising coupon-free cravats. She bought some small austere-looking roses from the florists, noted where the barbers' poles were, then investigated the restaurants where there was just a one step entrance. She chose one that had a view towards Portland Bill and made a booking for two for lunch. Then she went to the taxi rank just outside the station and talked to an elderly driver who reminded her of Cyril; he wore a pre-war chauffeur's outfit with a certain pride, touched his cap as she approached, yet looked strong enough to manhandle a wheelchair into the boot.

She sat inside and told him what she wanted to do.

'I've got plenty of money,' she said with her usual ingenuous candour. 'I want to pay you in advance because the man concerned might be a bit touchy on that score.' He nodded seriously. 'I want him to have the sort of day he could have had before he was wounded. It's a bit difficult for a woman to arrange this, so I'll need your help. Can you do it?'

'Only too pleased, madam. The young man is at the naval hospital, is he?'

She nodded. 'The rehabilitation centre.' She withdrew a notebook from her handbag. 'I've made a list of various shops and the addresses. And I thought we might have

lunch first of all. Here. I've booked a table for one-thirty.'
She ripped out the sheet of paper and passed it over.

He nodded judiciously. 'Perhaps the young man will have some emergency clothing coupons, madam?'

'Oh, that's an idea. I hadn't thought. I can ask the sister.'

'If so, might I suggest a shirt and sports jacket? Before lunch?'

Val smiled congratulations. 'What a good idea. I'll see what can be done.'

They arrived at the hospital at eleven-thirty. The small foyer and corridor beyond were both completely deserted. Val walked down to the sister's office, clutching her flowers self-consciously; did people bring flowers to men? She really had no idea. The dark red roses gave off a high, sweet smell, like a violin note. Much too poignant.

There was no-one in the sister's office. She sat in the visitor's chair and noticed that her white sandals were badly scuffed. She had brought an overnight bag in case of emergencies but no change of clothes. Yesterday's blouse and skirt felt suddenly shabby. Until now she had not given a thought to herself; her mother had said on the telephone, 'Oh darling – underwear!' and Val had laughed carelessly. She was on a mission; underwear was the least of her concerns. Now she was not so sure.

The door opened and a sister came into the room, stopping short at the sight of the visitor. It was not the same sister as before and Val half stood apologetically.

'Sorry. I was shown into this room yesterday, so I just . . . came . . .'

The sister held the door open.

'Visiting begins at two. If you would like to come back then.'

'Oh, you don't understand. I'm not visiting exactly. I've come to take someone out. For lunch.'

The sister showed her teeth indulgently.

'I'm afraid no-one in this hospital is fit to leave it. I

133

can assure you when they are they will be discharged. The beds are urgently required by others.'

'Of course.' Val tried one of her winning smiles. 'But it's quite all right. I've got a taxi outside and the driver is quite happy to take a wheelchair.'

The teeth were covered with horse-like lips. 'It's a question of stamina, Mrs . . .'

'Miss. Miss McKinley. From Clevedon which is near Bristol.' Unaccountably Val felt herself colouring.

The sister moved to the desk. 'You are a relative?'

'No. Not exactly . . . well, a cousin. Once removed.'

The sister revealed her teeth momentarily. 'I'm afraid visitors are confined to close family, Miss – er— '

Val felt her gall rise. She corrected her diffident smile to one of complete coyness.

'Well . . . it's not yet announced . . .' She simpered outrageously. 'I think my status is fiancée. I'm not quite certain. Yet.' The sister's teeth were tucked away disbelievingly. Val stiffened her spine and said, 'Stamina. Yes, I've got plenty of stamina.'

'I was referring to the patients' stamina,' the sister said sharply. 'The men are here to be strengthened. In mind and in what body remains to them!'

Val's smile disappeared and her blue eyes narrowed.

'Then I am the person you need,' she said silkily. 'I think I can manage on both counts where Berry Reid is concerned. Perhaps I had better go through and help him to get ready.' She swept past the sister as she spoke making sure the roses brushed the starched chest. And there, to her chagrin, was Berry, sitting in his wheelchair, listening to every word that was said, a stubborn non-cooperative look on his dark face.

The sister brushed at her apron and said happily, 'I don't think that will be necessary, do you, Miss . . .?'

Val couldn't bear it. She had set her heart on today's programme and now to be routed in front of this ghastly woman just because Berry was in a sulky mood was too much.

She simply had to brazen it out so she bent and kissed him.

'Hello, darling! I know you're going to give me the thumbs down but I'm afraid you'll just have to do what you're told for once!' She dumped the flowers in his lap and smiled again at the sister. 'I can imagine you're quite used to his stubborn ways, Sister. But I won't put up with them. Never have and never will. If we're going to be married he's got to learn to please me ... just occasionally!' She took the handles of the chair and began to push. Somehow she must keep talking so that neither Berry nor that ghastly nurse could get a word in edgewise. 'I told him we were going to buy the ring today. And he's not going to wriggle out of it.' She was level with the sister, already accelerating. Berry was trying to hold back the wheels but not quite hard enough. She said menacingly, 'There is still a law against jilting, you know!' And then just before they got well under way she said over her shoulder, 'Sister, I'm so sorry but your apron seems to have taken the brunt of Berry's roses! It's quite badly stained.' And while the sister tucked in her chin to look at her bosom, Val was almost running for the foyer. The taxi-driver came to meet them and that seemed to settle the matter. He touched his chauffeur's cap in a marvellous old-retainer sort of way, helped the chair down the ramp and opened the door of the cab with a flourish.

She had not realized quite what hard work it was. Berry was grimly efficient about extracting his crutches from the back of the chair and getting himself into the taxi, but she could see the effort it took. Yesterday she had been able to suffer with him as she watched from the window, today she had to pretend it was all a matter of course. If she so much as put out a hand to help him he would growl, 'Stop flapping, woman!' Nevertheless he had been tickled pink by her battle with the sister.

'I've never seen her bested before,' he crowed once inside the taxi. 'Poor old Murchison! When you said you

135

were my sort of fiancée! She'll be a long time getting over this!'

'She'd better get used to it then,' Val said, buoyed by her victory and Berry's unexpected acknowledgement of it. 'You've got a perfect right to come and go as you please from that – that – place!'

He sobered. 'It's a good place, Val. I'm a pigheaded so-and-so, but underneath, I know they're good.'

'The other sister— '

'Darwent.'

'All right. Darwent. She was so different. She wouldn't have tried to stop me.'

'Actually, she would. I'm on a very tight programme, Val. This will disrupt it badly.'

She was immediately aghast. 'What have I done?'

'It's all right, old girl. Doesn't hurt any of them to have a little mutiny on their hands. It will brighten the day for everyone in my ward I can assure you.'

'But I forced you— '

'Rubbish. If I hadn't half wanted to come d'you think you could have made me? I'm much stronger than you think, my girl.'

'You tried to hold back the chair.'

'I made a token gesture. Yes.' He made a sudden face at her. 'I didn't want you to think I was one of those men who'd go off with anyone.'

She laughed. So did he. 'Oh, Val,' he said. 'It's ages since I laughed.' He pecked her cheek. 'Thanks.'

She said demurely, as she would have done to Teddy, 'My pleasure, I'm sure!' Then she sobered. 'But you must tell me when you've had enough. It would be terrible to set you back.'

'All right. That's a deal.'

They drove sedately along the enormous bay of Weymouth and he pointed out various ships. As there had been no opportunity to enquire about clothing coupons, they could not splash out at the outfitters, but she bought him a cravat and tied it carefully around his naval sweater.

Lunch was the usual austerity fare. The grey national loaf had been toasted in thin slices and a liver pâté was served with plenty of green salad. Then came a solid fillet of fish which was doubtless whale, followed by cabinet pudding, also very solid.

'I say, that wasn't bad,' Berry said, sitting back replete.

'It wasn't a patch on what my mother cooks,' Val said. 'And as for your mother . . . may I talk about your mother and grandmother?'

'Of course. Fire away.'

She talked. How she talked. He seemed to enjoy it, listening attentively as if to a familiar tune he had not heard for a long time. She told him how Mrs Reid had continued to send food to the school all through that second year; how Granny had taught them to set traps for the rabbits.

'She tried to teach us how to skin and draw them. But we were hopeless. If Morag had still been there . . .'

He said quickly, 'Morag couldn't have skinned a rabbit to save her life.'

She was surprised. 'You're quite wrong about Morag, Berry. She would have looked on it as a necessary operation. She's never once fainted in an operating theatre. Her father was very proud of her for that.'

Berry was silent, moving the salt-shaker aimlessly around the pepper. Then when Val seemed to have come to the end of her news, he said, 'You mentioned yesterday . . . something about Morag and your brother.'

Val nodded. 'They were secretly engaged. She wanted time to herself after her parents were killed. So she came back to Gallenwick. She asked Teddy to look after Jannie and me. And he did.' Tears filled her eyes even now. She dashed them away quickly. 'He told me about the engagement. I was . . . so pleased.'

'You must have been.' He shook some salt onto the

137

tablecloth and rubbed at it with his finger. 'But she'll find someone else, Val.'

Val nodded. 'I know. A doctor I expect. She wants to re-create what she had before I think. Except that she would like a lot of children.'

'She said that?'

'Yes. She said she would never inflict on a child the kind of loneliness she had.'

He nodded judiciously and shook out some more salt then just as suddenly brushed it away and sat back.

'Tell me about the nightjars,' he demanded. 'Are they still there at Gallenwick?'

She smiled. 'I didn't hear them this time. It was too early. I drove round the stable yard and sort of greeted our old dorm window and then I went to the farm.'

'Tell me how they used to sound.'

He listened intently as she described their churring note and how she and Morag and Val had imagined they would protect them just as they had protected the nuns of old.

'The night Morrie's parents were killed . . .' She did not look at him. 'We missed out on the avenue that night. We'd been to Lyn Abbey and we were full of the story of the girl who killed herself. We went to bed early. And the next morning . . .'

'What rubbish,' he said strongly. 'Pure superstition and you know it! The bloody birds didn't protect the nuns very well, did they? Damned place closed after that stupid girl threw herself onto the cliffs— '

'Doc Willie's sister.' She had already told him that story.

'Yes. Quite incredible, isn't it? But come on. Admit that Morrie's loss had nothing whatsoever to do with the nightjars.'

'I admit it. I hope Morrie could admit it too. She is one of those people who feels guilty about everything and everyone.'

'Yes.' He stared out of the window. The statue of

George III, dominating the promenade at this point, seemed to stare back. 'Well . . . I suppose we are all responsible for one another. To a certain degree.'

Another silence fell and Val watched him covertly and wondered if the idea that had kept her awake half the night was crazy. Or brilliant. His profile was etched against the clear sky outside; it was very rugged, completely unique. Yet when he had fiddled with the salt and hung on to her every word, she had known he needed her protection.

She said suddenly, 'Berry. Have you thought any more about my suggestion?'

'Suggestion?'

'Living in the abbey.' She ignored his dismissive gesture and added sharply, 'Be honest, Berry! Come on, you said it was good to be straight with each other. Be straight now! Admit you've thought of it all night long!'

He turned and looked at her.

'Dammit all, Val! I can dream about it. It doesn't mean it's possible. It's not. It's absolutely impossible. You must see that.'

'I can see it's difficult. Yes.' She bit her lip and sat back in the chair as far from him as possible at the narrow table. 'There would be a way to make it less difficult. Much less difficult.' His brows lifted and she felt her face redden. 'All right. I will be straight with you, Berry. When I told your Sister Murchison that we were sort of engaged, it wasn't completely off the cuff. I'd been . . . considering . . . ways and means. Last night.' She snuffled an apology for a giggle. 'All night.' She put her hands out of sight on her lap and gripped them together hard. 'We could . . . actually . . . get married.' She did not look at him or wait for a reaction but rushed on. 'If we did – get married – it would be natural for us to look for a suitable house together. My father being in the business of properties would point out that the abbey is for sale.' She glanced at his face and saw it was wide with astonishment. That was better than being closed and angry. 'Don't you see,

139

Berry? You wouldn't feel this stupid thing about a man accepting a gift from a woman. It would be our wedding present. We'd have to have a few things done . . . but not many. And then I could look after you. You know. Legally.'

She stopped speaking and sat back. Her hands were aching and she unlaced them consciously and began to massage the fingers. Nothing happened for ages and she began to think it wasn't such an outrageous plan after all and he might even be considering it. When he started to laugh she was cut to the quick. She did not look at him but began to scrabble things into her bag intending to leave immediately; then realized she could not leave him sitting there. She clutched her bag and said fiercely, 'Shut up!'

He controlled himself with difficulty. 'Well . . . you are joking, surely?'

'No. I was not joking.' She looked at him and realized suddenly that his laughter had not after all been amused. She said tensely, 'What have either of us got to lose, Berry? I don't want children . . . I don't like men. You can't have children.' He flinched and she went on quickly, 'It would be an ideal arrangement. My life is going nowhere. We get on well together . . . this is something I want to do. Very much.'

He said raggedly, 'Be quiet, Val!' He stared at her. 'You don't know what you're talking about. You're a silly, spoiled child. Let's get back to the hospital and forget this ever happened.'

They faced each other, wide-eyed, breathing quickly. Then a terrible spasm crossed his face and he closed his eyes.

She reached over and gripped his hand.

'It's OK. It'll pass. Hang on . . .'

He turned his hand in hers and grasped her fingers hard. She closed her eyes too; tried to will the pain away for him. After an endless minute, his grip loosened.

'Sorry . . . and thanks.'

She said, 'Does it happen often? Do you need medicine?'

'No. To both questions.' He smiled tremulously. 'Val, I'm sorry. I deserved that. Ungracious swine. Can we – can we go back to where we were before . . . all that?' His smile steadied at her quick nod. 'What else have you got in store for me?'

They left the restaurant and went to a barber's shop. Berry looked more his old self after a civilian haircut. While it was being done, Val went to a jewellers' and came back with a watch. She waited until he was settled again in the taxi before giving it to him.

He protested vehemently.

'Val, you just cannot do this! It's an Omega! I can't accept it – honestly.'

Val tapped on the glass. 'Driver, can you take us for a run now? To the swannery perhaps. Then I think we had better go back.'

She sat back in her corner, holding the rejected watch, silent.

He said uncomfortably, 'You're not upset, are you? Val, it's been wonderful. You've somehow brought me back to – to my old life. Listening to you was better than anything that has happened since . . . for ages. I'm sorry if I can't go along with the – the game. You didn't really mean it anyway, did you – just a game. Hey? Val, look at me – you're not bloody well crying, are you?'

She looked up; her eyes were bright but dry.

'No. I'm not crying. I think I'm facing facts, Berry. You've been out now for three hours and you are exhausted. Don't argue, I can see.' She smiled suddenly. 'I'd planned something really exciting for tomorrow. I was going to abduct you and take you up to Gretna Green. But the elopement is off. Sorry, darling, but there it is.'

He stared at her while the taxi drew up by Abbotsbury pond.

'Val . . . I told you how it was. Don't make me say it

141

again. I can't get married – not properly. And it wouldn't be fair to you to— '

She interrupted him. 'Oh look at those two! They're mates, wouldn't you think?' Two swans were chivvying the other swans away from the bank where some children were backing off anxiously. 'Isn't that marvellous? Like sheepdogs almost. They're protecting the children.'

Berry said dryly, 'If the kids leave so does the free food. That's what they're protecting.'

'You would say that. It might be true but the two things hang together – they're inseparable. The swans have to protect the children if they want to ensure a good food supply. See how they work together? A pincer movement and . . . there they go!'

They watched as the bevy of swans took flight with some difficulty, flipping the surface of the water with their big webbed feet as they rose in a cloud of feathers.

'Are you trying to tell me something?' Berry asked quietly, his dark eyes following the birds longingly.

'I don't really know.' Val laughed. 'I'm no good at analogies and things. But it seems a shame to dwell on dark things when the sun is shining.' She looked at him. 'I don't care about . . . what you said. What I care about is that you are an artist. You need somewhere to work and someone to look after you and be a companion. Daddy can buy Lyn Abbey at a knock-down price . . . there's ways of doing that, you know, when you're a good auctioneer.'

He met her gaze squarely. 'What have I got to say to convince you? You go with the deal. Is that it? If I want Lyn Abbey I have to take you as well.'

Her face flamed angrily. She opened her mouth to speak then closed it again. Then she tapped on the glass and when the driver slid it back she said imperiously, 'Take us back to the hospital now, please.'

They did not speak until the taxi drew up outside the now familiar entrance. She stayed exactly where she was while Berry struggled to the edge of his seat, positioned his crutches and got into the road. The driver brought the wheelchair around and settled him into it. Berry replaced the crutches and sat back for an instant with closed eyes. Then he leaned back into the cab and said, 'All right. I'll have the watch.'

Her head whipped round in shocked surprise. She was still holding the gold Omega in one hand. Automatically she held it towards him. He extended one bony hand and as the sleeve of his sweater rode up she saw how scrawny his wrists were. She looked at him; his dark eyes were full of pain. Very gently, she slid the watch over his knuckles and wriggled it into place.

He said, 'D'you understand now, Val? It would be hell looking after me.'

She looked at him and felt a tenderness well in her that was quite separate from the pity he dreaded so much. Before he could stop her she raised the long bony hand to her lips. He gave an exclamation and whipped it away. 'Damn you, woman!' he said hoarsely.

She smiled. 'Can you manage?' She sat back. 'I'll call for you tomorrow. Same time.'

'I won't come. Murchison won't let me anyway.'

'Oh, I think you can manage Sister Murchison,' Val said blandly. 'Now let me see you go inside. Try to rest.' She closed her eyes, dismissing him. He stayed where he was for a long moment then laughed shortly.

'*Touché*, Vallery McKinley.' He backed the wheelchair and slammed the door. She watched him negotiate the ramp; the driver held the swing-doors wide open and the chair disappeared inside.

She stayed at Weymouth for a week. Physically and emotionally it was the most difficult week of her life. It was as if she were living for two people; Berry as well as herself. The effort of not helping him was almost superhuman, every evening her arms ached with the effort of being held at her sides. The mixture of tact and belligerence which coaxed him out of the hospital

143

every morning was exhausting. He liked her to 'chatter' as he called it, and she found herself making lists each evening of things she could tell him: funny stories, tales of her camping trips with Teddy, the gentle boredom of life in Clevedon, even poor old Titus Oates who was in love with her and who she only just tolerated for Teddy's sake.

During the early mornings before she collected him, and in the late afternoons after she had taken him back to the hospital, she shopped for luxuries that were not rationed. She queued for Continental chocolates supposedly smuggled in from Paris, American cigarettes, vitamin tablets. Through her teenage chambermaid, she contacted a small Cockney trader who dealt in the black market. From him she bought fresh underwear for herself, one of the new off-the-shoulder blouses, some pre-war white cricketing shirts and vests that were guaranteed not to tickle. Berry swore that the naval vests were giving him eczema.

Her father telephoned the hotel to say her mother was worried about her.

'How long do you intend to stay in Weymouth?' he asked, not entirely sympathetically. 'Do I need to employ another secretary? I don't actually recall you applying for holiday leave or giving me your notice!'

'Daddy – darling! Stop being all huffy and listen to me. I think it's all right. I'm having to work at this much harder than I thought, but I think I've given him a proposition which he might find . . . acceptable. Don't let anyone else buy the abbey, darling. Will you? It has become terribly important in my – er – negotiations.'

The noise on the telephone line sounded like a train going through a tunnel.

Eric McKinley spoke intelligibly at last.

'I don't know what you're up to, Val! What you really mean is that you want me to buy Lyn Abbey. Is that it? Cards on the table, my girl. It's the way you've always been.'

She might have grinned at this, but now she did not. She saw her future as destined; laid out for her.

She said, 'All right, Daddy. I want you to buy it. I really cannot go into the why's and wherefore's on the telephone and this line is frightful anyway. But – darling Daddy – if you love me just the littlest scrap, don't let Lyn Abbey go to someone else. You know how to arrange these things – I'm sure we – you – can get it cheaply. Brother Michael told me no-one would want it anyway and it would just crumble into a ruin. That would be awful, wouldn't it? You know how you feel about these wonderful old houses— '

'All right, Val. You've always got what you wanted and I suppose you'll get it now.'

She was shocked.

'Daddy! Am I really such a spoiled brat? Honestly, darling, I'm not doing this just for myself. It's just that . . . it's meant to be.'

'You're not spoiled at all in that sense, Val.' Her father sounded only slightly contrite. 'If you came into a million pounds and spent it in two days, you would not be spoiled because you'd probably spend it on someone else. But the fact remains, Val, that when you set your heart on something, you usually get it.'

'Oh, I hope so,' Val said fervently. 'In this case it's not one hundred per cent certain though. Berry Reid was always a bossy, self-opinionated sort, and now he's disabled he's worse than ever!'

There was a short pause then Eric said slowly, 'Val, are you getting me to buy Lyn Abbey simply to rent it to Berry Reid? That would be hopeless. My dear girl, he's going to need someone to look after him. He's bound to go back home. As I understand it both his mother and grandmother are there and will be able to make sure he's . . .' His voice tailed off and there was another pause. Then he said forcefully, 'Val, if you have any quixotic ideas about looking after this man— '

'Daddy dear, can you sit down a minute? I think –

145

I'm almost certain – I am going to marry him.' Val listened to the silence for a tense moment, then said quietly, 'Mother will understand, darling. Talk to her. Tell her that . . .' She paused. Tears were running down her small nose. 'Tell her that this is what I was born for. The reason I'm alive. Tell her that Berry Reid has given my whole life a – a reason.'

Eric's voice came back to her, small, helpless. 'Val. My darling girl. Please wait . . . come home and talk to us. You're being carried away by the terrible pathos of— '

She interrupted firmly. 'Far from it, Daddy. Let me tell you that this last week has been the hardest of my life, but the most satisfying. Since Teddy died.'

The pause this time was much longer. Val said, 'Daddy, are you there? You haven't passed out or anything, have you?'

'No. I am assimilating what you have just said. And what you have not said. And the fact that you are crying.'

She sobbed openly, surprising herself. 'Daddy. He reminds me of Teddy. He's not a bit like him – except that he has to live on the moor just as Teddy had to live in Clevedon by the sea. But he's – he's— '

Her father's voice came roughly across the hundred miles of wire. 'Val – be careful. Don't love him for Teddy's sake. It won't work.'

She swallowed her tears fiercely. 'I know. I'm not sure what I feel. It's not pity whatever you think. He's terrified that's all it is and that's why he's so . . . aggressive sometimes. But it's a kind of . . . Daddy, it's tenderness. I don't know another word. It fills me completely.' She was crying freely now, sniffing like a small girl. 'I feel so tender towards him. All I want to do is to be with him, look after him . . . Can you understand?' Her father did not reply immediately and she sobbed, 'I'm sorry. I shouldn't be talking like this to you. Mummy will know . . . but she's not well and I cannot burden her . . . you must tell her.'

He interrupted. 'I do understand, Val. I understand probably more than anyone else in the world.' He coughed and it was like an explosion in her ear. He said, 'I'll see what I can do about that abbey place. Take care of yourself as well as your young man. Give him my regards. And . . . perhaps my sympathy!' He managed a ragged laugh.

Val said, 'Daddy, thank you. Thank you.'

He said warningly, 'Nothing is settled yet, Val. Don't set your heart on . . . anything.' He sighed. 'I wish you could talk it over with your mother too. What about Morag?'

'Morag? Tell her about Berry?' Val stood still, chewing her lower lip for a moment. Then she said, 'D'you know, I think Morrie might be shocked. She's so driven somehow . . . by her ambitions to be a wonderful nurse. I think she might see this as awfully second-best.'

Eric McKinley sighed audibly. 'Perhaps she would. All right. We'll keep it to ourselves for a while, shall we?'

'Thanks, Daddy,' she said again. And replaced the telephone gently.

CHAPTER NINE

Morag's flat was plain to the point of being barren. Val, looking around it while Morag 'slipped into something more comfortable', felt a twinge of discomfort about her errand and wished she'd prepared the way a few weeks ago. She went to the gas meter and inserted a shilling then lit the fire. It wasn't really cold but she hoped the glow would help to brighten the room.

'More like a monk's cell,' she muttered surveying the bare walls. When she had suggested pictures before, Morag had reminded her that the pictures and photographs that meant anything to her were in her head.

'I don't want to come the martyr.' She had grinned to take off the awfulness of her words. 'But every last scrap in the Park Street house went up in smoke. And really, I'm not ready to replace it yet. I'll stick with these.' And she had tapped her forehead.

Val moved to the window and stared down at the devastation of the city. Already workmen were busy constructing an enormous new shopping centre. It was only five weeks since the end of the war in Japan, yet everything was hurrying frantically towards some kind of new era. Just as she herself was hurrying into this dedicated marriage, so the new socialists were laying their plans for a national health service for everyone ... The terrible war criminals were being tried at Nuremberg, the wonderful concepts of the old League of Nations were being enlarged and reinforced into the new United Nations ... Val's eyes filled with tears. She felt part of something splendid and idealistic. She turned back into the room almost reluctantly; its sterility seemed to negate everything that was happening outside.

Morag was in the corner which had been rigged up like a kitchenette. She was lighting the gas and putting on the kettle.

'I take it you've got time for a cup of tea?' She smiled at Val. 'You're looking wonderful by the way. You seem to be glowing!'

'Yes. That's how I feel.' But Val felt herself dimmed by Morag's room, by Morag herself. 'I've got heaps to tell you. But let's make the tea first and be cosy.' She drew up two wooden armchairs and fetched pillows from the bed to make them comfortable. 'Try to be cosy.'

'It's not cold,' Morag protested.

'No. But you've been on duty for over eight hours and I haven't stopped for four weeks. And I think we deserve a spot of pampering.' She drew up the table and put a carrier bag on it. 'Cakes. Mummy has someone to help her now and she made them. They're rather special.'

'Oh, I say.' Morag brought a tray of tea things to the table and peered inside the bag. It was as if she were trying to act a part. Enthusiasm did not come naturally any more. She poured tea and fetched plates for the cakes and they settled down.

'Come on then. I can see you're bursting,' she said, grinning hideously through jam and cream. 'If you've decided to smile on poor Titus, don't tell me. I couldn't bear it.'

'Oh no. Nothing like that.' Val felt suddenly nervous. 'How about you, first of all? What has been happening in men's surgical?'

'The usual. Exams finished. Think I'm all right.' She licked her lips. 'I don't want to count my chickens before they're hatched and so on, but I'm in line for theatre sister.'

Val grinned mightily. 'You'll have achieved your ambition, Mo! In four years! That's pretty bloody good, isn't it?'

'Val! You hardly ever swear!'

'I've learned how to do it. It releases a lot of tension.' Val

149

finished her cake, wiped her fingers on a rather grubby handkerchief because she still had not quite finished all her laundry, and decided that prevarication was at an end. She held out her left hand. The tiny diamond chip glinted in the September sunshine.

Morag gave the small scream expected of her. 'Val! You're engaged! Why didn't you tell me – phone or something! The last I heard, you were off men!'

Val recalled their phone conversation. 'I was, wasn't I? But I didn't know this particular man was alive even!' She took Morag's hand in hers; it was rough, the nails cut short. She said, 'Morrie, you'll never guess . . . not in a million years. It's Berry Reid!' Even as she spoke his name her eyes began to fill. 'Morrie – he's alive! All the Reid boys are alive! But Berry was flown home because he's lost a leg. The others are still out there waiting transport by sea. But Berry . . . Berry is here, Mo! And he's alive! And we're going to get married and live in Lyn Abbey . . . Oh, Mo— ' She choked on her own tears and put her face down to Morag's hand. 'I am so happy . . . more than happy . . . part of something more important than me! I wish I could tell you, Mo. I wish . . .'

There was an interval while she wept and Morag's hand stayed perfectly still in hers.

She began to babble again, unable to lift her head and look into those dark eyes.

'I know it's a shock. It was to me. When Mrs Reid told me – almost casually – I nearly died! I'd been to see the abbey – d'you remember I was going to catalogue the contents for Daddy? But there weren't any contents except the refectory table and chairs. But I saw the music room . . . and Brother Michael was still there and he's blind and he told me that the girl who killed herself for love was Doc Willie's sister! Would you believe it? And then I went to Gallenwick and looked at the stable yard and our room and then I went to the farm and Mrs Reid said . . .'

At last Morag moved. Val felt her other hand upon the back of her head, smoothing the curls down, combing them back up.

'Oh, Val . . . what a miracle. What a miracle . . .'

Val was so thankful to get a reaction that she sobbed again.

'Sorry about this, Mo. I can't cry in front of him. He would think I was pitying him. And it's not like that.'

She lifted her head at last. She could hardly see Morag; the dearly loved face wavered as if under water. She began to explain about the Radipole rehab. unit and Sisters Darwent and Murchison and how Berry was in so much pain but battled against it and was stubborn and often impossible.

'I have to be horrid to him, Mo. Really horrid.'

'I can imagine.'

'I kept buying him things . . . he says he's a kept man. We often laugh. Often.'

'He used to like a joke,' Morag said.

'Yes.' Val explained about Lyn Abbey and how her father had gone to the auction only last week and bought it far below the reserved price.

'And you're giving him that too?' Morag asked.

Val smiled ruefully. 'It was part of the bargain. If he wanted to live in Lyn Abbey, he had to marry me.'

'You are joking?' Morag said beginning to come into focus, looking like her Aunt Harriet, all buttoned up.

'Well, not really. I mean that's what we've said. And that is what is happening.' Val wished she could tell Morag about the impotence. After all, being a nurse, Morag would understand about that. But Berry had made her promise.

She said earnestly, 'You see, Mo, he's got to believe that I would go to any lengths to marry him. His confidence is at rock-bottom. In here— ' she tapped her head – 'he's been battered to a pulp. It's important that someone is desperate for him. Can you understand that?'

Morag frowned, obviously trying hard.

At last she said slowly, 'And you'd do that for him?'

'Oh yes.' Val looked straight into the curiously aristocratic face: yes, Morag was very like an Indian princess. She said again, simply, 'Oh yes.'

And Morag nodded, understanding. 'Then that is all right.' She smiled suddenly and took Val's hands. 'That is perfectly all right, isn't it?'

Val leaned forward and cast herself onto her friend. Morag held her as she had held her that first night at Gallenwick. She smoothed the riot of curls and said again and again, 'It will be all right. It will be all right.'

Berry insisted, abbey or no abbey, that he would not have a big wedding.

'Your parents, my Ma and Gran and that's it,' he said, his long mouth set in the stubborn lines she already knew so well.

'What do you mean? Abbey or no abbey?' Val said lightly, playing for time.

His face was dark that day. He had been home for a week now and knew that life on the farm as a 'spare part' was unbearable.

'You're always blackmailing me about the abbey. If we can't slip away and get married quietly, I don't care about the bloody abbey.'

She swallowed. She had not seen much of Berry since he left Radipole. There had been a great deal to do at home and she had spent three days at the abbey with her father discussing ways and means of making it habitable. Her mood of predestination had faded; there were long months ahead, years even, of hard work and expense. She had assumed Berry would immediately begin to make a living with his painting; her father had disenchanted her slowly and carefully.

'I know you think I'm an old grouch,' he had apologized. 'But I think you should know just what you are letting yourself in for. Art sales are right down – the war put the lid on that particular world. And you

152

will have to camp out in this place for years. It's probably damp in winter . . . not good for Berry's leg. That stump is always going to play up. Sorry, darling.'

'No, it's all right, Daddy.' She had looked around the music room slowly. It collected every ray of sun that was available, but on that particular day there was no sun. The rain poured down the windows monotonously. But it was still beautiful. 'We could live in this room, of course. It's big enough for everything. And perhaps convert the one through there into an enormous farmhouse kitchen.'

'Yes. That sounds the best bet.' Eric McKinley bit his lip. He had accepted back in August that this was what Vallery had to do. But he hated seeing her face such hardship. He said rallyingly, 'Don't forget you'll have Berry with you all the time. That makes everything worthwhile.' He was speaking from his own experience. Val said nothing.

She looked at Berry now, his strong dark face set in lines of pain. He had still not spoken of his years in the prison camp; sometimes she wanted to lift her fists and cry out against heaven at his experiences.

She said in a small voice, 'The abbey business . . . that's just a joke. Isn't it? If it doesn't work . . . if we can't afford it . . . we'll still have each other. Won't we?'

He looked at her sharply. 'Having doubts, Val?' his mouth twisted into a smile.

'No. I'm not having doubts. But when you talk of a hole-in-the-corner wedding and not caring about the abbey, I wonder whether you regret letting me talk you into this marriage.'

'I told you before. No-one talks me into anything I don't want to do.' His eyes suddenly softened. 'Val, you saved my life. Surely you know that?'

Her heart lifted ridiculously. She said, 'Don't be ridiculous, Berry.'

'I'm not being ridiculous. I'm a hulk – I can't give you anything – certainly not a family. You are a beautiful young woman who could marry anyone. And you want to marry me.'

'Don't talk such nonsense. You're my investment in the future. You're going to be a great artist. I know when I'm on to a good thing!'

He laughed and leaned up to pull her down on his lap. He gasped as his stump took her weight but held on to her firmly and pressed her back onto his arm and then kissed her.

She squirmed. 'Berry!' she protested as she came up for air.

He kissed her again, and then again and very gradually, she relaxed. She had hated it when Titus Oates had kissed her like this; she had hit him quite hard. She could not hit Berry and by the time he had finished kissing her she did not mind any more. She sat up, dazed, quite shaken. He slid his hand over her small, silk-covered breasts and said hoarsely, 'God, Val, you are beautiful . . . you are so very beautiful.'

She said nothing. She was completely unnerved. She stared into his dark eyes as if she had never seen him before.

He whispered, 'We'll manage, won't we Val? We'll manage?'

She forced her lips to move. 'Of course. Of course we will.'

He sobbed a small laugh. 'You are so . . . bloody . . . indefatigable!' And he lifted his face and kissed her again, but this time it was his usual affectionate peck. He sobbed again into her neck. 'Darling Val. Can you stand up now? My stump is killing me!' And she leapt to her feet and knelt by him while he closed his eyes tightly and clenched his fists on the arms of his chair.

'Oh, Berry – why didn't you push me off? Oh I'm sorry . . .'

At last he opened his eyes and grinned at her though his face was drained of colour.

'It's OK, baby,' he said with an American accent. 'I can take it if you can.' And then he clutched her hand suddenly. 'I'll get used to it, Val. And I'm going to. OK? I'm going to.'

She had no idea what he was talking about but at that moment she admired him more than ever before. Any sacrifice was worth making for this man. This hero.

She whispered, 'So it's all right? We will get married? I don't care where it is or how many people come . . . or don't come . . .'

'Of course we'll get married! If you back out now I'll sue.' He was grinning more normally now. 'But no guests. OK? We do it and we go straight to the abbey and we stay there for ever.'

She whispered, 'OK. Just your brothers and Morrie and Jannie— '

He threw himself back in his chair and lifted his head in exasperation. 'What have we just agreed? God, Val. Are you stupid? Ma, Gran and your parents! Got that?'

She felt so hurt and did not know why. He had been insulting before and it had not worried her. She said, 'But Hugh and Durston will be home by then. What will they think? And Morrie and Jannie are like my sisters— '

He straightened and looked at her. 'Have I got to kiss you again to get it into your skull that I cannot stand anyone witnessing such a charade!'

She gasped and stared at him, then stood up slowly.

'You . . . you swine!' she said inadequately. And left the room.

They were married in the smallest church on Exmoor just before that Christmas. In the event there would not have been room for Berry's brothers or Val's friends and she did not regret 'giving in' to Berry. The tiny church and the four people in the congregation became so significant she felt tears pressing yet again in her throat.

Berry waited for her, standing solidly without a walking stick, his mother by his side as 'best man'. The priest was a giant of a man, in charge of three of the enormous parishes on the moor. Val, glancing down, saw that beneath his cassock he had forgotten to take off his cycle clips. Even that seemed unbearably touching to her and she smiled into his eyes with all the confidence of her twenty-one years so that he blinked and had to refer to his prayer book before he could begin the service.

Margaret McKinley refused to cry. She looked unbelievably frail in a pre-war tea gown of apple-green silk covered by her ancient but beautiful chinchilla coat. Her ankles and wrists were like matchsticks; she had concealed ankles with snow boots and wrists with long kid gloves. Eric, joining her at the appropriate time, knew suddenly that he would not have her for much longer. He put an arm beneath her coat and around her waist and clamped her to his side as if defying death itself. She put her mouth very close to his ear as everyone rustled the pages of *Hymns Ancient and Modern*, and whispered, 'There will be children, darling . . . immortality . . .' He nodded and they both sang strongly, 'Love divine, all loves excelling . . .'

Peggy Reid looked unexpectedly dashing in the black coat she had bought for her husband's funeral. Berry had gone into Barnstaple with Val and bought a scarlet hat and silk scarf and gloves to go with it. He said she looked like a cavalry officer. She stood short and strong by his side, ready to provide physical support when he needed it. Jannie had been her favourite, but she knew that Vallery McKinley would be the best wife for her Berry.

Granny wore a fur coat of such age it was impossible to guess which animal had died for it. With her humped figure and short-sighted gaze, she resembled a mole. Whereas Berry in his demob suit, his left trouser leg draped carefully over the artificial leg, looked like one of the Exmoor ponies, head up, dark eyes questing the landscape, ready to burst free at any moment.

Val wore a utility suit of 'mixed fibres' with a very long skirt. It was heather coloured, almost purple; it made her eyes look violet. The small matching pillbox on her head sat among her curls like a bird in a nest. She had

156

applied a great deal of make-up and knew she looked like one of the wave of cover girls now all the rage. She carried a tiny nosegay of Christmas roses which she gave to her father almost immediately so that she could put her hand beneath Berry's arm. He did not shrug it away. He looked down at her and smiled and her heart melted.

Afterwards she thanked the priest prettily and said, 'You will come on to the abbey for tea, won't you?' And was thankful when he declined because she feared Berry might see that as breaking his rule. They got into the two cars: she drove Berry and Granny Thomas in Hugh's old Morris which still ran beautifully in spite of five years in the barn. The other three used her father's car, which by now almost knew its own way to the abbey. Incredibly they had discovered that the hairpin bends of the track could be negotiated by car and in spite of Berry sitting well back, closing his eyes and groaning 'Oh Christ' at every turn, they drew up outside the porch in less than an hour since the church service.

'There! What did I tell you?' Val asked triumphantly. 'We're still within easy reach of civilization!'

Berry prepared to get out of the car. 'What's it like going back up?' he asked.

'Just as frightening,' Val laughed and hurried round to help him. But this time he shook his head.

'Let me go in under my own steam, Val. If this is to be our home, I must be able to do that.'

So she hung right back and let him open the door and go inside on his own. She and Peggy had laid out a simple meal in the old music room; they had left the dining hall as it had always been. But Margaret and Eric had been here before the wedding and the enormous refectory table was a mass of banked foliage culminating in a fully decorated Christmas tree. Val gave a gasp of sheer delight. The darkness of the hall gave the tree mystery; the light from the open door glinted on the same bells and baubles she had known since childhood.

She said, 'Oh Mummy . . . Daddy . . . It's beautiful. When did you do it?'

'After we'd dropped you at the farm to get dressed.' Margaret smiled at Berry. 'It's not too bad at all driving back up the track. We brought all the stuff yesterday and stowed it in the butler's pantry or whatever it is. So we've done the trip twice. You'll soon get used to it.'

Berry put an arm across the thin shoulders and pecked both Margaret's cheeks in a very Continental way.

'Thank you, Margaret,' he said gently. 'Thank you for everything.'

He was in a mood to like everything; the hand-cranked lift he declared to be 'jolly'; he smiled his congratulations to Val at the layout of the music room and then stood in rapt delight by the enormous windows that looked out on to the shifting sea. Val had bought a deal table at Barnstaple market which would be a work table for Berry later. This was loaded with a proper farmhouse tea; a motley selection of chairs surrounded it. She had thrown an Indian shawl over the bed in the corner and put a few rugs down on the floorboards. There were no curtains at the windows, nor in the big kitchen behind the music room. Yet the whole effect was one of peace, tranquillity, even comfort. As Eric bent down to light the fire laid in the grate, she said quietly, 'I've done the right thing. Haven't I, Daddy?'

And he smiled up at her reassuringly. 'I think you have, my dear.'

Margaret hugged her daughter to her. 'I knew it from the first,' she said.

The wedding guests left just before darkness closed in at half-past four.

Val knelt on the window-seat in the kitchen watching the tail-lights of her father's car zigzagging up the cliff and then turning onto the road which would lead past Gallenwick and back to the farm. She tried not to feel lonely. This was what she had wanted; her life, her real life, was just beginning.

She went back into the music room and saw with horror that Berry had wedged himself by one of the windows which he had opened; he was leaning right out.

'Darling!' She rushed forward and caught the tail of his shirt; it was unbuttoned, half off his shoulders. 'What on earth are you doing? It's December! You haven't got your jacket on! You'll catch pneumonia!'

He looked round at her; she waited for laughter or annoyance. Instead his face was calm; more than calm. He seemed to exude peace. She felt unexpectedly confused.

'Darling . . . you look so . . . serene!'

He smiled. 'My God. That sounds saintly! Am I a saint then, Val?' He put an arm inside the casement and drew her to him. 'Come and be part of this, darling. Look and smell and taste . . . This is night. The world is leaning back from the sun and going into night. And tomorrow it will reach towards day . . . that's why this house was built here; to be part of the earth and the sea and the sky. Can you feel it?'

She was silent, trying to quell her anxiety for him, trying to reach his plane. It was bitterly cold. There would be a frost tonight, the air was already smoky with it; the first stars visible.

He said in a low voice, 'It is so necessary to know our place, Val. To know that we are part of all this. I tried . . . in the camp I used to go to the wire and look out and watch the soldiers and will myself to be part of all that. But . . .' he whispered a laugh in her ear, 'this is easier.'

She closed her eyes. It was the first time he had mentioned the camp.

He went on, almost to himself. 'It doesn't come naturally. We shall have to work at it . . . put down roots . . . civilization has spoiled us, atrophied our perceptions. When we were in the water, we became part of that water. And that is how it will be here.'

159

'Water?' she whispered.

He moved so that he could see her face, smiled suddenly and kissed her nose.

'Sorry, darling. I was thinking of someone else. Not that it matters. I am speaking of universals.'

She said brokenly, 'Oh, Berry!'

He kissed her. 'What?'

'I was only thinking . . . this is the window . . . that girl . . . Winifred . . .'

He kissed her again. 'I know. Don't you understand now? She was becoming part of this . . . just as her lover was . . . can you understand?'

He kissed her again and she gasped, 'Berry . . . don't think of death and dying. Please.'

He was unbuttoning her blouse as he kissed her. The air was like ice on her shoulders and then her breasts. His shirt was off and he held her to him and she could feel the heat of his body and the sweat on his face.

'Berry, you mustn't . . . this is not good for you . . . you said . . .' She could barely speak between his kisses.

He said hoarsely, 'You must help me. Val, you must help me . . .'

She did not know how to help him at first, but he showed her and she was not shocked. She wanted to give him whatever he asked. She had not counted on the sudden rush of emotion he released; the surrender to sensation. She had not dreamed of ecstasy. She had imagined she was frigid; that she was quite happy to remain a virgin all her life. She had seen herself as dedicated nurse and protector. Now, like an explosion, all her theories and ideals were scattered, childish. Again and again she supported him, uncaring as to his exhaustion or pain. When he slept at last, she cradled his head for a long time, staring into the darkness and smiling idiotically. She slept until the grey December light came through the uncurtained windows then woke to find him looking down at her.

He traced her face with his fingers.

'I'm going to paint you,' he said. 'Not today. I have to find out about you first . . . I have to know what goes on behind the curls and the baby-blue eyes . . . but one day . . .'

She smiled back, hardly hearing him, content as a cat. 'You have seduced me, Berry Reid! You led me to believe that you were impotent and the first opportunity you get, you seduce me!'

His smile broadened to a grin. 'Oh Val, did you think . . . you actually thought we were going to be friends! Confess!' His fingers went from her face to her body. 'Confess!'

She squirmed and laughed and shrieked a little. 'All right! But Berry, seriously now. You did say— '

He kissed her. 'Darling, I thought you would realize. It's simply that . . .' His eyes avoided hers. 'Val, I'm sorry but there will be no children.'

She cupped his face and forced him to look at her.

She said, 'I don't care. And you mustn't care either.' She kissed him as he kissed her. 'I love you,' she whispered, surprised at her own words. 'Oh Berry . . . I love you so much!'

He murmured, 'Don't sound so surprised, my darling. Why else would you have married me?'

She could not begin to explain all her motives. She whispered again, 'I love you so much. I am so happy . . . so happy.'

CHAPTER TEN

1951

Morag sat through the seminar at Birmingham University making notes automatically, her mind very much elsewhere. Her tutor was not much older than she was; ex-RAF, a boffin turned psychologist. His name, unforgettably, was Matthew Arnold. He knew her only through this course on rehabilitation, yet last week he had asked her to marry him. The proposal had embarrassed them both and she had not joined in the discussion or asked questions since. There were only five other people doing the seminars, so her silence was obvious.

Matthew was winding up the session.

'So ... although we have decided that each case must be dealt with individually, nevertheless can we generalize that our patients are likely to fall into one of two categories? The people who cannot relate their experiences, who are completely isolated from others. And those who are unable to stop talking. Who have become, in fact, obsessive.'

An older man, a doctor who had served in the Great War, leaned forward. 'May we investigate the first category at our next session, Matthew? I think obsessive behaviour might well be a common factor for what we used to call shell-shock. The obsessions might not be quite so obvious in the first category, but I have evidence to show that they are there.'

Morag made a note. 'Berry obsessive? About painting ... yes. Anything else?'

Matthew beamed. Morag thought, surprised, that he

was good-looking. He reminded her . . . dear Lord, he reminded her of Teddy McKinley.

Everyone was gathering books and preparing to leave. Jessica White, a midwife, said, 'Any chance of borrowing your surgical notes, Morag? I was up last night with my youngest and couldn't get down to it.'

Morag sifted through her bag and took some papers out of her file. Most of the medical students here were married with families. Jessica lived in Selly Oak; she could cycle from the Bourneville campus to where her small semi had survived the bombing but was succumbing to general disrepair after more than ten years without attention. She had jumped at the chance to become a doctor and her grant equalled her salary as a midwife. War-time hospital staff were being offered good grants by the government to qualify as doctors.

Morag had applied half-heartedly and at Aunt Harriet's instigation and sometimes felt it was unfair that she had got a place so easily. Aunt Harriet had brought down what she called the 'guff' on one of her visits to Bristol.

'It's not as if Birmingham were all that far away from home.' She had glanced perfunctorily around the flat as she spoke. It was so obvious that her niece did not intend this to be a home, merely a lodging. 'I can understand that you would not want to throw in your lot with me.' She held up her hand at Morag's dutiful protest. 'The feeling is mutual, my dear. I am set in my ways. But then I am over sixty. You are set in your ways and you are twenty-four. That is not good.'

Morag had smiled affectionately. She had grown close to her aunt; they respected each other; they set emotional limits beyond which they never strayed.

'You only see me when I am working, Aunt. When I have time off I spend it at Clevedon with Eric and Margaret McKinley.'

'Where, as I understand it, you take over the household duties and look after Margaret McKinley!' Aunt Hariet said drily. She put out a hand. 'I am not criticizing.

Mr McKinley tells me that you have made an enormous difference to their lives.'

'I don't know about that.' Morag stared through the window to where the Park Street house had been restored. But no oriel window. 'They miss Val, of course. Perhaps I fill some of that gap.'

'Perhaps.' Aunt Harriet remembered the holiday she had spent at Gallenwick with the seventeen-year-old Morag. She sighed sharply. 'I still think you should apply for a place at Birmingham, my dear. If you don't get it, then you've lost nothing.' She touched the back of Morag's hand. 'Life has to go on, you know. We can't stand still. Not ever.'

Morag could have reminded her that she was the youngest theatre sister at Bristol Royal; but she did not.

She avoided Matthew Arnold in the corridor and said goodbye to Jessica before running to Bourneville station for her train. It was a typically March day; a blustery wind forced her to hug her raincoat around her knees and close her eyes against a flurry of grit. The train creaked in, heavy with bodies; she squashed herself next to a man who was reading the *Birmingham Post* and thought longingly of her flat in Bristol, almost next door to the hospital, with its view over the city. However, this was her final year. She was already halfway through writing her thesis; it had to be in by mid-July. And then she could go and stay with Margaret and Eric for a whole month and think about what exactly she was going to do.

The train juddered to a halt at Selly Oak, then King's Norton, then Northfield and finally Longbridge. There was a car factory at Longbridge so nearly everybody got out; the evening shift began at six.

She turned out of the station into the little community of prefabricated houses already feeling for her key in her pocket. She had been lucky to get one of these small bungalows put up by the council after the war. The official tenant was doing a tour of duty in Nigeria and had no wish to lose it, so Morag was heaven-sent as far as he was concerned. She even tended the garden. And the tiny estate had somehow managed to retain a village atmosphere; it was framed by beech trees and a small brook ran through its centre; above it rose the steep Lickey Hills.

She fitted the key in the lock and was about to close the door after her when she heard a noise from the tool shed. The next instant the door was pushed open and Val's face appeared.

'Oh thank the Lord!' Val emerged and rushed at Morag. 'Oh I thought you were never going to get back! There's nowhere to telephone and – and— ' By this time she had hurled herself bodily into her friend's arms and was hanging on to her like a drowning woman. 'Oh Morrie – oh it is so good to see you – I left the car at Redley Lodge and came by train and had to change at Bromsgrove . . .' She began to cry helplessly and Morag, wedged in the front door, simply held her and patted her back and waited. After a very short time Val controlled herself. 'Darling, I'm sorry . . . it's just that, I thought you finished at three-thirty and I got here at three and when you hadn't turned up by four I thought you must have gone on somewhere for the evening and I – I— '

'Come on, Val. Let's sit down and I'll make some tea. Have you got a bag or something?'

'In the shed. Leave it. I have to tell you quickly, and there's no easy way. Mo . . . Mummy died last night. Oh Mo . . . I can't believe it! I can't bear to believe it! The world seems so cold . . . darling Mo, how did you cope? Tell me – help me— '

They were in the tiny sitting room by now. Morag let out a deep and audible groan, then they both sat down on the sofa and held on to each other while Val wept again. Morag stared dry-eyed over her shoulder at the small room which was not hers. Ten years since her own parents had been killed. And still she was homeless, without roots.

She said, 'Val, you've got your father. You must be strong for him. Oh my dear, he will miss her so much.' She spoke with the knowledge gained over the past years when she had spent all her holidays at Redley Lodge. Val nodded vigorously, knocking Morag's chin with the back of her head.

'I know. I know. That's what makes it worse. What will he do, Mo? What will he do?'

Mo took a deep breath of resignation. 'He will live, my dear. Day by day, he will live.'

Val drew back her head to look into the dark eyes so close to hers. Then she wailed anew.

'Oh Morrie – is that how it has been? My dear, how do you bear it?'

Morag smiled. 'Without too much difficulty now, Val. Like your father, I have everything I could possibly need in the way of creature comforts. I am well . . . so is he. I have a job I enjoy. So does he. And I have all these pictures up here –' she released Val long enough to tap her forehead, '– and so does he.'

Val subsided against the cushions, hiccuping on sobs, but calmer.

'I knew it was the right thing to do. Daddy suggested it actually. He said, there was nothing I could be doing and why didn't I come and tell you and bring you back with me.'

For a fleeting second, Morag thought of her thesis; of Matthew Arnold. Then she said quicky, 'He was right. I am so thankful you did.' She fished out a handkerchief and dabbed at Val's face. 'Is he expecting us tonight? Have we got time for some tea?'

'Of course.' Val shivered suddenly. 'I haven't been here before, Mo. It's cold. People always say it's cold in Birmingham.'

Morag knelt and lit the gas fire, then went immediately into the kitchen to put the kettle on.

'It's having to stay in that shed for two hours!' She turned and flashed a rallying smile at Val, noting the flattened curls, the white face behind the runnels of tears. 'Oh, Val. I'm so sorry. There's nothing to be said, but you know how much I love her too. She is so gentle . . . so completely kind . . .' Morag's voice tailed off at the sheer inadequacy of her words. She spread her hands helplessly.

Val crouched by the fire. 'I know.' She looked up, her face already twisting again. 'I like it when you use the present tense. She is still with us . . . isn't she, Mo? Isn't she?'

'Of course.' Morag crouched too. They both held their hands to the gas flames. 'I remember Doc Willie saying that they became part of us . . . our loved ones. And she should know after all.'

'Yes. Of course. Poor Winifred. I think of her so often.' Val nodded, staring through the window at the trees bending before a sudden gust of wind. 'Mo . . . is there a telephone kiosk somewhere? Shall I ring Daddy and tell him we'll come home tomorrow? Can you put me up? There's so much to talk about.'

'Yes. To both questions. We'll have tea . . . something to eat. Then we'll walk to the phone together.' She took Val's hand. 'We are together, Val. Remember that.'

She made a meal for them and told Val about the course, Jessica White, the doctor from the Great War, even Matthew Arnold. It was much later when they were in bed that she realized neither of them had mentioned Berry. She knew that he hardly ever left the abbey; that he worked like a fiend and was at last beginning to sell some of his work. That was almost all. When they met at Redley Lodge, Val rarely spoke of their day-to-day living. Morag had no domestic pictures at all of their life together.

It was not until the night before the funeral that she realized she would have to meet him. Somehow she had assumed that without Val he was virtually a prisoner in the house. Now, it seemed, he was not. He chose to stay there; he was perfectly capable of emerging when he had to. 'It's his work that keeps him there,' Val explained. 'That's all he thinks about. Painting.' She lowered her head. 'Well, almost all . . .' She cut open bread rolls fiercely. 'Hugh will collect him of course. Dusty will drive. They're very good.'

Morag was silent for some time, then she said, 'I've never met Dusty, have I? And Hugh only once. Or was it twice?'

'Dusty is a bit of a rogue I gather from Peggy. He's got various business interests in London, but no-one knows exactly what they are.' Val's face softened. 'Hugh is wonderful. He runs the farm now. Drives over and has a chat with Berry. You know, when he gets . . . down. Depressed.'

'Is that often?' Morag drained a tin of peaches and laid them artistically on a sponge flan.

'No. Not often,' Val said brightly. 'After all, Berry has got everything he ever wanted. And more.'

'More?' Morag raised her brows, surprised at Val's tone.

Val rolled her eyes self-mockingly. 'He wants – needs— ' she put on a voice 'lerve . . . he can't get enough . . . lerve.' She shook her head at Morag's blank expression and said normally and very matter of factly, 'He has to be loved. By one and all.' Morag had a sudden vision of Berry atop the haywain, ordering the girls about, joshing them, flirting with them . . . For some reason she remembered Caroline Prosser, weeping in a corner of the wagon.

She said directly, 'You're all right, Val? You and Berry?'

Val grinned. 'You never had to ask before, did you? How boring I must have been about my intense happiness!' She reached for the carving knife and began to cut ham fiercely. 'Sorry, Mo, but that sort of happiness doesn't last.' She popped a piece of meat into her mouth. 'But, yes, we are all right. We know each other very well . . . we're all right.'

*   *   *

The church was 'packed to the gunnels' as Val put it much later. Margaret had retired from most of the town's activities for some years now, but her gentle presence would still be missed. The secretary of the lawn tennis club said to Val, 'You two used to have such a good time, didn't you? It didn't matter whether you won your games or not, you did so enjoy them!'

Val said steadily, 'She made anything seem fun. Finding shells or wild flowers . . . even weeding!'

Morag said, 'Do have one of these rolls. Val, I think the rector would like a word.' She moved around the small groups in the living room and the large hall, trying to fend off the over-sympathetic from Val. Eric was empty-eyed, smiling mechanically, shaking hands. Morag was standing by him, not knowing how to help when a very tall, rather thin, but unmistakable figure approached them. She beamed involuntarily.

'Hugh Reid!' She held out her hand. 'You won't remember me. I'm Val's friend.'

His hair was almost entirely grey; he had a scar running from the corner of his left eye to the point of his chin. But he still looked like Lesley Howard.

'Morag Heyward.' He smiled and she was transported to the hayfield . . . sunshine . . . summer. 'Of course I remember you. We must talk. But I wondered whether now would be a good time for Eric to show me some of the Nailsea glass he is always talking about!' He moved slightly, blocking someone who was approaching. 'Remember last time you were at the farm, Eric? You said you'd just bought some from a sale in Gloucestershire?'

Morag watched them drift away. The McKinleys had spoken warmly of Hugh Reid in the past, they had found him easier to be with than their talented son-in-law. And she saw now that Hugh had not changed. She remembered that sensitivity from her two short previous encounters with him ten years ago. He was holding open the door of the dining room and shepherding Eric through to a few minutes' peace.

Just for a moment she was alone. And then she was not. The moment she had avoided for so long was there. She had seen Berry's dark head in the church, noted that he had not walked with the funeral cortège, hoped that he would avoid her too.

He said simply, 'Hello, Morrie.'

She turned and looked at him. He had not changed as Hugh had. His hair was as black and curly as ever, his eyes as dark. He was slightly shorter than she remembered, and then realized that was because of his aluminium leg. He was not using a walking-stick, but very casually he put a hand against the newel post and shifted his body round to face her. It made the meeting almost a confrontation.

She said, 'Hello, Berry. How are you?'

'You probably know already.' He smiled lopsidedly. 'And you? I hear you're going to be a doctor in our brave new world. Carry your father's torch.'

'Perhaps.' She remembered his abrasive tongue. 'And you're well on the way to being a famous painter. Val says you work all the time.'

'Of course. What else is there? You don't need two legs to be a painter.'

She refused to react. 'Quite.' Matthew's words about obsession came back to her. Was Berry obsessive about his work or simply dedicated? She smiled. 'So your predictions came true? Painting. Living in the abbey.'

He grinned suddenly. 'Is this your clinical approach? Reminding me of my blessings?'

She returned the smile. 'Probably.'

'So – *ergo* – I should be happy. Yes?'

'Ah, that is something else.' She kept her smile in place and turned to move to another group.

He gripped her arm suddenly. 'Don't you dare walk away from me now! Just because I cannot follow you!'

'I assure you . . .'

'And don't give me that calm Sister Morag line either! You and I both know what happiness is! We know it is a baptism of water, fear, love. Becoming one with that water, with each other . . .'

'Berry! Shut up!'

'We know what happiness is. We know how to find it. We know we have not got it now!'

'Berry! For God's sake be quiet! Someone will hear!'

'Ah . . . the Sister Morag shell is chipping, isn't it? So the old Morag is still there somewhere?' He pulled her against him. 'Do you remember how I broke that shell before? Do you ever think of it now?'

'No. Never.'

'I don't believe you. Val says your rented house is near a brook. Whenever you look at that water, do you remember— '

A voice said, 'Berry. Are you all right, old chap? You're hanging on to Morag as if your life depends on it!'

Morag looked around. She had been introduced to the oldest Reid before the funeral service and was delighted to see him again.

'Durston. I was going to get some more sandwiches.'

'Not for me, Morag. I was going to suggest that Berry and I slipped up the road for a quick one. What do you say, old man?'

Berry released Morag at last and turned to his brother.

'Good idea. Leave the women to their wailing, eh?'

Morag was shocked for an instant, then realized that was what Berry intended.

She said to Durston, 'Yes, I think he could do with getting away for a while.' She smiled at Berry. 'Just relax for a while in male company.'

If Berry was deprived of the final word, Durston made up for it. He laughed heartily.

'That will make a change, eh, old man?' He grinned at Morag frankly. 'Berry and I are rather fond of the ladies as you have doubtless heard!' He took Berry's arm and they made for the front door. Morag stared after them, trying not to be thoroughly disenchanted. She had tried so hard to see Berry as a 'case'. He had smashed right through that and reawakened all those feelings of that old war-time summer. And then had proceeded to smash those too. Helped, of course, by that final remark of Durston's.

Someone spoke to her and she directed them to the bathroom. Then Val was back from seeing the rector, her blue eyes bright with annoyance.

'Guess who has turned up, Mo? Jannie! She heard about Mummy just this morning and got Marius to drive her here immediately.'

'Marius?'

'The boss or the boyfriend or whatever! Anyway, they were getting out of the car as Berry and Dusty were coming out of the front door. So I introduced them and the next thing I knew they'd gone off to the pub – all of them! Can you believe it?'

Morag almost laughed. She felt suddenly an enormous sense of freedom. All these years she had thought of Berry Reid . . . in a certain way. And now she did not.

She took Val's arm. 'They'll be back at closing time. Two o'clock, isn't it? People are beginning to leave. We'll have tea by the fire in the sitting room like we've done so often before. We'll make some toast. Shall we? Your – father would like that.'

Val leaned against her. 'Mo . . . in case I forget to say it later . . . I couldn't manage without you. We'll always be friends, won't we?'

'Always,' Morag said.

It was amazing to see Jannie in the company of three men, each one determined to gain her sole attention. She had blossomed like a pale flower. Her hair was her chief feature, but the small face beneath it, though still waif-like, was strangely confident. She sat on the rug and leaned against Marius' knees smiling lazily into the fire,

172

contributing very little to the conversation, yet somehow being the centre of attention. Marius, twenty years her senior, appeared to be at ease, chatting with Morag and Val, but when Durston found a notebook and wrote down Jannie's address so that he could look her up in London, Marius picked up a tress of the satiny hair and casually smoothed it on his trousered knee in a way that left no doubt in anyone's mind that Jannie belonged exclusively to him.

Hugh and Eric McKinley came in from the dining room, still talking about Eric's collection of glass. Hugh grinned widely when he was introduced to Jannie.

'Of course! The water sprite! How could I forget!'

For a moment, Jannie's self-satisfied expression changed as she registered Hugh's grey hair and the scar. Then she smiled and drew him down to her.

'Sit here. Tell me about the farm. Your mother. I loved your mother.'

Hugh crouched but did not sit. 'Yes. She had a soft spot for you, didn't she? Thought you needed feeding up!' He patted the back of her hand. 'Look, we must talk another time. I'm doing some cataloguing for Eric. And you've got all the company you need!' His grin widened uncritically. Morag, listening to the exchange as she poured tea thought: he is entirely uncritical – takes people exactly as they are . . . he is so . . . unusual. And she smiled right at him as she said, 'You must have some tea first. And I think Eric would like us to make some toast.'

They sat either side of the fireplace with a toasting fork each and Eric drank his tea and held Val's hand and let his mind go back to other scenes just like this. Except that Margaret had been there.

Morag had always worked hard, but that spring and summer she worked harder than ever. Her father's advice about the therapeutic value of work held good. She came to terms with Val's loss and was able to write to Eric – even telephone him sometimes – with cheerful messages and reassurances that after July she would come to Clevedon as arranged. She managed to find Jannie's behaviour amusing too, though she and Val had discussed it afterwards and Val had confessed to being worried. 'You realize that Marius is – or was – Mrs Mears' boyfriend in the war? He was probably the reason she didn't come to see Jannie with Teddy and your mother. I wonder if Jannie is like her? You know . . . a bit . . . well, over-sexed?' Morag had laughed then, refusing to take Val seriously. As she sat in the university library, making endless notes, she smiled again at the thought of Jannie flexing her feminine muscles. That's all it was. Jannie, showing off.

Harder to accept was the small scene in the hall of Redley Lodge with Berry Reid. Morag refused to acknowledge that she had been shaken by such an aggressive confrontation. But sometimes, just as she was going to sleep, she could see again the pain and anger in those dark eyes. When she had returned from the funeral she had opened her notebook and stared at the words she had written about Berry's possible obsession with painting. Then she added a single word: sex.

The summer term began. Somewhere else, as if on another planet, the Festival of Britain was under way. All the medical students could talk of was the finals and their theses. When July arrived they met in the lecture room to hand in their manuscripts, all grinning with the sheer relief of actually getting rid of them after so long.

'I was a fairly carefree thirty-five when I started this lot.' Jessica White rolled her eyes. 'Now look at me. Almost forty, going grey, kids running wild because I'm always busy, house falling to bits— '

Morag laughed. 'You've done it, Jess. That's what counts. You'll get a job at the hospital, better money, do up the house.'

'I'm going to move.' Jessica smiled. 'Something rather wonderful has happened. My old GP can't cope with this

National Health stuff. He says I can move into his house lock, stock and barrel and take over. He'll ease me into it this winter and be gone in a year's time. What do you think?'

'Jess, it's wonderful. You'll be a marvellous family doctor. You'll specialize in pediatrics and maternity and all the young mums will hang on your every word . . . What's the house like?'

'Pretty decrepit. But that's what we're used to! And there's so much space! A bedroom each, would you believe! And a spare. You can come and stay, Morag, would you? Really? I hate to think we'll never see each other again!'

'I'll try. Of course. But I simply have no idea at all what I shall be doing. I'll write.'

Matthew Arnold appeared and suggested they all come to his room where he had some sherry and biscuits. There was a little party. Everyone became effusive, almost maudlin.

Matthew said to Morag, 'What will you be doing? Back to Bristol?'

She forced herself to meet his eyes. He was very like Teddy. And he was interesting. She sighed and told him about Clevedon.

'Well . . . gives you breathing space, doesn't it? You are lucky that you can take time and think about what you really want to do with your life.'

'I know.' Morag glanced at Jessica already fidgeting to get home to her children. 'I've no ties at all.'

Matthew said abruptly, 'Look. I'm sorry I messed things up last winter. We could have been friends I think. Can we start again? Will you have a meal with me tonight?'

She was tempted. After all, she had been almost engaged to Teddy McKinley.

She said, 'I don't think so, Matthew. It wouldn't be fair to you.'

'There's someone else?'

He was so direct, so vulnerable. He deserved more than

just a brush-off. She said suddenly, 'Yes. A long time ago. He's . . . gone now. But that's it. Can you understand?'

She saw his throat move as he swallowed. But then he smiled and said, 'Of course. Thank you for telling me. It's just . . . well, as you've probably heard dozens of times before . . . you are so beautiful.'

She opened her eyes, surprised. She had thought only one man considered her beautiful.

She got off the train at Longbridge probably for the last time, and turned into the huddle of prefabs. The afternoon sun filtered through the beech trees and glinted on the trickle of water in the brook. There was no-one about; everyone worked and the few children on the estate were at school. She could be in the heart of the country. A small copse in Exmoor perhaps. She stood by the water and knew that Berry had been right; every time she saw water, she had to push aside memories of them both in John Ridd's stream that summer of 1941. She said softly but very deliberately, 'I will never know another time like that . . . the intensity of feeling was almost too great. I never want to feel that again.' And she turned and walked up to the house, and there, sitting on the doorstep, was Hugh Reid.

CHAPTER ELEVEN

Morag could only think that something had happened to Val; why else would Hugh be here? So she stayed where she was, halfway up the path, rooted to the spot, staring at him, willing him to be an apparition.

He stood up. As usual he knew exactly how her mind was working. He held out his hands.

'It's OK. Nothing awful at all. I wanted to talk to you about one or two things. Dusty is at the farm, thoroughly enjoying the last of the haymaking, so I've taken a week or two off.' By this time he was holding her hands in his, massaging her knuckles with his thumbs. 'I've been at Redley Lodge with Eric McKinley for the past four days. He suggested having a chat with you. So . . . here I am.'

She was genuinely delighted. The feeling of anticlimax after the end of her course disappeared. She ushered him into the bungalow, sat him in the best armchair and put the kettle on.

'I was just staring into the brook wondering what on earth I was going to do with the rest of my life . . .' She laughed, deepening her voice theatrically. 'But especially what I was going to do with the rest of today – and now I know! How very nice!' She wondered how two brothers could be so different: Hugh was totally unthreatening. She sat opposite him and said as she would have said to Val, 'Tell me everything! How is your mother . . . why is Dusty at the farm . . . how are Val and Berry . . . especially how is Eric?'

'My mother is almost ecstatic. She adores match-making and she is really fond of Jannie, so she is in her element.'

'Jannie?'

He smiled. 'I didn't mention that, did I? Wanted to save it up. Jannie and Dusty have come to the farm together. Very much together.'

'My dear Lord!' Morag clapped a hand to her mouth. 'They met three months ago! And they are together?'

He laughed. 'Dusty's reputation has gone before him I do not doubt. And your Jannie . . . she has changed. She is still watery. But she has developed from sprite to witch.'

Morag laughed helplessly. 'Probably she was always like that. But Marius . . . he was so possessive! And Val told me that he was an old boyfriend of Eve Mears – Jannie's mother!'

He laughed too. 'The plot thickens!'

Morag got up and made tea. 'And your mother approves?'

'Not of the present situation. She is determined to get them both to the altar.'

'Well, if you've come for my help, I'm afraid— '

'No. Not at all.' He made a face as he helped her carry in the tea things. 'I just couldn't bear it any longer! They paw one another all the time. Ma doesn't seem to mind. I think she's given up on Berry and Val having a family and all she can see is potential grandchildren! Gran and Ma . . . they're quite basic, you know. Comes of farming I suppose.'

Morag laughed again. She felt light, happy . . . young.

She said, 'And Dusty is being a farmer too, is he?'

Hugh nodded. 'Things must have got hot up in London. And he wanted to get Jannie away from Marius.' He sipped his tea appreciatively. 'This is good. I left the car at the station. I thought you might see it and be forewarned. We could go for a drive later. Have dinner somewhere. Barnt Green looked rather nice.'

'It is. That would be fun! Can you stay? I've got a spare room.'

178

'I've booked at the George in Longbridge. Just one night. I hoped you'd come back to Clevedon with me tomorrow.'

She was delighted. They finished the tea and she walked him around the enclave of bungalows and then down to the brook while she told him about her thesis. 'My father used to say that a doctor was like an explorer. Pushing out frontiers all the time. I've taken the line that he is also a detective. Symptoms are his clues. But he mustn't simply treat the symptoms. They must lead him to the real solution . . . often nothing to do with the symptoms at all.'

Hugh said, 'What about if the patient has no symptoms, yet knows he is ill?'

'Ah. We had an interesting course during this last year. You are talking about a mental disease?'

'I'm not sure.' Hugh stared into the water as she had done, as if expecting answers there. 'Supposing a man had lost a leg and showed constant signs of aggression? I mean, the obvious cure would be to grow another leg. Impossible. How would you tackle that?'

Morag frowned. Val had said nothing about aggression. Ever.

She said slowly, 'I think he himself would have to deal with that. By using his other strengths to – to compensate.' She bit her lip. 'He may of course become obsessive about those strengths. It is difficult to say.'

There was a little silence. Hugh said eventually, 'Yes, I think you are right. So he would paint every minute of the day and sometimes half the night? To the point of ignoring his wife and his other family? That might be part of his cure?'

'I am not sure, Hugh. I would need to know a great deal more about the patient.'

'I am talking of Berry. You knew that.'

'Yes. I simply don't know anything about Berry now. And Val never discusses him.'

'She is loyal. She is a wonderful girl, Morrie. No-one else could do what she does for him.'

Morag's frown deepened. 'Is this one of the things you wanted to discuss with me? I cannot be more specific, Hugh.'

Hugh sighed and turned away from the brook.

'I suppose I wanted to ask your opinion. I always think of him when I see water. Before the war, he used to swim all the time. And he climbed John Ridd's stream once, did you know that?'

There was a pause, then Morag said, 'Yes.'

'Anyway, you don't have to be specific, my dear. I can see for myself that he is indeed obsessive about his painting. But perhaps as his success grows – and it will – he will become less so.'

They walked back to the house. It was time to go for their meal. Morag went to change and when she came back into the living room she said suddenly, 'You know, Hugh, Berry might not be able to climb John Ridd's stream again, but he could certainly swim. We visited a hospital in the West Midlands where they used swimming a great deal for paraplegic patients.'

Hugh nodded. 'Yes. Unfortunately, Berry will only tackle things which he knows for certain he will succeed at. Also . . .' he held out her coat for her and settled it around her shoulders, 'I think he is frightened of the sea.'

She turned and looked into his clear grey eyes. They were very close to hers. She thought of the three of them, Durston, Hugh, Berry, adrift in a boat in the endless Pacific. She shivered. 'It's not surprising,' she said.

They collected Hugh's car; it was still the Morris which had taken her back to Gallenwick that night ten years ago. She slid into the front passenger seat with a sense of familiarity that was disturbing. Was she never ever to forget that summer of 1941? When Hugh ground the gears, she said, 'You still have to double-declutch then?' And he nodded, unsurprised.

After all the Morris had belonged to the farm rather than him.

They drove sedately to Barnt Green and ate dinner in an inn overlooking the golf course. He entertained her with stories about Jannie and Durston and his mother's manoeuvrings and then talked about the farm itself as if she were part of it. It gave her a sense of belonging that was quite delightful. Margaret and Eric McKinley had always made a home for her in Clevedon, but she had never felt the same about Redley Lodge as she did now about Reid's farm.

'It's not a bad living these days,' he concluded. 'The government subsidies tide farmers over the lean times – flooding, drought and so on – and encourage new methods. I'd like to think Dusty and Jannie could make a go of it.'

'Dusty and Jannie?' She stared at him over the rim of her coffee cup. 'I thought he had interests in London? And Jannie . . . is she the right type for farming, d'you think?'

'Yes. I'm sure she is. She desperately needs the sort of basic rhythm of working with the seasons. What's more, Ma thinks she would be ideal.' He grinned. 'As for my brother . . . he should do something physical. All this wheeling and dealing will only get him into trouble.'

Morag was completely thrown. 'But what about you? I thought you were the one who intended taking on the farm?'

He smiled and speared a piece of Cheddar with the cheese knife.

'That's what I wanted to discuss with you, Morrie. It's what I've been discussing with Eric this past week. Something I should like very much. How do you see me as an auctioneer?'

She stared at him wide-eyed.

'I . . . don't know. I mean, there are exams and things. And a lot of experience is necessary. It's not just standing up at some country house and banging a gavel about.'

He burst out laughing. 'It's all right, you don't have to defend Val's father! I am very well aware of the hard work involved. But you see, Mo, I have always loved the land. Who is going to own it. Why they want to own it. What they will do with it. The same applies to houses and property. The unexpected find. D'you remember Eric's Nailsea glass?'

'I remember you were looking at it. The day of the funeral.'

'It came from a cottage in Wales. An elderly lady there – respectably married to a retired cleric – had been given that glass by a man before the First World War. They had been in love. He had been killed in the trenches. She knew at the time that he was married – just as she was. The glass was terribly precious to her. But she had recently discovered that his granddaughter needed money . . . Eric did not discover why. So she sold the glass and sent the money to her lover's only surviving family.'

'Oh my dear Lord,' Morag murmured.

'Eric probably paid over the odds for it. But it seemed worth it to him.'

'And to you,' Morag said.

'Yes.' Hugh cut his cheese into triangles. 'And Eric wants a partner. He's thinking of retiring within the next five or six years. He'd like the firm to go on.'

'So he'd train you.'

'And I would do the exams in my spare time.' The cheese crumbled unrecognizably. 'What do you think?'

'Is it what you want to do?' She shook her head. 'Stupid question. It is obvious. You just seemed so right at the farm. What does your mother think?'

'Dusty is the eldest son.'

'But if he's not keen?'

'That will make a difference, of course. I would have to think again.'

She said slowly, 'Well . . . it's all fairly hypothetical.

But . . .' She smiled suddenly. 'Hugh, it sounds marvellous! Really exciting! And terrific for Eric. Would you plan to live with him?'

'He suggested it. For the time being. He's got a housekeeper. Someone who helped Margaret and knows the house. She's willing to take me on too!'

Morag laughed. 'The two of you have worked it all out! I don't know why you gave me all that stuff about wanting to discuss it with me!'

He looked surprised. 'But . . . Mo, if you hadn't liked the idea, I would of course have forgotten it.'

She was astonished. 'But why? For goodness' sake, Hugh – how could my opinion affect you?'

'It would have affected me. But it's not just that, is it? I mean, Eric is hoping you will live in Clevedon. Live at Redley Lodge. He's told Mrs Knapp that you will be arriving this week and staying indefinitely. He seems to think you will practise in Clevedon.' He shook his head seriously. 'If my presence would queer your pitch, Mo, then I'm off.'

'But I hadn't . . . I was simply going to stay there while I made up my mind what to do.'

'And you still will do that?'

'Well . . .' She simply did not know what else to do. And actually Hugh's presence at Redley Lodge would make a great difference. She had been wondering how she and Eric would manage alone. 'I don't see why not. Do you?'

He beamed. 'I certainly do not! Oh, that is top-hole, Morrie! Eric was suggesting we might join the tennis club. What do you say?'

She did not know what to say. She laughed helplessly.

'What have you done to your cheese? You'd better ask for some more!'

The rest of that summer was idyllic. Sometimes Morag remembered guiltily that this time last year Margaret had ruled her little roost very quietly indeed. Now the house and garden were full of laughter and activity, much as Morag remembered it from before the war when she had spent weekends there with Val. Eric seemed content with the arrangement and could be seen smoking his pipe to keep the midges off, supposedly gardening, but really watching the tennis.

It was only when she went for an interview to join a practice in Cardiff that she realized how difficult the correct balance might be.

Hugh said, 'I thought we had agreed you did not mind me being here?'

'We did. And I don't. What on earth are you talking about?'

He had been there at the station as she stepped off the train. He was wearing one of Eric's old panama hats and his jacket pockets were bulging with the notes he had made from a visit to a manor house in the country.

'Well obviously, if you are going, it must be because . . . listen, I will leave. You know that. There is no need whatever— '

'Don't be ridiculous. It's not a case of you or me! If you weren't here I should still have gone for this interview.'

He opened the car door and she slid inside. It was so hot that the leather smell was all-pervading. He got in beside her and drove to the small sea front. He switched off the engine and they sat silently staring at the humps in the sea that were the Holme Islands.

He said, 'Well . . . have you got the post?'

She shrugged. 'I really don't know, Hugh. They'll be in touch. It was a big practice . . . I'm not quite sure that's what I want.'

'But you'll take it if it's offered?'

'Yes. But that has nothing whatever to do with your presence here. How can I convince you?'

He put his hands on the steering-wheel and stared at them.

'If I was still at the farm . . . if I hadn't taken Eric up on his offer . . . if—'

She said impatiently, 'If beggars were horses!'

He went on doggedly. 'You would have come to Clevedon as arranged. Looked after things at the house for a while. Started practising here. You know you would. It was absolutely cut and dried. So if you are changing that course of action it is because I am at Redley Lodge.'

She frowned at him, honestly perplexed. 'I cannot see . . . All right, Hugh. Your presence at the house frees me to a certain extent. I feel no sense of desertion— '

He said tightly, 'You must know that I am deeply in love with you.'

Morag stared at his profile. This had all happened before. In a car; on a hot summer's evening.

She said in a stifled voice, 'Of course I did not know. How could I?'

'Because I am so happy with you. And because I thought . . . you were happy with me.'

She swallowed. 'Well . . . I am. Of course I am. It's been the best summer since . . .'

He looked round at her. His knuckles were white on the steering-wheel. He said tensely, 'We could make it work, Morrie. We're already a family. I know Eric would be so happy about it. And Ma – Ma loves you three girls.' He looked at her. 'I know you're not in love with me like I am with you. But we'd grow together, my dear. I wouldn't . . . rush you . . . I love you too much to hurt you in any way— '

She said sternly, 'Hugh, stop. I love you too much to begin bargaining like this.' She took a breath. 'You think you know me. Everyone thinks they know me. They don't. Nobody on earth knows me, Hugh. I am not good enough for you and that is an end to it.'

He said something, very quietly. She felt her eyes distend, it was as if time stood still.

He said, 'Did you hear me, Mo? I know about Berry.'

She almost screamed. She could not bear it. Berry . . . talking about her . . . telling the others about what had happened.

Hugh looked away from her. 'It was when he was so ill. Rambling. He just said your name. Over and over again.' His hands relaxed quite suddenly and he spread them flat on the wheel. 'The thought of you . . . it kept him alive, Mo. I thought then that there wasn't a hope for me. And then . . . he married Val.' He flexed his fingers painfully. 'I knew then that you must have turned him down.' He tried to laugh. 'In a strange way I was angry with you. I should have been delighted because I loved you the moment I saw you. My Indian princess.' He tried again to laugh. 'But when we last saw Berry being taken off in a transport plane from Singapore, he was more dead than alive and I felt you must be heartless to say no at a time like that.' He glanced at her set face. 'I'm sorry, Mo. I didn't want to talk about it. But if it's all that . . . business . . . making you say no to me as well, then don't. I trust you. I know that whatever happened, you would have done what was right for Berry. If you don't want to talk about it— '

She said hoarsely, 'I don't!'

'Very well. But you mustn't let it block any happiness for the future. Please, Mo. Come down to the farm – let's have a holiday before the summer finishes. Let's go to the abbey. I think once you see Berry there, you'll know for certain that whatever decision you made was the right one.'

She turned and faced the sea again. The waves were lapping around the stilts of the pier and already the lights were lit in the pagoda on the end.

She said, 'Hugh, I want you to know, I am happier with you than anyone else. But I cannot seem to . . . exorcize old ghosts. I honestly think it would be best if I take the job in Cardiff and try to start a new life.'

He was silent for a long time; she thought he was accepting her decision.

Then he said, 'Will you come to the farm? Just for a weekend?'

'I cannot go to the abbey,' she said quickly.

'All right. Just the farm. See Ma. Chat with Jannie.'

She looked at him again. His grey eyes were so clear, so . . . good. He had no idea.

She sighed. 'Yes. Thank you, Hugh.'

'No, my dear. Thank you.'

It was strange, almost eerie, to be back at Reid's farm. She had told herself she would never go there again, never walk past Gallenwick, certainly never ever visit the abbey. Yet here she was at the first of those places, watching the line of geese come to meet them as Hugh opened the farm gate; staring out over the folds of the moor, russet in autumnal colours, where surely John Ridd's stream still poured over the step-like shelves and where the barn was next to the Doone Arms. So much had happened since that summer when she had been thrust cruelly from childhood into a strangely rigid adult life. And yet nothing had happened. Nothing had happened that could match those months at Gallenwick. Perhaps nothing ever would again.

She greeted Peggy Reid and old Granny Thomas as if they'd parted only a few months ago. Peggy was as white as her mother, but her shoulders were as broad as before and her short stocky body as strong. Granny was even more outrageous if that were possible. She no longer went to bed at night but slept in her wooden rocker by the range, a stout stick by her side, keeping an eye on the place.

It was unexpectedly wonderful to see Jannie. Away from Durston, or any other man, she was the old Jannie, her wide-open face seeming to wait for something to happen, something to change it.

She said, 'Isn't this marvellous? We must go over and see Val and be girls again! Oh, Morrie! D'you remember you said we'd always have each other? Those times are coming back. I feel it in my bones!'

Morag hugged her wholeheartedly, wondering whether it would ever be possible for the three of them to pick up the old threads again. Still she shook her head gently.

'Jannie, darling, I'm here for the weekend – you and Val must come to Clevedon. Say you will!'

Jannie closed her eyes and said intensely, 'I will! I will!'

The whole weekend Morag thought Berry would turn up unexpectedly. She suspected Hugh of having an ulterior motive. No-one had ever been that guileless. Except perhaps Teddy McKinley. Or even Matthew Arnold. Perhaps she knew only one man of guile and that was Berry Reid. Although during that first day at the farm she guessed that his older brother, Durston, was made from the same clay.

It was surprising to say the least to watch the complex relationship between Jannie and Durston. He was even more proprietory than Marius had been and had a way of putting his hand at the back of Jannie's neck beneath the waterfall of hair and either moving her towards him, or simply massaging her nape until she practically purred like a cat. But like a cat she was only half tame and would turn on him furiously for no apparent reason at all. Peggy Reid and old Granny Thomas took it all in their stride. Peggy simply shook her head in resignation. Granny was much more blunt.

'Matings is always stormy,' she commented on the first day when Jannie left the gorge table white-faced and angry because Dusty had 'taken her for granted'. She leaned towards her eldest grandson. 'You'd best go up to her and say you'm sorry.'

'I'm damned if I will!' Durston was just as angry. He had put his hand on Jannie's knee beneath the tablecloth. She had never protested before. 'She's got to learn to control that temper of hers!'

Morag was silent. She knew that Jannie did not have a temper in the sense Dusty meant. When she was hurt, really hurt, she went slightly out of control.

Morag thought of the much older – and definitely second-hand – Marius, and now Durston. How were they hurting Jannie?

Hugh said, 'You must be doing something wrong, old man.'

'What, for God's sake?' Durston exploded.

'If you don't know, how can we?' Hugh grinned. 'Go and make it up. She was nearly crying I think.'

'Christ. She's not a kid, Hugh! She's twenty-seven and very experienced. I'm telling you that. All right?' He avoided Morag's gaze and turned to his mother. 'You know her, Ma. She's unreasonable, isn't she? Flies off the handle at nothing.'

But Peggy Reid had kept the small waif in her heart for ten years now. She stood up and collected the plates.

'I'll put some of those blackberries in a dish. You can take them up to her.' She lowered her head to Durston's. 'And you will apologize for whatever you said or did. I don't care what it was. You will apologize.'

He looked away with an irritable shrug. 'Oh all right, all right. I sometimes wonder whether it's worth all this.'

Nobody asked him what he meant. Granny said again, sombrely, 'Matings is always stormy.'

In the afternoon, the quarrel obviously made up, the four of them walked around part of the boundaries, Dusty making notes of what hedging and ditching would be necessary that winter. In the role of farmer, with Hugh as his lieutenant, Dusty was at his best. All three boys had the land in their blood; like Berry they read the countryside unerringly. It surprised Morag to discover that Jannie was just as enthusiastic.

'We burned the stubble last week, Mo.' The small plain face seemed to glow.

'Cyril helped. D'you remember Cyril?'

'Of course. He had a brother.'

'He died. Just after the war. By then Hugh was back. He was wonderful helping Peggy and Gran to get the place running. Berry was out of it of course. And

Dusty . . .' she giggled, 'he was sowing wild oats as fast as he could in London. Funny thing was, Mo, when we met at the funeral we realized we had so many friends in common. In fact Marius had put some money into one of Dusty's films.'

'He's made films?' Morag was surprised again.

'Unsuccessfully.' Jannie laughed. 'He was fairly unsuccessful with everything until I persuaded him to come and take over the farm.'

Morag watched the two men waist-deep in a dry ditch clearing it against the winter rain.

She said, 'I'm having difficulty taking all this in. It's hard enough to imagine Val looking after Berry in that old abbey place. Now you and Durston . . .'

'I know. It's absolutely marvellous, isn't it? And the best of it is, Mo, I think we're going to get married.' Jannie beamed at her friend. 'We'll live here happily ever after and have children and love them to pieces and . . . oh, you know.'

Morag said slowly, 'It sounds . . . well, not like you, Jannie.'

Jannie was amazed. 'It's what I've always wanted! I thought you knew! Surely we must have talked about it? A home and a husband and children . . . oh yes!'

'What about . . .' Morag wondered whether she was being impertinent. 'What about Marius?'

Jannie laughed. 'Oh, darling. I just had to bring Marius to his knees! Just to show Ma what a fool she'd been!'

Morag nodded. 'I did wonder . . . but darling, forgive me, Marius was so . . . I don't know . . . domineering somehow. Val and I were a bit worried you were sort of in his power. Don't laugh!'

'I'm not.' Jannie turned her laughter into a rueful smile. 'That's how it is, sweetheart. You know . . . once you . . .' She rolled her eyes roguishly. 'Once you give in to them!' She shook her head at Morag's involuntary protest. 'It's not just me, Mo. Val's the same. And she's got a wedding ring too! But . . .' Jannie's small face puckered thoughtfully. 'Val hasn't got a family. That's how you get 'em. You get married and you have a family. Then they worship you. Look at Peggy and the boys. She looks after them but she's got the whip hand.'

Morag tried not to show how appalled she felt at this revealing little speech. Not least because of the comment about Val.

They had wandered on and were hailed by Durston.

'Come on girls! Lend a hand.' They went back to where a great pile of brushwood lined the side of the ditch. 'We want this hauled away and burned. Get cracking!' Durston glanced at Morag and added, 'The pair of you!'

The flames leapt and curled high as the sun set. Peggy brought out home-made sausages and when the embers glowed she sharpened hazel sticks and speared the sausages. They cooked them just as they had made toast at Redley Lodge. In the darkness as they sat around eating them Morag knew she was near tears. After fearing that Berry and Val would turn up at the farm, she suddenly wanted them there very much indeed.

Hugh's arm came around her shoulders. She leaned into him, felt the comfort of him and thought, 'I do love him. I do. He's so different from Berry and Durston. He would never want to own me . . . I would always be free . . . I want to love him so much that I must make it happen.'

She put her face up, grease and all, and he kissed it.

191

CHAPTER TWELVE

Morag Anne Heyward married Fitzhugh Warrender Reid on Christmas Eve of 1951. Almost exactly six years after her friend had married Berry. It was not so exclusive a celebration as that had been; but just as intimate. Durston was Hugh's best man and Jannie the only attendant. Morag had wanted Val to be an attendant too, but unexpectedly she had asked to be excused.

'Berry will need help to get in and out of church,' she explained, not meeting Morag's brown eyes. 'He won't accept it from anyone but me.'

Morag could understand Berry not wishing his wife to be part of this ceremony; but that Val had acceded to his wish was rather worrying. As it was, neither of them arrived until she and Eric had joined Hugh on the chancel steps. She heard the rustle of their arrival, glanced around to smile at Val and then was very conscious of their audible breathing.

Mrs Maitland and Dr Wilkie were on the bride's side of the church. Juliet Mortimer, now Sanderston, sat next to them with her husband and six-year-old twins. Juliet looked nervous, but Dr Wilkie sat the twins between herself and Mrs Maitland and they behaved impeccably. No-one had heard of Caroline Prosser since she left school. Behind Juliet sat Jessica White from Selly Oak. There were people from the tennis club and old acquaintances of the McKinleys who were under the impression that Morag was Eric's daughter.

Perhaps this was not surprising. Eric had suggested gently that Morag should wear Margaret's bridal dress.

'I wanted Val to wear it,' he said diffidently. 'But . . . well, Berry wanted it all very plain and it was just after the war. So she didn't.' He smiled. 'This is my second chance. Will you try it on? You can alter it how you wish. Margaret would be so pleased to know it was being used again.'

Morag had tried on the dress. It needed hardly any alteration. She said, 'I would love to wear it. There was nothing left from – from home. It would be wonderful to wear something that came from . . . then. But, well, it seems rather a – a liberty!'

Eric said very matter-of-factly, 'Listen, Morrie. I remember once looking at Margaret and Teddy and Val – right at the beginning of the war before you went to Gallenwick – and praying to God to keep them safe. Well, as you know He had to say no to that one. But He usually tempers the wind to the shorn lamb. He sent me you and now Hugh.' He smiled slightly. 'Could you not see it that way, my dear? You lost Lucy and Henry. But then you gained another family.' He turned and looked at the two of them in the mirror. 'In which case, you have a right to wear Margaret's dress.' His smile widened. 'I could come the heavy parent and say you have a duty to wear it!'

'Oh, Eric!' Her eyes were very bright. She smiled at his reflection. 'Thank you. I would love to wear it.' And with her hair almost invisible beneath the veil, she could easily have been Eric's second daughter, taller and slimmer than Val, rather like Eric himself.

Afterwards they went to the Esplanade Hotel, built into Clevedon's north cliff with windows around three sides of its Victorian reception room, all looking out on a quiet grey sea. The weather was typically English: a low grey sky like the lid of a tureen keeping the winds and weather at bay. Morag, swathed in Margaret's fur coat, stood by the be-ribboned taxi, breathing deeply as she looked up channel at the just discernible Welsh hills. Hugh stood by her holding the shoulders of the coat as if he expected it to blow off. They did not speak. The second taxi drew up and disgorged Jannie and Durston, Berry and Val and Eric. Durston put his hand on Jannie's neck.

'Let's get inside and have a drink, for God's sake,' he said.

Berry said, 'I second that.'

Jannie said, 'Wait! The bride and groom must go first! Morrie! Hugh! Come on – you've got all your lives to look at the view!'

Morag turned and looked at Hugh then, and smiled. 'So we have!' she said. And she held the coat with one hand, tucked the other into Hugh's arm and drew him into the hotel. Everyone laughed, even Berry.

After the speeches when everyone was milling around happily and Juliet was chasing her children from beneath the tables, Jannie managed to shepherd Val and Morag into an alcove.

'Isn't this just perfect?' she crowed. 'First Val and Berry, now you and Hugh, and next Durston and me!' She giggled tipsily. 'Honestly, girls! When I think of the three of us that summer in Gallenwick! Sex-starved! Having all those erotic fantasies about the Reid boys! And now they're coming true!'

'I did not have erotic fantasies,' Val said firmly. 'And I'm jolly certain neither did Mo! So speak for yourself, Jannie Mears!'

Morag said nothing. Jannie was brutally frank. 'Well, I certainly did! I couldn't wait to find out about sex! Mum and Marius used to go to town in the bedroom next to mine, so of course I went straight to him from school. He taught me everything. Got me ready for Durston as it were.'

Val said crisply, 'Jannie, shut up. You're drunk. And here is Doc Willie.'

Dr Wilkie and Mrs Maitland came into the alcove.

'Such a suitable match, my dear.' Mrs Maitland kissed Morag's cheek. 'D'you know when I met Hugh Reid at the farm I thought immediately how like you he was. Isn't that the strangest coincidence?'

Dr Wilkie shook her hand. 'So you are a doctor now, Morag? I am glad. Very glad, my dear.' She patted her hand. 'And very glad about this marriage. I hope you will continue with your career in spite of it?'

'I think so.' Morag smiled back noting that the marriage was seen as a threat to a career. 'We haven't actually discussed it.'

Jannie hugged Mrs Maitland effusively. 'You were like a second mother to me. Peggy too. My own mother was so hopeless . . .'

Val said, 'Shut up, Jannie!' She smiled brilliantly at Dr Wilkie. 'Marriage can be quite a career in itself, of course, Doctor.'

Dr Wilkie inclined her head. 'Indeed it can, my dear. A very worthwhile one too.' She smiled candidly, acknowledging her own restricted view. 'You know about my sister of course. I think of us as two sides of a coin. She chose love. And death. And because of that, I suppose I chose a career.'

Jannie giggled. 'You've been drinking, Dr Willie.'

Val said, 'For Pete's sake, shut up, Jannie!'

Dr Wilkie said, 'It is strange to think that you now live in that place. Naturally I think of it with horror. Almost fear.'

Val said suddenly, 'Listen. We are thinking of organizing painting weekends. We've got so much space it seems wicked not to use it. Would you like some of your art students to come down and try it? You could bring them.'

'Exorcizing old ghosts?' Dr Wilkie smiled.

'Well . . . I'm not sure about that.' Val smiled too. 'Simply look around. See its beauty and its mystery.'

Mrs Maitland was enthusiastic. 'I think it's a wonderful idea. Really wonderful.'

Val said, 'Why don't you talk to Berry about it? He's at the bar with Durston drinking far too much. Let's interrupt him and get him involved in something that really interests him.'

Jannie hardly waited until they were out of earshot before turning to Morag and saying in a stage aside, 'You heard that? The marriage is on the rocks, Mo. He's not interested in Val any more. It's work, work, work for him.'

Morag stepped in front of her hastily. 'You're wrong, Jannie. He takes her for granted, of course. He's innately selfish. But she is still the centre of his life.'

Jannie hiccoughed. 'Rubbish. She bought him the abbey. That's all he wanted her for!'

'Val is right, you are drunk, Jannie!'

'OK, so I'm drunk. We're supposed to be celebrating your wedding, remember? But learn a lesson from Val and Berry, Mo. Have children. Quickly. It's like I said to you back in the autumn . . .'

'Jannie, some couples make a decision to wait for a family.'

'Oh my God!' Jannie rolled her eyes. 'Does that mean you and Hugh are going to . . . what do they call it . . . get established, first? You'll be a good little doctor and take women's clinics and he'll build up the McKinley firm until Eric dies and it all belongs to you – the house – the business— '

Morag interrupted firmly. 'Let's go and have a coffee, Jannie. And talk about something else. Shall we?'

'I just want to ask you something. Something important.' Jannie blinked trying to remember what it was. Then she smiled broadly. 'Will you come to my wedding? It will be next month. In the new year. Nineteen fifty-two.'

Morag smiled. 'So he has asked you. Oh Jannie, I am glad. If that is what you want— '

'It is. You know it is. And he will ask me.'

'You mean, he hasn't asked you yet?'

Jannie's smile became secretive. 'Not yet. But he'll have to when he knows. His mother will kill him if he doesn't.' She hugged Morag's arm. 'I'm pregnant, darling. I'm going to produce the first Reid grandchild! And it will be a boy. To carry on the name, you know.'

Morag stared at her in horror. Then forced a smile.

'Oh, Jannie ... congratulations,' she said.

Juliet ran up to them, breathing heavily. 'Oh, girls – I was hoping to have a chance for a good old chat! But Peter says he's had enough of rounding up our two little horrors, so we're off!'

Morag hugged her. 'Thank you for coming, Ju. The twins are lovely. You must bring them down next summer when Hugh and I are settled. We can take them onto the beach.'

'That would be marvellous.' Juliet rolled her eyes. 'Don't go in for a family just yet, Mo. Life reduces itself to the lowest possible level. No time for anything else at all!'

Jannie said, 'Don't tell her that, Ju! I've just been advising her to start right in! After all it's still something only women can do!'

Juliet rolled her eyes again. 'More's the pity!' She looked towards the foyer. 'You don't suppose they've got out onto the road, do you? Peter – any sign of them yet?'

Juliet's husband, harrassed-looking and already losing his hair, dusted his hands together.

'I've locked them in the car. We'll have to go else they'll wreck it. All the best, Morag. Jannie. Goodbye.'

Morag watched them depart swiftly. She said to Jannie, 'I wish you luck, darling. Thank the dear Lord you've got Peggy to help you.'

Jannie said thoughtfully, 'Yes.'

Berry was unexpectedly delighted with Dr Wilkie's suggestion. He had admired her greatly in the short time he had known her as headmistress at Gallenwick. Her academic aloofness had acquired mystery when Val told him that the girl who had thrown herself from the window of the music room had been Doc Willie's sister, no less.

He said, 'We never took down the partitions that made up the monks' cells. We have at least ten of those small rooms. And now there is a bathroom on every floor . . .'

'It sounds a very practical idea as well as rather . . .' Dr Wilkie was unexpectedly at a loss for words.

'Inspirational?' Berry suggested.

'Indeed. And now that this new system of examination is established— '

'Afraid I don't really understand any of that.'

'It simply means that instead of passing or failing in a collection of subjects, entrants can obtain a certificate for each subject. It has made some of the less academic subjects more important. Needlework, art, drama. I think our parents would be delighted with the idea of art field trips. And with a teacher as prestigious as yourself— '

'Don't flatter me, Doctor,' Berry said but with a smile. He was proud of his burgeoning following. And now that Hugh was sharing the helm at McKinleys, there would be more contacts. Eric had done a good job but Hugh had a feeling for Berry's work. They were on the same wavelength.

'I did not intend to flatter.' Dr Wilkie's colour was high and Berry glanced at Val, amused.

Afterwards Val said incredulously, 'Surely you don't think Doc Willie will succumb to the famous charm? My God, she is old enough to be your mother!'

He kissed her nose. 'There lies the challenge, my darling.'

She scolded him humorously; it was how she dealt with his. . . flirtations. 'You are incorrigible, Berry Reid! I absolutely refuse to allow my ex-headmistress to be seduced into a mood of complete sentimentality by— '

'All I want to do is to paint her portrait.'

'That was how it started with the first woman who came to clean. As for that Miriam who replaced her— '

Berry ignored this and half closed his eyes. 'I wonder if I could persuade her to lie down. Reclining figure. That sort of thing.'

'Don't you dare!'

He leaned forward suddenly and kissed her. 'I'm glad you're not anyone else, Val. Jannie, getting herself pregnant to catch Dusty. Morag, all sensitive and so terribly bruised. You are . . . just right.'

She willed herself not to show how deeply she was touched by this.

She said, 'Because I let you get away with . . . everything?'

'I suppose so.' He kissed her again but this time she knew he was manipulating her. 'But you let me get away with it because you understand me, don't you, my sweetheart?'

She swallowed the tears which were now of disappointment.

'Oh yes. I understand you,' she said.

He focused on her and stared into her violet-blue eyes. 'You are so . . . obvious, Val. Your baby curls and complexion, your snub nose and wide mouth and blue eyes. Why do I love you?'

She said carefully, 'If you do love me perhaps you wonder whether there is anything else besides the obvious?'

'Perhaps I do.' He put a finger on the snub nose and pressed. 'One day . . . I will try to paint you. I promise that.'

She smiled. 'No. I don't think so, Berry.'

He was surprised. 'No. I mean it.'

'And I meant, that I would not allow it.' She kissed him properly and then looked at him again and saw the sudden awareness in his dark eyes. 'Sometimes, my darling, you are even more obvious than I am.' And she moved away.

They went to Paris for five days which was as long as their overseas allowance would last. They stayed at a small *pension* just off the avenue Foch and explored the city cautiously at first then with growing delight. It was strange to find a place so untouched by the war. The shops at home were short of goods, bread and meat were rationed; once in Bristol, there were still terrible reminders of the bombing. Here was a land of plenty; ancient buildings preserved for posterity, pictures and treasures of all kinds. They gorged on cakes from the patisserie on the corner of rue Georges and made themselves ill. They went to the top of the Eiffel Tower and the Arc de Triomphe, walked in the Tuileries and the rue de la Paix, knelt in the vast cavern of Notre-Dame and tried to ignore the beggars who were everywhere. By the time they went to bed at night, they were both exhausted. It seemed perfectly natural to lie side by side and go to sleep. Morag waited for Hugh to take her in his arms. She wanted, quite desperately, for him to sweep her away so that she would never again remember John Ridd's water slide and the barn by the Doone Arms and Berry's dark face. He, remembering how difficult it had been to persuade her into marriage, waited for her to kiss him, however diffidently.

On their last day, Morag said tentatively, 'We haven't spent our honeymoon very conventionally, have we?'

Hugh, who was already inspecting the *Guide Bleu* for today's outing, looked up and smiled reassuringly. 'We have been cementing our relationship, Morrie. Isn't that what is supposed to happen?'

She blushed. 'You know very well what I mean!'

His smile widened. 'I think so. I don't want to rush you, my darling. We've got the rest of our lives.'

She did not return his smile; her face became very red indeed. 'I don't doubt we love each other, Hugh. It's all . . . wonderful. I'll never forget these five days. But surely we should . . . I mean, we *should*— '

He put down the book and picked up her hand. 'You were talking to Jannie at the wedding – a great mistake.

She is playing a very different game, my darling, and you know it really. I want you to feel perfectly relaxed within our relationship. All this business about consummating marriage means nothing if it's looked on as a duty. Let it happen naturally, Mo.'

She wanted to tell him that there was a barrier to be broken and relaxation simply did not enter into it. She said stubbornly, 'It's nothing to do with Jannie. Isn't there a middle way between celibacy and – and – nymphomania!'

Hugh's face stretched then crumpled into laughter. 'Oh, Morrie! You are such a mixture of innocence and sophistication! We are not celibate, darling. And I don't really think Jannie is a nymphomaniac. At least . . . I don't think so. Is she?'

'I didn't know how else to put it.' She felt she might burst into flame at any moment. 'And if you are trying to turn the subject again, please don't.'

He was still, holding her hand, looking at her. 'All right. I am frightened of rushing any fences, Morrie. Everything is so perfect.'

'And please don't say how well we are suited! Everyone at the reception seemed to say that!'

'But we are.' He smiled again, the wonderful smile that was so reassuring yet held no passion. Then he pulled her gently towards him and kissed her very slowly. When he drew back, she stared at him and her eyes filled slowly with tears.

She whispered, 'It's going to be all right, my darling. It's going to be all right.'

They were very late leaving the *pension* that day . . . And they returned to it early, long before exhaustion set in. And Morag knew that it was all right. There was no betrayal with Hugh. It was different. That was all. Absolutely different. Before, she had been a child, and now she was a woman.

CHAPTER THIRTEEN

1952

Jannie had Julie on the twenty-first of July with the greatest of ease. Durston said proudly, 'Like a gypsy except she insisted on a bed instead of a ditch!' Val and Morag did not look at each other or Jannie. They were often slightly embarrassed by Durston's forthrightness. When he added, less proudly, 'Pity it wasn't a boy,' they both rallied immediately.

'How can you say that? She's so beautiful! So absolutely beautiful!' Val leaned over the crib gurgling ecstatically. It occurred to her, perhaps not for the first time, that this was something she could never experience. Not that she wished to do so, of course. That had always been quite clear in her mind.

Morag said, 'Girl babies are in the minority now, Dusty. I was reading up some statistics for my mother and baby clinic. Lucky you, to have one.'

Hugh said incredulously, 'Look at her fingernails! Just look!'

Everyone looked. Julie lifted her hands obligingly, fists clenched but thumbnails displayed. Dusty laughed.

'She can make a proper fist anyway.'

Berry leaned heavily on the mantelpiece, watching his mother fold nappies and stack them neatly on the washstand; he flicked his gaze momentarily towards the crib.

'The Japs would have a job to get a grip on those,' he said sourly.

Val and Morag ignored him; Jannie said, 'What do you mean, Berry?'

Dusty said, 'Nothing, sweetie. Do you think you should feed her now?'

Berry said, 'Our captors had a way with fingernails. That's all. They liked to remove them.'

Jannie understood and looked sick. 'Oh God!'

Val said quickly, 'May I pick her up, Jannie? If you're going to feed her in a minute.'

Hugh rounded up his brothers. 'In which case, is it time for us to look round the farm? I can't imagine Dusty doing such a good job as we did, can you, Berry? How about a spot of constructive criticism?'

Berry went grumblingly, Durston with alacrity. 'Women's work,' he grinned and held the door as his brother stumped through. Hugh caught Morag's eye as he brought up the rear and gave an apologetic grimace. But Morag had found the small exchange . . . interesting. It was a year since she had qualified and though her work consisted at present of pre- and postnatal clinics, she still thought occasionally of the seminars with Matthew Arnold and how some of the traumatic symptoms left over from the war might apply to her brother-in-law. Or her husband. She watched clinically as Peggy Reid unpinned the bindings around Jannie's swollen breasts and put Julie expertly into feeding position. When Jannie drew in a sharp breath, Peggy said soothingly, 'It'll be all right in a jiffy, my love.' And sure enough it was and Jannie smiled trustingly at her mother-in-law.

Morag thought wryly that when Jannie had married Durston she had also married his mother and grandmother. It was a bargain well worthwhile in Jannie's case. But she herself had married into a ready-made family; they still lived at Redley Lodge and Eric was there. And though she loved him dearly as a surrogate father, nevertheless somewhere inside herself she thought it was wrong. She and Hugh should have their own home. It seemed Val was the only one to launch out properly into marriage. Morag switched her objective gaze to Val who was still hovering delightedly at the way Julie 'knew exactly what to do'. And unbidden came the thought: poor Val. And then as the baby got into a rhythm of sucking, and Val had to wipe away a tear and Peggy laughed and Gran said, 'What's all the fuss? If pigs can do it surely yoomans can!' came another thought: when I was desperate he helped me . . . what can I do to help him?

But there was nothing. Nothing at all.

Peggy decreed a little nap after the feed and Morag and Val kissed Jannie, both strangely disturbed by the smell of milk rising from her bindings, and went downstairs for 'a nice cup of tea'.

'Not that I can imagine you making a nasty cup of tea, Peggy,' Val said moving easily to the dresser for cups and saucers. Val was as much at home in the farmhouse kitchen as Jannie was; more probably.

'Berry used to put salt in the teapot when he was a little boy,' Peggy said dotingly. 'That wasn't exactly nice.'

Val clattered cups and saucers unnecessarily. 'He was your favourite, wasn't he?'

'Don't know about that.' Peggy flashed her first daughter-in-law a look. 'He was the baby of course. Will wanted a little girl to end up with. So I suppose he was spoiled . . .' She rinsed boiling water around the teapot. 'How is he?' she asked.

Val looked up, smiling. 'Well, as you heard just now . . . he can be foul.' She stopped smiling. 'And then he can be . . . wonderful.' She sat down at the table and shrugged. 'It depends on the level of pain. There's been so much rain this summer . . . dampness does not help.'

Peggy made the tea and brought it to the table. 'What about these art students? How does he manage with people all over the place?'

'That depends too.' Val caught Morag's eye and grinned. 'You don't know about Berry's predilection for schoolgirls, Mo, do you? Don't be shocked. I don't mean that . . . as it sounds. He likes to paint them. Abstractions of course, but they still have to sit for him.'

Morag sat down. 'I thought the idea of the students was for Berry to hold classes?'

'He holds classes. They paint each other. He is good. Fierce but they don't mind that.' She laughed. 'They all fall in love with him, just as we did in the summer of forty-one.' She frowned. 'Trouble is, he works too hard. When we've got a full house he can't rest as he should do.' She drank some tea. 'That's probably why he had that little dig about the baby. He's tired.'

Morag said, 'Does he often refer to prison life?'

'Never to me. When he's with Dusty . . . then Hugh this afternoon . . . it's as if he wants to remind them. They seem to have taken it all in their stride. He can't stand that.'

Peggy sighed and stood up. 'He's a good boy really. It . . . it can't be easy.' She did not enlarge on that theme but went to the door. 'I'll just tell them there's some tea here if they want it.'

Val smiled at Morag. 'She always runs away. She wants everything to be . . . all right.'

'But so it should be. I can understand Berry, Val. He needs to talk about it. The dreadful time in the prison camp. For instance, they were adrift in a boat for over ten days. With Berry's leg terribly injured. They were picked up by a Japanese merchant ship and ended up just outside Singapore— '

'I know all that,' Val said impatiently. 'The actual events . . . I heard them from Peggy. But once they were in the camp at Singapore . . . the forced labour . . . that is what scarred Berry.'

'Well of course. And that is what he should talk about. Can't you encourage him to tell you— '

'D'you think I haven't?' Val stirred her tea angrily. 'My God . . . Mo . . . sometimes I think you can't see beyond the nose on your face! He has told me quite definitely that he will never talk about that time with me or anyone!'

'But . . .' Morag thought of the times at night after

she and Hugh had made love. Then . . . then everything was open between them and Hugh would tell her of the bandages he had made from banana skins, of Durston's beatings when he had been caught trying to talk to a girl through the wire, of the rotten, inadequate food and their efforts to grow vegetables. And of the stench of gangrene from Berry's infected leg. She said lamely, 'Hugh tells me things. Some things.'

Val smiled, understanding. 'Yes. Well. Obviously Berry does not talk about it willingly. There was a time . . .' She stood up and walked to the window and kept her back to Morag. 'Sometimes Berry talks in his sleep and one night he spoke a name. A Japanese name. Sounded like Akiko. Something like that. I mentioned it the next morning.' She stared down into her tea. 'He hit me.' She shook her head impatiently at Morag's gasp of horror. 'It didn't worry me. In a way, I was glad. I thought it might open the floodgates. But it didn't.' She moved to the Aga and poured more water into the teapot. 'Peggy doesn't know.'

Morag swallowed. 'Of course not. Oh Val . . . I'm so sorry. I knew it was hard but I did not realize how hard.'

Val said quickly, 'Don't get the wrong idea. It's hard at times. But there are other times . . .' She flashed a wide smile across the table. 'Besides which, you must know, he is my life's work!' She said it self-mockingly, but Morag knew she was serious.

They drove back through an evening glorious with sunset. Hugh sat well back in the driver's seat, smiling slightly, looking relaxed, happy. She turned sideways to study the view inland; the countryside was lush and heavy with foliage. There was no wind; the trees, fields, hedgerows, craggy heights seemed to be settling down for sleep. Hugh's profile was etched against a constantly changing background. The air from his open window blew his brown hair across his forehead and gave him a boyish look.

She said suddenly, 'You are the one certainty in my life, darling. Somehow you have managed to – to take in – to absorb everything that has happened and normalize it in some way.'

He flashed his smile at her. 'What has brought this on? Dusty's total lack of sensitivity? But you already knew about that. Jannie's dependence on my mother? Berry's bit of bad temper?'

'No. I have always known that you sort of polarize things. I simply wanted to tell you so. Too many things unsaid between us, Hugh.'

They began the hairpin descent down Porlock hill.

He said, 'Words are often better left unspoken, Morrie. I know you think that Berry should talk and talk and talk until the poison has all gone from him. It's not as simple as that.'

She widened her eyes at him. 'How did you know I was thinking of Val and Berry? And not so much of Berry actually.' She sighed and sat back, resting her head on the leather seat-back. 'She is – in some ways – so alone, darling. I wish there was something we could do.'

'There may well be in the future. We're here, waiting in the wings. She knows that.'

She put up a sun-warm hand and loosened the pins that kept her thick hair in place. 'Hugh ... she would not like me telling you this. Berry hit her. Because she asked about someone called Akiko. He said the name in his sleep and she thought ...'

He took a hand from the wheel and put it on her knee. The warmth of his palm struck through her cotton skirt and she realized that the sun was no longer reaching inside the car; her leg was cold.

He said, 'I'm sorry, my love. I can see how you must feel. But ... did Val mind very much?'

'She said not. But ... Hugh, it's awful.'

'Yes. I know. But it's not unforgivable. She has evidently forgiven him.'

'She would forgive him anything.'

'Are you saying she is besotted with Berry?'

'No. Not a bit. It's strange. She says he is her life's work. And that is what he is. How ever laughably self-sacrificing it sounds . . . that is what he is.'

'That's tough for him.'

'I suppose so.'

'That's why he is resisting her. Buttoning himself up against her . . . he is refusing to let himself be anybody's life's work.' They had reached the Minehead road; the enormous hump of the moor cut off the sun and it was almost dark. Hugh switched on the headlights.

Morag said slowly, 'I can understand what you mean, although it shows such a cruel streak in him.'

'Yes. Not cruel. Perhaps hard and manipulative. We all have it. We are all farmers at heart, Morrie. Farmers have to be hard . . . cruel to be kind . . . that kind of thing.'

She was startled. 'You are not like that, Hugh!'

'I could be. Life has been easy so far. But I could be.'

'Life has not been easy for you – you've had as much to contend with as Durston and Berry!'

'Darling, I have got you. I fell in love with you when I saw you that first time in the rain by the stream. I knew then that I would move the world to be with you always. Waiting was the hardest part. Waiting for the war to finish. Waiting to be repatriated. Waiting while Berry and Val settled in at the abbey and Durston mucked about in London and I helped Ma get the farm up to scratch. And then waiting for you to finish your training . . . to be at a loose end . . . to be looking for something new. Then I moved in. Inveigled you to Redley Lodge. Laid siege . . .'

They were both laughing, Morag incredulously, Hugh with the dramatic snarl of the stage seducer. She put her head on his shoulder, told him to stop it. They fell silent while the headlights flickered over the new flat landscape of the Somerset Levels. He thought she was asleep and was surprised when she spoke out of the darkness.

'They should have a baby. He would not feel the need to keep painting other women. And Val . . . Val would have another life's work.'

He said nothing. It was as if he knew she had not finished.

At last, after they had left Bridgwater, she spoke again.

'Perhaps . . . should we have a child, darling? What do you think?'

He gave her space to change her mind. 'I've heard that women feel broody when they see a new-born child, but surely not Morag Reid? Dr Morag Reid?'

But she did not withdraw her words. And after a very short pause he said, 'You must know how I feel about that, my dearest Morrie.'

She pushed her head a little harder into his upper arm. As they wound their way through Weston-super-Mare, he flexed his hand, realizing it was numb from the pressure. She shifted slightly and murmured something incoherent. And he knew she was asleep.

Jannie watched Durston as he came into the darkened bedroom fresh from his bath. His large silhouette went to the cot and he stared down at his daughter with a kind of disbelief.

She whispered, 'For the good Lord's sake, don't wake her up, Dusty darling. I can't face giving her another feed.'

He chuckled as he came to the bed.

'Thought you were asleep, old girl.' He kissed her forehead chastely. 'You'll have to feed her again some time or other, sweetheart.'

'I know. But in the morning. When your mother is here to help me.'

'I'll help you, baby. You know that.' He put his hand around her throat and kissed her properly. She surfaced quickly.

'Darling, don't get . . . like that. I can't. Not for ages yet.'

'Who says so?' He was undoing pins. Her breasts fell about in a way she loathed. She began to cry.

'There. There. Dusty will make it better.'

The trouble was he was irresistible. She held the brass rails at the top of the bed and tried to stifle her cries of ecstasy. But Julie woke all the same and in a way it was a relief. She wanted to sleep but she also wanted to get rid of the milk that ran from her once the bindings were undone.

Durston watched the whole process dotingly.

'I love you so madly, Jannie. You are a pocket Venus. Perfect . . . absolutely perfect.'

She smiled, delighted. This was what she had always wanted; adoration. And she had known that one day she would get it. The smile widened, remembering that it was Berry she had fastened on, wanting to bring him to his knees. Not any more; Berry was so horrid; no-one would ever bring him to his knees, not even Val. Dusty was different. He was like one of the moorland ponies, strong and tough; dominant and protective.

She let him take the child back to its cot and did not protest when he refused to re-pin her bindings. She curled into his arms, her face in his neck and settled for sleep.

'Love you . . .' Durston murmured again.

'And you don't mind that Julie is a girl?'

'Don't mind . . . next one will be a boy.'

She laughed gently and then just before sleep, she said, 'I wonder how Berry and Val manage?'

But he was already unconscious. And did not wake even when Julie began to cry. But Jannie did not mind this time. She sat on the edge of the bed, naked and beautiful, and fed her baby and felt the first stirrings of love.

*   *   *

Val said severely, 'You behaved badly. And you know it.'

Berry sat on the edge of his bed and began to unstrap the harness which held his aluminium leg in position.

'And you're not going to forgive me,' he observed, pretending not to watch her as she undressed in front of the uncurtained window. Where that stupid girl had thrown herself onto the rocks.

'I might forgive you if you admit it and then apologize.'

She was delightfully plump. A Botticelli cupid with her curls and curves.

He said, 'Anyone can see you. You're absolutely brazen.'

She glanced out at the blackness of the sea, the indigo horizon, the pale moon.

'Not a ship in sight. And if there were, it would need a very powerful telescope to pick me out.' Even so, she went to the door and snapped off the light. 'And stop changing the subject,' she said with the sternness of a nanny. 'Admit to me that you were being deliberately horrid this afternoon.'

'Deliberately horrid,' he mimicked her. 'Deliberately horrid. Deliberately horrid.'

'Thank you. Now apologize.'

'Dammit! I wasn't admitting to anything!' He was suddenly furious with her. 'You're always badgering me to talk about prison life! That was part of it!'

She was indignant in her turn. 'I have never badgered you . . . not about that! Not about anything except taking life a bit more easily— '

'Laying off the booze, laying off my work— '

'Not all your work. Painting women. Distorting them. You call it abstraction. I call it voyeurism. Perversion— '

'I've never made love to anyone except you since we were married – and you bloody well know it!'

'There are ways of making love, Berry. And you know that too!'

She realized they were in the middle of a full-blown row and wondered how it had happened.

He said cruelly, 'Yes. And you know most of them, don't you?'

She was silent, cut to the quick. She stood over him, a plump silhouette. Val, cuddly and selfless and loving. Yet none of those things.

He said, 'Look. I'm sorry. Forget I said that.'

She said in a low voice, 'Do you object to the way I make love, Berry?'

'No! Never. I said – forget that. Forget it. I love you. Surely you know . . . I can't help the way I am. But I love you. I'll always love you!'

She knelt above him, leaned down, kissed him. 'It's all right. I know. I shouldn't have asked for an apology. I don't want you to be apologetic, my dear. Not ever. About anything. I want you to be free.' She kissed him again, slowly, insistently.

He said, 'You never say you want me to be happy.' He cupped her head away from him and tried to see into her blue eyes which were black in the darkness.

She sobbed a small laugh. 'What is happiness, Berry? Maybe when you are free, happiness will follow.'

They made love as they always did, without a great deal of tenderness but with overwhelming passion. Afterwards he propped himself onto his elbow and looked at her.

'You are . . . Byronesque,' he said, pushing her curls across her forehead with his forefinger. 'My lovely ordinary Val. Byronesque.'

She said, 'Shut up and go to sleep.'

He kissed her and this time there was tenderness in his mouth.

He whispered, 'I'm sorry I was a pig this afternoon. You know why.'

'You don't want anyone to forget . . . anything,' she murmured sleepily.

'No. I want to father a baby.'

She was wide awake after that. He slept, exhausted, the stump of his leg on top of the sheet, twitching even in his sleep. And she wept. Very quietly. She wept.

CHAPTER FOURTEEN

1956

Jannie woke to Peggotty's monotonous wail. It was still dark but Durston was not by her side so the milking had started already. She cursed the day they had decided to begin dairy farming; sheep were a pain at lambing time but otherwise they kept decent hours. Still, Dusty had always refused to get up to the girls at night whether he was there or not.

'Woman's work,' he said when she complained of being tired all the time. 'And, sweetie, in case I haven't mentioned it before, I cannot stand women who whine.'

She had long ago given up protesting that she never whined. When Peggy had been there it had been different. Peggy would not allow a breath of criticism to fall on Jannie. She had been delighted with the marriage, delighted with Julie, still delighted with Rosamund. But when Gran Thomas died, Peggy had decided to travel.

'I've been tied to the farm for over thirty years now. We came when Berry was three. I've never been away from it for longer than two days – do you realize that? I want to see something of the world before I get decrepit!'

The family had protested that she would never be decrepit. But they saw her point. It would have been incredibly selfish to try to keep her. Even so, Jannie had told her how much she would be missed.

'I'm sorry to be such a wet week ...' She had started to cry which she knew Peggy hated. 'It's just that I'll miss you so very much. I – I— '

She mustered her courage and blurted, 'I love you, Peggy!'

'Oh, my dear girl.' Peggy had overlooked the tears for once. 'I love you too. But in a way I'm doing this for you. You rely on me too much. I'm sapping your confidence, Jannie. You're well able to look after Dusty, run the house . . . you don't need me, but you think you do. That's not good, chicken. And anyway, I'll be back.'

That seemed unlikely now. Peggy had left home in 1954 and had landed up in Australia last summer. She had married a sheep farmer on a station of four thousand acres. The nearest town was Melbourne, two hundred miles away. She loved it.

Jannie still mourned. 'Oh Peggy, Peggy.' She felt for her slippers that April morning, desperate that the baby would wake Julie and Ros. 'I'm glad for you of course, but . . . I can't cope here. I just cannot!'

Her head still throbbed from last night. She had said to Dusty, 'Look, I didn't want Peggotty. And I certainly don't want any more.'

He had ignored her of course, and she was quite unable to resist him, in fact as she cried out, gasping and holding the bedhead, she did not care that her health visitor had told her she was one of those rare people for whom most known forms of contraception were a waste of time. She was proud of the fact. As she had said defiantly to Morag and Val on one of their rare get-togethers, 'I'm fecund. That's what I am. Fecund, fecund, fecund.' She had said something like that before, and Val said, as she had said then, 'For God's sake, Jannie!'

She shuffled across the landing into what was laughingly called the nursery, bent over the cot and scooped Peggotty into her arms. The child immediately stopped crying and began the peculiar blind movement of her head in an effort to find food.

Jannie pulled down her nightdress with practised hand even as she walked back to the bedroom. She flinched slightly as the baby found her nipple, then it

214

became less painful and she sat on the edge of the bed and rocked, murmuring all the time. The dawn turned the natural linen curtains to pale cream and revealed the big room, furnished as it had been when Peggy and Will Reid moved in, but derelict with discarded clothing, a potty, a clothes-horse of nappies, a basket containing a jumble of pins, cream, cotton wool.

She chanted soothingly, 'I love this room, Peggotty. I love the fact that it's been here for so long. It's so substantial. The window overlooks miles of fields – not a soul to be seen. I love it. It's perfect for you to grow up in. And the walls are thick . . . you'll never hear Daddy and me through them. But I wish it wasn't like a tip. I wish I could get someone really ugly to clean it. When Peggy was here – that's your Granny, my darling – Daddy left the cleaning girls strictly alone. The house seemed to run itself. Now . . .' She kissed the downy head. It smelled sweet and milky.

She lifted the little girl onto her shoulder and patted her before transferring her to the other breast. Immediately the crying started again.

She whispered, 'There . . . my darling. I'm sorry, baby. I don't think I've got much for you any more, have I?' She fought against putting Peggotty onto a bottle. She had read somewhere that you couldn't get pregnant while you were breast-feeding.

Peggotty gave up the struggle for food and turned her head to yell frantically. Jannie tried jiggling her, taking her to the window to 'see Daddy', cuddling down with her in bed. Nothing helped; Peggotty was still desperately hungry.

Jannie sighed and struggled into her dressing-gown and slippers. Annoyingly the crying stopped as she flip-flopped downstairs and into the kitchen, but it restarted while she boiled milk and took the bottle out of its pan of boiled water and waited for the milk to cool.

Durston came in just as she had tucked the teat into Peggotty's mouth.

'God! I could hear you from the milking sheds!' He had taken off his boots in the porch and padded around the table in his socks assembling bread, butter, marmalade. 'Couldn't you have got some bloody breakfast while you were waiting for that milk to cool?' He stared at her without affection. 'Honestly, Jan, you're hopeless! You're not even dressed!'

She said plaintively, 'Well, if you could hear Peggotty from the cowsheds, you know why I'm not dressed.' She whimpered suddenly. 'Actually, I don't feel all that special.'

'No. You don't look it.' But there was no sympathy in his voice and when he trod in some water as he filled the kettle, his irritation overflowed.

'You messy cow! You can't even make the baby's bottle without slopping water all over the floor!'

Angry tears spouted down her cheeks. 'How dare you call me a cow! How dare you! I hate you! You never try to see my point of view! I've a good mind to leave you with the girls and go home to my mother— '

'Except that she wouldn't have you!' He had no idea that he was hurting her so terribly. 'Or rather her latest boyfriend wouldn't have you!'

She lowered her head over the baby's and squeezed her eyes tightly shut. It was so horribly true. If she went to see her mother she invariably stayed in Clevedon with Morag in the McKinleys' house. Eve professed to be in seventh heaven to see her daughter and granddaughters, but of course she simply did not have room for them in the house on the Downs and the kitchen was much too small for the preparation of meals on the scale that they would need. Jannie opened her eyes in time to see a large tear plop onto Peggotty's nose. The child released the rubber teat and screamed once, then recalled her mission in life, grabbed the teat again and sucked frantically, rolling her blue eyes as if demented. Even her baby preferred bottled milk to hers.

Durston commented, 'God, I thought she was going

to start up again.' He stuck the kettle on the range and came to peer down at his third daughter. 'Look at that. She's starving. You ought to put her on the bottle full stop, Jan. She's obviously much happier with cow's milk.'

Jannie, almost as outraged by his easy-goingness as by his ill-temper, said in a stifled voice, 'Well, that's all right then, isn't it? As I'm a cow!'

He laughed and ruffled her hair. 'Come on, old girl. Cheer up. You know there's only one worse thing than a woman in tears and that's a whining specimen!'

He went about getting some breakfast: great hunks of bread and marmalade washed down with tea. Jannie was only too well aware that in Peggy's day it had been ham and eggs.

Peggotty fell asleep, mouth open, milk residue trickling down her chin. She needed changing; the smell of ammonia was strong. But Jannie could not bear to take her upstairs and wake her now. She laid her gently on the battered old sofa and sat at the table pouring tea. Durston was talking about the arrival of the vet this morning with semen from a champion bull on the other side of the county.

'I rather like the idea of building up a pedigree herd, Jan. The Reid herd. It's got a ring to it, don't you think?'

She said dully, 'You do realize you're talking about a lifetime of pre-dawn milkings? Which means early nights and no social life whatsoever and— '

'For God's sake, Jan! You're doing it again! It was you who wanted to be a farmer's wife! When I suggested starting dairy farming – it was you who thought it was a good idea because of the milk subsidies! You liked the early nights – my God, there was a time when you couldn't wait to get upstairs! Now everything we do brings on the vapours!'

'That's not true! And anyway, it's not us any more! You just said everything we do! But all I can do is look after babies!'

Peggotty roused at her raised voice and let out a cry echoed immediately from upstairs as Rosamund woke.

'And you're not much good at that!' Durston said bitterly.

Jannie looked at him tragically. 'I sometimes wonder why you married me!' She could have bitten out her tongue because she knew the answer to that one.

Thankfully he didn't give it. Instead he leaned over the table and put his calloused hand around her neck.

'Shall I tell you? Even better . . . shall I show you?'

She bleated a protest. 'Peggotty . . . Ros . . .' But he had the energy of a dervish; the regularity of farm life suited him. As she surrendered helplessly, she thought of the bull who was servicing their cows at long-distance. That was how she felt; powerless. Just like a cow. Tears ran down the side of her nose and he licked them and said, 'Come on, my darling. I love you – I love you— ' But she did not respond.

The vet arrived with the artificial insemination pack at midday and Dusty called Cyril on the telephone and he and his nephew, Maurice, duly arrived. They all went into the cowsheds. Jannie had managed to mix a cake in between taking Julie to kindergarten at Gallenwick and putting Peggotty and Rosamund down for their mid-morning nap. She just hoped it wouldn't drop in the middle this time. Cyril always said, loyally, it tasted just as good that way, but the vet had taken a look at the last one and said he was not supposed to eat between meals. She put out cups and saucers and plates, made herself some tea and collapsed onto the old sofa, still damp from Peggotty's sojourn there this morning. She was so tired her head buzzed. It was like a gift from the gods when she heard the warning honk of the geese then the familiar engine note of Val's car as she drove carefully into the yard. She prayed Berry would not be with her. And he wasn't.

'Darling! What a wonderful surprise! Come and

collapse with me!' She hugged Val who was as plump as Jannie was skinny.

The contrast did not escape Val. 'Jannie, how do you do it? Look at me – talk about middle-aged spread!'

There was a time when Jannie would have told her very tactlessly how to do it. Now she said, 'Val, don't talk like that. We are not middle-aged!'

'Thirty-two, my dear. Another three years and we shall be right in the middle of our three score years and ten!'

Val took off one of Berry's old hats and shook out her curls. Under her jacket she appeared to be wearing Berry's shirt and trousers too. Jannie remembered how pretty Val had always looked in the gingham summer frocks that had been school uniform. Her present mannish clothes did not suit her.

Jannie smiled ruefully. 'I give up trying to be cheerful. I feel middle-aged. In fact I feel positively elderly today!'

'Rubbish! You're still our little Orphan Annie,' Val said affectionately. Then she frowned slightly. 'Perhaps you're rather too waif-like since Peggotty. Morag was worried about you at Christmas. D'you feel all right? I know that you're as tough as old boots in spite of looking so delicate, but . . .' Her voice died away as Jannie's eyes filled and overflowed again.

'Oh, Val. I'm sorry. I don't know why I keep crying like this. It's driving Dusty mad. Take no notice. Please. I'll put the kettle on.'

'No you won't. I'll put the kettle on.' Val sprang up, put Jannie's feet on a stool and made for the range. 'You're tired out. That's all it is, Jannie. Don't get worried. Morrie was telling me about some of her patients . . . oh, darling, don't cry. Everything is going to be all right.'

But the floodgates were open now and Jannie could not stop. She told Val how much she missed Peggy and how impossible it was to get any domestic help because Dusty was so – so boisterous. She looked anxiously at

Val as she used the inadequate word and was grateful when Val simply nodded.

'I'm no good at anything much, you see,' she sobbed, watching Val make tea without slopping water or dropping a cup. 'And I'm so frightened I'll have another baby. I never told you, but I had a miscarriage in between Julie and Ros. If that had gone full term there would be four under-fives!' She looked at Val, appalled. 'Can you imagine it? I feel sometimes as if I'm just a baby machine!'

'Oh my God!' Val crouched and encircled her friend with loving arms. 'Darling, surely you know about birth control? You've got that nice Mrs Merrydown as a health visitor— '

Jannie told her what Mrs Merrydown had said.

'Well then, surely Dusty . . .' Val coloured slightly. The three girls had never talked really intimately and for the past fifteen years there had scarcely been the opportunity to do so.

'Oh . . . Dusty's hopeless,' Jannie said, wiping her eyes on the sleeve of Val's shirt, feeling a bit better already. 'You know what he's like. There's no stopping him . . . sorry, Val. But, you know.'

'Yes.' Val stood up, poured a cup of tea, handed it to Jannie and sat down opposite her. 'Would you like me to ask Berry to have a word?'

Jannie smiled ruefully. 'Darling, it's no good blaming Dusty. I'm as bad.' Her face tightened again. 'There's something wrong with me, Val. I must have too much – too much – something or other.'

Val looked down at her lap, embarrassed.

Jannie said, 'I think it would be all right if we'd had a boy. Dusty needs to bring up another farmer. Perhaps when Julie is a bit older . . . though I think she's going to be little like me.' She looked into her teacup, willing away the tears. Val could not possibly understand. Not really. She said determinedly, 'Peggotty was a big baby. So perhaps . . . later on . . .'

220

Val said suddenly, 'I can smell something burning. Have you got a cake in the oven?'

Jannie gave a wail of despair that threatened to wake the sleeping babies upstairs.

Val said, 'Now don't move! I told you, I'll see to it!'

She removed the blackened cake, turned it out immediately and gently crumbled away the burnt sides.

Jannie wept, 'It's flat! Completely flat! It will be inedible!'

'Of course it won't! I'll butter-ice the top and shove lots of walnuts and cherries into it . . . you'll see.' Val smiled. 'Now go on upstairs. Lie down for half an hour. Then get in the bath and come down for tea at four.'

Jannie said, 'You don't understand. The vet is here. And Cyril and his nephew Maurice.'

Val helped her up and escorted her to the stairs. 'I'll call you later. Do as you're told.'

'The girls,' Jannie bleated. 'Julie . . . kindergarten . . .'

'What did I just say? Go!' Val stood at the bottom of the stairs until Jannie was on the landing. She shook a fist as Jannie hovered looking over the banisters. Jannie surrendered. Her bed was still unmade. She fell into it, drew the covers over her until she was buried in them and immediately was asleep.

Val mixed some scones and put them in the oven and turned her attention to repairing Jannie's cake. Her mouth was set in a thin line; she could have gone out and given Durston Reid a piece of her mind for two pins. Not that it would do any good. He and Berry were two of a kind. Water off a duck's back. You had to play them like an angler with salmon.

The cake was ready, the scones buttered, when the men came in and began to wash up at the sink. Val poured tea and put out plates.

'Where's Jannie?' Durston asked belatedly as they sat down, laughing, full of themselves, no more than

221

foolish, overgrown schoolboys. Val breathed deeply, calming herself with difficulty.

'Not well.' She smiled dazzlingly at Durston. 'How would you like to drive my car, brother dear? Just to pick up your daughter from Gallenwick.'

'Jannie will do it. She likes the other two to have the trip.'

Val cut him a piece of cake, poured more tea for everyone.

'Sorry, Dusty. She really isn't up to it. And I haven't woken Ros and Peggotty yet. Will you do that and I'll go for Julie?'

Dusty stood up immediately. 'No. I'll get her.'

Val turned her smile on the other three men. 'Now don't rush off. You can help me with the babies. I'm a complete amateur.'

She fetched Ros first and put her on Cyril's lap. He fed her pieces of scone and jiggled her delightedly. Then she made a bottle for Peggotty and brought her down. By the time Durston arrived with Julie, both babies had been fed and changed, the vet had gone and Maurice and Cyril were crawling around the floor with Ros.

'I say, this looks rather domesticated.' Durston grinned, pleased to see the washing-up had been done for once and the table properly cleared and scrubbed. 'Just like the old days,' he added.

Val kept her smile in place somehow though she hoped fervently he never said that sort of thing in front of Jannie.

She said, 'I've just made a fresh pot for Jannie. I'm going to take a cup upstairs. Would you like one, Dusty?'

He slid an arm around her waist and squeezed gratefully. 'Lovely. And I don't just mean the tea. You are what is known as cuddly, Val.'

It almost put her off her plan. But then she thought of Jannie so horribly frail, so – so much a victim. She said, 'Dusty, how would you like to exchange wives for a while?' She forced her smile to become roguish and was glad when he removed his arm quite quickly. 'Not in every sense, brother dear!' She laughed as she made for the stairs. 'Just to give Jannie a break from *les enfants* for a week or two. Think about it. We've got no paying guests at the abbey for the rest of this month and Mrs Murchison can cope with Berry. If the weather continues like this, Jannie could sit out on the rocks and have a few gentle walks.' Val took Julie's hand and they started to plod up the stairs. Durston watched them, frowning slightly.

'You're serious? You think Jannie is ill?'

Val was delighted with this evidence that Durston really cared about his wife. She waited until she and Julie reached the landing then said, 'I think she might be ill if she can't have a change.'

Strangely, it was Jannie who put up the most resistance. She clutched the jumble of bedclothes around her and stared at Val wide-eyed.

'I couldn't. I couldn't leave the farm.'

Val frowned. 'My God, don't tell me you're going all . . . what d'you call it . . . agoraphobic?'

'Of course I'm not.' Jannie changed tack. 'It's the children. I can't leave them!'

'I shall be here, idiot! Or don't you trust me with them?'

Jannie began to cry. 'Of course I do. They've known you since . . .' She hiccuped and said, 'Berry doesn't like me, Val! You know he doesn't. He'll just hate the idea and you'll talk him into it and then he'll be all frosty and peculiar.'

Val laughed even as she dried Jannie's eyes and noted that Julie took absolutely no notice of her mother's distress.

'Listen, idiot. You don't know Berry very well, obviously. He probably won't even notice that I'm not there! Jannie, he paints. That is what Berry does. If I took away his palette and banned him from the music room, that would be quite different.' She cupped Jannie's tear-stained face

223

and looked right at her, shocked that no-one had noticed how ill Jannie was. 'Please do this, darling. I am worried about you. If I can't help in some way, I'm going to be very unhappy, and you don't like me being unhappy. You know you always rely on my cheerful and optimistic nature!'

Jannie smiled tremblingly and unwillingly and gave the ultimate foolish excuse.

'Dusty won't let me go, Val. He needs me here.'

Val was glad she could be truthful about this one.

She said, 'Darling, I've already put it to Dusty. He's concerned about you. Very concerned. He'll agree to anything if it will make you well.'

Jannie swallowed and made an enormous effort.

'For your sake then. I can't let you become morose and bad-tempered!'

Val hugged her, laughed obediently and began to plan how she would tell Berry.

CHAPTER FIFTEEN

It was the first of May. Jannie was always glad when Easter was over and done with. The awfulness of Good Friday never seemed quite expiated by the resurrection of Easter Sunday. She could so easily believe in the horrors that man inflicted on man. Not so easy to assimilate the empty tomb and all it implied. How could anyone, even God, forgive all that? She spread her towel on the little pebble beach that was revealed at low tide around the abbey, and sat on it, thinking about the things Doc Willie used to say about grace and how it never had to be earned; it was simply given. Jannie had had to earn everything she had ever wanted in life. Except this. Val had given her this precious time because she loved her. Jannie's eyes filled as they so often did. She thought: I love Val more than anyone else in the whole world. Then she felt guilty because of Julie and Rosamund and Peggotty. She dashed the back of her hand across her eyes and told herself to shut up. Then she laid down on the towel and tried to give herself up to total relaxation like Morag had told her to do.

The trouble was, ever since those evenings of isolation in the Clifton house, Jannie had rarely been alone. She had loved boarding at Gallenwick for that very reason and when she left and found her mother had a new boyfriend, she had deliberately sought out Marius and offered her services as secretary. They had both known what she meant by that; Marius had taken every advantage he possibly could. But he had also been sensitive enough to understand her terrible inner loneliness. He had given her his protection in the Victorian sense of the word.

She had always known that men would one day want her company. She was prepared to earn theirs.

The pebbles were hard beneath her towel. She sat up and rearranged it. It was very warm in the shelter of the house and cliffs. She glanced around almost surreptitiously, then took off her cardigan and unbuttoned her blouse. The cardigan made an adequate pillow. She lay back again. It was three o'clock. Berry slept till four then worked until supper at seven. Four hours. Four hours of being alone seemed like eternity. She closed her eyes against the sun and noted the dusky reds and purples that formed against her lids. The sun must be doing her good, surely? Perhaps tomorrow or the next day, she would stop this stupid weeping and begin to act like a human being again.

Over the next hour she had divested herself of most of her clothes and she was still hot and uncomfortable. She dreaded the stern Mrs Murchison coming around the house to call her for tea. Not that Mrs Murchison would do such a thing. She considered Jannie a personal burden and treated her with icy disdain. She was some relative of a nursing sister who had looked after Berry at the hospital near Weymouth and she guarded him like a dragon. Jannie sighed and wondered how on earth Val coped here by herself with only Murchison for company. No wonder she had put on weight; there wasn't much to do except eat.

She rolled over onto her side and wedged her petticoat beneath one hip. The tide was coming in; she would have to stop relaxing and move soon. Her heart lifted slightly. Though what she could do with the rest of the afternoon she could not think. She wondered how she would manage to keep up a conversation with Berry again that evening. He had gone on and on last night about the situation in some place in the East. North Vietnam. Apparently everywhere else in the area was independent and North Vietnam was still Communist controlled. She could not see what was wrong with that. 'If that's what they want,' she had ventured timidly. 'After all, Berry, Communism is just sharing everything.' He had shot her a look that made her wither inside. He would not discuss his work and for that she was grateful. She had caught glimpses of it in the music room and couldn't make head or tail of it. Most of it seemed to be rather slapdash pictures of rock formations. There were some that looked vaguely like human figures; but distorted, as if they were writhing in pain. She had asked brightly, much as she would have asked Julie, 'Tell me about that picture, Berry.' And he said, 'Sorry, Jannie. I don't talk about what I'm doing.' But at least he had spared her another of his looks.

She sighed sharply, put on her clothes and trailed up the rocks towards the small postern that gave to the cellars.

Far above her, Berry sat uncomfortably on the window-seat of the music room, his peg-leg straight out in front of him, his good leg bracing his body towards the open casement. He had a sketch pad on his lap and a piece of charcoal in his hand. Several discarded sheets of paper lay around him; the one on which he was now working showed a wavering outline of a human figure as if under water. A swatch of hair hid the face and billowed over the humped shoulder; the hip, exaggerated, skeletal, rose high above the rest of the sketch, then trailed away into oblivion. The hair and that grotesque hip-bone were the only definite features; the rest of the body, though suggested, was indecisive, almost irrelevant.

Berry watched Jannie make for the postern and cursed under his breath. Another hour and he might have sketched something he could have worked on. He closed the pad carefully and sat on thinking about Jannie Mears. She had been in the house a week now. At first she got on his nerves with her incessant weeping, but now that he had incorporated the tears into her general wateriness he thought he could bear the next two weeks which Val had promised him would be the extent of it all.

And in spite of himself she was interesting him. She had been practically brought up with Morag and Val, yet she was so different and he wondered why. For one thing her apparent frailty juxtaposed fascinatingly with her stamina. Until this last postnatal thing – whatever Val had called it – she had never been ill. Val had migraines and a bout of flu most winters; Val relayed news from Clevedon about Morag's miscarriages. 'She might look strong,' Val had said worriedly only last Christmas. 'But she's not. I remember how that haymaking business drained her. She used to come back covered in midge bites and hardly able to speak for exhaustion.'

Berry had said, 'You can't worry about everyone, Val. You've got me right under your nose, now Jannie. Let Hugh worry about Morag, for God's sake.'

She had walked over to his painting table, kissed him and said, 'Whatever makes you think I worry about you?' And they had both laughed and felt a moment of complete closeness.

He had long ago told her how possessive he was, how jealous of her other interests. He also told her when he had been with other women; the art students, the sycophants who came every summer. He could tell Val everything and always did. Sometimes when he saw her china-blue eyes flicker with pain, he wished he could shut up. But he never could. He knew he would tell her about Jannie and his urge to paint her; about these surreptitious sessions when he leaned uncomfortably from the music room window and sketched her naked body down on the rocks.

He said aloud, 'Of course there's her fertility. That's what it is. Her bloody fertility. She and Dusty . . . couple of bloody rabbits.' He closed his eyes and kept swearing as if he were repeating an incantation.

Jannie wore slacks that night. She did not like trousers on women, but Val had bustled her into leaving the farm without bothering with proper packing. 'You can wear whatever you like of my stuff. Don't bother with clothes.

228

Nobody will come to the abbey and Berry won't notice what you wear. Honestly.'

Val's dresses were enormous on her, but there were trousers galore, obviously from before the time Val had put on weight. She found a pair in black moygashel, belted them fiercely over her laciest blouse and tucked her hair behind her ears. She hadn't bothered with make-up for ages and her face shone bleakly without its frame of hair. She stared at herself in the mirror over the dressing table and thought how ugly she really was. It was no wonder Dusty had so low an opinion of her. Her eyes began to fill again and she turned away impatiently and went into the big kitchen where Mrs Murchison was putting a jar of cowslips in the middle of the deal table as a sign that the meal was about to begin.

'Shall I lay up?' Jannie asked, leaning over the cowslips and sniffing appreciatively. 'These are lovely. Did you pick them this afternoon?'

'Yes.'

Mrs Murchison was heavily monosyllabic; her unspoken words suggested to Jannie that other people could have gone looking for flowers rather than lying about on rocks. She brought a bundle of cutlery to the table and plonked it down. Jannie began to lay it around three sides of the table. She dropped a fork just as Berry stumped into the room.

'I'm sorry . . . sorry . . .' She picked up the fork and Mrs Murchison took it from her, put it in the sink and gave her another . . . Jannie swallowed instant tears.

Berry sat down heavily. 'Stump's a bugger,' he commented to no-one in particular.

Mrs Murchison said, 'I'll get you in the bath after supper.'

Berry gave her one of his looks. 'You know bloody well I can get in the bath and out of it on my own, Murchison!' he snapped. 'And before you can make any more of your so helpful suggestions, I can put the horse-liniment on myself too!'

Mrs Murchison was completely unaffected by this outburst. Jannie retreated to the window and stared out at the cliff, radiant in the evening sun. Not a cowslip in sight.

Berry said, 'What's this? Not another casserole? Why can't we have fish?'

Mrs Murchison said equably, 'Because there's none in the freezer and I can't drive the car and Mrs Reid isn't here. So I am unable to go into Barnstaple to buy fish.'

Berry snorted a laugh. 'I like your dumb insolence, Murch. You're very like that sister-in-law of yours at the Radipole hospital.' He grinned. 'Gosh, how she hated Val for besting her!'

'I expect she had your well-being at heart, Mr Reid,' Mrs Murchison said with a faint smirk of pleasure at having won Berry over.

He nodded. 'I bet she did. And I know you have too, Murch. That's why I forgive you so much.' His grin widened at this piece of brazen cheek. He went on blandly, 'But you're mistaken about Mrs Reid, you know. She is in fact here, though she is trying desperately to melt into the background. She is a good driver and will take you shopping any time you wish.'

Jannie stammered, 'Of course. I didn't realize . . . of course.'

Mrs Murchison was none too pleased at this but she inclined her head graciously and even drew out a chair for Jannie before seating herself and serving the braised steak. It was delicious of course. The sort of good farmhouse food Jannie was used to. She thought of the meals she and Marius had eaten in London during her previous life. Dainty, imaginative meals. Fish in sauces and spun-sugar concoctions for puddings. Had they ever cooked anything in the flat? She frowned; there had been sandwiches and cocktail bits. That was all. Marius had told her she could not cook and she had believed him.

'This is scrumptious, Mrs Murchison,' she said. 'I'm hopeless at cooking.'

Mrs Murchison softened visibly. 'You can't be hopeless, Mrs Reid! You feed your family every day.'

She pictured Dusty hacking himself off a corner of the loaf and spreading it with butter and marmalade. She remembered the cake that Val had 'tarted up'. She said, 'Well . . . families . . . they're easily satisfied.'

Berry was looking at her with his unfathomable black eyes. Dusty was dark too but she was thankful that she could always see into his eyes and know what he was thinking.

Berry said, 'Tell you what. Why don't you go and get some fish tomorrow, Jannie? And cook our supper? You'd enjoy doing that without the kids to interrupt. You could tootle around Barnstaple – look in the shops – you've been here a week and you must be bored to death.'

She was appalled. She so rarely drove the car further than Gallenwick to pick Julie up from kindergarten. As for finding the fish market and choosing fish, then bringing it back and cooking it . . . she imagined the eyes staring at her on the passenger seat of the car.

Mrs Murchison tried to rescue her. 'I'll come with you. I know which fish Mr Reid prefers.' She forestalled Berry's objections quickly. 'I shall be glad to look round the shops myself. We could meet up again to come back.'

'Oh. Thank you, Mrs Murchison.'

Berry said plaintively, 'I shall be here by myself then.'

They both stared at him. One of his chief clarion calls was for 'complete solitude'.

He shrugged ungraciously. 'All right then.'

Against all her expectations, Jannie enjoyed the morning's shopping expedition. Mrs Murchison chose trout, 'We get a lot of sea fish. This will be a change.' Once she had left Jannie for the 'nice dress shops', there was a terrific sense of freedom. Jannie could not feel lonely in this bustle of people. She wandered through the streets, not even wanting to cry. In a dark, old-fashioned grocer's she bought some almonds and unsalted butter. In a bookshop she bought a cookery book. Next door to that was a shop called 'Nine to Nineteen' full of frilly summer frocks. Frills were definitely in that year. She bought two in a size eight, wore one and put Val's trousers and shirt in a bag. The dress was a deep blue and gave some colour to her eyes. She found a beauty salon and went in for a shampoo and facial. She read the cookery book while she was under the dryer. Trout with almonds did not sound difficult at all.

She returned to the car park at the appointed time. Mrs Murchison was waiting by the car and her eyes widened as Jannie approached.

'I must say, my dear, you look very nice.' This was a paeon of praise from Mrs Murchison and Jannie knew it. She thanked her profusely.

'I think I am beginning to feel better,' she said. 'You're looking after me so well.'

Mrs Murchison smirked as she put the fish carefully on the back seat. 'My sister-in-law has had a lot to do with your kind. She talks to me, you know.'

'My kind?' Jannie edged carefully out of the car park and joined the line of traffic heading east.

'You know. Nerves.'

Jannie said nothing. Her hands tightened on the wheel. Was that what was wrong with her? Was she going mad? People – some people – did go mad after a birth and all the crying had started after Peggotty last October. Suddenly she wanted to see Peggotty so badly she almost turned off at the Gallenwick junction. But then she did not. Mrs Murchison would be annoyed. And probably Durston would be too. And even dear Val . . . no, she could not risk that kind of disapproval. So she continued the next ten miles to the track and, sweating profusely, negotiated the hairpin bends down to the abbey.

They sat down to supper very late that night. Berry had made no comment on her appearance at all. Now he said, 'You shouldn't let them mess about with your hair,

Jannie. And you ought not to mind being thirty-two. It's a wonderful age to be.'

Before she could speak Mrs Murchison said repressively, 'I like the curls.'

Berry said, 'Well you would of course. I expect you like the trout too, do you?'

'Very nice.' Mrs Murchison smiled at Jannie. 'I quite like the nuts, dear. A very good idea.'

Jannie knew she was being treated as a 'nerve case'; she felt her throat begin to constrict.

Berry leaned across the table and gave her one of his looks; but his eyes were full of laughter.

'Oh, so do I. Don't you, Jannie? So much tastier than having the fish pure and unadulterated. Rather like your hair and dress!'

She waited for the tears to come as they always did when Berry was sarcastic. But he was grinning openly now; grinning at her; excluding Mrs Murchison.

Unexpectedly, surprising even herself, she began to laugh.

'Oh, do shut up, Berry!' she said.

He sat back, well pleased. He said, 'After supper, will you shampoo your hair? Leave it wet. I'm doing a portrait of you as a water sprite. You can sit for an hour before bed.'

She was amazed. She stared at him speechlessly until he said, 'You're not going to start to cry again, are you?'

She shook her head. 'It's what Hugh called me. When I was seventeen.'

'Is that the reason for the frilly dress and the curls?' She said nothing and he added incredulously, 'You're not still in love with Hugh, are you, Jannie?'

Mrs Murchison said, 'There's no pudding. We thought cheese and biscuits.'

'Excellent.' Berry pushed aside his plate. 'And coffee. Lots of it, Murch. You can bring it into the music room. Mrs Reid is going to wash her hair now.'

* * *

She sat on the window-seat with a towel around her shoulders while he sketched busily and the coffee cooled and the biscuits and cheese were untouched. Occasionally he asked her to do things with her hair. 'Forward over your face. Now pressed flat to your head – bugger the drips, let them drip!' When her hair was dry, he said, 'Take off that bloody stupid dress. It's soaking wet and makes you look like a tart.'

She giggled. 'All right. I'll go and change.'

'For God's sake, Jannie! Take it off and sit by the fire.'

She gazed at the carefully placed logs. 'It's not lit,' she said feebly.

'Then light it, girl! The matches are on the mantel-piece. I want to see your shoulders now. With your hair drifting across them . . . comb it out, can you?'

She put a match to the kindling and went to her bag for a comb. He was making growling noises of impatience and she caught her finger in the zip of the bag and fumbled for ages before she could find her comb and then, of course, it was unbelievably tatty because that was yet another job she had not done for ages. She held it up, tears in her eyes.

'For God's sake, Jannie.' He heaved himself up, grabbed his stick and stumped at her so that she cowered. But when he put the stick against the wall and leaned over her, his strong, blunt fingers were gentle. 'Use your hands, woman. Like this. It's rather like tossing hay. It spins and catches the light.'

Now it was his kindness that made her weep. When Dusty wanted her he was rarely gentle. She sobbed, 'It's all right. If you want to go to bed . . . it's all right.'

He straightened, slowly and painfully, gazing at her with his black eyes full of astonishment. For a long time there was silence in the big music room, broken only by Jannie's sobs.

Then he said slowly, 'Is that what you think this is all about? A kind of prolonged, artistic foreplay?'

She wailed, 'I don't know . . . I don't know anything any more. I don't know what people – men – want of me. I can't do anything except sex. So . . .'

'So you think sex is all you're good for?'

His frankness released her in some way; gave her the freedom to be honest herself.

She said, 'Well, you know I can't cook. And I'm hopeless with the girls. And I can't seem to produce a boy . . . you said yourself I looked like a tart.'

He went on staring at her, amazement changing to horror.

'My God, Jannie. I'm sorry. I knew you didn't have much self-esteem, but this . . . this is absolutely ridiculous. My dear girl, you cooked that trout perfectly. You looked like a tart because I made you sit there with water dripping all over your dress. I don't know a thing about the kind of mother you are, but Val seems to think you do all right. And it's a well-known fact that men's contribution to the creative process determines the sex. Shame for Anne Boleyn that Henry the Eighth didn't know that!' It was an attempt at a joke, but neither of them laughed.

She gestured helplessly. 'Then what is all this about? You don't paint proper pictures. Of people.'

His black eyes sparked then and she thought for a dreadful moment he might hit her. And then, quite suddenly, he began to laugh. He tipped back his head and roared and Jannie, watching him, still frightened, thought that he looked and sounded exactly like a lion. A big black lion with only one leg.

He continued to laugh as he staggered back to his painting table, and gradually she too smiled, stood up and raked her hands through her hair, then with one swift movement drew her new frock over her head and sat down on the fender.

He was still. With tears streaking her face and her petticoat clinging to her childish shoulders, she looked more like an orphan than ever. He said tentatively, 'Is this all right? Are you sure?'

'Of course. It's no trouble, is it? To sit by the fire.'

He said, 'Oh yes it is. To some people.' He picked up a brush and looked at the stretched canvas in front of him, then at his palette. 'I'll tell you something, Jannie Reid. Sitting is an art in itself. And you can do it.'

She said, her voice very small, 'Thank you.'

He paused, narrowed his eyes at her, then said, 'I'll tell you something else. I can paint proper pictures. I'll paint you, Jannie. I'll paint you so that you can recognize yourself and know that you are a proper person. How's that?'

'Oh, Berry,' was all she said.

They sat together for the rest of that evening, not speaking. Berry worked like a dervish, eyes flicking from model to canvas again and again, as if he expected her to get up and leave at any moment. But Jannie relaxed into her pose, resting on one arm, cheek on shoulder, hair almost covering her face, her bare legs stretched sideways, gradually turning pink in the warmth from the fire. The May sun dipped into the sea and the light from the enormous windows gradually faded and still he worked on. It was almost dark when Mrs Murchison tapped on the door and immediately entered and switched on the lights.

'Good heavens!' she exclaimed, staring at the discarded frock, the half-naked girl in front of the fire and then leaning against the wall with relief as she registered Berry sitting safely at his work table. 'I thought you'd gone to bed . . . you can't possibly be working in this light!'

Jannie jumped up, confused and guilty again. She grabbed her frock and slid it expertly over her head. Berry turned angrily, then just as suddenly relapsed into his chair.

'You're right, Murch. I can't. And I'm done up anyway. What's the time?'

'Time for you to go to bed,' Mrs Murchison scolded and then saw the coffee. 'And you didn't drink your coffee! I'll fetch you a hot drink— '

'I'll have whiskey, Murch. And so will Mrs Reid. We'll see to it. You get off.' He waited while she hovered for a moment and left. Then he said to Jannie. 'In the bureau, Jannie. A double for me.' He smiled wearily. 'You've scrambled into your clothes often before. You did that like an expert.'

She did not flinch. The long evening had done something for her, she hardly knew what. She put two glasses on a tray and poured whiskey and then a brief squirt of soda. Marius had taught her that too. She said, 'Yes. I suppose that is something else I can do.'

'Sorry . . . sorry . . . wasn't thinking.' He took his glass and gulped.

She smiled. 'No, don't be. I need to remember the things I can do as well as the ones I can't.' She tossed back her own drink and said, 'Thank you, Berry.'

He stared at her. 'God. Hugh was right. You are very . . . watery.' He closed his eyes. 'I must go to bed. Can you take the cover off, Jannie? And fetch my stick?'

She went to the bed in the corner, pulled off the printed cover and turned down the covers. Then she went for his stick.

She watched him walk across the room very stiffly and collapse onto the edge of the bed.

'Can I do anything for you?' she asked.

He grinned. 'No thank you, Jannie. It would be practically incestuous.'

Her colour flamed. 'I mean . . . help you to put on your pyjamas or something.'

'No. Nothing. Go to bed, there's a good girl.'

She had reached the door when he said curiously, 'You never had the chance to answer my question. Are you in love with Hugh?'

She opened the door and went onto the dark landing. Below her the refectory table gleamed dully and she wondered why Winifred Wilkie had not thrown herself over the banisters and killed herself inside the abbey.

She said, 'Of course not. What a ridiculous idea.'

She went to the bathroom and began to get ready for bed. Her face in the mirror looked back at her, startled, terribly aware. She thought that it had happened while she lay in front of the fire and Berry painted her. She wondered if he had some way of stealing the souls of his sitters. He must never know, of course. And Val must never know. Especially Val. She probably loved Val more than she loved Berry.

But as she undressed and slid into her single bed, she knew from the slow steady thump of her heart to the ache in her loins, that she had fallen in love with Berry Reid. And she knew too that she had never been in love before.

CHAPTER SIXTEEN

Jannie knew, as day succeeded day in the sealed bubble of Lyn Abbey, that happiness was something that was very close to grace. It was unearned; it was as ephemeral as a butterfly, yet it grew and took root and glorified each small action, each small event. Every morning after breakfast, Berry would position her with great care. 'If you can hold your head like that for just ten minutes, I can pin it down on canvas . . . then you can rest and let me concentrate on the feet.'

They lunched early and he went for his rest and she had the whole afternoon to herself. She smiled to think that time had hung so heavily that first week. Now there was not enough of it. She rambled around the cliffs gathering armfuls of wild flowers, putting jars of them everywhere in the dark hall, on each of the stairs, along the window-ledges. She explored every corner of the abbey, inside and out. The cellars, which must surely have been a smugglers' hiding place when the house was first built, had their own doors leading onto the rocks, one to the east and one to the west. Now they were laid out like a self-contained flat with the living rocks protruding inside at various places and the constant sound of the sea felt as well as heard. She remembered Brother Michael and another of the Franciscans had lived there while the house was being sold. It was used now by other artists and teachers who came through the summer to learn from Berry.

The stone staircase at one end of the kitchen led into the big, gloomy refectory which seemed now to be merely a store room for canvases, deckchairs, umbrellas, wellington boots. She cleared all that to one side to make room for more flowers; she was fast running out of containers.

The big rooms off the refectory were carpeted and furnished now and as beautiful as their counterparts on the landing floor. The one directly beneath the music room was equipped for a dozen painters. She wandered between the easels and then broke into a dance of pure joy, leaping across the room as if trying to catch the dust motes. Then she climbed to the landing floor, checking each jar of flowers as she went, and joined Mrs Murchison in the kitchen. After a very little while Mrs Murchison handed her a duster and suggested she should clean some of the monks' cells ready for the summer visitors. Jannie did not mind; she sang tunelessly as she rubbed at the windows overlooking the sea, and brought a surreptitious gleam to the dark oak cupboards and chests which had belonged to the monks.

Mrs Murchison's partisanship had died a death when Jannie had suddenly been 'cured'. As a patient she might be interesting; as a zany, dancing, flower-picking sprite, she was just another of Mrs Murchison's chores. She was keeping Mr Reid happy and that was all that mattered. She could be ignored, and she was.

Jannie barely noticed. She would dust and polish and peel potatoes and never expect a word of thanks. Several times, in an effort to bring a high gloss to the banister rail, she would slide down the last flight, feet held high above the jars of flowers, hair flying backwards. Mrs Murchison forecast disaster. But Jannie knew she was leading a charmed life.

When the sun was really hot she would lie on the rocks, sometimes completely naked, glorying in the heat on her limbs, rolling onto her stomach to tan her back, her hair pulled back with a rubber band. She did not care any more that her face was so plain; in fact she wondered if this intense happiness might have changed it. You read things like that in books; perhaps it was all true. Perhaps love really did change everything.

Above her, uncomfortably perched on the window-seat, Berry went on with his other portrait; the one she would never recognize. Sometimes he ceased to see her naked body objectively; sometimes, he simply stared at her as he did when he glimpsed her dancing, or sliding down the banisters. It really was like having a sprite around the house.

After supper every evening she would sit again for him, happy if her neck became cricked and her hip hurt because the discomfort was a kind of offering. She asked nothing more than to be in Berry's presence while he painted her. Sometimes, fancifully, she would imagine that his brush was caressing her real body; that he was making love to her; that he was, in fact, creating her anew.

On the fourth evening, he said, 'Talk to me, Jannie. I want your face to be mobile. Move your hands if you like.'

She did not want to talk. It was in the deep silences that she felt closest to him. When she talked she so often said the wrong thing.

She said hesitantly, 'Well . . . what shall I say?'

'Anything. What you are thinking now.'

She almost blushed. How could she tell him that?

He said impatiently, 'All right, woman! Go on with what you were saying at supper. About Vietnam and Korea.'

She did blush then, remembering the way he had so obviously held back from any comment when she had inserted a timid contribution to the conversation.

'Well . . . I simply thought that if countries want to be Communist we haven't got much right to tell them they cannot . . .'

'Good. Good.' He leaned back from the canvas, stared at her. 'Go on. What about if they don't want to be Communist countries and they're being forced into it?'

'Well, can't they vote on it?'

He guffawed. 'No. Communists don't vote.' He leaned back again. 'Go on – go on! What have you got to say to that?'

She frowned slightly. 'You know I have nothing to say to that. I suppose that is what the United Nations are for.' She looked at his face. He had his bright-eyed, feverish expression. She said, 'Are you up to your tricks, Berry? Are you trying to make me cry?'

He stopped working and looked up, startled. 'For goodness' sake, Jannie! Why would I do that?'

'To get the watery bit?' She smiled. 'I think I'm too happy for you at the moment.'

He said, still surprised, 'You are, aren't you? Being an artist's model suits you.' He sat back and consciously relaxed for a moment. 'I'm sorry, Jannie. You must ignore me if I shout. Did I shout?'

'No. It's just that . . . you know I can't talk about politics. I don't understand them.'

'Why should you? You live intuitively, which is the best way to live.' He picked up his brush again. 'Talk about something else then. Tell me about the Bluebell School before the war. How you met Val and Morrie and became friends.'

She rested her head on a footstool and smiled at the ceiling, happiness escalating further because he thought to live intuitively was good.

She said, 'We were ten. Ron was still at home then. He wanted me to be a Bluebell. He had met the Heywards at some posh dinner and he thought they were the bee's knees and Mr Heyward said his daughter was going to the Bluebell School and that was enough for Ron. He thought I was as good as Morag Heyward any day of the week!'

'And so you were. Who is Ron?'

'My father. I called him Pops but Eve didn't like that. She was always having rows with him and she liked me to join in. She said we were a trio, Eve, Ron and Jannie, so we should be in on whatever happened. When she went

242

out with other men she often took me along. So that I could tell Ron that everything was hunky-dory!' The fire was hot on her buttocks and she moved slightly and then apologized. 'Sorry, Berry. Put me back how I was.'

'Certainly not. You were probably frying.' He had stopped working but he kept his head down and a brush in his hand. 'How did you feel about the . . . other men?'

'Well, I didn't realize at first. I don't think there was much in it. Flirtations. Eve needed her ego brassoed and poor old Ron didn't somehow cotton on.' She rolled onto her back without thinking and gazed at the ceiling. 'When they kissed her – the other men – she would make a meal of it. Then she would lift me up and tell whoever it was that I wanted a kiss too. And when they pecked me she would shriek and tell them to do it properly.'

Berry said involuntarily, 'Christ.'

'Oh I didn't mind. But it was better when I went to the Bluebell School. I think Mr Heyward must have told Morrie to keep an eye on me. She always did. From day one until that last awful term at school.'

'How was it awful?'

'Well . . . her parents, you know. Then you and Dusty and Hugh. Then Teddy . . . Morrie went into a shell and as far as I know she never came out of it.'

'Not even now she's married to Hugh?'

'I don't think so. Not entirely.'

'Oh dear God.' Berry mixed a new colour with great concentration, then said, 'And Val? How did you become friends with Val?'

Jannie crooked one knee and scratched a bare foot. 'Everyone liked Val. She was as straight as a die and she was fun and she wasn't too clever or silly. Her parents and brother came to everything and bought ice-creams for everyone and . . . oh they were just perfect. I loved Val.' She straightened her leg and looked at Berry and quite suddenly tears were pouring down her face. 'I love her still.'

Berry swallowed and forced himself out of his chair. 'No tears please! Session over for tonight.'

She sat up dashing the back of her hand across her face. 'Sorry . . . sorry, Berry. I don't know what brought that on.' She looked up at him and her face was raw and vulnerable and plain to read. 'I'm still happy. I've never been so happy. Even if I did cry!'

He turned away abruptly and reached for his stick.

'Good. I'm glad to hear it.' He stumped across the room. 'We'll have a day off tomorrow. I want you to drive me to the farm. Is that all right?'

'Of course. You want to see Val . . .' She could accept that because she expected nothing of him. But then her voice dropped. 'Or are you taking me back?'

He said, 'That is entirely up to you. And Val. Yes, I want to see Val. And I wouldn't mind seeing my nieces.'

She followed him to the door and said tentatively, 'The only thing is, Berry . . .'

'What?' He turned and gave her one of his looks, black eyes opaque. She shivered.

'Don't go drinking at the Doone with Dusty. Please. Val doesn't like it.'

He guffawed loudly. 'God, I've got two of you nagging me now!'

'Not nagging. Caring for you. About you.'

He crossed the landing and gripped the banisters, staring down the flower-filled stairs to the table. 'Murch will go mad at all these jamjars,' he commented gruffly.

'I've told her I'll keep them fresh and clear them away before I leave.'

'Right.' He stared at her in the dim light. 'I'm going to the bathroom. Good night, Jannie. And thank you.'

She watched him stump along the landing. And then she turned for her own room.

Val was in two minds about life on the farm. In one way she was in her element. In another she was simply plain exhausted.

At the very core of her being was a need to care for people she loved; Berry repudiated this so violently she had to hide it always. But the three girls, Durston, even the animals, lapped it up. She refused to push Dusty out of his room so she slept in the nursery on Granny Thomas' feather bed, which, as the old lady had so often said, was warm in winter, cool in summer. Into its downy nest she took Peggotty nearly every night. It was absolutely against all modern advice she knew, she would not tell Jannie, certainly not Morag, and the local health visitor would have a fit. But the baby thrived on the limitless supply of cow's milk and the constant proximity of this doting aunt who was as plump as the feather bed on which they lay, and even more comforting. Val got up each morning when she heard Durston moving next door. She carried Peggotty expertly on one hip and sang and joggled her while she made the first cup of tea of the day and boiled milk for the first feed. Durston appreciated coming downstairs to the gurgling baby, the housewifely sister-in-law, the hot tea and the spotless kitchen. Sometimes he felt bound to show his appreciation and hugged them both. Val could cope with that; it was when he came back in for breakfast, after she had bathed Peggotty and put her down for the morning, before the other two had got up, that it became difficult. In the end she had to say, 'Look here, Dusty. Get on with your breakfast and stop acting like someone in a book!'

She expected him to feign complete and bewildered innocence and was a little taken aback when he said seriously, 'All right. But it's a bloody shame. You're wasted out in that ghastly hole!'

She scooped eggs out of the frying pan onto his plate. 'Of course I'm not wasted! You of all people should know that!'

For once he had no reply, which again nonplussed her. She poured tea and told him she would want him back in the house by nine o'clock to mind Ros and Peggotty while she took Julie to kindergarten.

'The vet is coming to look at those cows,' he said, cutting his bacon appreciatively; it was neither too hard nor too soft. 'But I'll be around.'

'Not good enough,' Val said crisply. 'Ros will be in the playpen and Peggotty upstairs. No good if you're in the barn with the vet. I'll leave coffee on the range. Offer him some. I'll be back by ten.'

He looked up at her. She was like his mother only squashier. A butterball of a woman. Yes, Val was a woman. Jannie was still a girl.

'Any chance of having him to lunch?'

'Of course. There's that ham and cold chicken. Plenty of salad. I'll boil new potatoes.'

'Sounds good.' He finished his breakfast and sat back, replete. 'Thanks, Val.' He watched her as she scrambled eggs for the children and laid another breakfast at the end of the table. 'You're a good 'un. Sorry I said ... what I said. I suppose I thought that probably Berry doesn't appreciate you.'

Val grinned at him. 'He likes to think he doesn't. But he does. Don't worry about it, Dusty.'

He grinned back like an overgrown schoolboy.

'Thing is, Val . . . he wants you all to himself. You should have kids. Lots of kids. You're a natural mother.'

She nearly screamed the truth at him. But the telephone bell rang urgently like a warning bell and when she answered it Berry was on the line demanding to come and see her.

'I don't think I can stand much more of this,' he complained. 'When are you coming home, for Christ's sake? You are my wife – have you forgotten?'

'No, my darling. I never forget that.' She turned her back on Durston and said quietly, 'You know we said three weeks. And I realize more and more how much Jannie needs a break. It's hard work here.'

'Can't I come and see you?'

She thought of the children and the vet and probably Cyril as well. She said rallyingly, 'Come to lunch. Jannie is probably up to driving now, isn't she?'

He said sourly, 'I made her take Murch into Barnstaple last week. Yes, she's up to driving. She wants to see you.'

'Well then. I think you'll see that she needs the rest of her holiday. Is Murch looking after her?'

'She's driving Murch mad. She drifts around like thistledown and bring flowers into the house.'

Val frowned. 'Doesn't sound like Jannie. You are being nice to her, Berry?'

There was a pause. 'Yes,' he said at last in a curiously flat voice. 'I am being nice to her.'

'All right. Perhaps it's a good thing to come here. I'll be able to check up on her. If you're being sarcastic and unkind I'll kill you, Berry!'

'Sounds fun,' he said and rang off.

By the time she had washed and dressed Ros and Julie, given them their breakfast, wiped them clean again, settled Ros in her playpen, checked the contents of Julie's minute satchel and called in Durston and the vet, she was tired again. It was only nine o'clock and although she had been up since four it was more than that. In a way, although life on the farm was exhausting it was very straightforward. Whereas life at Lyn Abbey was never straightforward. Next week she would be preparing for Doc Willie to bring in half a dozen sixth-formers for the Whitsun art week. Not only were the girls an unknown quantity, so was Berry. If the weather continued to be fine, he would sit in the window-seat when he should be resting, and sketch the girls as they swam and cavorted on the tiny foreshore. Val hated that. She hardly knew why, but she hated it.

Julie said, 'Why you drivin' fast, Aunty Val? Is we late for school?'

'No, we isn't late,' Val smiled at the small girl lovingly. Julie had Jannie's straight straw-coloured hair and pale eyes, but she was as tough as her father. 'I'll slow down, shall I?'

'No. I likes going fast. It's summer now. I likes summer.' She thought a while then said, 'I likes winter too.'

'Perhaps you likes everything, Julie?'

'Praps I does,' the little girl said, surprised. ''Cept Daddy hurting Mummy.'

Val looked round in surprise. 'You must be mistaken, sweetie. Daddy would never hurt Mummy.'

'She cries out in bed. Like this.' Julie made animal noises.

Val said, 'Oh my dear Lord!' She bit her lip uncertain whether to laugh or be appalled. 'Listen, darling, Mummy has dreams and she talks when she dreams. She used to do it when we were at school. That's all it is. Nothing to be frightened of.'

Julie was instantly reassured, Val not quite. Should she have a word with Jannie? It would be the height of impertinence, but if Julie could hear things like that, perhaps Jannie – and Durston – should know.

It was strange to chug up the elm avenue of Gallenwick and see the old hockey pitch laid to lawn again. Val tried each morning to close her memory against those days. The loss of Teddy coloured all her schooldays.

She turned the car expertly into the stable yard where the children were already gathered around matronly Mrs Pargeter ready to 'make a line'. The pre-school group was held in the old stable block and Val stood by the car, waving and watching as they trooped in importantly. She knew that their 'task' for that day would be to hunt the deserted grounds for wild flowers. The new owners of Gallenwick were Americans and hardly ever in residence. They allowed Mrs Pargeter unlimited use of the grounds.

She drove slowly back wondering whether the nightjars still flitted in the trees as the sun set. Just before she reached the roofed bridge which led to the road, she stopped the car, switched off and sat for a few precious solitary moments. It was a mistake. Before she knew it she was bent over the wheel, sobbing like a child. And she had no idea why. As she dried her eyes fiercely, she said, 'Oh Berry, Berry, I'm sorry. We made a bargain and I've no intention of breaking it. I'm sorry, darling.' And she drove back to the farm.

Jannie was a different being. Val watched, amazed, almost bemused as her friend darted around the kitchen, laying the table, smiling congratulations at Val for the prepared lunch, the salad, the enormous enamel bowl of new potatoes. She seemed lit from within, in a world of her own. Hard to know whether she was cured of her postnatal malaise, or whether she was breaking down completely.

When they stood side by side at the sink, washing up, she said, 'Val, I can't thank you enough. It's been marvellous to have all this time . . . my time . . . my very own time.'

Val smiled uncertainly. 'Berry says you have filled the house with flowers and polished the banisters . . . sounds as if you have been busy.'

'I've done things. Yes. But I didn't have to do them.' Jannie aimed a peck at Val's cheek almost shyly. 'Darling, the thing is, I can do them. You know . . . I am able to do them.' She laughed depreciatingly. 'I didn't think I was good for anything – d'you know that awful conviction? Because the children take up so much time, I've had to let a lot go and I thought I couldn't do it. But I can.'

'Of course you can.' Val folded the tea towel and hung it over the range. 'But it's more than that, isn't it? You're different, Jannie. You look so well.'

Jannie said simply, 'I am happy. I don't know if I'll be able to hang on to it, but at the moment, I am happy!' She looked at Val, her pale eyes wide. 'D'you know, Val, I don't think I can have been happy before. Even when I thought I was. Isn't that amazing?'

'Yes.' Val could think of nothing else to add to that.

She looked through the window to where Berry and Durston were talking to the vet. The three men leaned on the roof of the car talking across it like women would around a tea table. Berry stood easily, his weight on his good leg. He had been pleasant enough since he arrived; attentive to his nieces, smiling at Val. But she had sensed an unease about him. Something different. Just for a second she wondered whether it had anything to do with Jannie's happiness. But then, if Jannie were sleeping with Berry, she would not be happy in Val's presence . . . would she?

As if in response to this thought, Jannie said suddenly, 'You know, Val, I have to tell you something. I love you. I realized it quite suddenly while I was using your house, your cutlery and crockery and bed linen and . . . everything. I've always been rather in awe of Morag. But I love you.' She smiled, embarrassed. 'Sometimes these things should be said.'

'Oh Jannie.' Val thought she might cry again. 'I love you too.'

'I know you do.' Jannie laughed. 'That's the wonderful thing. You must love me to let me borrow your – your life! That's what is making me happy I think. Love!'

Val sobbed a laugh too. 'If Morrie could hear us! We sound unbearably soppy!'

'But we're not being soppy!' Jannie looked defiantly challenging. 'Are we? It's simply a straightforward fact! You see . . . I'm not even trying to thank you. That would be soppy. Wouldn't it?'

'Yes.' Val wanted to hold Jannie as she held Peggotty. She wanted to apologize for having underrated her for so long. She said instead, 'Darling, I'm so sorry but I've been taking Peggotty into bed with me and giving her as much milk as she can possibly hold. And carrying her on my hip wherever I go. I've spoiled her terribly.'

Jannie looked at her, waiting for more and when nothing came she burst out laughing.

'Oh, Val. Thank you. Thank you for spoiling my baby.'

She stopped laughing with difficulty and added, 'There. You've forced a thank-you out of me!'

Val said, 'It's easier, you see, Jannie. She doesn't cry and I get a good night's sleep. I know it's wrong but if it works, does it matter?'

'Of course it doesn't matter! That's one of the great things about Mrs Merrydown. She always says, if it works it doesn't matter whether it's in the book of rules or not!' Jannie patted Val's arm. 'She has to visit a lot of the gypsy camps, you know.'

'Oh thank you, Jannie! I have felt a bit guilty about it.' Val grinned. 'There, I've thanked you too!'

They both laughed.

Val said, 'And since it seems to be confession time . . . oh this is embarrassing . . .'

'Go on,' Jannie encouraged. 'Whatever it is, go on.'

'It's just that . . . oh God, Jannie, I hate to say this. But Julie hears you. You and Dusty. When you . . . you know . . . cry out and things.'

For a moment Jannie looked genuinely puzzled. And then it was as if a curtain covered her eyes. She said, 'I didn't think she would hear. The walls are so thick.'

'Yes but you leave the door open to hear the baby, don't you?'

'I'm such a fool, Val. Such a damned fool.'

Val was horrified at the effect of her words. 'Darling, you're not a fool. It's perfectly natural. It's only that it might not be good for Julie. She thinks Dusty is hurting you. I told her you always talked in your sleep.'

Jannie said, 'Did I? I didn't know that.' She seemed to be looking at something beyond Val, though she was only watching through the window as the car departed with the vet. She said quietly, 'Another ten days . . .' Then she focused on Val and said almost sharply, 'The boys are coming in. I'll get Peggotty. Would you mind if I went with Dusty to fetch Julie? I need to be with him alone. Would you look after Ros and Peggotty for me?'

It was as if their previous conversation had not taken

place. Val nodded, suppressing her sense of shock at Jannie's sudden reversion. She knew with a sinking heart that she would have to stay at the farm for the intended three weeks . . . maybe longer. Lyn Abbey was healing Jannie, there was no doubt about that. But the cure was not yet complete.

Berry watched her give Peggotty her bottle; his dark face was set in the way that Val called sulky. It was much more than that, but the childish word seemed to make his obvious misery more acceptable to both of them.

He said, 'I know it's only another ten days. But I was hoping we could do the swap today. You can see she's OK now.'

'She's better, yes. But something happened just now and she seemed to go back into herself in such an odd way. I'm sorry, darling. I simply cannot suggest to her that she comes home now. She's absolutely counting on the next ten days.'

He said sharply, 'What happened – just now? Did you say something to her?'

She removed the flattened teat from Peggotty's frantically sucking lips and let the air bubble back into the bottle. She reconnected the baby and then looked up directly into her husband's dark eyes.

'What do you think I might have said, Berry? Do you think I asked her if you had made a pass at her?'

'Don't be ridiculous, Val.' He seemed unconcerned by the implied accusation. 'What did you say to her? Was it anything about her mother?'

Val was surprised enough to lower the bottle for an instant. Peggotty's yell brought her back to earth.

'I just . . . No, I didn't mention her mother. It was to do with Julie. Hearing things. Jannie and Dusty . . . oh, you know!'

Berry said nothing, staring now at Ros in the playpen. The small girl stood his glare for a full minute before bursting into tears.

Val snapped. 'Oh my dear Lord. Now look what you've done.'

'It's OK . . . don't fuss, woman.' Berry got up with difficulty, leaned into the playpen and hoisted Ros out and onto his knee. He jiggled her inexpertly but to some effect. She hiccupped into silence and stood on his lap to clutch his hair.

'Oh . . . Christ . . .' Berry closed his eyes as her small bare feet connected with his stump. But still he waved Val away. 'It's all right! Get on with your job. You know very well there are times when I don't mind.'

She looked at him, half smiling, remembering the other times he did not mind. He grunted as Ros settled herself on his good leg and began to go through the pockets of his jacket.

He said, 'Don't stare at the child, you know she doesn't like it!' He grinned too. 'She's wonderful, isn't she?'

'Yes.' Val swallowed convulsively.

Berry said, 'The thing is, apparently Eve Mears was some kind of pervert. She used to include Jannie in some of her activities. Probably Jannie thought you might be saying that history was repeating itself.'

'Oh . . . oh Lord.' Val stood up and put Peggotty over one shoulder to wind her. 'Yes. She used to say things in her sleep when we were at school.' She frowned down at her husband. 'How have you discovered all this? Have you talked to her properly?'

'She says things sometimes. It all sounds quite grim.'

Val nodded. 'But Morrie reckons that it's good to talk things out. So you're helping her, Berry. Please don't mind too much.'

He held Ros' hands and rocked her back and forth. 'See-saw, Marjorie Daw . . .' Outside the car drew up and disgorged Julie, frantic to see her Uncle Berry. 'I don't mind, Val.' He stared up at her as she jiggled Peggotty. 'I want you back. Just remember I said that.'

She was confused. She watched as Julie ran into the kitchen and began to tell Berry immediately about her day. The little girl, so like her mother, waved a huge branch at him. 'They're like cats' tails, Uncle Berry. See? See?' Val put Peggotty into the playpen and retrieved Ros. Jannie stood in the middle of the kitchen looking around as if she'd never seen it before. When there was a gap in the general hullabaloo, her high voice enquired with a kind of desperation, 'Is it time for us to go home now, Berry?'

Berry was still looking at Val, waiting for her to do something and she did not know what.

She said prosaically, 'Let's have a cup of tea first, Jannie. Shall we?'

And only then did she realize that Jannie had called Lyn Abbey her home.

CHAPTER SEVENTEEN

As they drove back to the abbey, Berry understood exactly what Val had meant. Jannie kept her eyes on the windscreen with a kind of burning concentration that had none of the happy anticipation of their journey that morning. Neither of them spoke until they were ten minutes from the cliff-top path, then Berry said, 'When I get my next decent cheque, I'm going to get one of those cars. The hand-controlled ones.' There was an unresponsive silence and he prompted her impatiently. 'Well? What do you think?'

She spoke in a new voice; almost sullenly. 'Why not? I'm surprised you haven't done it before. Obviously Val is a much better driver than I am.'

He stared at her. Her hair had come away from its rubber band but it straggled around her face without any of its usual shine. He realized with a small shock that she looked worse now than when she had first arrived at Lyn.

He said abruptly, 'What's up? Were the kids too much for you? Or do you hate Val for coping?'

She spoke in the same hard monotone, 'I love my children. And I love Val. I would like to go right away – an island somewhere – with them. And stay for ever.'

He went on staring at her. He wondered just how seriously unstable she was.

She braked at the top of the cliff and put the car into first to begin the descent. Over the years the track had been surfaced and pushed further sideways into the cliff, but it was still a difficult manoeuvre.

Berry did not take his eyes from her face. 'Val was

afraid she might have upset you. That business with Julie hearing you and Dusty making love— '

'Shut up!' she cut him off sharply. He had never heard her speak like that before. 'Just shut up about it, will you? You – Dusty – probably Hugh too, all tarred with the same brush! You think it's funny, don't you? Making me sit every evening and talk to you while you practically rape me on your bloody canvas!' The car was going much too fast, she pulled hard on the wheel and they took the first hairpin at twenty-five. 'Do you know, when we drove to fetch Julie from school, I told him. I tried to tell him . . . how I felt about it. History repeating itself. That sort of thing.' She wrenched on the wheel again. 'He couldn't stop laughing. He thought it was great. Like you with your painting – like Eve sharing her blokes with me! He stopped the car and practically pulled me onto the grass – just where we used to sit and listen to the nightjars – and he – he— ' She was weeping profusely; she could not possibly see the next bend. Berry reached for the handbrake and pulled on it fiercely, the car slewed, stalled and stopped with its front wheels half an inch from the cliff face. She put her head onto the steering-wheel and wailed helplessly.

He sat back and waited for the sweat to dry on his face, then he turned and lifted her bodily onto his lap. He thought grimly that his stump was having to take a lot of punishment today. It did not matter.

He held her against his shoulder just as he had held Ros earlier, and waited until she had cried herself out. Then he put his chin on top of her head and began to talk very slowly, feeling his way, praying that he would not put his foot in it as Val so often accused him of doing.

'Dusty made love to you on the bank at Gallenwick. And somehow you felt . . . used. I am painting your portrait – it is not unduly erotic – but again, you feel used. That is probably because, as a child, you were used.' He frowned through the windscreen at the view of the abbey roof below them. 'You have a low opinion of yourself, Jannie. Very low. I thought, after your ten days at the abbey, you might have realized that you are worth . . . a great deal. You have enormous talents. You have qualities – innate qualities – which make you special. You are fey and interesting, rather like a will-o'-the-wisp. You are elusive. And beautiful.'

She tried to laugh and sobbed instead. He moved some of her hair from his nose and combed it down over her shoulders. Val's hair was short and crisp. This was like strands of seaweed.

He said, 'Why don't you talk to Morag sometime? She would be able to explain it all to you. I can only . . . feel.'

There was a long pause, then she nodded very slightly. Encouraged, he said, 'And I'll stop painting. Of course. But I can't stop barking at you. Can you bear it?'

At last she managed a proper, gasping laugh.

'I don't want you to stop painting. I don't want Dusty to stop . . . what he does. That's the problem, Berry. I'm the problem. Not Dusty, not you.'

He swore then, furious with her that she had turned his words full circle yet again. Then he lugged her up, his hands beneath her armpits, and dumped her back in the driver's seat.

'You little fool!' he yelled. 'You could do anything! And all you do is denigrate yourself! Can't you see it's the most egotistical, narcissistic trick in the book? Or do you think you're some Christ-like figure that can earth everyone's sins for them? Well – I'm not pandering to you any longer! You can sit for me, or you needn't! You can pick your bloody flowers and stick them round the house, or not! You can polish and clean the place till it's raw for all I care!' He shoved her legs beneath the steering-wheel, stuck her hands on it. 'I'll tell you one thing, my girl! You're going to back this bloody car off the cliff edge and drive us safely down to the abbey! And when we get down there, you're going to cook the bloody supper!'

She wailed, 'But I said – I want to sit for you—'

'Well, we're not sitting or painting or talking any more drivel tonight! Because you're going to be much too busy cooking and laying the table – which you can do perfectly well so don't start telling me how impossible it all is!'

He stopped, simply because he had run out of breath and for a long moment there was panting silence in the car. Then, startled, but obedient, she put her feet into position on the pedals, checked the gear lever and switched on the engine. With infinite care, she edged the car away from the cliff face, then pulled on the handbrake, changed gear and began the descent again at four miles an hour. They drew up outside the house. The front door was open and in the twilit interior the banks of flowers covering the refectory table seemed to glow with a light of their own.

He was about to apologize and thank her for getting them safely down, when she said almost calmly, 'What would you like for supper?'

He breathed carefully, twice.

'Scrambled eggs,' he said hoarsely. 'And a great deal of tea. With a great deal of sugar.'

She got out, went around the car and opened his door and lifted out his left leg.

He said, 'You know I hate you doing that.'

She looked at him, there was the faintest glimmer in her sea-blue eyes.

'Well, we've all got our crosses to bear, I suppose.'

He watched her go into the house and wondered what would happen next.

Apparently, nothing much. Mrs Murchison's nose was put thoroughly out of joint by her take-over of the kitchen, but when Berry took her aside and explained that it was a therapeutic exercise she professed to understand completely.

'She had a relapse, did she?' Mrs Murchison oozed sympathy.

'She bloody near killed the pair of us,' Berry snapped. 'I want her to take responsibility for the place for a while. If you can make yourself scarce I'd be grateful.'

She did not care for that. 'If it weren't for the proprieties, I would go to see my sister-in-law in Weymouth.'

'Yes, well that's not on, is it? In the circumstances.' Berry could feel his nerves fraying by the minute. He stumped into the music room, shut both doors and rang Val. Then, when he got her, he could not bring himself to tell her what had happened.

Instead he said, 'She's cooking supper. Seems a bit more normal.'

'Darling, you're an angel. But you sound so tired. Are you in pain?'

He was but he had forgotten that. 'I just want you back. Remember I told you . . . I want you back.'

She said, 'Darling, I know. And I want to be back. Only another seven days. You can see how things are.'

He said feelingly, 'I certainly can.'

'And whatever you are doing is right, sweetheart. Until I put my big foot into it, she was such a different girl. Happy.'

'Yeah.'

'Don't sound so sarcastic, Berry. I'm offering you one of the biggest compliments you're ever likely to get!'

He grinned. 'And I love you too.'

The scrambled eggs were slightly rubbery but Mrs Murchison rolled her eyes and said they were absolutely delicious. Jannie had one mouthful and watched as Berry ate his. He found he was hungry; he was missing his wife, saddled with this peculiar girl, and still he was hungry. He washed everything down with four cups of tea and began to feel slightly better. He wondered whether he might spend an hour on his portrait of Jannie: the one she would not recognize. It might well make him feel more normal.

Mrs Murchison said, 'I'm feeling rather tired tonight.

Do you mind if I go to my room, Mrs Reid? You could leave the clearing up until the morning if you like.'

Jannie smiled briefly and began to clear the table immediately. Mrs Murchison did not protest. Berry wondered whether she was overdoing her new role; surely Jannie would suspect something. But neither of the women seemed to find anything odd about this incredibly odd situation. Jannie washed up, he dried. She even laid the table for breakfast. It was all done in complete silence.

He said, 'I think I'll have an early night too, Jannie. All right?'

'Yes.' She brought a jamjar of wild columbine to the sink and began to rearrange the flowers. 'It's good to be back. I'm perfectly all right, Berry.' She glanced up from the flowers, already her eyes were darker, more focused. 'Thank you. Sorry I was a pain. Thank you.'

He did not look at her for too long; he had no wish to see that awful, raw adoration in her eyes again. Perhaps it had gone for good; perhaps her passionate interlude with Dusty on the grass at Gallenwick had its good side. Thank God he hadn't said anything to Val about it. He had been sorely tempted to use it as a weapon to get her home again: 'If you don't come back now – immediately – Jannie's going to get into bed with me whether I want her or not!' He would have hated himself for saying that.

He went into the music room and wedged himself into the window-seat for an hour, gazing out at the drowning sun, thinking about Jannie's life as a small girl, understanding her love of Val and her respect for Morag. And then his thoughts stopped as they so often did when he reached the wall of his feelings for Morag. He closed his eyes against the molten sea and would not allow himself the indulgence of memory. But when he pushed himself off the window-seat and began to prepare for bed, a very precise thought came into his head. If only he had made Morrie pregnant all those years ago. His one chance of immortality.

* * *

260

He slept fitfully and during the night was conscious of people moving around on the landing outside his door. At six o'clock when it was properly light, he sat up, suddenly awake, suddenly afraid that Jannie had left the abbey. He strapped on his leg and pulled on his old painting flannels and a shirt and made for the kitchen. It was empty, pristine, the flowers back in the middle of the table, breakfast laid for three. The kettle was still warm and a cup was standing in the sink. Jannie had made herself some tea quite recently.

He went to the window and stared at the cliff, still in deep shadow. There was no sign of a figure struggling up the path and the car was where they had left it yesterday outside the porch. He stuck his head out of the door and listened. The tall old house was silent. Which of course was how it should be at six o'clock in the morning.

'Damn!' he murmured. 'What's she been up to now?'

He hovered uncertainly on the landing, then shrugged and made for Jannie's room. The door was ajar. He did not move it and peered inside with some difficulty. The bed was made and empty.

He swore again and made for Murch's little flatlet on the third floor. It was hell getting up the stairs; Val had said something about a new invention, a chair-lift, rather like a dumb waiter. He'd have to go into it some time. He swung himself along the landing and heard her long before he reached her door; she was making a moaning noise, like an animal. And then came Jannie's voice, low and soothing. 'Don't worry, you'll be all right in a minute. See if you can sleep now.' He stood still, his hand on the wall, waiting. After a few minutes, Jannie appeared, backing out of the room very quietly, pulling the door gently behind her.

She saw Berry and gave an enormous start, then put her finger to her lips and pointed back to the stairs. They descended slowly but quietly and went back to the kitchen. He turned and faced her.

'Poor old Murch! Case of Delhi belly I take it?'

Jannie's face was wide open with worry; the buttoned look had gone, this was normal anxiety.

She said, 'Oh, Berry! It must be the scrambled eggs! She's been so ill through the night! I didn't know whether to call the doctor or what! I feel horribly responsible.'

'Don't be a fool! If it was the eggs I'd have it! I feel as fit as a flea!' And quite suddenly he did. He sat down at the table and began to laugh. 'I've wished it on her, Jannie! It's my fault. I wanted you to take over the housekeeping reins and I told her to back away – of course she wasn't keen – you know what she's like! Now this!' Relief overwhelmed him; he laughed helplessly. 'Sorry, old girl! I know you've been up all night coping with this, but it just strikes me as funny! Sorry!'

She sat opposite him. 'Of course. You had more than anyone. So it can't be the eggs.' She ran her hands through her hair and scooped it into the elastic band. 'But I think we ought to have the doctor, Berry.'

'She'll be all right. It's a long way for him to come.'

But for once she was adamant. 'I'll ring him at eight o'clock. He'll be getting ready for his morning surgery then.' She sat back, glad now that the decision had been made. 'I was so worried in the night. You hear awful things about food poisoning.' She managed a small smile. 'Poor old thing was ashamed of vomiting in front of me. The times I've sat with Julie. Things like that don't bother me.'

He said, 'I'll make some tea – no, sit still, you've been up all night.' He filled the kettle. 'You know, Jannie, you're a strange mixture. Doesn't it occur to you that there are a great many people who could not sit up all night holding a bowl for a middle-aged woman?'

She shrugged. 'Oh well . . . you know. Things like that . . .'

She stretched hugely. She was wearing one of Val's

shirts which was much too big for her. It emphasized the mixture of child and woman in her. He thought for a moment of holding her slight body between his rough palms, like a sculptor moulding a figure. He took a deep breath and turned back to the kettle.

'You should have this tea and go back to bed. I'll phone the doctor. You must be bushed.'

She laughed comfortably. 'Don't be silly. I'm used to getting up and down throughout the night. You'll have to take care of Val when she gets home . . . oh no.' She shook her head at herself, her pony-tail flicking across the shirt collar. 'I forgot. Val is sleeping with Peggotty . . .' She smiled. 'Good old Val. I'll be able to do that.' She pulled the jar of flowers towards her and sniffed appreciatively. 'I don't want to be pregnant again. Ever.'

She was not talking to him so there was no need to reply. He made the tea.

The doctor diagnosed a 'virus' and said there was nothing he could do for Mrs Murchison except prescribe rest, plenty of fluids and a light diet when possible. She seemed already on the mend, propped up among her pillows, assuring them weakly that she did not want to be any trouble, suddenly overwhelmingly grateful to Jannie, unexpectedly clinging too.

'Could you stay a little while?' she said, holding Jannie's small hand as if she expected her to run away. 'You were such a comfort to me in the night. I thought I was going, you know.' She looked up at Berry. 'I didn't want to disturb you, Mr Reid, but I really thought I was going.'

Jannie said easily, 'Of course I'll stay. And when the papers arrive you can look at them while I make some soup for lunch. Peggy taught me how to make proper farmhouse soup. And I can manage quite nice ice-cream too. How would you like some ice-cream?'

Mrs Murchison's eyes filled with tears. 'I've met all you girls and I always said, you were the softest one.'

Berry said hastily before he started to laugh, 'I'll go

and see if the papers have come then, shall I?' He could hardly wait to get to the phone in his room and tell Val that Murch thought she was a hard case.

That afternoon, while Mrs Murchison slept the sleep of recovery, Jannie took the easy way to the tiny foreshore through the cellar postern. She carried a book and some sun oil, but she knew she would not be reading. In spite of her words to Berry that morning, she was exhausted; when she was exhausted at the farm there was no hope of rest. Now she luxuriated in having at least three hours to herself. There was enough soup and ice-cream for their supper and Mrs Murchison was settled. Presumably Berry was resting too. She placed a towel carefully, rolled her cardigan into a pillow and wriggled out of Val's trousers. In five minutes she was asleep.

She was never sure what woke her. It could have been a gull, or simply that she was too hot. She lay for a long moment, orientating herself, knowing – yet almost frightened to know it – that the elusive happiness was with her again. Before, when she had acknowledged it, it had gone away. She tested it gently, forcing herself to recall the apalling fact that Julie had heard her cries of shameful ecstasy . . . but on the other hand, Val had not seemed to think it was dreadful. Not really. And it need never happen again . . . she would make sure it never happened again. She closed her eyes against the sun and wondered whether she might become celibate. Was it possible? Would it enable her to stay happy . . . for ever? Like someone in a story?

She felt a trickle of sweat run between her small breasts and hoped that she wasn't coming down with whatever Mrs Murchison had. Mrs Murchison had said she was the softest of the three sisters-in-law. And though Berry had obviously interpreted that as being the most stupid, Jannie knew that Mrs Murchison had meant something else.

She unbuttoned Val's shirt and let the sweat dry in

the sun. And remembered Dusty pushing her onto the bank at Gallenwick in spite of her protests . . . and then remembered how her protests had died and she had held him fiercely.

She turned her head, expecting to weep. But there were no tears and the happiness was still there, inside her somewhere. She sat up slowly; she was very hot indeed and the hard lights from the sea dazzled her into dizziness. She put a hand to her hair and removed the rubber band. Then she shrugged off the shirt and edged, crabwise into the water.

She was no swimmer and the winter storms around the abbey terrified her. But the last ten days had been calm and windless and bathed in this wonderful spring sunshine. There was nothing to fear. She lay in the shallows, letting the water wash over her body, feeling her hair stream out behind her, letting her love for Berry return with each small wavelet. She felt it was rather like a baptism. This must be what Doc Willie had meant all those years ago, all unearned, unsought. But instead of grace, this was happiness. She smiled blindly into the sun wondering whether grace was happiness all the time and no-one except herself realized it. She turned her head away from the sun and the water washed her face. She thought that perhaps she was having a moment of pure epiphany and at any minute now she would see a vision, hear a voice.

She did not have to listen very hard. The voice bellowed from above her, 'What the hell are you playing at, Jannie? Get out of that water! D'you hear me? Now!'

She rolled onto her stomach almost lazily; this of course was the voice she wanted to hear. She lifted her head. Berry was almost suspended from the window of the music room; he looked wild, like an animal. A bear or a lion.

She smiled at him beatifically. 'Hello, Berry,' she said inadequately.

'Get out of that water, Jannie! Get yourself up here!'

'Yes. All right.'

She knelt, lowered her head so that her hair hung over her face into the water, then flicked it back. Droplets flew everywhere aureoling her head and crouching body. She stood up. It did not worry her that she was naked. She was glad that Berry wanted her to sit for him again. That was when she was happiest; that was when she felt part of him.

She left the book and trousers, picked up the shirt and draped it over her shoulders and went through the door into the cellar. Her bare feet left prints on the ancient stone and on each step as she went up to the first floor. She smiled. They would dry and disappear in minutes. Nothing lasted. Only happiness.

Berry was waiting for her on the landing; his face was black in the darkness and he practically dragged her into the music room and then turned her to face him, holding her by her upper arms, his weight on her a measure of his pain.

'Don't you ever try anything like that again, my girl!' He looked grim and he shook her quite hard. 'Who do you think you are? That poor Winifred Wilkie? Are you trying to relive something in that crazy head of yours?'

She did not mind any of it; he was simply showing her that he cared about her. She smiled up at him.

'I was hot. But when I got into the water, it was wonderful, Berry. Quite wonderful.'

He said, 'Christ. So you weren't trying to drown yourself?'

She laughed gently. 'Like Ophelia? Oh Berry . . . is that what you thought?'

'What else? You tried to do us both in yesterday. You hardly slept all night. You've been working all morning – probably exhausted. You're in a deeply depressed state. What would you have thought if positions had been reversed?'

She went on laughing. 'I don't know. But believe me,

I don't want to commit suicide. I am happy. Why would I want to end that?'

He released her as if suddenly conscious of her nakedness. He turned to his painting table.

'Sorry. Sorry, Jannie. You'd better put that shirt on properly.'

She went slowly towards the empty fireplace and began to throw down cushions.

'I'll sit for you now, shall I?' She sat down and then rested on one arm. 'I've had a good sleep. Have you?'

He stared, nonplussed.

'Well . . . yes. But I thought . . . I told you there would be no more sittings.'

She smiled. 'Only because of what I said. But as the water washed over me, Berry . . . it was . . . I wish I could tell you . . .'

He said dryly, 'A purification?'

'More positive.' She did not want to say the word baptism; he would laugh. 'It was a glorification.' She smiled again. 'That's what it was, Berry. I was filled with glory. Don't laugh. Please don't laugh.'

'I'm not going to laugh.' He was staring at her; her thin shoulders and small breasts; the shirt not concealing the thrust of her hip bone. He looked at the work he had been doing while she lay below him on the rocks. A creature of the sea and the sky, the sun and the earth. He picked up the brush he had thrown to the floor when he thought she was drowning. He began to clean it.

He said, 'Can you put your head back? Look at the ceiling? I want that line of throat going between the clavicles.'

She tilted her head in exactly the right position. He almost gasped with pleasure. She was perfectly still; five minutes, ten, half an hour.

He said, 'All right. Relax. Sit up and move your arms.'

She sat up, pushed her legs out in front of her, stretched mightily. He sat there looking at the painting and then at the model.

She said, 'May I see?'

'No. It's not at a viewing stage yet.'

She stood up, reached down, pulled on the shirt and buttoned it up. All her movements were calm, unstudied, exquisite. She said quietly, 'My portrait is against the wall. Over there, Berry. What have you been painting this afternoon?'

He was like a schoolboy caught cribbing. He stammered something; stopped himself, began again.

'I'm doing two. One that's . . . kind of . . . allegorical. In a way.'

'You're doing a nude. Why don't you say so?'

'No! I mean, it happens that . . . it's to do with you being a water sprite. That's all. Nothing important.'

She walked to the window, her bare feet making a padding sound on the old floorboards. She put one knee on the seat and looked out. Then she turned.

'You have been sitting here. Painting me while I sunbathed.'

'Jannie – listen – I'm sorry! I'm really sorry! It's not like you think – voyeurism – all that stuff. It's simply that you are completely unconscious of what is happening – and the juxtaposition of human, sea, rock, it's irresistible.' He held out his paint-stained hands. 'I'm sorry. Please come away from the window.'

She smiled. 'Berry. Stop it. I'm not going to go crazy again. I told you . . . everything is so different now.'

'You mean . . . the glorifying experience?'

'You're humouring me!' She laughed. 'I don't mind. Honestly. I know it sounds funny and pretentious. But what it did for me was . . . Berry, I know my own worth. I know I have a place – an important place – in the world.'

'Well and so you have. Mrs Murchison thinks so. I think so. Val thinks so . . . we can't all be wrong!' he tried to laugh.

She shook her head at him gently. 'I needed to know.

For myself.' She stood up and moved towards him. 'I needed to know the things you've told me – shown me. That they are good things. Not shameful at all. When I give myself to Dusty, I do it wholeheartedly. Berry . . . I am good at physical love.' She gestured towards the piled cushions. 'That's what this is all about, my dearest. I am good at it, because I am giving myself to you. Can you understand that?' She threw back her head and laughed with a kind of triumph. 'Oh, Berry . . . I thought I used sex to get what I wanted from life. I did not understand it was a celebration of what I already had!' She put one hand on his shoulder, another against his cheek. 'I am good at having babies, suckling them. I am rotten at a lot of other things – politics and philosophy and – and books and painting . . . but when I'm good . . .' She giggled, a schoolgirl again. 'When I'm good, I'm very, very good!'

She brought her face close to his and then looked sideways at the painting. Her breath caught in her throat. He waited for her to drop away with disappointment. But she did not. She stared at the canvas, her mouth slightly open in sheer astonishment. At first she could see nothing . . . a molten mass of fiery sea and black rock and seaweed . . . a great deal of seaweed. And then she saw herself; part of earth, air and water. She was being born, an adult woman, being born of the elements.

After a long moment, she turned and looked at him.

'So you know. My God . . . you've known all the time.'

She kissed him, tenderly and then with mounting passion. Somehow he carried her to the bed. There was nothing else to be done. But as he was engulfed in her passion, he knew with terror and delight that he had started something impossible. Part of him regretted it, mourned for what he had had and was now losing. But the other part soared high above the two of them, like an eagle, freed of the terrible impairment of his leg. Sometime during that late afternoon he called a name. Jannie held him close, hardly hearing. It sounded like 'Akiko'.

CHAPTER EIGHTEEN

Jannie was never to forget the next three days. Past and future disappeared; not once in that time did she think of her children, her husband, her best friend. She had been washed anew by the sea, and was no longer Jannie Mears or Jannie Reid. She was a creature of water and air; she could do anything. And she did. She cared for Mrs Murchison with a tenderness that overwhelmed that lady; she whirled around the abbey, opening windows, renewing flowers, polishing the dark wood until the whole place seemed to gleam with secret lights. She made simple but delicious meals and carried them on trays, first upstairs, then into the music room where she and Berry would eat as they sat on the window-seat far above the quietly shifting sea. Every evening after she had settled Mrs Murchison, she would sit for Berry. And then, as the darkness made his work impossible, she would go into his arms and they would hold each other. And then they would go to bed.

At first, the sense of doom which Berry had had to block out, sat on his shoulder waiting for him to come out of this suspended state. Sometime during that first night he woke and wept silently for Val, for Jannie, for himself. Finally, grief exhausted, his mood changed and became childishly defiant. He wanted to go to Val and shout at her. Tell her it was all her fault, that he had warned her and she had ignored that warning. But as dawn paled the windows, the sheer weight of guilt fell on his shoulders and he looked at Jannie, pale and insubstantial beside him, and whispered, 'Oh God. I am so sorry . . .'

But then she too woke and it all started again. Her

intense happiness was indefatigable; she refused to recognize the foreboding in his dark face, she was illuminated from within and when she knelt above him he seemed to be bathed in her light. He whispered wonderingly, 'You are like an angel, Jannie.' And she smiled and leaned over him. 'Juliet's mother used to say something like that. Kissed by angels.' She kissed him lingeringly. 'There. How was that?'

He cupped her face in his rough hands. 'You are beautiful. It is as if you are giving me your beauty.'

And after the first day, that was how it was. She was giving herself to him so completely, there was literally no room for guilt. He finished the two paintings, completed another. When she was flitting around the house, he listened to her childish, minor singing voice, and continued to work like a dervish. He used greens, every shade of green. He did not know whether he could capture the off-beat quality that was so near madness. But he could try. Greens had to be predominant.

So, for three days, their peculiar charmed existence, ethereal and almost spiritual, yet also very domesticated, continued. The physical love-making was quite a small part of it and inseparable from the minutiae of the rest. They did not need to be in each other's presence; Jannie spent a lot of time with Mrs Murchison; Berry was happy to be alone in the music room with his work. But as long as they were within the abbey or just outside it, the cord between them was unbreakable. When Jannie sunbathed she could feel his eyes on her body. When she played Scrabble with Mrs Murchison she held him inside her head, seeing him mix paints, clean brushes, lean avidly over his canvas as he leaned over her each night. She knew he was trying to capture her for all time. He could not do it physically; already both of them knew the transience of their communion. But on canvas . . . that was something else. On the third night when she came to him to see what he had accomplished during the sitting, she stared at the points of green scattered everywhere over the canvas and drew in a deep breath.

'I like this one best.'

He put his face close to hers, breathed in the essence of her. 'It's called pointillistic,' he whispered. 'You need to lean back from it in order to see it.'

'But you have not leaned back.'

'No . . .' His eyes were half closed. From his waist down he throbbed with pain.

She smoothed her hands over his face and felt the sweat. 'Only you. No-one else will come close to me again.' She kissed him. 'This must be the last time. I think you are ill, dearest. Tomorrow you will rest and I will look after you.'

She spoke so matter-of-factly as if their union had been a party and the party was over. That night she made love to him tenderly, then fiercely, then tenderly again. She told him he had made her well and he stared up at her, his dark eyes feverish and said, 'Don't leave me, Jannie.'

She pillowed his head, stroked his rough curly hair and smiled into the darkness.

'When I was seventeen, I swore I would enslave you one day. I thought that would make me your master.' She kissed his forehead. 'It has made you mine.' She kept kissing him. 'You know I would die for you, Berry. You must know that.'

'Be quiet. Don't say things like that. It must never happen again – never again.'

'Do you mean this must not happen again?' she asked as she kissed him.

'I meant dying. Nobody has the right to die for someone else. It is too heavy a burden to carry.'

She thought he was referring to Doc Willie's sister again but then he turned his head into the crook of her arm and said, 'Akiko!'

She slid down in the bed until her head was level with his. He was hot, very hot.

She said, 'Who is Akiko, Berry?'

It was as if he had heard a gunshot. His body stiffened against hers; he rolled onto her fiercely, his arms spread-eagled as if to protect her. She thought he would stifle her.

'Berry! Let me go – darling – please— '

For a terrifying moment, the pressure of him increased; he pulled his right arm around and put his hand over her mouth; his good knee pressed into her groin agonizingly. And then the pain in his stump must have become unbearable. With a grunt of surrender he relaxed his hold on her and his body seemed to crumple and fall away from hers. Terrified she propped herself up and looked at him.

'Berry – my God – say something!'

He lay, his eyes rolled up, his breathing shallow and fast. She scrambled over him and reached for the phone. Dr Harris answered after the second ring.

'Has she taken a turn for the worse?' he said when Jannie announced herself. 'Not Mrs Murchison? Tell me the symptoms.'

Jannie looked at Berry, flat on his back on the tumbled bed. The pathos of his disabled body suddenly overwhelmed her so that she could barely speak. The doctor interrupted her stammered words.

'I'll be with you in about twenty minutes. Can you keep sponging him with tepid water? If he comes round try and get him to drink.'

Jannie ran for water, then tore down the stairs to open the outside door. When she returned Berry had moved. He was on his side and his eyes seemed to be focusing somewhere towards his invisible canvas.

She knelt by the bed and began sponging him with a wrung-out face flannel. He did not speak but he smiled slightly. She leaned forward and kissed his mouth.

'You're going to be all right, my darling,' she whispered.

He moved his head as if in assent. She squeezed the flannel again and mopped his face gently. She thought he must have had a stroke. Suddenly the future – which had not existed for three days – was there, pressing on them. She sobbed.

Immediately he said very clearly, 'Don't be frightened. I am all right.'

'Oh, Berry – thank God. What can I do? The doctor is on his way.'

He smiled again. 'Well . . . would you prop the canvas so that I can see it? And then I think you had better switch on the lights and perhaps find a dressing-gown somewhere?'

She sobbed again but this time with laughter.

'Oh, Berry . . .' She darted around the room. 'I'd better tidy the bed too. Although you hardly look respectable . . .' she paused and looked at him. It was like a farewell. 'Oh, Berry . . .' was all she said.

He whispered, 'You said it was the last time, Jannie. You must have known somehow.'

She knelt again and began to sponge him.

'I knew you were tired to the bone. I did not know you were going to be ill.'

They heard the doctor come in and call to them. Jannie started up, but he moved at last and caught her hand.

'Did I hurt you?'

'Of course not. It wouldn't have mattered if you had.'

His dark eyes were as she had always thought of them; impenetrable. He said, 'That is exactly what Val said.'

Val was at Gallenwick when Jannie arrived. She was counting the days until the end of this third week. She refused to call Dusty anything worse than incorrigible, but found even his incorrigibility was becoming unbearable.

He had said last night, 'Doesn't Berry go in for much of the old slap and tickle then?'

She had flared back, suddenly furious with him. 'Berry gives me respect – I am not and have never been his plaything!' She had turned back to the sink where he had trapped her and added, 'Honestly, Dusty, I simply do not know how Jannie puts up with it!'

He laughed comfortably as he moved away at last. 'She loves it,' he said.

But Val refused to go along with his indifference. 'Probably because you don't offer her anything more.'

He was irritated. 'Oh for goodness' sake, Val! I expect Morrie to be pious – not you! Perhaps if the two of you relaxed a bit, you might get pregnant and stay pregnant!'

She knew he did not mean to be cruel. He had been sweetness itself to Morag when she had miscarried the last time. And of course he had no idea of Val's passionately sterile relationship with Berry. Nevertheless she flinched. He was instantly contrite.

'I say, old girl, I'm sorry. Thoughtless idiot – that's me.' He pushed his face near hers. 'Hit me. Go on – punch me on the nose. Serve me right.' She laughed helplessly and went for a towel to dry her hands. He said seriously, 'Listen, kiddo. Jan and me – we've talked about you. Only natural. And we both think that although the abbey is hopelessly unsuitable, and Berry is the most selfish devil on God's earth . . . we think you should start a family. Adopt if there's no other way. They're crying out for adoptive parents.'

Val kept her back to him, her mind whirling. Did he know about Berry? Was it not the close-kept secret she had imagined? She decided to take his suggestion at face value.

'Well . . . maybe. Though I have to admit I did not realize children could be such hard work.' She looked at him. No, he had no idea about Berry. She said suddenly, 'Do me a favour, Dusty, would you?'

'Anything, old girl.' He was like an eager puppy.

'Help her more. When she comes home. Don't take her for granted.'

He had been going to protest; she knew it. But then he said seriously, 'All right, Val. I promise.'

276

Now, threading the lanes and turning over the bridge-gate into the grounds of Gallenwick, she wondered how long his good intentions would last. She thought of his proprietorial hand on Jannie's throat and shuddered. Mrs Merrydown, visiting the girls last week, had told Val that Jannie would not carry another child and would have to be sterilized for her own safety.

Julie said, 'Is Mummy coming home today, Aunty Val?'

'No.' This was a daily routine. 'At the weekend, darling. Not long now.'

'I don't want you to go away, Aunty Val.'

'Don't say that, darling. You know I have to go back to the abbey to look after Uncle Berry and Mummy has to come home to the farm to look after you.'

'I want you both to stay at the farm. There's room for Uncle Berry too. An' I could help him with his painting. Mrs Pargeter says I'm a good little painter.'

'Listen, Julie. When you're properly four, would you like to come and stay at the abbey for a while? By yourself ? You could – perhaps – paint with Uncle Berry then.' She crossed her fingers on the steering-wheel. Berry could be lovely with the girls; he could also be unlovely.

Julie was much too excited at this prospect. She jiggled about and got her sandal caught on the gear stick so that Val was forced to warn her that such behaviour would put Uncle Berry right off.

Julie calmed down sufficiently to get out of the car, jump on the base of the flower-decked pump in the stable yard and whirl around Mrs Pargeter yelling her news at the top of her voice. Val shrugged helplessly at the older woman and waved to Julie. She drove back down the avenue of elms and wondered what she had let herself in for.

All such forebodings were swept to one side, how-ever, when she recognized her own car parked in the farmyard. It was not quite ten o'clock, much too early for a social call. Something had happened to Berry or to Jannie or to poor old Murch.

Jannie was bustling around the kitchen as if she had never been away. Dusty sat at the table, Ros on his knee, a huge smile making his face look quite moon-like. Val hung on to the doorpost and took a deep breath. She was quite certain now that Berry had thrown Jannie out.

Jannie did not run and hug her as usual. She said quite calmly, 'Val . . . my dear. I'm sorry to arrive like this – no phone call or anything. But . . . Berry didn't want you to be worried unnecessarily. And apparently this has happened before— '

'What?' Val could have choked her. She came into the kitchen and looked at her friend. 'Are you all right?' She turned to Dusty. 'Is she all right? When did she arrive?'

Jannie laughed. 'I am here, Val! You can address any questions to me!' She still made no attempt at a proper greeting. She said, 'Sit down. I'll make you some coffee. I think everything is all right – I am, thank you very much! But I have to tell you that although Berry is all right – the doctor says he is definitely all right – he was ill in the night. The doctor says it has happened before. Overwork. Tension.'

Val said flatly, 'He had a fit. Is that what you're saying?' She looked at Dusty as he exclaimed. 'Hasn't he told you?' She refused to sit down even though Jannie was pouring her coffee. Instead she hung on to the back of a chair and lowered her head. 'It's like an epileptic fit. He works and works and becomes exhausted and then . . . it happens.' She closed her eyes. 'Jannie . . . tell me. Did he attack you?'

'Not exactly.' Jannie pushed the coffee mug along the table. 'Drink this.'

Val reached for the mug but did not raise her head. 'What time did it happen?'

'I'm not sure.'

Val sat down slowly, staring at the mug of coffee all

278

the time. Somehow everything was suddenly askew. Just off-centre. Jannie, who was so inefficient, seemed to exude control. Val who had been coping with everything at the farm, had lost it. She sipped her coffee. Berry had not actually hit Jannie. And he had not hit her in the middle of the night sometime. She shivered and put her hands around the mug.

'What happens now?' she asked dully. If Jannie suggested returning to the abbey, she would know for certain exactly what had happened during the last two-and-a-half weeks.

Jannie said brightly, 'Well . . . obviously Berry will have to rest. He wants you back, Val.' She too sat down. 'He wants you back where you belong.' She laughed. 'And I think I should come back where I belong. Don't you, darling?' She reached across the table and put her hand over Dusty's. He took it almost gratefully.

'I'd almost given up on getting you back again,' he said. 'I've been doing my best to seduce Val. In case you decided to stay with Berry!'

It was Dusty's idea of a joke. Jannie played along with it.

'Did you succeed?' she asked lightly.

'Don't think so.' He put Jannie's fingers to his lips. 'She's a cold fish, Jan . . . Not like you.'

Val wanted to scream. She said, 'I'd better get back. Mrs Murchison is all very well but she gets on Berry's nerves at times.'

'Oh, I forgot to say . . . she's in bed with some gastric trouble.' Jannie's casual acceptance of all these crises was unnerving.

Val stood up immediately and made for the stairs. 'I'll pack. The baby is asleep, Jannie. Don't forget to pick Julie up.'

Jannie rolled her eyes. 'As if . . .' She made no attempt to stand but did add, 'D'you want any help?'

'No.' Val took the stairs two at a time. She wanted to get away from the farm now. She did not know whether she wanted to go home, but she did know she had to get away from the farm. And Jannie.

The weather changed as she drove back to the coast. A treacherous little wind blew up from the northwest and she had to wind up her window. The car smelled of Jannie; a faint flowery perfume which she had never noticed before. As she parked the car and went into the enormous hall, it struck her afresh. And then she saw why; the place was full of wild flowers, some of them wilting but most of them burgeoning from their vases and jamjars, spilling pollen, blossom and their amalgamated scent with a profusion that was profligate . . . brazen. Val stared in amazement as she climbed to the landing; on each step there were flowers; dog roses, shamrock, cuckoo flowers and cowslips. A tiny fishpaste jar of late violets sat demurely between a milk bottle full of cow parsley and a single glorious thistle. The flowers brought out the deep colours of the wood; the long gleaming line of banister and the lustre of the wall panelling. She came to the landing and looked along its length to the guest bedroom; everywhere there were flowers and scent. She hated it. It was unreasonable, perhaps petty of her, but she hated the flowers and their scent . . . and their intrusion.

The door of the music room was ajar and she went inside, dreading to find it decked out. It was as usual, sparsely under-furnished; great spaces of floorboards, Berry's painting table, cupboard and bookshelves, stacks of canvases. And the bed.

Berry looked at her. He was hollow-eyed as always after one of his attacks, his dark colouring somehow paler, a faint yellow tinge under his skin.

She said, 'You're only thirty-six. You're going grey.'

He said, 'Geniuses always age prematurely.'

'Geniuses' wives age even more prematurely.' She came to the bed and stared down at him. 'How are you?'

'Better. Tired, but better.'

'Yes. I can see.' She knew she should kiss him and go and make tea. But she could not. 'How did it happen?' she asked.

'I don't know. Hasn't she told you?'

'She?'

'Jannie. Murch doesn't know anything about it.'

'Jannie told me what happened. But then, I would already know that, wouldn't I? How did it happen? When? Was she with you all night?'

She looked down at him, her sky-blue eyes hard and bright. She was filled with such hatred she thought she might burst open.

He stared back for a long moment without speaking. Then he held up a hand. 'It has been a difficult time, Val. What do you want me to say?'

'I want you to tell me the truth.' Her voice was as cold as iron and as hard. She ignored his hand.

He said, 'Val. I don't think you do. I love you. I want to be with you until I die. Isn't that enough?'

She said, 'Tell me, Berry. Tell me.'

For another moment he held her eyes and kept his hand there for her. And then with a sigh, he turned away to face the wall.

She went back onto the landing and began to clear away every flower in the house.

The days passed. She disliked the fact that Jannie had coped so well; that Murch was full of her praise, that there were gooseberry pies in the fridge and everything was so clean. She hated it that Jannie had worn her clothes and washed her hair every night . . . 'Mr Reid was doing her portrait, see, and he liked it wet. Seaweed he used to call it,' Murch enthused as she gradually took the reins back into her hands.

Val said, 'I wonder she didn't catch her death of cold.'

'It is a wonder, Mrs Reid. A miracle too because if she'd been ill I think I would have died. I think she saved my life.'

Val wanted very badly to say a rude word.

Berry did not get better and Dr Harris prescribed rest and more rest.

'We've got Dr Wilkie and four of the girls coming for Whitsun,' Val said. 'Shall I cancel them?'

The doctor looked at Berry who made no comment at all. 'Yes. Yes, that is all you can do,' he said. He hesitated at the door waiting for Berry to protest and when he did not, he led Val into the kitchen.

'He certainly needs to rest, my dear.' He went to the window and gazed up at the cliff. 'But he's not ill. It's as if he's opted out for a while. No good trying to push him into any teaching just at the moment. The whole thing would be a complete fiasco.'

Val could imagine. Besides she was in no mood to deal with five extra bodies around the place. After her hectic life at the farm, she should have been finding life practically boring here. But it was as much as she could do to get through each day. And the nights were worse. She lay by Berry's side waiting for him to turn to her or even put his arm beneath her neck. He never did.

Dr Harris had turned from the window and was now looking at her.

'You could do with a rest too, Mrs Reid. Just as well if there are no visitors for a while.'

Val said unguardedly, 'I wish I could go away. See my father. Morag . . .'

Dr Harris narrowed his eyes. 'I can suggest an excellent nurse. She would live in.'

Val shook her head, smiling. 'I wasn't serious. I couldn't leave him. Not until he is better.' She made a face. 'Then he'll start work again and he won't notice whether I'm here or not!'

Dr Harris smiled. 'Quite.' He paused on his way out and put a hand on her arm. 'You do very well, my dear. Very well indeed.'

She watched him go downstairs then went back into the kitchen and made some tea so that she wouldn't cry. As far as she knew she had very little to cry about.

May went out in a series of strong breezes and showers and the first two weeks of June were warm and bright. Berry got up and went through the cellar door onto the rocks to sit in the sunshine. Val was all prepared to deny him his sketch book, but he did not ask for it. He unearthed an old panama from his wardrobe and sat for hours with it tipped over his eyes, apparently sleeping. She looked out of the window and thought he was thinner. He would no longer allow her to help him in the bath, so this was the first time she had seen him without his shirt since April when she had gone to the farm. Even from far above him she could see the shadows of his ribs. Before her heart could contract with its usual love for him, she tried to imagine life without him. Berry dead. No Berry. She felt nothing; no horror, no sense of terror. It was simply . . . unimaginable. She waited then for the tenderness to flood her. Again, nothing happened.

She slid off the window-seat and walked the length of the room. Then back again to peer out at him. She thought dully that perhaps this was the end of her strange love affair with Berry Reid. A void. Nothing.

She started to walk in earnest. Down as far as the paler square where the harpsichord had stood so long ago. Back to the window. Across to the fireplace, then to Berry's painting table, then diagonally to where half a dozen fresh canvases were stacked against the wall. She repeated the pattern again and again until she was exhausted. For the first time in her married life, she felt trapped. She suspected her husband of seducing her dear friend who was ill. But her husband was patently ill himself and needed her care more than ever. And she knew nothing of what had gone on here during the two and a half weeks they had been together. Jannie had obviously worked like a demon herself. Mrs Murchison had nothing but praise for her. Perhaps . . . perhaps these dreadful, soul-destroying suspicions were wrong. And if they weren't, what could she do? She could not leave him: she could never leave him. She was . . . trapped.

She walked another circuit of the music room and paused by the stack of paintings. Berry did not like her looking at his work without him. He liked to point out various techniques. 'See what I'm getting at here? The shape of the rocks coming through the sea . . .' He painted the sea always. A still life would be set before a window and the sea was there. There were seascapes by the dozen. She knew he was frightened of the sea; he thought by painting it he could control that fear.

She lifted the top canvas away from the others and peered down at it. A nude figure . . . lying on rocks . . . surrounded, almost engulfed, by water.

She knew immediately it was Jannie and that Berry had leaned from the music room window to get the first sketches. She looked at the next painting and the next. They were all of Jannie. There was a conventional portrait of her lying in front of the fireplace, her hair wet and in rats' tails around her face. There was a strange ghostly figure, half-woman half-water, covered in seaweed, very pantheistic. She began to lift out the pictures and range them along the skirting boards. There were eleven. All modelled by Jannie. She fetched Berry's chair and sat on it to stare at them. After half an hour she stood up, replaced the chair and the pictures and went into the kitchen to start supper.

There was nothing she could do. He was ill and he needed her. She began to cry as she washed the lettuce. Then cursed herself for a fool. Her relationship with Berry was different; special. It did not rely on their love-making; it certainly did not – could not – rely on any family. She had wanted to devote her life to him; and that was what she was doing. She had long ago accepted that there was a part of Berry's life she could not share; it did not matter because no-one else shared it either. But now she wondered. She could not

284

share what he had had with Jannie. Whatever it was it had resulted in those paintings. Wonderful paintings. Had he been able to tell Jannie about his experiences in Singapore?

She arranged a bunch of shallots in a glass bowl. The sharp smell of them made her weep again. She said angrily, 'Your nose has been put out of joint, Vallery McKinley! Just because he's never painted you! But then . . . look at you! Short and dumpy and the typical matron! Who would want to paint you!'

And she put the kettle on for tea.

Somehow they established another sort of relationship. She moved into the guest room that night, but she helped him in the bath, she padded his stump when it became raw, she talked to him almost naturally about books and television programmes. Eric had brought them down a brand new television set on his last visit, and unexpectedly Berry was addicted. He asked if supper could be earlier so that he could settle down in time for Cliff Michelmore; he thought it was absurd that everything closed down on Sunday evenings to give people time for church. When a letter arrived from one of the programme controllers suggesting an interview, he was as thrilled as a schoolboy. It helped their domestic relationship enormously. Val thought that by the time the interview had been done, they would be almost back on their old footing. She had started to kiss him goodnight and he hung on to her sometimes. On the second of July he took his sketch book with him when he sat outside. It was the first time he had done any work since his illness. While Murch was washing up that evening, she joined him in front of the television.

'Shall I move back into this bed tonight?' she asked with her old directness.

He looked up at her, his face suddenly young again. 'Yes, please,' was all he said, but he reached for her hand. And that night she made love to him as she had always done. She knew it worked; it worked for both of them.

The next day he painted properly, sitting at his table, cleaning his brushes, mixing the kind of colours he loved, glancing at the sketch he had done the day before, laying the paint on thickly in a pointillistic style. She left him to Murch's tender care and took the car into Barnstaple for groceries. She still could not bring herself to call at the farm on the way home; it was almost seven weeks since she had seen Jannie.

But as she began to negotiate the cliff track down to the sea, she saw there was no postponing their meeting any longer. Jannie's car was outside the hooded door of the abbey; she was just getting out.

Even at this distance, Val knew something was wrong. She felt a definite pang followed by a dull sense of dread as she took the bends as fast as she dared and pulled up behind Jannie's car. She took the stairs to the landing two at a time; the door of the music room was open, she stood just inside. They knew she was there; Berry threw her an anguished glance, Jannie turned completely, her wide-open face clouding for a moment.

'Oh, Val, I'm sorry. It will be awful for you, I know that. But there can't be much left between you and Berry and I know you'll understand. You always understood, Val. Next to Berry I love you more than anyone in the world. It was as if . . .' She turned back to Berry and her face was illumined again. 'It was as if you were giving me Berry! I saw that . . . as soon as I got home I realized that was what you had done.'

Berry said hoarsely, 'Shut up, Jannie! Just shut up and go home! We don't want you here!'

'Of course you've got to say that, my darling. But Val sent me to you. Have you forgotten? She insisted . . .' Again she turned, staring at Val beseechingly. 'Tell him, Val. Tell him how you had to bully me into coming. You wanted this to happen. Didn't you?'

Val moved her lips somehow. 'What? What did I want to happen?'

Berry shouted now. 'Jannie! I've told you! It was madness – you are mad! Val and I are together. Completely. Can't you grasp that?'

Jannie said swiftly, 'You haven't told her. Val . . . I shall have to tell you— '

Val said very levelly, 'I know. I've seen the pictures. I know.'

Jannie stared. 'And you're staying with him? When you know he loves me with all his soul and body?'

Val looked at Berry. Besides Jannie's radiance he looked terrible. He looked old.

She said slowly, 'I think . . . really . . . I think it's up to Berry. Don't you?'

Jannie was suddenly wild. She looked from one to the other with a kind of desperation.

'No. I don't think so. I think it is up to me. I have left my husband and children to come to Berry. Not only because I adore him and he adores me. But because I am carrying his child.' She spread her hands dramatically across her abdomen. 'I am giving him something you cannot, Val. Or will not.' She registered Val's expression and became defiant. 'I know that's cruel. But it has to be said.'

There was a silence in the room. Val waited for Berry to speak; to tell Jannie how completely wrong she was. When he said nothing, it seemed the worst betrayal of all. She counted ten inside her head. Then she turned and left.

CHAPTER NINETEEN

Hugh insisted that Morag should accept Matthew Arnold's offer of a place on his course.

'Listen, darling. It's no good you marking time like this, waiting to have a baby. You know yourself that's not the way to live your life. You've always been interested in the psychological side of your work. You know this chap – you liked his teaching when you were at Birmingham before . . .'

Morag nodded, smiling, knowing that although he was absolutely right she still wanted to snap his head off. Perhaps that was the root cause of her discontent . . . no, hardly discontent . . . lack of content. Because Hugh was so good, so kind, so understanding, she had nothing to come up against. No arguments, always discussions. It was surely something to be deeply thankful for.

She said, 'I know, I know. What you're really saying is that perhaps I'm never going to be able to carry a baby full term, so I might as well get on with my life— '

'I am not saying that, Morrie, and you know it.' But his voice was not angry; not even hurt, just . . . reasonable. 'I am saying that as a mother as well as a doctor, it would be good to have as much understanding of human nature as you can grasp. And this is the perfect opportunity.'

She was almost contrite. 'Darling, of course. I'm being pig-headed again. There are absolutely no obstacles to me disappearing for a couple of months, are there? I can arrange for someone to cover my clinics, I can give up my locum stuff. Between them Eric and Mrs Knapp run the house . . .' She had been going to add that she was redundant, but looking at Hugh's increasingly quizzical expression, she was forced to stop and smile. 'All right. I'll go.'

'And I shall miss you,' Hugh said.

'And I shall miss you too.'

But going up on the train she had to admit to a sudden sense of freedom. She watched the telephone wires dipping and rising outside the window of her compartment and wondered just what was happening to her. She had read somewhere that when a relationship stagnated, it died. Was it possible that the sheer security of her relationship with Hugh was also stagnation? And did Hugh know that too, and that was why he was practically packing her off? Or did he simply need a break? And was that all it was for her too?

She changed trains at Worcester so that she could catch the stopper up through the Lickeys. She was getting off at Selly Oak and staying with Jessica in the big doctor's house overlooking the canal. She had been once before and Jessica had brought her children to Clevedon. They could not keep in close touch; there were too many other things happening in both their lives. But their friendship was easygoing because of the distance. In some ways Morag was more pleased to be seeing Jessica than she would have been to see Jannie or Val.

The train stopped at Bromsgrove for the bank engine to be coupled, and they were shunted up the Lickey bank to Barnt Green. She remembered when she and Hugh had had a meal here just after she had qualified. It was changing; several new estates clustered behind the trees but the expanse of the golf course could not change. She stood up and put her head out of the window. The Lickey air was supposed to be a tonic.

It was good to see Jessica again. She had not lost her harum-scarum look. She erupted from the surgery as Morag came in through the open front door, her white coat open, her stethoscope swinging around her neck. Her hair was cut neatly into her neck in the latest style but the front frizzed upwards uncontrollably and though the blouse and skirt beneath the white coat were both simple and smart, they were both slightly askew.

'Don't go into the waiting room, Mo!' she begged as she hugged her greetings. 'You'll be just appalled at the queue! I can't seem to keep it down!'

'That's because they all want to see you,' Morag said. 'I told you that's how it would be.'

'Yes. That's all very well . . .' Jessica leapt down the hall and opened a door marked private. 'Come on into the den. Shirley's around somewhere catching up on homework. She'll make you a coffee and show you your room and I might be through by then.'

Morag went through to the living quarters and found Jessica's eldest, now eighteen and taking A levels at any minute, up to her eyes in textbooks. There was a break while they talked and drank coffee and Shirley said how impossible life was if you had any conscience at all, and Morag suggested that the Clevedon air might suit her during the summer holidays.

'Could I bring a friend, Aunty Mo?' Shirley bargained.

'Male?' Morag asked.

'I think so. He wears trousers.'

'I don't see why not.' Morag was laughing. 'I'll consult with the doctor, if you don't mind.'

So began a very happy six weeks. It was good to work with Matthew Arnold again. They visited psychiatric wards; she watched – with horror – as patients underwent electric shock treatment. Nobody could explain its good effects; nobody suggested there might be bad ones. She was amazed and excited by the experimental approach to psychiatry. Drugs, counselling, confrontational therapy, group therapy, drama therapy, art therapy. There seemed no end to the possibilities.

Matthew came to supper one night with the Whites.

'Basically,' he said seriously as Jessica argued fiercely for a patient's right to privacy, 'it is vital to both respect that privacy, and to share it. A person displaying a great many physical symptoms can be deeply troubled by an experience almost entirely forgotten. Deliberately forgotten. When this is admitted, brought out, looked at, it often happens that he or she can now bear it . . . deal with it. The symptoms disappear, often immediately. Time has made it bearable.'

Jessica remained unconvinced. Morag nodded. She had found herself thinking of Berry again. As far as she knew, he had never spoken to Val as Hugh spoke to her.

Jessica went into the kitchen to make coffee and Matthew turned to Morag.

'You can understand what I mean because of your personal repressions, Morag. I think Jessica is far more . . . what the Americans call upfront. She cannot conceive of a past unhappiness gnawing away at her physical health.'

Morag raised her brows. 'My repressions?'

He smiled. 'You see? A classic case. You do not realize you are suppressing events that have hurt you. Cocooning them in forgetfulness.'

She stared at him. She could hear Jessica in the kitchen. She said in a low voice, 'How do you know?'

He was surprised. 'Well, of course, your original application form. Parents, both dead. I take it during the blitz?' He smiled. 'You never ever mention your parents, Morag. Don't you realize that?' She was relieved that he had not – somehow – guessed about Berry, but startled at what he had said. 'No . . . I did not realize that.' Jessica came in and poured coffee. Morag said, 'Hugh – my husband – never knew them.' She looked at Jessica. 'My parents. They were killed during the blitz on Bristol. He never knew them.'

Jessica said comfortably, 'You've shown him snaps, I expect.'

Morag swallowed. 'Everything was destroyed. Every-thing.'

Jessica glanced from one to another. She said rallyingly, 'Well then, you've talked about them . . .' Her voice died. She coughed and said, 'Is this a consultation I'm interrupting?'

Matthew laughed easily. 'Of course not. Just showing Morag an example of repression.' He changed the subject. 'You remember Howard Greenaway? He was older than the rest of you – a doctor doing a postgrad course.' Morag said nothing so Jessica nodded vigorously. Matthew said, 'He's quite famous now. Works on post-war traumatization. He's done a couple of excellent papers.'

Morag looked up at that. She frowned slightly. 'You mean he was very interested in shell-shock?' Her frown deepened. 'Do you know about Berry too?' she asked.

'Berry?'

Her eyes suddenly crinkled into laughter. 'Sorry. My brother-in-law. He was a prisoner of war in Singapore. With my husband and another member of the family. When you spoke about post-war traumatization I thought . . . Sorry! I'm showing signs of neurosis! You see, it doesn't always do to unearth the past!'

Matthew smiled too and agreed wryly. 'That is what is so difficult about analysis. How far to go.'

They talked a little longer, then Matthew said, 'I am hoping to be able to take a few of you into my course on criminology. It will mean another six weeks away from home. How would you feel about that, Morag?'

She asked him for more information and he explained about his research into criminal tendencies and possible rehabilitation techniques.

She said, 'I'm not sure. It's really out of the field of general practice.'

'Not a bit of it. If these tendencies can be diagnosed early enough, something might be done.'

Jessica said, 'And we could have another six weeks together, Mo. It'll go into the school hols. We could have picnics and things.'

'I'll see.'

But it was during the next week, the second Wednesday

of July when she was thinking in a desultory way about a fourth birthday present for Julie, that she had the telephone call from Hugh to say that Val had arrived at Redley Lodge to be with her father.

Morag had just come in from the university; it was hot and oppressive, thunder on the way. She scooped her heavy knot of hair from the nape of her neck to let the air dry the sweat.

'Is Eric ill?' she asked, her heart in her mouth. She had long given up protesting that they should get a home of their own. Eric was indeed like a father to both she and Hugh.

'No. But he could do with some help. I know you want to complete the course – but I knew you would want to know what was happening.'

He paused and she prompted him. 'Go on.' She was filled with sudden foreboding.

Hugh sounded tired. 'Mo . . . I'm so sorry. Val has left Berry. Eric can't cope and neither can I. She needs you.'

Morag clutched the receiver with all her strength as she stammered incredulous rhetorical questions. 'And what about Berry?' she concluded. 'Who is looking after Berry?'

He answered the last question only. 'Darling . . . apparently Jannie has moved in. That is what this is all about. Jannie has left Dusty and gone to live with Berry.'

Morag felt as if she was bleeding. Some kind of strength seeped from her body.

After a moment, she said, 'I'd better come home now I think.'

Hugh's voice lifted with relief. 'There's a train at six. From New Street. Can you make it? I'll meet you at Temple Meads. It gets in just before eight.' He paused then said, 'Darling, if you could just stay a few days . . . you could go back. That other course you were telling me about . . . I think you should do it.'

'Do you?' She could not think about that now. If he wanted her gone for the whole summer, she would think about it later. She closed her eyes just as Shirley came bouncing in from the garden. 'I did OK in English Lit., Aunty Mo!' The young voice was so normal. It could have been Val of fifteen years ago when they'd all matriculated.

Morag said, 'I'll be on that six o'clock, Hugh.'

She replaced the receiver and turned to tell Shirley that she was going home.

When she saw Val, waiting for her in the porch of her old home, her heart contracted. She recalled, as she had not recalled for years, her own mother's voice telling her that she could make things better or worse for Jannie and Val. 'That is the sort of strength you have,' she had said, sitting behind the teapot and the toast rack. It was the thought of her mother that was Morag's undoing. She went to Val who was dry-eyed, self-contained, put her arms around her and wept.

Val and Eric were horrified. 'Darling, I'm so sorry – what am I doing to you?' Val drew her friend into the familiar sitting room, unaltered since Margaret's death. 'Hugh . . . perhaps a drop of whiskey.'

Hugh was strangely unmoved. 'She's tired out. The course . . . these things are never easy. Anyway whiskey doesn't suit her.'

Eric said, 'It's gone cold since the rain started. We should have lit the fire.'

Morag said, 'I'm really hot. I'm just so sorry. It was seeing Val.'

The two of them fussed around her as if she had just suffered Val's terrible loss. Only Hugh seemed to realize the irony of the situation. He brought in some supper on a trolley: watercress sandwiches and iced tea.

'Enjoy this together – just the two of you,' he advised. 'Eric, let's leave them. Come and have a drink at the New Inn.'

So the girls were alone with nothing to do but talk and eat. For a long time they did neither. Morag had had a long time to think on the train, and she knew she was feeling as much betrayed as Val. And by Jannie of all people.

She said at last, 'Val . . . you'll have to tell me what happened. I've only had the bare facts from Hugh. I simply cannot believe that Jannie . . . that Berry would succumb . . . I mean, Jannie is so obvious!'

'Yes.' Val sighed and picked up her glass of tea. She said, 'I thought she was going to die, stuck on the farm with Dusty and the girls and no help whatsoever . . . she can't weigh much more than seven stone. And her confidence had gone . . . nil. It was awful. I had to do something.'

She began to talk about the last two and a half months. Quietly, unemphatically, she described her time on the farm; even Dusty's 'incorrigibility'. Then she mentioned the visit Berry and Jannie paid and how she insisted that Berry should keep her the full three weeks.

'Apparently Dusty could hardly wait to get her to himself. On the bank at Gallenwick . . . I think that hurt her more than anything. Yet . . . yet she wanted it – needed it – as much as Dusty did. I think she hated herself so much she almost killed them . . . Berry and herself . . . in the car.' Val choked slightly as she sipped. 'It was almost funny. Berry was outraged. Furious with me. Blaming me for risking his life with her.' She glanced up at Morag. 'Perhaps I was to blame, Morrie. I don't know. I never thought . . . for one moment . . .' She sipped again and spoke in a new hard voice. 'I knew of course when I got home. All those blasted flowers . . . and Berry as ill as he could be. He'd had one of his fits. Tiredness. Or guilt. I don't know what it was. But we worked through it, Mo. We were getting it together again in our own peculiar way, when she arrived. Said she was having his baby.' She paused as Morag let out a low cry. 'Exactly. Didn't leave me in much doubt about what had happened, did it? What would you have done, Mo?'

'I don't know . . . I don't know . . .' Morag pressed her hands together. 'What will they do? What on earth will they do? She can't stay with him, Val! She's got three daughters— '

'She doesn't care about them any more. Only the wonderful child of this wonderful union which was obviously made in heaven, so how can I possibly understand— '

Morag pushed the trolley away and gathered Val to her.

'Don't think about it, darling. Push it to the back of your mind. After a while you will forget it ever happened. You might be able to forgive Jannie . . .'

Val spoke into Morag's hair which had escaped its knot and was cascading in black tails down her back.

'Morrie, you don't understand. Jannie has betrayed me . . . yes. But she was ill – she still is ill. I think she might need help from one of your psychiatrists, my dear. It's Berry . . . it's Berry's betrayal I can't stand.'

'But – you said yourself – she's acting crazily. What could he do if she – you know – threw herself at him?'

'Morag.' Val's voice was very quiet. 'I promised him I would never tell a soul . . . but now I am going to tell you. Berry cannot have children. There was an infection . . . something happened at the POW camp in Singapore.'

She waited. Both girls became still. Morag breathed, 'Oh my God . . .'

Val said steadily, 'You see now? All he had to do was to tell Jannie the truth. But he did not.'

Morag whispered again, 'Oh my God.'

Val gave her friend a quick peck as she released herself and moved back to her own chair.

'There. Now I too have done my bit of betraying.' She smiled brightly. 'It hasn't made me feel any better at all. But at least someone else in the wide world knows about it.'

Morag said, 'You knew this when you married him?'

'Of course. He told me. But you see, darling, I thought

that meant he could not actually make love to me. And that suited me very well because . . . well, I thought I was peculiar in that way.' She managed a laugh. 'It wasn't like that. And I got a booklet from the rehab. unit on how to help disabled people to enjoy a full sex life. Oh, I was determined to do the whole job properly!' Her laugh soured. 'What a naïve fool I was!'

Morag said quickly, 'No. Never think that, Val. Whatever you have done for Berry has been right. You know that in your heart.' She leaned forward. 'Listen. Jannie will go home. Berry will want her to and he will tell her the truth. Or if not, he will still want her to, and Dusty will arrive . . . she will go back.'

'I don't doubt it. Berry can't stand that kind of responsibility.'

'Well then . . .'

'And I return? Everything swept under the carpet? Everything hunky-dory again?' Val shook her head gently. 'I don't think so, Mo. Do you?'

'Not quite like that. No. You make it sound pat. But you'll work at it, Val. You said yourself you were beginning to get everything back again when Jannie turned up. You can do it. You know you can.'

Val let out a gigantic sigh. 'Maybe I can. The thing is, do I want to? I'm not sure.' She picked up a watercress sandwich. 'It hasn't affected my appetite anyway.' She grinned. 'Daddy has suggested that I go to work with Hugh. What do you think about that? He reckons I picked up quite a lot when I was in the office back in the forties. He says I could take on the selling and buying of houses and let Hugh concentrate on the antiques.' She chewed stolidly, looking suddenly lost. 'I suppose it's better than hanging around here.'

Morag said, 'I suppose it is.' She stared at the sandwiches and decided against them. 'I'm supposed to be cheering you up. I don't know what to say or do, Val.'

'You don't have to say anything about Berry or Jannie!

Tell me about your course. And tomorrow we'll go and play tennis. And perhaps at the weekend we could have a long walk.'

'Yes. All right.'

They spent a week forcing themselves to exercise, do housework, behave 'normally'. By the following Wednesday, they were exhausted. Hugh suggested they should come with him the next day to assess some silverware in one of the pocket castles along the River Wye. Morag looked at him, recognizing his kindness, grateful for it, yet unmoved at the same time. He smiled at her.

'It's OK, Mo, you don't have to come. But I think you should, Val. You could take some notes for me, get the feel of everything again.' He put a hand on her shoulder. 'When you're working you simply do not have time to think of anything else.'

Morag said suddenly, 'My father said that.'

Both Hugh and Val looked round at her, surprised. Val said, 'You hardly ever mention your father.'

'No. I've been thinking about him lately.'

Hugh said slowly, 'Come with us then. I'll drop you off in Bristol. You could go into the infirmary and look up some of his old colleagues.'

But Morag shook her head. 'No. I can't do that. Not yet.'

She wanted to be by herself. She wanted the house to herself too and it was a relief when Eric made for the golf course and Mrs Knapp announced she was visiting her sister. 'I expect you'll be all right, Mrs Reid? Deckchair on the lawn?'

'Sounds good,' Morag agreed. But she waited in the hall until it was quiet enough to hear the house creak around her, then she drew up a chair to the telephone and dialled the number of the abbey.

She expected Mrs Murchison to answer and it was at once a relief and a shock to hear Berry's familiar voice.

'Hello. Is that you, Dusty?'

She drew a deep breath. 'No. It's Morag. I'm calling from Redley Lodge.'

'Morag?' Berry's voice sharpened with anxiety. 'Is it Val? Is she all right? What has happened?'

'Nothing. She and Hugh have gone to look at some silver. It seemed an ideal opportunity to talk to you.'

'Oh God. Listen, if you're going to tell me what a fool I am, go ahead. But why hasn't she phoned? If it hadn't been that Hugh kept in touch, I wouldn't know where she was.'

So Hugh had kept in touch, had he?

Morag said, 'She is doubtless waiting for you to phone her, Berry.'

'It wouldn't do any good. I'm in a mess and I know it. At least I know it.' He paused. 'Mo . . . if I could see you, I think . . . I think it might help.'

'Help? You? Or Val?'

'Mo, don't go all frosty on me. You always understood. Don't start pretending you don't know what I'm talking about, either. Mo, listen. Can you come down? Please?'

She said, 'Don't be ridiculous. If you think I'm going to help you with Jannie— '

'She's gone. Dusty came and fetched her . . . I rang him every hour . . . Murch has gone too. She thought it was all too disgusting for words. She was right of course. Mo . . . please come down. I want to paint you.'

'You want to . . . what?'

'Paint you. It's the only way I can . . . lay you to rest. I think I'm going mad, Morrie. You could save me.'

'Oh . . . rubbish!'

'I think this place is haunted. That sister of Doc Willie's. I thought Jannie was going to follow her example . . . Mo, please come down.'

She replaced the receiver and sat staring at it until it rang. When she picked it up his voice kept repeating, 'Please come down' and she replaced it without speaking.

It was almost too easy to hoodwink all of them. She telephoned Jessica and warned her that if any phone calls came through she was to say that Mo was too busy to come to the phone. Jessica asked no questions; after a brief and startled pause, she said, 'Yes. All right. Will you tell me about it later?'

Morag said, 'Yes.'

She looked up the trains from Clevedon into Bristol and then began her note to Hugh and Val. After several abortive attempts it read very simply. 'Darlings, bit of an SOS from Jessica, so I'm catching the midday train into Bristol and the one-fifteen to Birmingham. Will phone tonight.' She tore up the note that said how sorry she was; there was absolutely no need to apologize. She signed it and left it by the telephone then ran upstairs to pack.

The local train was empty at midday. She changed at Yatton and caught a stopper into Bristol. There was an express calling at Exeter which left Bristol at twelve-forty-five and she caught it by the skin of her teeth. At Exeter she waited for an hour for the Barnstaple train so she went into a phone box and telephoned the garage outside Barnstaple station to see if she could hire a car. It was waiting for her when she arrived. The garage owner showed her proudly around the controls, put her case into the boot. He said suddenly and unexpectedly, 'I remember when you all arrived here in 1941. Snowing it were. We had to get a plough to clear the road for you to Gallenwick.'

She stared at the man, amazed.

'I'm afraid I don't really remember . . .'

'I was the station master then, m'dear. I retired last year and bought this garage so that I could keep an eye on the station.' He grinned. 'I see you still got that Bluebell label on your case. I'll never forget all them Bluebells arriving that snowy day.'

Morag settled herself behind the wheel. 'Neither will I,' she said.

She drove carefully, trying to avoid the potholes,

feeling as if she were quite literally driving back into her own past. Once the road opened out slightly, she took a hand from the wheel and unpinned her hair letting it stream out in the wind. As she passed Gallenwick and the turning for Reid's farm, her own deception almost overwhelmed her. She braked, half thinking she would turn back. But then, she took her foot off the brake and continued towards the coast. She stopped thinking, 'What am I doing?' And began to think, 'What have I done?'

And then, quite suddenly she was at the top of the cliff path, beginning the hair-raising descent to the abbey. And as she negotiated the last bend, Berry emerged from the porch and stood waiting for her. She pulled up and switched off the engine and in the sudden silence he walked around to her door.

'I knew you would come,' he said simply. And opened the door for her. She got out of the car and stood, the door between them, looking into his dark eyes.

'I shouldn't be here. I've told a lie.'

He said grimly, 'We've all told lies, Morrie. Perhaps you've been living a lie for a very long time.'

He did not attempt to touch her and after a moment she went to the boot and got her case. And then he led her into the abbey. She had never been inside. She followed him up the stairs, interested to see that the flowers Val had described so bitterly were back again, all of them dead or dying, shedding pods and seeds everywhere. They gave the place a deserted, derelict look that was chilling.

She followed Berry along the landing, noting his emphatic limp, realizing with her doctor's objectivity that it meant he was in pain.

She did not know how, but she was absolutely certain that she could help him. And what was more, he could help her.

CHAPTER TWENTY

Hugh dictated the list slowly, checking each hallmark, sharing with Val the discoveries, never explaining, never condescending.

'Just look at this creamer!' He held it towards her. 'Go on, handle it. Feel the solidity of it, look at that spiralled fluting. The Georgians knew how to make an object substantial without undue weight. About combining exquisite workmanship and – and practicality!'

Val put down her notebook and held the creamer gingerly. She said, 'I thought I was going to be doing the house sales. Daddy said they were on the increase since the war.'

Hugh turned to the teaset and ran his finger lightly over the teapot.

'Eric and I . . . we wondered whether Morag might feel able to telephone Berry and Jannie . . . if she were in the house on her own.'

'What?' Val put down the creamer and stared at Hugh. 'You've been discussing this behind my back! Don't you think it would have been . . . good manners at the very least . . . to tell me what you had planned?'

Hugh smiled wryly. 'Planned. That makes it sound easy, doesn't it? We haven't planned anything, Val. Except to make sure we did this trip on Mrs Knapp's day off. We have not discussed it with Morag at all. She was invited to come with us today if you remember. But she decided against it.'

He stopped smiling and picked up the teapot to look at its underside. 'Whether Morag will use that time to phone the abbey, we simply do not know.'

Val watched him while he read out the hallmark. He

glanced at her, saw she was going to do nothing about it, picked up her notebook and wrote it down himself. Val's eyes were enormous and she did not look pleased.

She said at last, 'All right. I accept all that . . . for the moment. I know that you and Daddy aren't devious, like Berry.' She forced a little laugh, then said, 'But why Morag? You could have spoken to Berry. You are his brother after all.'

He checked her notes carefully, then took her arm and led her into the next room.

'Morag is a doctor, Val. And she is very interested in the psychological side of health. You know yourself, she believes a healthy body is dependent upon a healthy mind. And Jannie is . . . well, you know Jannie best of course, but you cannot talk to her any more. Perhaps Morag can.'

'And Morag has no idea that you and Daddy were making an opportunity for her to . . . still sounds rather hole and corner to me.'

He looked suddenly very tired. 'That is up to her, don't you think?' He glanced around the room. 'Nothing here of much interest, Val. Shall we go and have some lunch?'

She glanced at her watch; it was twenty to one.

'We could be home by two if we left now.' She looked at him. 'But then, you don't want to be home early, do you? It might not give Morag the opportunity she needs.'

'Val, you are imagining secret machinations— '

'I don't know what to think.' She strode through the mediaeval hall into the July sunshine. 'After Jannie . . . I can smell rats everywhere.'

They stood beneath the disused drawbridge and looked across the valley. The house was on the borderline between Gloucestershire and Wales; it looked over the River Wye; a miniature fortress guarding the Marches.

Hugh said, 'Makes you feel fairly insignificant, doesn't

it? Everything that has happened here . . . and we are still fretting and fuming.'

She shivered. 'Hugh . . . I know you are trying to help me. And I thank you. I suppose . . . I want Berry to be happy. And if that means living with Jannie, then . . .'

'He won't live with Jannie,' Hugh said quietly. 'There might have been a time – a few days – when she pulled him into her crazy world and they were both suspended together for a time. But that is all. Berry is enchanted by certain women. Jannie was one of them.' He smiled at her. 'Your Doc Willie is another.'

She smiled back and after a while nodded. 'I think I understand that. Doc Willie . . . yes. So perhaps Jannie too . . . are you saying that he will want me back?'

Hugh led her to the car and handed her in. She was so unused to this kind of attention; to someone else looking after her. It was quite wonderful.

He said, 'That is – perhaps – what Morag will discover.'

When they got back and found Morag's note, Val was all at sea again. She did not know who or what to believe any more. It was a ghastly feeling.

Hugh was very quiet. It was obvious the note was a shock. He showed it to Eric when he came in and Eric put his arm around his daughter and held her tightly to his side.

'Morag hasn't worked anything out, darling. She is acting intuitively. She is waiting to see what she will find when she gets to the abbey.'

'So you're sure she's gone there?' Val could not understand his acceptance of Morag's dreadful deception.

'Well . . . no, of course we're not sure.' Eric spoke almost indulgently as if this were a game. 'But we know Morag is interested in Berry's case. Prisoner of war trauma she calls it. And she knows that Jannie is messing everything up hopelessly. So . . .'

Val repeated, 'Berry's case. Berry is a case to Morag,

is he? Jannie too. My Lord. My dear Lord.' She moved away from her father's arm and sat in her mother's armchair next to the fireplace. 'He is my husband and Morag's case.' She gave a hard little laugh. 'I don't like this. I hate this.' She looked at Hugh. 'If she does ring tonight, I want to speak to her, Hugh. I want to know exactly what is happening.'

'All right.' He sat by her. 'Val. Be fair on Morrie. Perhaps she really has gone to Jessica's again. And as for Berry being her "case" . . . surely you have always treated Berry as someone to be cared for? You married him to look after him— '

'This is interference!' She looked at him; he was less than six inches from her. His eyes were grey. He was very like Leslie Howard. Suddenly, without any warning at all, she wanted quite desperately to lay her head on his shoulder and admit that she was tired to the bone and needed looking after herself.

She deliberately whipped up her anger. 'It's – it's an invasion! First Jannie – now Morrie!' She saw his expression change and said hurriedly, 'Not that I think Morrie . . . It's just that, why didn't she discuss it with me? Ask my opinion? Make the suggestion – openly – that she should go down and – and— ' she spluttered a laugh, 'and give him a consultation!'

'Oh, Val . . .' Hugh sounded tired again. 'You know Morrie better than that. When does she ever discuss things, explain her feelings . . .'

Val felt as if she were on the brink of some discovery. She thought at first it might be about Morrie. And then Hugh smiled apologetically and she knew it was not only about Morrie. Hugh was telling her something about himself as well. And his marriage.

Her father said, 'Mrs Knapp's left some salad in the fridge and there's cold chicken from yesterday. Shall we have supper early?'

'Yes. All right. I'll do it.' Val began to stand up

automatically but Eric said, 'No. Stay where you are, my dear. I'll do it.'

As she relapsed into the chair again, the phone began to ring. He picked it up on his way to the kitchen, listened, said something like, 'All right. Yes, I'll tell them when they get back.' Then he replaced the receiver and reappeared in the doorway.

'She's all right. And she is at the abbey.' He spoke matter-of-factly, entirely without emotion.

It was Hugh who said, 'Did she tell you that?'

Eric hesitated then said, 'No. But I could hear the gulls. I take it there are not many seagulls in Birmingham?'

Val said, 'I wanted to talk to her . . . what the hell is happening?' But she spoke without her former conviction and her father did not reply. He closed the door carefully behind him and they heard him moving about in the kitchen.

Hugh said slowly, 'So . . . I hoped, very much, that she had gone to Jessica's.'

Val did not voice her surprise. She looked into his grey eyes. 'Do you think . . . oh my dear Lord . . . is she in love with Berry?'

Hugh did not look away from her and after a while she asked, 'Is he in love with her?'

He took a breath. 'I don't know. What is being in love . . . what does that mean, Val? Is it not more important to love than to be in love? Love can grow and grow but can a person stay in love? There was . . . an explosion of feeling between them. A long time ago. But explosions do not last.'

Val could not look away from him. She said very steadily, 'When did the explosion happen?'

'In the war. Before Berry joined our minesweeper.'

Val looked back into the past. 'After her parents were killed . . . yes.' Then she whispered almost to herself, 'I have lost Jannie and now Mo.'

Hugh held her against his shoulder and she wept at

last. Both of them realized that she said nothing at all about losing Berry.

After the first hurdle of Morag's arrival had been negotiated, a strangely anticlimactic time followed. Berry made no more mention then of painting her portrait; he showed her the kitchen, the guest room and the music room – 'This is where I sweat it out,' – with the same objectivity as a house agent. There was none of the old provocative aggression in his manner; in fact there was barely any hint that he knew her. If he hadn't greeted her with those words, 'I knew you would come,' she would have wondered whether she was welcome. He was very definite that for a while they must live their own lives. 'Explore everything,' he said briefly.

'Take your time. There's food in the fridge. I want you to feel free. I want you to feel this place around you . . . comfortably around you.'

She took over the guest room, living out of her suitcase, spending most of the day in the kitchen or walking the coast path or cleaning the unused rooms at the top of the house. Every evening she rang Redley Lodge, making no mention of her whereabouts, as if such prevarication made the implicit lie slightly less horrible. She had lost a real sense of purpose. It had been there during the train journey and the drive across the high moors to the coast; now it was gone. She and Berry ate breakfast, lunch and supper together. She knew she should leave; go to Jessica's and make a lie into a truth. But although the guilt was always with her, she did in fact begin to get the feel of this place. She would touch the stone of the porch as she went in or out, sit at the refectory table as she renewed the flowers and assimilate the twilit feel of the enormous old hall, look out of each of the windows at the different views. She made up her mind every night that she would go the next morning, but the days seemed to melt into each other and on the fourth morning she was still scrambling eggs and making tea when Berry came into the kitchen.

She wondered whether he had left the house at all since she had arrived. His colour was awful, like a plant kept in the dark. He had indeed been sweating it out in the music room. Since that first evening she had not been inside the room again.

She said now, 'Berry ... I don't want to interfere with your routine, but your room ... shall I clean it or anything?'

He looked at her properly. She realized he had avoided looking at her during meal times and his conversation had been almost entirely about the news of the uprising in Egypt.

He smiled. 'I didn't ask you here to be a cook or housewife, Mo. Thank you for getting the meals – letting me share them— '

'For goodness' sake, Berry!'

'I know. It's my house, et cetera et cetera.' He smiled. She had forgotten that smile; so boyish and open. No wonder Val could see Teddy in him.

'I thought you needed time. I needed time too. I don't quite know what is happening, Mo. Do you?'

She made a face. 'No.' She poured tea and sat down opposite him. 'I cannot believe that I came here simply because you asked me to.' She sipped her tea and coughed. 'They think I'm in Birmingham, you know.'

'Yes. I rather thought you must have had to cover your tracks.' He looked beyond her, his eyes opaque. 'Two sinners, Mo. But then, we knew that already.'

She almost broke down then. 'Ah ... Berry,' she said on an indrawn breath.

He focused his gaze again and said quickly, 'Has the place helped? Do you feel ... in a separate world?'

'Oh yes. But that's not good enough, is it? Not really. Because it's completely false. Jannie is ten miles away, probably very unhappy indeed. Val and Hugh and Eric are seventy miles away and I am deceiving them – lying

308

to them with every minute I spend here.' Her voice shook with shame. 'I even phoned Jessica and asked her to cover for me. It's horrible!'

He interrupted her fiercely. 'Listen. You must live in the present. You are here. No-one can get you – no-one even knows you are here! Shut everyone else out of your thoughts.' He leaned forward. 'You know I am in love with you, Mo. Since then . . . fifteen years ago . . . I shut you out – think I've forgotten you, then I know I haven't. You're like a – a ghost – worse than that, an albatross – my albatross . . .' He began to laugh and then stopped suddenly. She knew he was right. Because he was her albatross too.

She blurted, 'I know – I know. If only . . . I can't seem to – to – feel my parents any more . . . because of you!'

His face became very gentle; she had forgotten this side of him too.

He said, 'Ah . . . Mo. That is hard. That is hard indeed. I might get rid of my albatross by painting it out of me. But you . . . what of you?'

She said helplessly, 'I don't know.'

He picked up one of her hands and held it tightly. 'Should we stay together, Mo? Live together, sleep together, eat together . . . is that our destiny?'

She made a sound of protest. 'Hugh . . . I love Hugh, Berry. And Val and Jannie. It would be the end of all that.'

'Yes. But should we do it?' He gripped her hand hard. 'Morrie . . . I could do great things if you were here with me. I could paint murals. I could live my life properly. It wouldn't matter about my leg or anything. Nothing else would matter except being together.'

She looked down at their linked hands. His was so rough . . . calloused from his work. Hers had been red and raw too since her nursing days. She knew suddenly that this was what she had come for. However she had covered up her true motive, this was it. To be with

Berry; to feel his hand in hers, his body against hers. But when she remembered that time at the top of the water slide, those same hands had been smooth . . . they had been young.

She said slowly, 'My dearest dear . . .' She lifted her head and stared at him. 'I will love you always. But I think it is too late.'

He said urgently, 'Why? You're wrong – I'll prove you're wrong. You'll sit for me and I shall woo you in paint . . . I know I can do it . . . turn the clock back . . .'

She shook her head. 'Ah, Berry. You can do it with Jannie. But you see, my dear, it's already happened for us.' She glanced at their hands. 'Berry, there was a time when this would not have been enough. We would have been in each other's arms.' She stood up, leaned across the table and kissed his forehead. 'There. Do you see what I mean? Nothing stands still. And our love hasn't stood still. It has developed into something very strong indeed . . . strong enough that we can bear the albatross . . . perhaps we could not live without its weight any more.'

He watched her as she went to the stove for the teapot and poured more tea. He spoke objectively as if discussing someone else. 'I suppose I should have told Val about you right at the beginning. When I was in hospital. But it seemed unbearable then . . . anchoring you to a wreck of a man . . . I didn't even want you to see me. And when Val told me about Teddy and how you wanted a big family . . . I couldn't do it.'

She did not look round. 'Don't you see? It was too late then. We were different people. We'd touched the sky together . . . it wouldn't have happened again.' She turned. Her eyes were very dark. 'If I had still adored you as I did then, you could not have borne the weight of it.' She shook her head gently. 'You know how heavy the weight of adoration can be. Remember Jannie.' She gave him his fresh tea. 'Perhaps Jannie's craziness shows you – and me – exactly what a burden love can be.' She sat down. 'So I would have been your nurse. Not a caring amateur like Val. A professional nurse. Could you have stood for that, Berry?'

He moved his head slowly from side to side, again and again.

She leaned across the table and gave him his spoon. 'Stir your tea,' she suggested gently. 'Be glad it happened. But no albatrosses. Please.' She waited until he stirred obediently and returned her smile, then she said briskly, 'When do you want me to sit for you?'

He sighed deeply. 'How can we talk like this? I've thrown away everything . . . my wife, my brothers, my friends . . .'

'That's why I'm talking like this.' She nodded at him. 'Drink your tea. Look, the sun is coming out. We'll take the car and get some groceries this morning. Then you can rest. Then we'll start.' She said very seriously. 'Come on, my love. Think about the portrait. Otherwise, perhaps we'll both end up like Jannie!'

He said, 'Poor Jannie. Oh God . . .'

'Shut up, Berry! Drink your tea.' She picked up her own cup and drained it slowly. Then she sighed sharply and said, 'They're asking for homes for the Hungarian refugees. Perhaps you should think about it. This big place all to yourself . . . it's immoral.'

'Oh God . . .'

'And another thing. You should get out more. Tomorrow, instead of resting on your bed, I'll put up a chair and you can sit outside.'

'No thanks. I'd prefer to sit in the window-seat.'

'So Val told me. I'd like to swim and I'm not having you peer down at me like some lecherous old man. You can swim with me.'

His face blanched at that. She swept on regardless. 'And I'll have a word with Val about one of the cars which are operated by hand. It's ridiculous that you can't drive yourself. You need to visit galleries. Other artists.'

311

He said, 'You'll have a word with Val?'

She had forgotten just for a moment. She said quietly, 'Yes. I will. I will.'

Jannie lived in a grey haze of misery; scrambling haplessly through her chores, hating Dusty's coldness more than she had hated his previous ardour. Berry's rejection had hurt, but she could have coped with that, hugged their precious secret to her and fed upon it in private. He had to reject her; she was married to his brother and she had three daughters . . . He had reminded her of those facts over and over again as she hugged him weeping, telling him that none of that mattered because she was carrying his child. A love child. A love child in the fullest meaning of the word. But when Dusty arrived to take her home, Berry had been so obviously relieved and thankful, her weeping had escalated into hysteria and she had allowed Dusty to hustle her downstairs and into the car like some recalcitrant child. He had locked her in. He had shouted at her to shut up and behave herself. He had told her that her place was with her husband and her children and she should never have gone to the abbey in the first place. Even then, as she battered at the windscreen with her fists and tried to bite his hand when he restrained her, even then she was certain that once they were home he would take her upstairs and there would be the usual comfort. But that had not happened. She was back to where she had been all those years ago. Nobody loved her. She agonized about Berry. She felt bereft without Dusty's constant – and so often unwelcome – attentions. But most of all, she missed Val. She grieved for them all; but there was a hope of retrieving Dusty . . . he would want her again, surely. Even Berry . . . she would visit Berry when she knew he was alone and he would be completely unable to resist her. But Val . . . her wiles would get no reaction from Val. She had lost Val for ever.

She told no-one about the baby. Berry knew and Val

knew, but no-one else. She wondered whether she had imagined it; after all, her periods were bound to be erratic; they had been ever since she had Peggotty. But there were the other, all too familiar signs. Her breasts, beautifully small since Val had taken over Peggotty's feeds, began to swell and throb again; already her waist had lost its elfin slenderness. She had imagined that another pregnancy would kill her and had determined to get rid of any future baby before it could grab at her emotions. But this was different. This was the product of her love for Berry and his love for her. Perhaps it was over now; but it had been a time of magic. She never wanted to forget it.

She said nothing to Mrs Merrydown, and she kept away from Dr Harris. She knew she was ill; she could keep no food down and one morning when Peggotty woke her very early, she kept seeing things: half-women half-fish . . . mermaids . . . floating around the room as she fed the baby. When Dusty came in for his breakfast, she was hanging over the sink heaving uselessly on an empty stomach. She forced herself upright and tried to smile.

Dusty said, 'You look like death warmed up. What the hell's the matter with you?' He slammed around assembling bread, butter, marmalade. Jannie, who had intended to be organized for once, stood by the sink, saying nothing.

He said bitterly, 'I thought you went to the abbey to be cured. Suppose it was one of those classic cases – you saw Berry as your doctor and fell for the poor bugger. No wonder he was put out. Christ, no leg and a wife who doesn't want kids and you start your shenanigans!' He glanced up. 'Are you deaf? Or just dumb?'

She forced out words; her voice sounded husky. 'I think I hallucinated. In the night. I . . . I'm not sure.'

He laughed shortly. 'I can guess what you saw. Berry on a white horse. Rescuing you from your wicked husband!'

Jannie flinched. Then said, 'It – they – were sort of mermaids. Black and green.'

'Oh . . . for crying out loud.' He cut bread. 'Sit down. Eat this.' He put bread on a plate, daubed it with butter and pushed it towards her.

She sat down and looked at the food.

'I can't eat it. But thank you . . . thank you.'

He drew his chair towards hers and sat down, staring at her, frowning, champing on his own breakfast with relish.

She whimpered. 'Don't look at me, Dusty. I know I'm a mess. I'll be better soon.'

He stopped chewing and said slowly, 'You're pregnant. That's what's the matter with you, my girl. I've seen it often enough.' He made no move towards her. Tears began to trickle miserably down her face.

He said, 'That time you came over to see the kids. When Val was here. On the bank at Gallenwick. Was it then?'

'I don't know.' She waited for him to reach the other alternative.

He said musingly, 'It must have been. Unless it was before then.' He began, quite suddenly, to laugh. She watched him through her tears wondering whether she was hallucinating again. It was horrible; she was ill and terrified and he was laughing at her.

He swooped suddenly and gathered her up. 'My God, Jannie! That's why you were going all moony over Berry! You're always like that when you're pregnant!' He kissed her, dried her face with his rough palm and kissed her again. 'If only I'd known! I could have saved all this flap and anxiety!' He kissed her almost frantically. 'Darling Jannie! Didn't you twig yourself? You know how randy you get when you're expecting!' He was kissing her and laughing and drying her tears all at the same time. She thought she must faint. He was going to make love to her and she could not bear it, yet it was what she wanted too. She saw with split-second horrible clarity, that as he entered her she would go mad.

He sat down with her on his knee and sobered with difficulty.

'Now. Darling. We have got to be sensible. I promised Val I would look after you and that is exactly what I am going to do. You'll have to behave the way you look ... like a little nun!' He laughed again. 'Come on. Be a good girl. Eat this up. Even if you're sick at least you'll have had some nourishment from it.' He leaned forward awkwardly around her body and cut the bread and butter into tiny pieces and began to feed them to her. Amazingly, she could eat it; chewing carefully and swallowing each piece when he told her to. He held a cup of milk to her lips and she drank. Then he carried her to the old sofa, laid her down and pulled a rug over her.

'Just lie still, baby. If you don't move it might stay down. I'll get Julie up and off to kindergarten.' He stared at her sternly. 'And listen. We have got to have someone in to give you a hand. I mean it, Jannie. You can't do it any more on your own.'

She spoke. It was the old Jannie's voice. 'No-one will come to work here. Your reputation has gone over the county!'

They both laughed. It was better than making love. They had not been so close for ages.

He said, 'I'll think about it. Leave it with me.'

After he had taken Julie off and Peggotty and Ros were sharing the playpen, she got up carefully and began to clear the table. It was a mistake. Almost immediately she was back at the sink bringing up her breakfast. When she was still hanging weakly over the plug holding the taps with hands that sweated with weakness, she heard a car above the cries of the two girls. She looked up and tried to focus her eyes. It must be Val. It had to be Val. And Val would only come if she were going to forgive her. She sobbed at the thought. Dusty believed in her – he actually believed that this baby was his. And Val was going to forgive her.

The car pulled up and someone got out. Everything

315

was blurring hopelessly, but when the door opened, she said faintly, 'Eve!'

And then she collapsed on the floor.

Eve Mears stared in horror at the crumpled cobweb that was her daughter, then at the screaming infants in the playpen.

She spoke to them loudly. 'You'll have to get on with it. I was never any good with your mother when she was your age!' And she lugged Jannie onto the sofa yet again and bathed the smell of vomit from her mouth and patted her face until she opened her eyes.

Jannie looked up and saw that Eve was no hallucination after all. She smiled tremulously. 'Oh Ma . . . I am so glad to see you,' she whispered.

Eve did not protest at being called Ma. She too smiled and kissed her daughter, then stood up and looked around.

'The kettle is on the range,' Jannie murmured. 'But there are drinks in the cupboard.'

'It's nine-thirty in the morning, darling,' Eve said. 'Even I can't start as early as that. I was looking for a baby's bottle or something. To shut up the frightful row.'

Jannie said, 'Pick Ros up. Put her at the table. Give Peggotty to me.'

'Certainly not. You've just fainted.'

Eve sat Ros in a chair and put her handbag in front of her. 'Go through that, little one. Your mother always enjoyed my handbag.' She lugged Peggotty up and sat with her gingerly on her knee. 'This one is wet. And she smells almost as bad as you.'

'Sorry.' But Jannie smiled. 'Can you change her?'

'I hardly remember . . . Ron used to do you. All the time.'

But Eve found the nappies and followed Jannie's instructions. Dry and happier, Peggotty crawled around the kitchen floor. Mother and daughter looked at each other.

'You look terrible, darling. Are you ill?'

'Pregnant again. A lot has been happening.'

'Perhaps . . . if I stay . . . you could tell me about it.'

'Can you stay?' Jannie moved her head eagerly then fell back. 'Will you stay?'

'I can. I want to. If . . . what about your husband?'

'Dusty will be only too pleased.' Jannie closed her eyes and fought off nausea. Then she said, 'But why? I thought you were so happy with that . . . what's-his-name?'

'Roger. Roger Vallender. Yes, I was.'

'Not any more?'

Eve spread her hands. For the first time Jannie noticed her mother was not wearing gloves; or a hat.

'My own fault, Jannie. I don't know what is happening to me. I've changed. I don't like it very much, but I know it's happened.'

Jannie closed her eyes again. Her mother was still so beautiful, so vivid, so unlike Jannie herself. It hurt to see her.

Eve cleared her throat. 'I don't know how to tell you this, Jannie. I know how you felt about him. What I didn't know, was how I felt about him. Now . . . it's as if nothing much mattered. I had to come to see you. You are his daughter, so you matter.'

Jannie opened her eyes and looked up. 'What are you saying, Eve? Is it Ron? Is it Pops? Is he still alive? After all these years?'

Eve said slowly, 'We thought he'd gone in the war, didn't we? I suppose if I'd made a few enquiries . . . there was no widow's pension after all . . . Anyway darling, I suppose it makes it less of a shock now. He died last winter. Pneumonia. Caught a cold and neglected it. He was living with a woman . . . she didn't know about us . . . you and me. And then she found some old snaps he kept – he was such a hoarder. And she went into things and wrote to me . . . just after Christmas.'

'Pops . . .' Jannie was strangely hurt. Why hadn't he got in touch with her? She was married . . . he had grandchildren. She said, 'You've known since Christmas? It's August now!'

'I didn't want to upset you. We haven't seen him since the war, darling. I didn't think it would upset me. But it did. I can't be bothered any more . . . with men, you know. Dressing up, going out . . . what's the point?' She laughed wryly. 'Perhaps I did it just to shock Ron. D'you think that was it, darling? D'you think I did it just to cock a snoot at Ron? Like you slept with Marius to cock a snoot at me?'

Jannie groaned aloud. Had it all been so horribly simple as that? She tried to think back to last winter when Pops must have died. It had been the usual dreadful time; Peggotty crying even as she sucked, Julie having a perpetual cold, her nose running into her mouth like a slum child. Ros had had that rash . . . And all the time their grandfather – the only one they had – had been dying.

She looked at Eve and realized suddenly that her mother was crying.

She said, 'Oh Ma . . . what a waste . . . what a terrible waste . . .'

Eve put her arms around her and sobbed into her neck. Jannie thought of all the times she had wanted this contact with her mother. And now . . .

She said, 'Ma . . . sorry . . . I have to be sick.'

She reached the sink just in time.

CHAPTER TWENTY-ONE

After their talk in the kitchen on her fourth morning at the abbey, both Morag and Berry felt something had been accomplished. They had acknowledged the amazing experience they had shared all those years ago, recognized the enormous impact it had had on their lives. Berry went so far as to greet her the next day with a rueful, 'Good morning, Albatross!'

Morag took over their two lives with a renewed sense of purpose. Her instinct had not let her down after all; she had come here to finish something that had been started fifteen years previously. She did not know how it would be finished, or even whether it could be finished. But during this time of waiting, she cooked meals, cleaned the tall old house, enjoyed the small events of the day in much the same way as Jannie had.

It was a strange, platonic relationship that grew between them; without passion, without any of the intensity that had threatened at first; certainly with none of the craziness of Jannie. Morag posed for him very matter-of-factly, never asking to see the work in progress. She used all her nursing skills to make him physically comfortable, making certain he never became overtired, bathing his stump each evening, getting used to strapping on his leg and administering painkillers. She let him talk about Jannie in the hope that some of his appalling guilt could be assuaged.

She did not have Jannie's ability to pose for hours in one position. She sat in the window-seat, knees crooked, for an hour each morning and another in the evening. At other times she was busy to the point of exhaustion.

He said sourly, 'You've got a great deal in common with

Jannie, haven't you? No wonder you were friends.' She cocked an eyebrow at him and he enlarged grudgingly. 'She couldn't stop working around the place. It was flowers with her. It's bloody polish with you.'

She smiled. 'I hadn't thought of it. Yes . . . we are alike in a lot of ways.' She added flatly, 'We both love you, for instance.'

'She was mad, Morrie. And you . . . do you love me? You never show your feelings.'

'I am here. That shows my feelings, Berry. Jannie knows only one way to show hers. But the flowers . . . they were special. She wanted to show that your time together was beautiful.'

He narrowed his eyes at her, mixed more paint. 'The damned things died within an hour of her leaving.'

Morag risked nodding her head. 'Quite.'

There was silence while he laid his colour on the canvas. She thought how weird he looked, his smock daubed with paint, bits of dried paint in his thick hair. How had Val coped all these years? And would she be able to cope again?

She said quietly, 'I have been here a week, Berry. I must go in another week.'

His head came up, concentration gone. 'One more week? I need more time!'

'Every day we risk everything going wrong, my dear. You know that as well as I do. If Val – if Hugh – ever guessed for one moment that I was here with you alone, the awfulness would be irreparable.'

He shifted slightly, groaned, shifted again. 'Mo . . . I don't think Val will come back. Are you going to leave me here alone?'

She smiled. 'Stop dramatizing. I will find a way around it.' She glanced down at her watch. 'Now get on. There's twenty minutes left. I want a swim while the tide is in.'

'My leg is hurting.'

'Shall we stop now?'

320

'No.' He went back to the canvas. 'You've become very hard, Morrie.'

'Objectivity. Doctors need to be objective.'

He said a rude word and she smiled. He looked up and smiled back.

They went shopping, the hired car almost jibbing at the steep climb up the cliff. He told her about the near disaster with Jannie and she was privately horrified. He went on to describe some of Jannie's life as a child, then later at the Bluebell School. 'It was the happiest time of her life, that year at Gallenwick with you and Val,' he said. 'You are both so special to her.' He glanced sideways at Morag's classic profile. 'Don't let her down, Mo, will you? She looks up to you and she relies on Val's goodness. She thinks she has lost Val. But you . . . you could still help her.'

She said, 'I'll do my best. I hope she is all right. At the farm. With Dusty.'

'He loves her. But . . . well, he can't resist . . . women.' He grinned suddenly. 'If it weren't for what happened in Singapore I suppose I'd be just the same.'

She could have told him Singapore had not changed him. Instead she said suddenly, 'What did happen in Singapore?'

'Hadn't you noticed? I lost a leg.'

She said flatly, 'Just like that. You lost a leg.'

'Oh, you're after the gory details, are you? Objective medical interest?'

They were entering Barnstaple. She concentrated on driving and did not reply.

After the shopping expedition he was suddenly exhausted. She made him lie on his bed and she massaged him. It could have been erotic; he would have liked it to be; it was not.

'You're a cold fish, Mo,' he grumbled.

She ignored that. 'You must learn to relax, Berry. I'm serious, it can be learned. Your painting is part of you, I know that. But you must look out for danger signals, know when to stop.' She worked on his neck for a while, then said, 'Tomorrow, will you come and swim with me? Please?'

His head was turned on the pillow and she saw his eyes close. 'You know I can't do that.'

She said, 'Hydrotherapy is so important, Berry. I'm not trying to get you to come to terms with your fear of the sea. But there's all that water out there and it could help you so much.' She began to explain to him that he could strengthen his limbs by using the buoyancy of the water.

He said, 'Shut up, Morrie. Just shut up.'

She said equably, 'And another thing. I thought tomorrow I would ring Doc Willie.'

His head jerked. 'Why? We cancelled her art group. It's all settled.'

'Oh yes. I understand that.' She let her thumbs follow his ribs. 'Relax a little more, Berry, you're still too tense here.' She swept up his vertebrae to his collar-bone. 'I thought she might take over from me when I go to Birmingham.'

His voice rose to a falsetto. 'Doc Willie?'

'Yes. You could paint her. You know you want to. And I think it would help her a great deal to live here. What was it you said to me when I arrived? Let the place feel comfortable around me? If she could feel comfortable here, it would help her accept that awful thing that happened back in 1917.'

'Oh my God . . .' He closed his eyes. 'Are you still harping on about that? It's nearly forty years ago, woman!'

'Yes. Quite.' She wiped her oily hands on a towel. 'I've finished. I think you should try to sleep now.' She went to the door. 'I'll see you in the morning. Think about what I've said. I can't force you to have Dr Wilkie here, but it would give me great pleasure to think of you with her.'

He propped his chin on his hands and looked at her.

'You're more cunning than I am, Morag Heyward. We would have made a wonderful pair.' She did not move and he added swiftly, 'We still could.'

She closed the door on him very gently.

There were times during the next few weeks when Val forced herself to stop and wonder what was happening to her. Most of the time it seemed to her that she was moving in a new country, full of sunlight, where she was completely protected, yet independent, where for the first time in ten years she did not have to think or plan someone else's life.

There was a comfortable, seductive routine to her days which she could pretend made everything very above-board and simple. She drove each morning to Bellevue Road – either in her own car or with Hugh and her father – opened the windows in the big old room above the auction hall, looked through the post before the part-time typist arrived, and spent a very enjoyable half-hour deciding whether any of the letters merited a change in that day's plan. Sometimes she would take her own car and pick up would-be house purchasers from the station to show them what Clevedon had to offer. The small town was growing in popularity; only half an hour by train from Bristol with easy access to almost anywhere in the West Country. She could reel off its advantages with absolute sincerity and add a potted history to add interest.

But what she liked best was helping Hugh. He would catalogue and pack each of the lots for the next auction with loving care. A special silver sale took place in her second week at home – she was already thinking of this escape as coming home – and she acted as general dogsbody, displaying each item on the table by the rostrum, listening raptly as Hugh described it. 'A piece made in the time when Clevedon was a tiny village . . .' She told him teasingly he was a romantic and he accepted that as a compliment. But he was more than that. He had a great sense of his own place in time; he said to her, 'It would take such a few of us, standing side by side with outstretched fingers just touching, to bridge the whole of our known time.' He smiled at her expression. 'I'm not being romantic now, Val. Absolutely realistic. My father was knocking on when he had me and his father was the same, and he . . .' his smile widened, '. . . my grandfather fought in the Crimea. He could remember Florence Nightingale very well.'

Val was thrilled. 'Mo never told me that! How amazing!'

Hugh said, 'I've never told her. At least I don't think I have. She likes me to talk about my childhood . . . losing Pa . . . being in the war.'

Val said, 'You're bigger than that, Hugh. You should tell her . . .' And then she remembered. As far as they knew Morag was still with Berry; still deceiving them all. She turned away. 'Sorry.'

He said, 'Don't be. I've told you. Surely we need not be so exclusive in what we confide in people?' He put out a hand and turned her to face him. 'This is what I meant the other day, Val. I fell in love with Morag the moment I saw her out on the moors. But I can love someone else.' His grey eyes were so honest she could have wept. She was horribly used to Berry and his deviousness. 'Am I not allowed to love you?'

She said, 'Oh Hugh. Of course. Of course.' She managed a smile of reassurance and told herself that this small exchange was one of the things she would think about later. After all, it could well be that he was simply making a conscious effort to boost her confidence after what had happened.

So she went on enjoying the busy routine of this new life. There was hardly time to think about it anyway; she helped Mrs Knapp with the meals, went to the hairdresser for the first time in years, she even bought some new clothes.

Her father was delighted.

'You're looking better every day, my darling.' They both kept telling her how nice she looked, even Mrs Knapp was in on it. 'You haven't changed an iota since you were at school!'

Val said, 'I've lost weight. That's all it is.'

But Eric shook his head thoughtfully. 'No. I know you're much thinner – no wonder. But you don't look ill. Not at all. And don't tell me it's the hair-do and your pretty summer frock because there's something else as well.'

Val hugged him. 'Oh, Daddy. It's being with you. You and Hugh and Mrs Knapp . . . you're spoiling me.'

But she knew that if she gave herself time to stop and think she would know exactly what it was.

In the middle of August a chilly wind came off the sea and whipped some of the dryer leaves from the trees. Val stood by the window where she had been sitting when she first saw that Lyn Abbey was for sale.

'Autumn's not far away.' She shivered involuntarily. 'I hate winters at the abbey.' She peered between the houses opposite to catch a glimpse of the sea. 'I'm glad we can't see much of the channel from here. I'm not that keen on sea views.' She looked round at Hugh, her face open and suddenly frightened. 'I think I mean that I don't like the abbey. Full stop.' She forced a tight smile. 'Oh my dear Lord. What am I saying?'

He had been reading a letter; now he put it down on the top of his desk as if it were fragile. He said, 'It's been two weeks. Only two weeks. That's not a lifetime after all.'

It sounded irrelevant but she knew what he meant, exactly. Two weeks ago Morag had gone away and they – the three of them – had manufactured this easy routine, this easy relationship, this new life. And it seemed much longer than two weeks.

She said quietly, 'I don't think I can go back, Hugh.'

He picked up the wooden letter-opener and fingered

325

it thoughtfully. 'The longer she is away, the harder it will be to . . . accept.'

With a shock Val realized she had not after all known exactly what he meant. His thoughts had been on Morag, not on Val at all. She knew a flash of pure jealous anger.

'Surely you won't accept it? Not now?' She walked quickly away from the window, reached the other side of his desk, leaned across and seized his wrist. 'Hugh. I won't let you go back to how we were! I cannot! Berry does not want me any more than I want him! He has made that plain over and over again! And Morag does not – cannot – want you!'

He looked down at her fingers around his shirt cuff. He put down the paper knife and covered her hand with his. 'Ah Val. If only it were that simple.' He looked up at her, his smile glinting. 'We would simply change over then, wouldn't we? You and me. Morag and Berry. Is that how you see it?'

She faltered. It was ridiculous of course. She rallied the remnants of her pride and common sense.

'I'd prefer to live here than in that draughty old abbey with the grey sea lapping its walls all the time.' She released him and sat on the edge of the desk, changing the subject subtly. 'D'you realize that if there's snow or ice, we're marooned there? We can't get a car up the cliff and no-one can get down to us?'

'I know. It worries Morrie a great deal.'

'It does, does it?' She could not resist a last burst of ire. 'That's why she's gone down there, is it? To find out for herself?'

He said nothing. When she looked at him he was staring at the paper knife and she thought for a frightful moment that he might be near tears. She stood up briskly.

'Come on. Let's get cracking and forget the abbey and its inhabitants for another day. I have to take Titus and his obnoxious wife and children to see a house in Kenn.'

Hugh roused himself as she bustled around putting papers into her briefcase.

'Take a cardigan,' he said. 'It's cold today.'

He left the room and she looked at the door and faced the thought that had been there all the time. She did not only love Hugh. She was in love with him. It was not that she could not face the abbey, or Berry's infidelities, or his constant and unpredictable pain. She had married the wrong man. She said quietly, 'It's time you went home, my girl. Time to remember the status quo.'

There was a funfair on Bristol Downs. It had been started annually during the war to boost the Holidays at Home campaign, and it proved so popular it continued afterwards.

Eric said, 'You never go anywhere just for fun. And this really is fun. Hugh, take an evening off and take my daughter to the fair – make her have some fun!'

Val said nothing. She looked at Hugh with a kind of defiance. She wanted to challenge him somehow; to say, 'Dare you forget Morag long enough to take someone else out?' When he returned her look with his usual smile she felt small and mean.

'It would be rather special, wouldn't it, Val?' He clapped Eric on the shoulder. 'Why don't you come too? You're a crack shot – you'd win every time on the rifle range!'

But Eric was adamant. It was almost as if he wanted to push them together.

Val put on a cotton dress in red gingham, strappy sandals and a panama of her father's. 'I'm meant to look like a cowgirl, from Oklahoma!'

Hugh decided against dungarees and wore flannels and an open-necked shirt. It was still windy but the temperature was climbing; they were in for a thunderstorm. It was good to wind down the windows of the car and let the warm air rush in. They crossed the suspension bridge just as it was getting dark; far below, the tide swelled the river. It was like crossing a drawbridge into another country. She thought, I'll take tonight, then tomorrow, I'll telephone Berry . . .

Hugh said worriedly, 'I'm not sure where to park the car, shall we go along to Blackboy hill?'

Val had an inspiration. 'Let's park outside Jannie's house. Opposite the observatory. I'll direct you.'

'Are you thinking of calling?' She did not reply, wondering whether that had been at the back of her mind. He said, 'Mrs Mears won't know what is happening on the moor. She doesn't keep in touch.'

'No . . . quite.' Val leaned forward to direct him through the mass of traffic past the zoo. 'Anyway we'd never get the car in along here.' She paused, added, 'Left at the top of the road.' Then sat back. 'It's the first house. We'll drive up to the garage. I'll have to knock. Otherwise she will wonder what's happening.'

He followed her instructions; it was the only thing to do, the Downs were crowded with people; there were horses, painted wagons, cars, every type and condition of transport. Smoke rose from half a dozen fires; the sun was setting at the mouth of the Avon and the light was luridly, foggily red. It had a mediaeval, Hogarthian look. Val felt a surge of childish excitement. If only she could turn the clock back; if only she were calling for Jannie now and they were meeting Morag . . .

She knocked on the door. The porch light was on and inside the hall was suddenly lit. The door opened and a man stood there.

'Oh.' Val was horribly taken aback; she had forgotten Eve's penchant for young men. This one looked like a Twenties matinée idol. 'Sorry. I'm a friend of Eve's. Is she in?'

'I'm afraid not.' The young man smiled showing a mass of white teeth. 'I'm Roger Vallender. Her . . . her . . . paying guest. She is staying with her daughter at present. I'm not quite sure when she will be back.'

Val felt her eyes open very wide. 'I see. At the farm? At Reid's farm?'

'Yes. I've got the phone number if you want to— '

'That's all right. I've got it too.' Val forced a laugh. 'Look. It's just that, we're old friends. May we leave our car on the drive for a couple of hours? Everywhere's so packed.'

'Of course. Of course.' Roger Vallender emerged and came to the car to shake Hugh's hand. 'Delighted to meet you and your husband. I know so few of Eve's friends. It seems ages since she left.'

Hugh said, 'When did she leave?'

'A fortnight ago.'

Val looked at Hugh in the lurid light. He met her gaze for a moment, then said, 'It's good of you to let us park. We won't be long.'

He got out of the car and locked it. They shook hands again. Roger Vallender asked them in for drinks later, it was obvious that he was lonely. 'Eve has no idea when she will be home,' he told them. 'Apparently her daughter is very ill.'

Val said, 'Yes. We know.'

They walked back into the road, crossed it and joined the thronging crowd on the outskirts of the funfair. Above them loomed the blackness of the observatory. There was no hope of talking; the noise was deafening; each ride had its own signature tune roaring out of loudspeakers. Val felt herself jostled sideways and made a grab for Hugh's arm and he looked at her, his grey eyes lit by the neon and suddenly put his arm right around her and fastened her to his side. It was as if their thoughts flowed together; Jannie had been at home for some time ... Morag and Berry were alone ... together ... in the abbey. No Jannie, no Mrs Murchison. That sea-bound isolation holding them together.

Morag wrote to Dr Wilkie telling her as much as she

possibly could. The doctor telephoned her as soon as she received the letter.

She was crisply concise as usual, unable to deal with the emotions that were obviously running high around Berry.

'Do I understand that Vallery has left the abbey for good?' she asked.

Morag replied in a similar vein. 'I don't think so. As I mentioned she has no idea I am here. That might change any feelings she has about returning. I would think she would come home. Quite soon. I simply wondered if you would hold the fort over this difficult time.' She cleared her throat. 'As you know, Doctor, Berry has wanted to paint your portrait for some time. It would be a good opportunity.'

'That is why you went down I gather.'

'It is one reason. But of course I was hoping to resolve the situation.'

'Have you had no success?'

'Some. Certainly the – the incident – with Jannie is easier for him to accept.'

'How is Janice?'

'I don't know. I could only deal with one thing at a time.'

'I see.' The telephone wire hummed emptily for a while then the older woman said, 'Is the invitation from you or from Berry?'

Morag said hastily, 'From Berry, of course! I am sounding you out. He will write to you himself if you think . . .'

'Mrs Maitland could do with a holiday. Perhaps if we came together, we could manage. It is difficult, Morag. I am sure you realize that.'

'Of course. It was a long shot . . . asking you to step in. But I know you have an affinity for the place. And my position here is really untenable.'

Dr Wilkie said again, 'I see.' Then on a sudden note of decision she added, 'All right. Give me three or four days to make arrangements. Maitie and I will come down for two weeks' holiday. How does that sound?'

'Very good. In fact, ideal. Thank you so much. Berry respects and likes both of you very much. He will be delighted.'

Morag replaced the receiver and sat staring out of the kitchen window. She thought that after all she had not accomplished very much. She and Berry, they were like old lovers, tired old lovers who could be easy and frank with one another but that was all. It seemed a poor compromise after she had thrown her hat over the windmill and come down here so secretly, risking her marriage – and his. On the other hand, Berry was well again and thinking straight about Jannie. And the old dream that he must have carried all these years . . . that she too had carried all these years . . . was somehow now acceptable. Perhaps even laid to rest. She sighed, recognizing in a moment of desolation the impossibility of one human being helping another, wondering if she would ever be a good doctor. Then she shivered and stood up briskly. It was time to wake Berry and bully him into climbing down the stairs to the cellar and through the small door to the rocks where she had set up his chair. 'If you're going to watch me swim, that's where you must be,' she had told him in her nurse's voice.

'What difference does it make whether I watch from the window or the beach?' he had groused.

'One makes you a peeping Tom, the other makes you good company,' she had replied patiently.

She was glad to see he had changed into shorts; he had no inhibitions at all now about her seeing his leg. She settled him, unstrapped the aluminium contraption from his thigh and cushioned the stump carefully.

'I'm going to miss you,' he said, looking down at the centre parting in her thick black hair. 'Will you do me a favour?'

'If I can.'

'Unpin your hair. Let it float in the water.'

'Like Jannie used to?'

'You are so different. Jannie was like seaweed. You are a rock.'

'Thanks,' she said dryly, but she unpinned her hair before she slid out of her towelling robe and entered the sea quickly. She still had inhibitions about him seeing her in her swimsuit.

It was glorious to swim out to the point of the small peninsula. She floated on her back, at one with water and sky. The sea took her hair and massaged her scalp and she let all the anxieties of the past two weeks drift away. Doc Willie was coming ... she herself could go to Selly Oak and be with Jessica – the complete normality of Jessica was like a beacon of hope. And Hugh and Val need never know that she had been at the abbey.

She swam back to the beach slowly, savouring the movement of her arms and legs. In the shallows within reach of his bare foot, lapped by the wavelets, she bounced gently off the shingly seabed and told him about her telephone call.

'So you need a formal invitation from me?' he asked.

'Yes please.' She tipped her head to look at him. 'You do see it is the perfect solution, don't you?'

'Acceptable to all parties?' He sighed. 'I suppose so.'

She kept staring at him though she could not see his face against the brightness of the sky. She could not find the energy to pull herself up and out of the water. She was in a kind of trance.

'Mummy and I used to go to Clevedon sometimes. Just the two of us. To swim.'

For a moment she was not sure whether she had spoken the words aloud. And then Berry spoke.

'Not with Val?' he asked.

She went on slowly, carefully. 'Before I knew Val. When I was really quite young. I don't think Mummy could have any more children ... I'm not sure. We didn't talk about it. But we were friends anyway. She liked my company. Not just because I was her daughter.'

He said nothing. He seemed to be waiting. She said, 'I remember her bathing costume . . . that's what they were called. Bathing costumes. Not swimsuits. She had knitted it . . . small sleeves and quite a high neck and proper legs. The bottom half . . . the shorts . . . were blue, and the top half was white. She looked very beautiful.'

Berry said very quietly, 'Your father wasn't with you?'

'He was working. Even in the summer he wore formal clothes . . . he said they were one of his many idiosyncrasies. I thought he meant they were hideous crinklies. I always called them . . . that.'

He almost whispered. 'I imagined you as a threesome. You and your mother and father.'

'We were. We had picnics on the Downs. He didn't like swimming. We sledged in the winter. It was such fun. And afterwards we would have tea and sit in the oriel window and look at the people slipping and sliding down Park Street.'

Now she had started she could not stop. She told Berry about that last operation she had watched and how even now they were beginning to experiment with making smaller and smaller incisions. 'He knew they would,' she said. 'He was very . . . far-seeing.' And then she told him about her mother's visit to Gallenwick with Teddy McKinley. 'It was as if she knew . . . as if she had come to say goodbye. If only I'd known . . . if only . . .'

She realized she was weeping because she could no longer focus on Berry's silhouette. She heard Berry say, 'Mo . . . please don't . . . please don't . . .' But once she had started she could not stop. He leaned down and tried to take her wrist, but she had floated away from the tiny beach and he could not reach her. He pushed himself forward and the next instant he was out of his chair, lying chest down in six inches of water. She caught her breath on a sob, blinked hard to clear her eyes and saw a moment of sheer panic wipe his face of all other expression. She cried out, 'Berry . . . don't be frightened.' She kicked with her legs and reached out for him. Her hands held his; she drew him towards her. He held her, floating automatically, suddenly able again, the frightful handicap meaningless in the shifting water.

She wept again; this time with sheer joy for him. When he kicked his good leg to guide them into the shallows again, she lifted her head from his shoulder and said, 'No – no, Berry. This is John Ridd's stream again! Can't you see? You are strong and whole in the water . . . come . . .' she let him go and began to swim into deep water, '. . . follow me, my dear. I followed you before . . . I trusted you. Trust me now.'

There was a split second of irresolution as he looked back at the shore and the safety of his chair. And then he turned and began to swim after her. His arms were powerful and he had no difficulty in catching her up.

He gasped a laugh and said inadequately, 'It's cold . . .'

She smiled. Her thick hair was everywhere; she pushed it away from her face and swam to him, put her arms around him and quite naturally kissed him.

'Oh, Berry . . . Oh, Berry, I am so pleased.'

He held her too. 'Are you all right? I shouldn't have encouraged you to talk about your parents.'

'Yes, you should.' She snuffled a laugh into his neck. 'I came to help you. And you have helped me . . .' She looked up. 'Do you know, I haven't cried like that for ages . . . not since the day I knew that they'd been killed.'

He stared at her face for a long moment before he kissed her. It was a long kiss, very gentle. It was a forgiving kiss . . . forgiving of the past. After it they both swam back to the shallows and there, waist-deep, he let her tow him back up to the beach and into his chair. And then, while they dried off in the sun, he told her about Akiko in two sentences.

'She was a nurse in the hospital where they amputated

my leg. She was kind to me – they thought . . . never mind what they thought . . . she was killed.'

Morag said nothing. The weight of his guilt was so obvious that there was nothing to say.

He said, 'It was after that they experimented on me . . . I didn't care. It seemed a just punishment. But of course, I knew then that I would never be able to marry you.' His dark eyes stared into hers. 'I didn't want to marry anyone else, Mo. Not then.'

Morag spoke at last. 'I know . . . And I am so thankful you married Val.' She stretched in the sun, no longer embarrassed by her scant swimsuit. 'You do realize that it is the perfect match? You and Val?'

He smiled slightly, 'Yes. Of course I do. I hope she feels that too.'

'I think she does.' She looked up at him. 'You and me, Berry . . . it wouldn't have worked.'

'You mean two albatros don't make a pair?'

Suddenly they were laughing; almost weeping too.

'I'll do this every day,' he promised her. 'And I'll get Doc Willie to join me too.'

She shook her head at him, smiling. 'You are incorrigible.' She handed him a towel. 'We must get your leg on and go back upstairs. You mustn't get cold.'

'Yes, Doctor,' he mocked. But he wrapped himself in the towel and struggled out of the chair as soon as he could. Morag was thankful to reach the music room. She left him in the window-seat and went to run his bath; then she helped him into bed and brought supper in on trays.

He said, 'Don't look so sad. I know you're leaving tomorrow. I can finish the paintings now without you.'

'Is that all that matters to you?'

'Of course. It means I can see you whenever I wish.'

She stopped eating and pointed her fork at him. 'Listen, Berry. When Val comes back, those paintings must go away. Jannie's portraits were bad enough – if Val sees mine as well— '

'I thought you'd understand, Mo. Your portraits – they will make Jannie's acceptable. Don't you see?' He leaned back in his chair, suddenly tired again. 'I shall paint Doc Willie as well. And then . . .' He closed his eyes and smiled. 'And then I think, I can do Val's. After all this time . . . I shall paint Val's portrait.'

She stared at him for a long time. She did not need a picture of Berry; she knew she would never forget him.

When she saw he was asleep she took his tray, tucked him in gently and left the room. Tomorrow she would return the car and catch the train to Exeter and then to Birmingham. And very soon, she would be home again with Hugh.

CHAPTER TWENTY-TWO

The roar of the fair receded as they moved closer to the edge of the gorge. Val would have fallen if Hugh had not held her up; by the time they leaned gratefully on the sea walls and stared into the chasm beneath them, her breath was catching on uncontrollable sobs.

He said without conviction, 'Ah, Val . . . dear Val. There's nothing to cry about . . . nothing.'

She could not argue; he knew why she was crying. She tried to breathe deeply of the sea-scented air, but a ludicrous hiccup checked her and she put her head onto her arms surrendering helplessly to grief.

Hugh put his hand on the back of her neck and ran his fingers upwards through her curls. Far below, the lights of a tug, probably the *Bristol Pilot*, punctured the darkness. The tide must be flowing. He thought of Morag and Berry alone in that old Victorian house practically in the sea. There was something about the sea . . . he could feel it now . . . vast and eternal, it made the rules and regulations which men called morals and ethics seem petty and meaningless. The sea was mastered only by the moon; the moon which also governed all lunatic impulses.

He drew a breath unhampered by sobs and tasted the salt and the wildness. Morag and Berry alone with that wildness. Mrs Murchison's dry and proper presence removed.

He said aloud, 'I trust Morag.' His voice sounded defiant and he modified it and said quietly to Val, 'Val, we can both trust Morag.' He ran his hand through her hair again. There was something perennially schoolgirlish about Val. How could Berry hurt her so badly? And now . . . Mo.

She lifted her head but it was as if she had not heard him. 'It's funny really, isn't it? Berry ... Berry has sampled the three of us. Apparently he started with Mo. Then it was me. Then Jannie. And now it's Mo again!' She laughed crazily. 'My God. We thought Dusty was naturally unfaithful but he limits himself to a swift cuddle at the sink!'

Hugh said doggedly, 'We can trust Mo.' He cupped her head, traced her left ear with his thumb.

Val turned on him furiously. 'Oh yes! We can trust Mo! She sneaks off telling us she's going to Birmingham ... she's alone with him in that – that place! Oh yes, we can trust Mo!' She lifted her face to the night sky in agony. 'I should have done something straightaway – talked to her on the phone and called her bluff and made her come home!' She focused on Hugh again. '*You* should have done it, Hugh! What possessed you to let her carry on with such a charade? You should have ordered her back home where she belongs.' She began to hammer on his chest with clenched fists. 'You're too reasonable – too kind – too easygoing! No wonder she's always hankered after Berry – he's none of those things! My God, I know that! He's totally selfish and amoral and— '

He kissed her.

He hardly knew why he did it. He had loved her as a friend, as a sister, but there had been moments that came close to something else. And now her anguish seemed to turn their relationship inside out. For an instant she held back, and then, quite suddenly, her anger and grief distilled into a fierce passion. He had spoken of 'changing partners' and quite suddenly she knew that that was his intention. But anyway none of that mattered. They were here under a fickle moon, both rejected, both in pain, both needing ... something. She would show Morag ... she would show Jannie ... she would show Berry Reid. She pressed herself to him frantically, opening her mouth to his kisses, pushing her hands inside his shirt to his flat stomach and small hips. As they knelt in the shelter of the sea walls, he whispered, 'Val . . . are you sure?' and she laughed, because she had never been more certain of anything in her life.

It was fierce and over quickly. They lay, half-crouched, dishevelled, covered in the dry dust of scuffed grass; scratched and sore, terribly conscious of their excesses. Val had used all the wiles she had learned with Berry and was now sure she had lost Hugh's respect; she had brought him down to the level of Berry . . . how long before he sought out Jannie? He said, 'Val, I'm sorry . . .'

And that was the final straw. She turned silently and crawled away from him to retch into a thicket of brambles. And that was the last straw for Hugh. He watched miserably as she cleaned herself with his handkerchief then offered his arm for the return walk. When she ignored it, he put his hands in his pockets. They felt like hams on the ends of his arms. When he remembered how they had clutched Val's ample body, he hardly knew what to do with them. He wanted to howl into the fair's cacophony . . . howl a name that was not Val's . . . 'Morrie!'

Val walked well away from him, terribly conscious of the smell of vomit hanging around her. Surreptitiously, she pulled at the drawstring neck of her frock until it was almost choking her. They did not knock on the door of the Mears' house; as they reversed into the crowded road and drove off, an upstairs window opened, but they ignored it. Val sat huddled in her seat while Hugh wound down the window and paid the toll man at the suspension bridge. The lights were left behind. They turned into Beggar Bush Lane and darkness finally closed around them.

Hugh spoke so suddenly she jumped.

'Val. I'm sorry. I don't know what else to say. I behaved abominably and I'm deeply sorry.'

She said nothing. He must know it had been her doing; he must also know that she loved him. She did not think she could bear it.

He waited while the headlights ripped through an

avenue of beeches. Then he said, 'Can we forget it? Is that possible? Pretend it never happened?'

She rallied the last remaining shreds of pride. 'Of course. There's really nothing else we can do.' She had hoped – hoped so much – he would say he loved her and they must be together for always. Even now she waited, holding her breath, then said, 'Is there?'

'I suppose not.' He slowed as they came to a bend; in the beam of the lights a fox's brush showed for an instant. She saw the flash of his eyes as he glanced at her. 'We comforted each other, Val. We felt betrayed and we comforted each other.'

She tried to fight back. 'We *were* betrayed, Hugh. We have been and we are being . . . *betrayed.*' She moved slightly, straightening her back. 'Let's face facts, Hugh. Please. Berry and Morag are living together. I rather think I have left Berry and Morag has left you.'

There was another protracted silence. Then he said heavily, 'Yes.'

She felt suddenly better and sat up properly. 'The question should be, not what have we done. But what are we going to do?'

Another silence while they negotiated the village of Failand. Then, again, he said, 'Yes.'

She wanted to remind him that he had suggested they might simply change partners. She swallowed, waiting for him to reach the inevitable conclusion without prompting. All change partners. Like in a square dance.

He cleared his throat and said with sudden decision, 'I'll go down there. Tomorrow. I'll have it out with them.'

'You'll go down there?' She was not quite sure why she did not want that. 'Why? There will be a row . . . don't go, Hugh.'

And then he said, 'It would be worth a row . . . worth a hundred rows . . . if she would come back.'

Val crumpled very slowly into her corner again. She

said nothing else, but as they drove past the manor house, she wiped her eyes surreptitiously.

Eric found her the next morning making tea in the kitchen. It was very early and heavy dew hung on every flower petal in the garden. He leaned over the sink to look out of the window at it and commented without turning round, 'You look rather dewy too, my dear. Is something wrong?'

'I didn't sleep very well.' She poured an extra cup of tea and pushed it along the counter. 'We dropped in to the Mears' house last night. It seems that Jannie is back at Reid's farm being cared for by her mother. So Morag and Berry have been alone all this time.' She sounded completely matter-of-fact. 'Hugh is going down to the abbey today to try to find out if they have any plans.' She sipped her tea, replaced the cup into its saucer with a clatter and said, 'I didn't know, but it seems that Morag and Berry ... they had a bit of a fling when we were all children. And she ... he ...' She looked at her father in sudden distress. 'I don't quite know whether I'm coming or going, Daddy. It seems that my wonderful idea of looking after my very own wounded sailor has been a bit of a sham!'

Eric gathered her into his shoulder and rocked her gently saying nothing while she wept. When the worst of the outburst had subsided he said, 'Listen to me, Val. I know Hugh and Morrie now very well. Whatever has happened in the past, they are right for each other.' He rubbed her spine as she hiccupped like a child. 'And I think that you are right for Berry. I wish it weren't so because your life with him must be difficult – I know that. But I think it is worthwhile and in the end that is what is important.'

'Daddy, you don't understand. Berry does not love me. He loves Morag. And I don't love him. I love Hugh— '

'Sh-sh-sh ...' He soothed her as her voice rose

helplessly. 'Don't upset yourself, my darling. Hugh is the one conventional Reid brother. He happens to be living in your old home. Don't you see? This is a very natural reaction against your peculiar lifestyle in the abbey. Hugh is kind, Berry is not. Hugh is whole and . . . Berry is not.' She gasped a cry of pain into his neck and he said swiftly, 'You make him whole, Val. You are his other half . . . that is what marriage is.'

'Like you and Mummy . . .' She wept again. 'But not like you and Mummy. You loved Mummy. Berry does not love me.'

'I think you are wrong.' He held her away slightly so that he could look into her blue eyes. 'Phone him, Val. Come on . . . seize the nettle. Phone him now.'

She was shocked. 'It's too simple. What shall I say?'

'Ask him if he wants you to come home.'

'But . . . Morrie will answer the phone.'

'I don't think so, do you? If she is really playing a double game it would rather give the whole thing away.'

She whimpered. 'I can't . . . I can't do it, Daddy. If he says no then that will be that. And if he says yes . . . I don't want to go back . . . I want to stay here.'

'Oh Val . . . poor darling. The devil and the deep . . .' He pecked her cheek and sat her down. 'Will you let me do it?'

She was aghast again. 'I don't know. I'm not sure . . .'

Eric went to the wall-phone in the kitchen, lifted it and dialled the operator. When he asked for the number Val made a low moaning sound but did not move. From where she sat at the table she could hear the operator's impersonal voice, 'You are connected, sir,' and then the steady buzzing sound of the phone ringing by Berry's bedside and in the kitchen. She could almost smell the paint and visualize the oriel window and the all-pervading sea outside. Unexpectedly she felt a pang of homesickness.

Then the buzzing stopped and she saw her father frown.

He said, 'Have I got the right number? This is Eric McKinley speaking from Clevedon. Who is that please?' Then the frown deepened. 'Dr Wilkie? This is most unexpected!' The frown disappeared and he smiled. 'Certainly it's a pleasure also. But you are the last person I expected to hear.'

Val stood up in response to her father's urgent beckoning and stood close to him. She could hear Dr Wilkie's unmistakable voice saying, '. . . nearly a week now. The weather has been simply marvellous. However, you wished to speak to Berry? I've unplugged his telephone receiver so that he will sleep late. He still gets very tired of course. I will see if he's awake.'

Eric said quickly, 'Don't wake him, Doctor. It's just that we were anxious about him, and Vallery and Hugh were thinking of coming down to see him.'

The doctor's voice became warm. 'Oh, of course. That would be grand. Mrs Maitland and I thought we would not see Vallery this visit.'

'Mrs Maitland is with you?'

'Yes. She needed a holiday and as Berry is painting my portrait Mrs Maitland has taken over the housekeeping.'

Val moved to the window. So . . . Berry had got his way yet again. He was painting Doc Willie's portrait just as he had said he would. Suddenly she began to laugh. The laughter turned to tears then back to laughter. When her father replaced the receiver and turned to her she shook her head.

'I'm all right. Honestly. It's just that . . . how much would you bet that he has done Morrie's portrait as well? The only person he cannot bring himself to paint is . . . is me!'

When Morag returned home, she took Shirley White with her. She was never quite sure whether this was because

343

she needed protection or because she had promised the girl a holiday in Clevedon anyway. The fact that Val was back at the abbey and Hugh had not come up to Birmingham to fetch her at the end of her course seemed ominous. She had continued to telephone home, just as she had from the abbey, and when Eric told her that Hugh and Val had gone to see Berry, she did not know what to think. She had not asked Doc Willie to lie on her behalf so it was more than likely that Val and Hugh would be told of those two clandestine weeks. If they were, what would they make of it? While she was with Berry, Morag had known she was deceiving her husband and her friend; but she had envisaged telling them about it later . . . perhaps much later. But the full significance of her stay at the abbey could never really be understood if she did not include that time in John Ridd's stream. And that . . . that could never be told. As the train drew out of Cheltenham she tried to imagine some kind of explanation for what she had done. 'You see, we were very close once . . . when we were children. And we had to remember that time together and then put it behind us. We called it . . . our albatross . . .' But how could anyone understand that? Especially how could Hugh and Val understand? How could she explain the sheer miracle of talking about her parents to Berry . . . of swimming together . . . of Berry's brief confession and expiation of terrible guilt?

By her side Shirley said, 'I wish you'd told your husband about me coming, Mo. He might not think it's a very good idea.'

But Hugh had not telephoned or come to see her. He had stood aside. He so often stood aside.

She said, 'Oh he'll be glad to see you, Shirley.'

He was. He was on the platform at Clevedon, his fair brown hair neatly brushed but curling over his ears and forehead because he had forgotten to go to the barber's. He wore a tweed jacket and grey flannels and he looked so good she wanted to run into his arms and tell him how much she had missed him but that she loved him

344

more than ever. But when he moved toward her it was to pick up her suitcase; his smile was terribly controlled: she felt a moment of pure terror. Had she lost him?

She said, 'Darling . . . this is Shirley White. Jessica's eldest. D'you remember I asked her if she would come and stay during her long vacation?'

He immediately put down the case and pumped Shirley's hand enthusiastically. Shirley gazed at him, her face wide open.

'You didn't say he was so good-looking!' She spoke with her mother's candour. 'Oh . . . hello Mr Reid. Do you mind me turning up like this?'

Hugh laughed at last, his grey eyes crinkling endearingly. 'I am delighted, Shirley. Where's your bag?'

Shirley reached back into the compartment, chattering away the whole time. 'Mum says I disrupt everything and everyone, so you might not stay delighted!' She turned and gave him a full smile. 'But I am. Delighted I mean. My father was killed in the war and the only older men I know are teachers and an awful old uncle in Handsworth who smells of pigeon droppings!'

They moved up the platform past the buffers, laughing uproariously and almost naturally. Morag knew that Hugh was thankful for the presence of Shirley. Just as she was herself.

Everything was different. Val had moved the furniture in the sitting room so that her mother's old chair was in the window and whoever sat in it was somehow separated from the others. Morag found herself sitting in it simply because Eric sat in his usual chair by the fireplace and Shirley curled up by Hugh on the sofa. Morag had always lined the kitchen window-sill with pot plants: they were all gone; the tiled surface gleamed bare and white. Morag realized they must have reminded Val of Jannie's proliferation of wild-flower arrangements. She remembered that she too had picked flowers and put them around the abbey. Would Val sweep them away as she'd swept Jannie's away, with fury and disgust?

345

But more than the rearrangement of the house, was the attitude of the people. Hugh and Eric had changed. And they had changed in the same way; they both avoided her. Just as she felt awkward and ill at ease with them, so they did with her. They were all thankful for the presence of Shirley White. When she said goodnight each evening and went into Val's old bedroom, it was like switching off a lamp. After ten minutes with the *Bristol Post*, Eric would announce he was off to bed. Morag would leave with him and lay the table for breakfast in the dining room. When she returned to the sitting room, Hugh had either gone or was preparing to go. Either way there was no breaking the barrier once in the bedroom. Their love-making had always sprung from affection, passion building slowly between them as they shared the intimacies of bedtime with desultory conversation, laughter, sudden kisses. All that had gone. She found herself commenting on the weather; Hugh might suggest that they picnic on the beach the next day so that Shirley could swim. He and Morag always swam together; now they went to the beach so that Shirley could swim. It grew hotter and hotter; Morag found herself longing for a thunderstorm, as if with a sudden flash of lightning they could break through the awful wall between them.

Shirley stayed for ten days and then it was time to go home for the results of her A levels. She cried on Morag's shoulder, blurting out her feelings with the brutal honesty of youth.

'I think I've fallen in love with your husband, Mo! I'm so sorry. But I have these wonderful dreams where you go off with someone else and I look after him and mend his broken heart and one day he looks into my eyes and tells me that— '

'Darling, it's all right. I know the rest. And I promise that if I go off with anyone else I'll give you advance warning.'

'Don't laugh at me, Mo!'

'I'm not. As a matter of fact if you don't stop crying soon, you'll start me off.'

'He's so lovely, Mo.'

Morag said quietly, 'I know.'

Shirley lifted her head and said, anguished, 'But it's not just that. He makes my thighs quiver!'

Morag did not know whether to laugh or cry. She did neither. She said again, 'I know.' And she thought of Berry and the sea and the sun. That had been so different. Her thighs had not quivered then.

Eric had heard that the manor house was 'going' to the National Trust.

'The family are in some difficulty it would seem,' he said when they sat down to supper the night after Shirley's departure. 'There may well be some private sales to be negotiated. I wondered if you would like me to make contact, Hugh. I'm sure if there is anything to be sold, they would prefer it to be dealt with locally.'

Hugh was suddenly animated. 'You play golf with Sir Monty sometimes, don't you?' He grinned. 'My goodness, Eric, that would be a coup! To deal with the Montagu silver! And the pictures . . . it's rumoured there's a Holbein in the gallery. We could get Berry to take a look at it perhaps.' He checked himself, glanced at Morag, then said, 'Probably not. Val tells me he's still not really himself.'

Morag said, 'You've been in touch with Val? Why didn't you tell me? I'd love to talk to her.'

Eric stopped eating for a moment, then continued to chew slowly. Hugh said, 'I expect she was busy.'

Morag said, 'She telephoned?'

'Yes.' Hugh drank some water. 'I think you were out with Shirley.'

'But you didn't tell me.'

Eric said, 'It would be worth asking her if Berry would be willing to look at the pictures. I'm sure I could arrange it.'

She looked from one man to the other. Suddenly her

normal control slipped. She said loudly, 'Perhaps you should ask me about Berry's health and fitness. After all, I am the doctor in the family. I am the one who went to the abbey and found him alone and neglected and ill and nursed him back to health!'

If she hoped to cause an explosion of amazement, she was disappointed. Both men looked at her, surprised, but by no means shocked. She realized that they knew about her deception. They had known all the time; Val knew. She began to shake.

The silence stretched out unbearably. It was a kind of torture: they hated her enough to want to torture her. It was all clear now. She had not imagined the wall between her and the rest of the household.

She controlled her trembling somehow and said, 'In my opinion – medical opinion – Berry should be able to come here and inspect any pictures. In fact if he takes my advice he will have bought a hand-controlled car and be in a position to drive himself here.'

It sounded concise and objective; almost professional. It worked with Eric. He took a long breath and let it out very slowly. When it became apparent that Hugh was not going to speak, he said slowly, 'We knew you were at the abbey, Morrie. We understood that you felt awkward about it and kept it to yourself. But . . . I think you should know that you hurt Val. A great deal.'

She looked at Hugh and immediately his gaze slid away. She said, 'I'm sorry. It was foolish. But . . . after Jannie . . . the way things were, I felt it might be better . . .'

'Maybe at first.' Eric was not going to back down on this point. 'But after you had arrived and found him obviously ill and alone, then you should have told us the truth. You lied every time you phoned, Morrie. That is what hurt Val.'

'Oh dear God.' Morag put her elbow on the table and rested her head on her hand. 'If only she had said . . . that's not an excuse. I'm so sorry.' She looked sideways at Hugh; he was now staring fixedly at his plate. She said, 'I think I saw myself as the one person in all of this who could help ... who could go in and – and – tidy everything up.' She sobbed a laugh. 'What a fool!'

There was another silence, then Eric said quietly, 'Yes,' and stood up.

Suddenly, unexpectedly she felt a spark of anger. She said loudly as he reached the door, 'He was on his own, you know. Ill and alone in that enormous place.'

Eric opened the door, turned and said, 'Thank you for looking after him, Morrie.' He closed the door gently as he left and Morag stared after him, shaking again. She looked at Hugh. Incredibly he too was standing up.

She blurted, 'Are you running off too? Am I to be sent to Coventry?' She forced a laugh. 'It's like being at school again!'

He began to stack the plates as he spoke. 'Don't be silly, Mo. You know I understand your motives perfectly.' He looked in her direction but could not quite meet her eyes. 'As a matter of fact, you were the only person who could help Berry ... sort it out. And it seems that you did. After all, Val has gone back home and even though Doc Willie and Mrs Maitland are back in Bristol, it seems ... all right.'

He was being sweetly reasonable, as always. And she hated it. She said loudly, 'Berry told me about the prison camp. There was a girl ... a nurse called Akiko. She fell for him. They killed her and then experimented on him.'

Hugh piled the plates near the hatch and came back to put away table mats and cruet.

'Yes,' he said in a withdrawn voice. 'We knew. Of course.'

She was aghast. 'You knew? Why haven't you talked to him?'

Hugh leaned on the table and looked at her at last.

'There are some things best left unsaid,' he told her with unusual authority.

She protested at that. 'He needed to tell me!'

'He needed to tell you. You, Morag. Not me ... not

anyone else.' He straightened and turned to leave. 'If it helped him . . . if it helped you . . . then I am glad.'

'What do you mean by that?'

'What I have said. I am glad.'

She followed him up the stairs; she wanted to hit him. She would never be able to explain to this oh-so-reasonable man what had happened in the sea at Lyn. In the bedroom he stripped off his tie and unbuttoned his shirt. She said angrily, 'I don't know why you're behaving like this! If you're so glad why are you so – so disapproving!'

He sat down to unlace his shoes. He said heavily, 'We . . . Eric and I . . . we are worried about Val. She is so alone. First Jannie, then you . . . and, of course, Berry.'

'She need not worry about me! My God . . . you didn't think . . . Hugh, there was never any question of – of *that*! You surely didn't think?' She was aghast, staring at his downcast head.

He continued doggedly to take off his shoes. 'We knew . . . naturally . . . that there had been something between you back in the Gallenwick days— '

She said, in agony, 'Val did not know!'

'I knew. Berry loved you. He intended marrying you. If he'd been a whole man.'

'Oh my God! And you told Val!'

'She was utterly bewildered by what you had done. She needed some explanation.'

'You told her! And naturally she thought I'd gone to him – she thought I'd left you and gone to Berry! Oh my dear Lord!'

He said nothing; it was as if he could not meet her eyes. She felt anger beginning to boil inside her.

'Why did she go back to the abbey? I don't understand that. She was here? She had Eric. And . . . apparently . . . she had you.'

Her choice of phrase hit him like a physical blow and he flinched. And then . . . at last . . . she knew.

She said slowly, 'Oh no. Oh my God . . . no.'

He said as if she had not spoken, 'Eric telephoned the abbey. When Doc Willie answered, Val decided immediately to go home. I drove her down that same day.'

Morag tried to control herself. She was good at self-control. All her life she had hidden her own emotions, concerned herself with others. Years ago, when she was seventeen and had climbed the water slide with Berry Reid, she had let herself go completely. And last month in the sea at Lyn it had happened again in a different way and her long pent-up grief had been released. But this was different. This was pain and anger to a degree she had never known before.

She went to the window and looked out into the gathering dusk and breathed consciously. To her left was the tennis court, used often while Shirley was with them, now with the net slack and rolled. She imagined Val and Hugh playing singles there, imagined them walking into the orchard afterwards, Val's cardigan slung around her neck just as it had been when she was at school, her mop of curls in childish disarray, her enormous blue eyes sad and lost. She imagined Hugh, the eternal comforter, telling her everything would be all right, perhaps putting an arm around her shoulders. Val was a curious compound of schoolgirl and woman, everyone knew how 'marvellous' she was looking after the recalcitrant genius that was Berry Reid. Yet from her curls to her plump calves she looked young and unprotected. Yes, Hugh would most definitely have put an arm around her shoulders.

Morag heard her own voice saying loudly, 'You slept with her, didn't you?'

She sensed Hugh's sudden stillness behind her. It infuriated her further. He had always had this waiting quality. Hadn't he said he waited for her until she was 'established'?

She turned and screamed at him, 'Answer me, Hugh! For God's sake be honest with me!'

He stood up and faced her. His grey eyes met hers

at last. She saw the grief there and had her answer. She thought: I have lost him . . . I have never truly given myself to him . . . and now I have lost him to Val's open honesty.

She said loudly as if to placate some fate: 'All right. I fell in love with Berry Reid when I was seventeen! He came home terribly maimed and he married Val and I married you and I thought it was second-best! But it wasn't – d'you hear me Hugh? It wasn't second-best at all! And when I went down to Lyn and looked after Berry, I knew that it wasn't second-best! I knew that even if there had been no war and Berry and I had been together since 1941, it would not have worked. I knew that I was – always have been – in love with you.'

He said, 'And what now? I thought you had left me. Val thought she had left Berry. We comforted each other. Once.'

She could not imagine it. She stared into his face at once dearly familiar yet now, suddenly, the face of a stranger. It was the stranger she addressed.

'I have never felt like this before.' It was a tremulous confession; the kind of thing Shirley White might have said. She whispered, 'We have always been friends, Hugh. Our . . . friendship . . . got in the way.' She sobbed on a laugh. 'Isn't that ridiculous? It is only now . . . when we have stopped being friends . . . that I realize we have also been lovers.' She cupped his face and kissed him with desperation. 'Have I lost you, Hugh? You have barely looked at me since I came home. Do you hate me?'

He whispered, 'How could I hate you? I have not dared let you see into my face. And I have not dared see into yours.' He leaned back to focus her properly. 'You never lost me. Not once. Did I lose you?'

She shook her head and kissed him again. He returned her kisses. They began to undress with a kind of frantic haste as if time was running out for them. As they made love she heard herself cry out and was reminded of Jannie. It was as if, by sheer physical effort, they could crash through the walls that had been built between them over the past month. Some time during that autumn night she said, 'Things will never be the same for us again.' And when he asked if that was good or bad, she replied, 'I don't know.' He did not try to reassure her. But after a long silence when they held each other with the same desperation, he said, 'We have somehow gone beyond civilization, Morrie. But it will never be dull, never dull.' And he pulled her to him as if trying – literally – to make their bodies one.

In the morning they got up early and walked to the sea. Only then did they realize that there had been a storm in the night. The promenade was covered in seaweed and there were sandbags at the doors of the houses.

Morag said, 'We needed it. Everything was drying up.'

He said, 'Like us?'

'I suppose so.' She leaned on the rail and looked out at the tide. 'After those two miscarriages, I suppose I felt sterile, Hugh. Barren. This time I think it will be different.'

He knew what she meant. 'Don't set your heart on that, Mo. It won't matter. We've got something . . . you and I. It can survive a great deal.' He put an arm around her and she smiled as her thighs trembled.

The air was damp and cold after the rain. 'All right. But . . . I still think I am pregnant. And I still think this time it will be all right.'

Jannie was strangely but wonderfully happy during the rest of that summer and autumn. Eve was not like Peggy Reid of course, but Julie made her laugh and Rosamund unexpectedly adored her grandma and called her Evie and would do anything for her, so Jannie was immediately relieved of two-thirds of her children. With new-found confidence Jannie took over the cooking again. She stockpiled fruit puddings and cakes as she had done so happily at the abbey and cooked enormous joints of meat in the slow side-oven so there was always a meal half done. Eve, soon bored with preparing vegetables and cleaning the bathroom, contacted an agency in Barnstaple and they ran through half a dozen 'home helps' until Mrs Skinner turned up, a small workhorse of a woman who fell in love with Durston to the extent of cleaning his wellingtons each night and standing them in front of the Aga.

What was the best thing of all, however, was that Eve 'had a word' with Durston. Jannie never knew what she said, but during those first awful days when she had wept and clung to her mother and told her things that afterwards she wished she hadn't, Eve had understood that Dusty must leave Jannie alone at least until after this baby was born.

She had held Jannie, rocking her like mothers did. It had never happened before and Jannie thought she was in heaven.

'Surely if you just tell him, darling? He wouldn't . . . well, he wouldn't rape you, would he?' Eve tinkled a laugh to show she wasn't serious, but Jannie clung to her fiercely.

'It's not like that, Eve! If he . . . I can't hold out against him . . . you don't know what I'm like!'

Eve glinted a grin at the waif-like face on her shoulder. 'Oh I do, darling. It's me you're talking to. Remember?' She kissed Jannie's nose reassuringly. 'I'll talk to him, sweetie. Don't give it another thought.'

Jannie had not been hopeful but, amazingly, whatever Eve said had worked. Durston had moved into the back bedroom and was all consideration. He had never fussed over her during her pregnancies before, but this was different. He was forever fetching a stool so that she could put her legs up, checking on her diet, bringing her grapes and peaches from Barnstaple market. When Julie started at the primary school he took and fetched her. He drove Eve and Jannie around the shops and came in with them to buy the layette.

'I can't believe it,' Jannie said to her mother when the clocks went back and the evenings suddenly drew in. 'He's always been loving but I thought it was only because . . . well, because he wanted to sleep with me, frankly!'

Eve said, 'He thinks this baby is going to be a boy.' She sighed. 'Men are so strange like that. I think it was when you were born and turned out to be a girl that Ronnie started to look elsewhere.'

'Pops?' Jannie stared across the hearth to where her mother was curled up on the sofa trying to manicure her splintering nails. 'But I always thought it was you who – who looked elsewhere!'

'Well of course, I wasn't going to be left on the shelf, darling! That's not me!' Eve stretched languorously, displaying beautifully slim hands and legs. 'Not bad for almost fifty, am I?'

'You're beautiful,' Jannie said honestly, knowing full well her mother was over fifty. 'So it was because of me that you two drifted apart?'

Eve arched her brows. 'Oh I don't think so, do you? Ronnie was so dull. If you'd been a boy he would probably have been duller still!' She tinkled her infectious laugh and Jannie found herself echoing it.

She said confidently, 'Actually, I think it's going to be a boy too.' She patted her stomach, already enormous. 'Yes,' she stared into the fire. 'Yes, I want to give him a son. He will be . . . pleased.' She thought of Berry, crippled, unable to do so many things. He could watch his son grow up whole and healthy like he had been.

Eve said curiously, 'Will you want to sleep with him again? After the baby is born?'

For an instant Jannie almost told her mother that she would sleep with him any time and anywhere he wished. But then she hardly knew how much her mother knew about the Berry business.

She said slowly, 'I don't know . . . I suppose so. He won't be willing to be celibate for much longer.' She

355

looked at her mother's smiling face knowing that Eve
enjoyed this kind of woman-talk more than anything.
She said humorously, 'I can't quite believe he's celibate
now. D'you suppose he sleeps with Mrs Skinner?'

They both laughed helplessly and Durston, coming in
from the cowsheds, paused at the door thinking what a
perfect pair they were, sitting together in the firelight,
laughing happily.

He said expansively, 'You know, you two make me feel
good. Very good.'

They both knew what he meant: he thought he was
entirely responsible for their happiness. They laughed
more than ever.

Just before Christmas, Morag visited the farm. She
brought an enormous sack of presents for the children,
a hamper for the adults and some baby clothes. What
she also brought was the news that she was pregnant.

'Oh, my dear.' Jannie was so pleased to see her she
could not let go her arm. 'Oh Morrie, how wonderful!
Oh you must keep it this time, surely? Do you rest
each afternoon? Are you eating properly ... taking
your orange juice?'

'Of course.' Morag was delighted with her welcome;
she had not known what to expect. It seemed Eve Mears
was doing a good job. 'Remember, I am a doctor!'

They talked as they had not done for years. It was
a wonderful day. It was only when Morag said she
must leave that there was the faintest suspicion that
all was not completely well. Jannie came to the car and
stacked her own presents onto the back seat. Eve stood
in the porch clutching the children around her, out of
earshot.

Jannie said, 'Have you seen Val? Or Berry?'

Morag said, 'No. Not yet. Val and I are not quite ...
after all that business in the summer.'

'I know.' Jannie's small face quivered suddenly. 'I love
her so much, Mo. And of course she will never speak

to me again. I don't blame her. I just wish it could be different.'

'Of course she'll come round,' Morag said confidently. 'We need time. That's all.'

'That might be all right for you,' Jannie mourned. 'But not for me. You see . . . this baby is Berry's and Val knows that. And she knows I still love him and always will.'

Morag was more surprised than shocked. She had thought that somehow Jannie would by now have accepted that Berry could never father children. Everything seemed so wonderfully normal at the farm she had assumed that Jannie was 'cured' of that terrible infatuation. Just for a moment she was tempted to tell her through the car window that her baby must be Durston's; and then she did not. Perhaps Hugh was right and there were things that had to be suppressed.

She gazed into the blue eyes that were so unlike Val's and swallowed.

'Listen, Jannie. We shall always be friends. You and Val and me. Whatever happens. You know that.'

Jannie smiled sadly. Then said, 'Drive carefully. Happy Christmas. Take care of your baby. Just think, we're pregnant together!'

'So we are!' They both laughed and Morag had actually started to drive away when the geese began their honking and another car drove into the yard.

It was a car neither of them recognized, but when the driver blasted the horn, they knew instantly who it was. Jannie clutched her heart theatrically and Morag jerked to a stop and leapt out into the mud.

'Berry!' She put an arm around Jannie who looked about to faint. 'Jannie – it's Berry – he's got one of those special cars! At last!'

Berry wound down his window. His face was thin, almost hollow, but his dark eyes were alight.

He said, 'By all that's holy! Morrie! Val sent me down to mend matters with Dusty and Jannie! I had no idea you were here – where's Hugh?'

'At the manor. Still valuing . . . you were going to come and look at the pictures. Remember?'

'I will. I will. I promise.' He began the long job of clambering out of his car. 'What d'you think?' he grunted. 'I've had her three weeks. Been everywhere, done everything. Like having wings.'

They all went back into the kitchen. Jannie did not speak. She looked as she had looked back in the summer; like a ghost.

Eve deployed the children and put the kettle on. Durston came in and after lowering like a threatening bull for a few moments, decided to talk about the car. Morag began to make her second farewells.

'Just a minute – hang on Dusty – ' Berry banged his fist on the kitchen table for silence and the children gazed at him wide-eyed.

'Nobody wonders why I've come now . . . no questions?'

Eve said diplomatically, 'Well . . . Christmas and all that sort of thing . . .'

Berry laughed. 'Nothing to do with Christmas. We haven't got a single card or present yet!' He looked at Morag, held her gaze determinedly. 'Val wanted me to tell you. She's pregnant. Baby due next May.' In the silence that followed he continued to hold Morag's gaze. 'We're delighted,' he said emphatically. 'Absolutely delighted.'

Duston let out a sigh like a trumpet blast. 'My God. So am I. Surely this can be the end of the feud . . . all that ridiculous nonsense over Jannie's portraits . . . Congratulations, old man! I couldn't be more pleased . . . well that's not true because I'm much more pleased with my own baby!' He snorted a laugh and Julie joined in. Eve clapped her hands and looked at Morag and Jannie.

'Well . . . isn't that amazing?' she asked everyone. 'You three girls are all pregnant! At the same time!'

Jannie recovered first. 'Amazing,' she echoed obediently. 'Isn't it, Mo?'

Morag managed to look away from Berry's hypnotic dark gaze.

'Yes.'

The really amazing thing was that her voice did not falter. It sounded strong and completely normal.

CHAPTER TWENTY-THREE

Jannie's baby boy was born by Caesarian section on the twenty-eighth of February 1957.

When Mrs Merrydown had called on St Valentine's Day, there had been some concern because the violent kicking which made Jannie so sick had suddenly stopped and it seemed to the health visitor, listening through her stethoscope on the mountain of Jannie's abdomen, that the heartbeat was fainter. She decreed that Jannie should 'go in' for observation.

'I'm having him at home,' Jannie said with the sudden stubbornness that had characterized this pregnancy. 'I had the others at home and this one is very special. He will be born at home.'

Five days later Mrs Merrydown was blunt.

'My dear, if you don't allow a Caesarian section to be performed very soon, your baby will die and I think you will be at risk too.'

When they made the incision, the wall of the uterus was so thin it was possible to see the baby-shape through it. There was no question of any more children for Jannie. As soon as she was strong enough they talked about sterilization. She was glad. If there had been a chance of having more children by Berry it would have been different. As it was, she thankfully agreed to whatever they suggested.

Durston boasted at the Doone Arms that it was the only way to avoid another baby. 'It doesn't matter what precautions we take. She gets pregnant immediately I go near her!'

Berry who had driven over to wet the baby's head, said drily, 'Might be something to do with Jannie as well as you, Dusty!'

Durston looked into his mug thoughtfully. 'Yes. She's not a bad little lass.' He glinted at Berry. 'As you well know, brother!'

'Look. Can't we gloss over that unfortunate period?' Berry said. 'Christ. I was trying to help you over a bad time— '

But Durston was laughing. 'Don't worry, old man. I know you can only shoot blanks.' He hiccupped loudly. 'Must be OK sometimes though. Else how did your Val get that bun in her oven?' He looked suddenly alarmed. 'Hope you don't think it was anything to do with me, brud! She wouldn't let me within a yard of her the whole time she was at the farm!'

Berry forced a laugh and put up a hand to order more beer. 'No. I don't think it was anything to do with you,' he said and wondered whether Durston had always been so insensitive. He thought of Jannie, so small and frail, and frowned. 'You're going to have to take care of that wife of yours for sometime to come,' he said. 'This must all be a frightful strain on her.'

Durston scoffed at that. 'She's as strong as an ox!' he boasted. 'Like a vixen. Or a little shrew.'

Berry shook his head. 'More like a harvest mouse.' He suddenly remembered the trembling mouse that Morag had kept in her pocket years ago. Busy Lizzie. He said, 'Hang on to Eve Mears, for God's sake. Jannie will need all the help she can get.'

'Oh, I'll do that all right,' Durston said and upended his mug.

Because Val and Morag thought Jannie might die, they both went to the hospital and met for the first time since Val had left Berry last June. It was not easy. They sat either side of the hospital bed, holding one of Jannie's hands and looking assiduously at her and not each other. Jannie was very weak, her face waxy, her breathing shallow. But she was happy and triumphant too.

'I shall call him Ronald after Pops,' she whispered.

361

'Dusty isn't keen. He says it sounds like a band leader. Ronnie Reid. But I don't care.'

'You're entitled to choose the name,' Morag agreed. Val nodded quickly.

Jannie moistened her dry lips and murmured, 'I hated you at first, Val. Having Berry's child. And then I thought ... it's wonderful. It's something else we share.' She looked intently at Val. 'We can share this, can't we Val? We can see each other again? Be together?'

Val said woodenly, 'Of course we can.'

'When are you due? It must be sooner than May. You're so big!'

'I think it might be towards the end of April.' Val tried to smile. 'I was always fatter than either of you, remember.'

'And what about you, Mo?'

'May.' Morag smiled at Jannie. 'We shall have to come and get some hints from you, darling. As soon as you're well again perhaps we can get together?'

Val risked a quick glance sideways. She smiled too. 'That would be nice, wouldn't it, Jannie?'

They were talking to her as if she were a child. She looked like a child; her teeth too big for her mouth.

But Jannie surprised everyone. She brought Ronald home four weeks later and apart from having to rest every afternoon, she seemed as good as new. She doted on the baby, but then she had always doted on her babies. Peggotty was relegated to the playpen with Rosamund, and Ronald spent his days in his mother's arms, often attached to one of her nipples.

Eve tossed him up one day and said, 'My God, you're heavy, Ronnie Reid! A little roly-poly, that's what you are!' She laughed down at her daughter. 'Ronnie Roly-Poly!'

Julie took up the new name and Rosamund, almost two and a half, shouted 'Roly! Roly! Roly!' And Roly Reid he became. Jannie was duly sterilized and came home thinner and whiter than ever and with a lost look about her.

She said to her mother, 'It was something I could do, Eve. Have children. It makes me feel so . . . odd.'

Eve was amazed. 'Darling, you really are idiotic! Think what fun you can have now! And no worries at all!'

'Yes,' Jannie said doubtfully. The only 'fun' of that sort she wanted would be with Berry and he hadn't shown himself since that day he had announced Val's pregnancy. She heard he was having one of his frantic working periods and Val was making him lie down with her every afternoon. She hated that. The thought of them side by side on Berry's bed in the music room, Berry's aluminium leg against the wall, Val with her pregnancy now absolutely obvious . . . it made her want to cry. She knew there would never be anyone else for her. Not really. Sometimes she looked at Durston when she announced she was going to bed. But he did not meet her eye and continued to sleep in the guest room. If it had not been for Ronnie she knew she would feel just the same as she had last summer. As if she were nothing . . . nothing worth having. Ronnie and Eve. They were her saviours.

By the time Val had known for certain that she was pregnant, she and Berry had established a relationship that was close to the one they had shared before their wedding. Val told Berry what to do and, grumblingly, he did it. Except that now she told him what not to do. 'You mustn't work longer than two hours at a stretch.' 'You mustn't go without breakfast . . . lunch . . . supper.'

He had a series of sketches of Dr Wilkie, all of which he wanted to develop into portraits. Dr Wilkie was at once girlishly flattered and professionally cautious.

'You know what he's like, Vallery dear. He goes out of his way to be outrageous. I caught a glimpse of some of the work he did with Jannie and can quite understand it caused a rift between you.'

Val had smiled. A rift. What a gentle word for the battle that had raged – was still raging between all of them. She could have borne it where Jannie was concerned . . . Jannie was incorrigible and that was that. But Morrie . . .

'I don't think for one moment Berry would produce anything that could embarrass you, Doctor. He thinks very highly of you.'

Dr Wilkie blushed, she actually blushed. 'I think he does, Vallery. And I am . . . honoured.' She looked around the music room, empty of Berry because Val had chosen to come into it.

'It has been such a strange experience, my dear. I know I have been here with various groups of young painters, but this . . . just your husband and myself in this room. With the sea all around it.' She forced a smile. 'The place lends itself to melodrama, Vallery. And I can understand only too well why my sister did what she did. One feels the strangest sense of – of – presences. Being out there, waiting.' She laughed uncomfortably. 'I am not at all metaphysical as you know, child. But I always had a horror of this place. And now . . . those presences are comforting, Vallery. Can you understand that?'

Val shrugged helplessly. 'Doctor, I am so – so *pedestrian*. To me this is . . . was . . . a very beautiful house practically rising from the sea.'

Dr Wilkie raised her brows. 'Was?' she queried.

Val smiled ruefully. 'A touch of homesickness I think. As I said, I am pedestrian. And . . . basically, quite urban.' She smiled properly. 'But I am so glad you feel happier here now. Please come often. Berry enjoys your company very much.'

For a moment Val thought the older woman might embrace her. Then she turned away. 'I'll remember that,' she said.

The few days they shared at the abbey were good for Val. She and Mrs Maitland got on excellently in the kitchen and she and Berry were able to treat each other politely, almost as fellow guests in their own home. When the two women left there were days when she hardly saw Berry. She knew he was working like a dervish on his sketches and she took trays of food in at regular intervals, changed the sheets on his bed, even pushed the vacuum around. She felt as if she were there simply waiting for Berry to collapse. Then she could take up her role as his nurse. In the long hours of loneliness she walked along the cliffs and stared out to sea almost hoping Dr Wilkie's 'presences' would make themselves felt. Was this all there was to the rest of her life?

Once she telephoned the office at Clevedon, desperate just to hear Hugh's voice. When a female answered, she was taken aback. It was too early for the part-time secretary to be there.

'It's a personal call,' she said. 'Either Mr McKinley or Mr Reid.'

'They are both at the manor house at present. May I give them a message?'

'No. I . . . I'll telephone Morag. Dr Reid.'

'I say, you're not in luck! Morag has a clinic this morning. That's why I'm here. Something to do. I'm staying at Redley Lodge.'

Val realized suddenly that this must be one of Jessica White's children. She felt a pang of sympathetic understanding for Morag. They both needed a third person in their marital relationships!

She said, 'It's all right. I can ring any time.' She replaced the receiver before the girl could become embarrassingly helpful. She felt worse than she had before. It was this damned house. So cut off, so isolated.

October blew itself out in a series of gales that brought sea spray pouring over the window of the music room. Her father came for a week especially to tell her that Morag was pregnant again. He knew it would hurt her, but she did not react at all. He was suddenly alarmed at what he called her 'peakiness'.

'Darling, you looked so well in the summer. Is something wrong?'

Val smiled wryly at him. They were sitting together at

the kitchen table which was in the deep shadow of the cliff. It felt like mid-winter.

'You know something is wrong, Daddy. Don't let's pretend. Not when we're alone like this.'

Eric put his hand over hers. 'You are so like your mother. You are able to open your heart, Val. It is a splendid talent.' He patted the hand briskly. 'Of course I know that things are difficult here between you and Berry. More difficult than usual.' He smiled too. 'You've never had it easy, Val.'

'But it was always worthwhile, Daddy. There must have been something between us – love – whatever it was – that made it worthwhile. Now, I am simply a housekeeper and nurse.'

'Can't you have it out with him? Even a row? If you hate him, let him know. See what happens.'

'I don't hate him. Not really. I don't feel anything at all.'

'What about Morrie?'

'Same applies. You tell me she is pregnant. I ought to hate her again for that – but I don't. Jannie is quite poorly with this new baby, but I don't care about that either. I love you and I love Hugh. And that is that.'

'Perhaps you could go away for a time. Stay with Juliet. Or Dr Wilkie.'

But she was suddenly decisive. 'I can't leave Berry.'

It seemed they had come full circle; he stared at her helplessly. 'Well then, will you have a check-up with Dr Harris?'

'Daddy, I know what is the matter with me – I don't need a check-up. I've got a bad case of the miseries!' She laughed because this was a phrase from childhood. But Eric did not laugh. Instead, before he went back home, he spoke to Berry very seriously.

'I know all about a father's natural anxiety,' he concluded. 'But keep a weather eye open, Berry. There's a good chap.' He could have added bitterly that Berry was not the only sick person in the abbey, but he did not.

Berry looked at him for a long moment, then nodded briefly.

And so November began its endless march; Val's least favourite month because it was then that news of Teddy's death had come through. She felt as if she were being sucked into a black pit. Berry found her sitting on the stairs one day her head resting against the banisters.

He said abruptly, unused to opening any kind of conversation, 'Is anything the matter?'

If she'd told him her stomach ached, or she was depressed, he might have grunted and passed by. When she said, 'No. Nothing,' he knew he had to do something.

'Come into the music room,' he said tentatively. 'I know how you feel about me, but I'm another human being. And it's light in there and the sea is looking rather special.'

She followed him in listlessly because it would have been harder to resist him. He sat her in the window-seat and told her he would make some tea and she was to use her eyes and 'see everything'. When he came back she took the proffered mug and held it so that the steam warmed her face.

He nodded to the window. 'Isn't it marvellous?' he asked.

She looked over the mug, which offered warmth and comfort, to the steel grey of the flat sea which offered cold and menace.

She said, 'I hate it.'

'Why?' he was amazed.

'Grey upon grey. Slightly depressing.'

'Is that what you see?' He eased his good leg alongside hers and took the mug from her. She had to force herself not to shrink from his closeness. 'Look,' he said gently. 'Look again. See the silver flashes? See the shifting blacks and greens? An element filled with life, Val. Teeming with it.'

367

She stared. Of course he was right. But it made no difference; it was still cold and menacing.

He said, 'Now look at the sky. Just grey?'

She did not reply. Obviously there were colours there she could not see.

He said very quietly, 'Dr Wilkie could see her sister out there, Val. Can you see your brother?'

It was as if the steam from the mug he held melted some ice behind her face. She began to weep. And then, quite suddenly, bile seemed to flood up from her stomach; the room began to tilt upwards. She heard Berry's voice, 'Oh my God! Val . . . what is it?' And then, in a riot of hideous sensation, she fainted.

Somehow Berry must have lugged her across the floor-boards and onto the bed. She came to with the same fright-ful swimming nausea and groaned long and loud. Berry's voice reached her from the other side of the bed.

'I'm phoning the doc, Val. Lie still. Concentrate on breathing.'

She obeyed him, closing her eyes and fighting the awfulness in her chest and throat with all her strength. She heard Berry stump around to her side of the bed and did not open her eyes.

'It's all right, my darling. He'll be here within half an hour.'

She felt his arms holding her and clutched at his shoulders frantically. He had called her his darling. She said his name loudly, 'Berry! Berry!' And he continued to make soothing noises and do wonderful things like smoothing her curls and touching her face and kissing her closed eyes. She wailed again, 'Berry!' She began to move.

'What is it, Val? Try to stay still.'

But she gasped, 'Sick! I'm going to be sick!'

And she was.

Dr Harris looked at them quizzically.

'I'm surprised you haven't guessed what's the matter.

For goodness' sake. Your wife is pregnant, Mr Reid! Over three months pregnant I would say at a guess.' He grinned broadly, reminding Val of Dusty for a moment. 'It happens, old man. It's a miracle, but it happens.' He had helped Berry to clean up and examined Val carefully. Now he prepared to go to the bathroom to wash his hands.

Val bleated, 'But I haven't missed a period! I'm as regular as clockwork.'

Dr Harris paused by the door. 'Not all women cease menstruation immediately. But if you continue to menstruate, please let me know.' He smiled again. 'However, as far as I can tell everything is perfectly normal. You need some iron and some vitamins and you'll be as fit as you were before – if not fitter.' His smile was congratulatory. 'You have an ideal body for child-bearing, Mrs Reid.' He left the room and Val dared to look up at Berry.

There was a very long silence. They heard water running, soap being lathered vigorously, more water.

Val said tremulously, 'Berry . . . I'm sorry. I've been sorry ever since it happened.' She moved her hands on her bare knees. 'I seem to have . . . sort of . . . thrown away . . . just about everything.'

Berry said nothing and she could tell nothing from his dark eyes. He stood, holding the edge of his painting table, taking his weight on his good leg. He smelled horribly of her vomit.

Dr Harris came back in grinning like a Cheshire cat. 'This is the bit of my job I really enjoy,' he announced almost smugly. 'We'll make an appointment for you both to come to the surgery and we can organize relaxation classes . . . do you know anything about relaxation, Mrs Reid?'

She glanced again at Berry and said dryly, 'Not very much, no.'

He repacked his bag, talking all the time, and at last stood to leave.

'The best of this . . .' he swept Berry with that knowing grin again, 'is that you can relax with your wife! This baby will make such a difference to you. And I rather think the first thing is that you will have to take over the kitchen for a while.'

He laughed as if he'd made a joke and made for the door. 'Don't come down the stairs, I know my way around this old place quite well now.'

They listened to him going down, crossing the hall, closing the porch door.

Berry said, 'I'll make some more tea.'

'Go and have a bath.' Val swung her legs to the ground. 'I'll make the tea.'

He did not move. They stood, looking at each other. He cleared his throat.

'Will you stay?' he asked.

She heard the plea in his voice and felt her heart jump just a little.

'Where else would I go?'

'To your father.'

She swallowed. Hugh lived with her father and she was having Hugh's baby.

She whispered, 'You know I cannot do that.'

His eyes were like black holes in his face. 'But you love Hugh.'

'Ah . . .' She lifted her head slightly, closed her eyes. 'He does not love me. He loves Morag.' She opened her eyes, 'Just as you love Morag.'

He said steadily, 'I was quite desperately in love with Morag when she was a girl and I was a boy. I love her now as a patient loves a doctor. It's quite different, Val.'

She shrugged. 'I don't know. I thought I was the one who nursed you.'

'Is that all it's been all this time?'

She said again, 'I don't know. I don't know anything any more.'

'You know you are pregnant. And . . . it seems that you will stay here. With me.'

She said, 'If that is what you want.'

He was silent for so long she moved away towards the door. She almost missed his whispered words.

'What I want – what I have wanted for years – is to have a child.'

She checked for an instant. Then she went on into the hall and the kitchen and she made tea.

It was after they had eaten and drunk together that he said, 'Val . . . tomorrow, if you feel better, will you sit for me?'

She covered her eyes; he must have known she was weeping and that it was not because she was unhappy.

He said briskly, 'Then I must get one of those cars that have hand controls. I shall have to do the driving. Especially when you go into labour.'

Hugh wanted to move into their own house. He felt suddenly that Eric's presence was inhibiting his relationship with Morag. It was all too obvious that Eric was frantically anxious about Val alone – as he saw it – in the Gothic house on the cliff. When they heard of Val's pregnancy it was hard enough on Morag; he knew she had felt desperately unhappy after her meeting with Val at Jannie's bedside. But it was also hard on him: Eric and Hugh had always enjoyed a special friendship. That disappeared overnight. Eric blamed Hugh for Val's situation. It was as simple as that.

Strangely, after lobbying for their own house in the past, Morag was unwilling to make the break now.

'Don't you see that if we branch out on our own now, it will be for negative reasons, not for positive ones.'

'You can't face being alone with me,' Hugh said matter-of-factly.

Morag had a sense of *déjà vu*. Hadn't he coerced her into staying on at Redley Lodge back in 1951 in much the same way?

They were both busy so the wrangling had to be limited. Morag's clinics had developed into prenatal

371

and postnatal sessions; in the circumstances of her own pregnancy she was very popular with the young mothers of Clevedon. She took the regulation relaxation classes with them and was always willing to discuss the more mundane aspects of maternity care. But there was an element of truth in Hugh's childish accusation. On the night of the storm when they had both broken through their reserve, it had been easy to love him unreservedly and to accept that in spite of Val, in spite of Berry, he loved her too. But Val's pregnancy had made a difference. There was no suppressing this particular memory. When Val's baby was born it would be impossible not to remember day after day that the child was also Hugh's.

She had taken up her usual role of supporter.

'We shall learn to live with this, Hugh . . . don't worry about it. And while we're learning, Eric's presence is surely comforting— '

'He is a constant reminder of – of what happened!' Hugh simply did not know how to cope with any of it any more. Eric's presence at the office was bad enough. To have it at home as well was too much.

'We'll see. Give it until this arrives,' she touched her abdomen. 'See how we all react to having a baby in the house.'

She put his hand where hers had been and then began to kiss him. Morag had learned a great deal in the last few months and she knew exactly how important sex was now.

It was only the next day that Eric dropped his bombshell. He waited until they had cleared away the supper things and all assembled in the sitting room. Very deliberately he sat in his wife's chair in the window. It was a long way from the fire; a long way from the sofa where Hugh and Morag sat ready for the nine o'clock news.

'Before you switch on,' Eric held up a detaining hand, 'a house came in today. Someone selling one of the big red brick properties in Gardens Road opposite the office.'

They both knew exactly what he meant. Morag looked round in surprise. Hugh stared at the carpet.

'It would be ideal for you. Three enormous reception rooms, Morrie. One would be ideal for a surgery. A sheltered garden . . .' He cleared his throat. 'For the pram.' He fished some papers from his pocket and put them on the coffee table. 'And of course so near the office.'

Morrie picked up the papers and glanced through them. 'Yes. I see what you mean.' She passed them to Hugh. 'You know about it I expect.'

'No.' His voice was strangled. 'No, this is Eric's idea.'

'What do you think?' Eric asked, as if politely interested.

'Of course.' Hugh still could not look up. 'If this is what you want. Of course.'

Morag continued to stare at Eric. 'You want us out!' she said almost disbelievingly.

He said steadily, 'Not quite like that, my dear. You know you are like my family. But in fact you are not my family. My family is Val. And she might want to come home. But of course she cannot do that if you are here.'

Morag said, 'I have been so selfish. You are right. We are stopping Val from coming back home.' She glanced at Hugh. 'I'm sorry, my dear. I should have realized what you were getting at.' She looked again at Eric. 'Hugh has suggested this before.'

He stammered, 'I wasn't . . . I'm afraid I wasn't thinking of Val.' He stood up suddenly. 'This is such a mess. Of course we must go.' He leaned on the mantelpiece and said to Eric, 'Do you want me out of the business?'

Eric was genuinely astonished. 'Of course not! My God, I plan to retire fully soon. In any case you bought a partnership into the firm almost six years ago . . . it's more yours than mine now.'

Hugh said almost violently, 'No! It's still yours, Eric. And Val's.' He looked over at Eric. 'Is she that unhappy?'

Eric seemed to withdraw into himself. 'Happiness has very little to do with anything now, surely?' He relented slightly and added, 'She is not unhappy. I simply wonder if the situation will become . . . untenable. In the future.' He shrugged. 'Who knows? But I can certainly see that the abbey is not a suitable place for a young child.'

For a wild and uncontrollable instant, Morag let herself imagine Val's child at Redley Lodge and Morag's own child two miles away in Clevedon. Half-brothers. Half-sisters. She wondered just how 'tenable' that situation might be.

She said brightly, 'We'll go and look at it, shall we Hugh?' She saw his bewilderment and said, 'The house. In Gardens Road.' She turned to Eric. 'They're lovely, I quite agree with you. I'm so glad you thought of it.'

Eric looked at her sadly. It was almost as if she were fastening some inner suit of armour.

Val's baby girl was born at a small nursing home just outside Minehead on the twenty-first of April. She was in labour for just two hours, refused the gas and air and was sitting in a chair watching Berry rock the baby when Jannie and Morag arrived.

'I could have managed alone,' she boasted. 'It was a piece of cake!'

Morag felt as she did with so many of her 'mums'; a great sense of pride. She did not allow herself to look at either Berry or the baby.

Jannie said, 'It's your hips, darling. They're made for child-bearing.' She did not look at Berry or the baby either. She was conscious of a terrible gnawing jealousy. This baby was a mere two months younger than Roly. How could Berry have been unfaithful so soon? She herself had not slept with Dusty since that time.

Val laughed easily, 'Bitch,' she commented without rancour. Suddenly she could forgive the whole world. Hugh might well have impregnated her but this was Berry's daughter. The child had gradually become visible in each of the portraits he had made during the last five months. He had said only last week, 'She's a girl, Val. She wants me to paint her and she knows I only paint women!'

She had smiled at him, certain that he was right. She had said, 'And you only paint the women you love.'

He had not denied it. And she had stretched her arms above her head and yawned mightily as if filling herself with a kind of glory.

Now she looked up at Morag: she had long ago accepted that Berry loved Morag in a special way, but that too had become something to be grateful for. Morag had seen Berry through what Val thought of as a 'bad patch'. Val took her hand wishing so much she could talk openly to Morag ... wishing there were words to describe how she felt. Wishing – praying – that Morag did not hate her for loving Hugh. She looked down at the red knuckles and unexpectedly kissed them.

Morag kept herself still and managed a smile. 'It's natural to feel euphoric,' she said as if trying to explain Val's sudden demonstration of affection.

Jannie said, 'Yes, that's true. It doesn't last. You'll feel terrible when your milk comes in.'

'Oh thanks!' Val rolled her eyes at Berry. 'I'm so glad you came!' She was suddenly still, holding Morag's fingers, looking at Jannie. 'I am. Seriously. So glad we are all together again. Aren't you?'

Jannie said doubtfully, 'I suppose so.'

And Morag said heartily, 'Rather!' But she retrieved her hand from Val's as soon as she could.

Hugh said quickly, 'What names have you come up with?'

Val said, 'Berry's thought of something quite wonderful.'

Berry grinned. 'My sense of drama. I thought Edwina. For Val's brother and for Doc Willie's sister.' Edwina opened her heavily hooded eyes and surveyed Berry gravely but with a kind of approval. Berry leaned his leonine head closer. 'Hello Edwina,' he said softly. And Morag remembered the harvest mouse.

Henry William Reid was born at the new house in Clevedon one month later. Neither Val nor Jannie could leave their babies long enough to visit Morag, and she was glad. She had never known such happiness as this and she was terrified of anything that might spoil it. Eric and Hugh walked over from the office practically every hour to check that everything was going smoothly. The young mothers from her clinics called regularly; Jessica brought Shirley down; Aunt Harriet took up residence and organized everything in her orderly fashion. It was a time of quiet, milky peace, disturbed only by young Harry when he was hungry.

Hugh wished it could go on for ever and knew it could not. When Aunt Harriet went home and the callers diminished, he said tentatively, 'Berry is going to drive Val and Edwina up to Eric's for Whitsun. That will be nice, won't it?'

Morag was feeding Harry. Her hair was down and a few threads of grey emphasized its darkness. Involuntarily, she pressed Harry further into her breast.

Hugh said gently, 'Mo . . . Edwina can't harm Harry.'

'Of course not!' Morag rallied instantly. 'And they are . . . cousins. After all.' She tried so hard to be objective. Edwina was Hugh's daughter; of course he would want to see her. She said, 'We'll have a picnic. Shall we? On the beach?'

'It might be awfully difficult for Berry managing on the shingle.'

It was not a reproach but she apologized swiftly. 'I didn't think . . . yes of course. It must be here.'

He cupped her face. 'Darling, just let it happen. Please. Don't fight so hard.'

'Oh, Hugh.' She laughed and turned her mouth into

the palm of his hand. 'You talk as if we're engaged in some kind of battle!'

Before he could reply, Harry moved his head to avoid suffocation and voiced a protest. They both laughed.

CHAPTER TWENTY-FOUR

1957

On the fourth of October 1957 when Roly Reid was eight months old and concentrating every ounce of his energy into learning to crawl, the Russians launched Sputnik I and the space race began. Jannie, who felt she had been in some kind of competition all her life, said to Val, 'Just you wait. If you think Edwina has been hard work up till now, just you wait till she's on the move. You won't have a minute's peace with all those stairs!'

Val, who had forgotten that Jannie might think Berry had fathered Roly, laughed comfortably.

'We've already wire netted all the banisters and had gates fitted!' She shook her head at her daughter so that her curls bounced like ping-pong balls. 'Who's got a doting daddy then?' she cooed.

Jannie thinned her lips into nonexistence. 'You're lucky! I hardly see anything of Dusty these days!'

Val looked up, surprised. 'Oh Jannie! He's absolutely crazy about Roly! You know he is!'

'Only because he's a boy!' Jannie wished she had the nerve to announce to the whole world that Dusty's pride was misplaced. But that would be the end of everything with Val. And they at least had some trace of their old friendship. 'Anyway, I meant me. Dusty hardly spends a minute in my company!'

Val remembered Dusty's awful selfishness when she had been living at the farm last year. She said sympathetically, 'At least your mother is staying on, Jannie. Which is lovely after all these years, surely?'

Jannie nodded. 'The one good thing to come out of . . . all this.' She crossed her fingers mentally and added, 'Besides Roly, I mean.' She went to Roly and picked him up just as he had reached his goal of the cupboard where the biscuit tin was kept. He screamed. She said loudly, 'I'm terrified she'll get fed up with it all and leave. That friend of hers – Roger Vallender – he's keeping the house going in Clifton. But if he leaves— '

'He's hardly likely to give up free accommodation of that standard,' Val commented.

'No, but . . . well, there's nothing much happening here.'

They both knew what she meant. No men for Eve. No nightclubs where she might meet men.

Val said, 'There are her grandchildren. And her daughter.'

But Jannie said nothing. Granted Eve adored the children when they were good. But as for Jannie herself . . . their relationship had always been difficult.

Berry and Dusty walked across the farmyard. Berry was using a stick; he wore a panama in deference to the autumn sun and because he was losing his thick black hair. He was unexpectedly upset about it; Val had bought him the panama after Edwina's birth. Julie and Ros tagged behind him adoringly; Eve brought up the rear, holding Peggotty's hand. It made a charming picture and Val reached down for her camera and took a quick snapshot. She had always liked photography and Berry was encouraging her to take it seriously.

Everyone groaned but Berry called, 'Turn around, Val – take the geese! We can put the two pictures together!'

Val did so. Jannie, holding the yelling Roly, felt the taste of envy in her mouth. Dusty would have dismissed any hobby she might take up. He did not even sleep with her now. And, after all, that was all she was good for.

By the time the visitors left, she was exhausted.

'Eve, can you cope? I'll just have to go to bed.'

'Of course I can cope, darling. Dusty will help. And Mrs Skinner has left supper all ready.'

Jannie trailed upstairs and into the big double bedroom which now seemed so enormous. Everything was neat and tidy thanks to Mrs Skinner. Jannie went to the window and looked out. It was already dark; she shivered at the thought of winter. How was she going to get through another winter knowing there would be no more pregnancies, no more babies to give her stupid life any rhyme or reason? She stared at the night sky and wondered where the Russian space probe was. Perhaps that was what all the stars were, just space probes? She shivered again. She had always been terrified of the thought of eternity. Nothing could go on endlessly . . . unless it was this pointlessness . . . this vacuum. Perhaps this *was* eternity.

She opened the window wide and undressed in front of it letting the night air chill her to the marrow. Then she got into the cold bed and hoped she had got pneumonia and would die before the morning. No-one would miss her, not really. At one time Val and Morag would have been broken-hearted. Not now.

She rolled over onto her stomach and tried to stop her chaotic thoughts. Perhaps she should go to Berry and ask him to meet her . . . just occasionally. Somewhere in the country where they could make the kind of wild passionate love which had so transported her eighteen months ago. He could drive now so it shouldn't be a problem. But even as the thought occurred to her she remembered his humorous call to Val, 'Turn round and take the geese.' He was so utterly domesticated . . . all the wild wonder driven out of him by Val and her plump ordinariness.

Outside her room Julie's voice suddenly pierced the silence. 'Shall I go in and say night-night to Mummy?' Eve's murmur came back, 'No darling. Mummy will be fast asleep by now.' Other treads could be heard on the landing carpet. She identified them: Ros, Peggotty stumbling by her father, Dusty murmuring to Roly who was doubtless asleep in his arms. Her children. All of them happy without her.

The hours seemed endless: this *must* be eternity. She was still cold, her tiny body unable to fight the chill of the pristine sheets. She thought of Dusty, always warm: she thought of his chest, matted with the curly hair, the smell of him, the comfort to her soul and body as he said, 'Come here, old girl . . . come on . . . come to Dusty . . .' And suddenly she sat up, astonished at herself, astonished at the simplicity and obviousness of the solution to all this. He was her husband! Marital duty was a two-way business. She needed *him* – Dusty – urgently. Not Berry who was miles away in body and spirit. Not Val and Morag who had never been as close to her as they had been to each other. Not her mother or the children. She wanted her husband.

She slid out of bed and padded, naked and still shivering, to the door and onto the landing and past the nursery towards the spare room. That door was slightly open so that Dusty could hear if Roly cried in the night. She glided up to it and slid through sideways, suddenly proud of her tininess, her wraith-like quality. It was what Dusty had always adored. And then she stood very still, her eyes dry and burning in the musty room. Dusty had not drawn his curtains either but the window was closed against any freshness. The two bodies on the bed seemed to be performing some dance. They writhed silently, pantingly, sometimes together, some-times prising themselves apart to change the rhythm of movement, the pattern of the dance. Jannie had long been an expert in the mechanics of sex; but she knew she could never match her mother. She flattened her bare back against the wall and watched, transfixed as Morag – so long ago – had watched her father perform an appendectomy. She remembered Eve saying once to Ronnie, 'I know how to give a man a good time.' And that piece of information had somehow ended the argument preceding it.

When one of the bodies straightened in ecstasy and Jannie saw it was her mother's, she slid out of the room again as invisibly as she had slipped in. In any case, she was certain that had she given in to her instincts and started to scream the house down, no-one would have heard her. She probably wasn't there at all. She was probably in the universe with the sputnik.

She went back to her room and crept into bed. In the morning they found her there, sucking her thumb and staring at nothing.

Eve telephoned Val a week later. She was almost hysterical with anxiety and a need to escape a suddenly impossible situation.

'I think I've done my bit, Val!' she said defensively before Val could comment on the ghastly news. 'It's all very well but I can't take everything on to my shoulders! And my tenant back home has given notice – I simply must go back and check that everything is all right there!'

Val said, 'Do you mean she is in a coma? I don't quite understand.'

'Not a coma. Though she might as well be. She's like a zombie. Won't dress, eat . . . won't actually *do* . . . anything!'

'What happened? We were there the day before if you remember.'

'Exactly. I was hoping you could shed some light – did you say anything to her? To upset her?'

Val felt her hackles rise. 'No. But obviously we both know that she had an affair with my husband.'

'My dear, she was having a nervous breakdown! That's why I came to look after her!'

Val rolled her eyes in a kind of furious resignation. 'Look, I'll come over. Later on. I don't want Berry to know about this.'

'Still insecure?' Eve's voice was jocular, yet at the same time almost sly. Val suddenly hated her.

'Not at all,' she came back coolly. 'Berry is not well and Dr Harris is coming to see him after surgery. When I've talked to Jannie, I'll give Berry a proper report.'

Eve turned petulant. 'Well, I can't hang about indefinitely. I was planning to leave after lunch.'

'Perhaps you'd better revise that plan. Until Dr Harris has seen Jannie.'

Val replaced the receiver before Eve could say another word. She stood there, fuming at the sheer heartlessness and audacity of the woman. Edwina was sitting in the middle of her playpen next to the window that looked out over the cliff. Val suddenly scooped her up and held her close. From across the years she seemed to hear Jannie's sleep-hypnotic voice crying, 'Don't let him Ma . . . I'll tell Pops . . .' Val kissed the nape of Edwina's neck and wondered fiercely just what Eve had been up to.

Dr Harris examined Berry's throat and thought it might be a virus.

'Difficulty swallowing . . . no sign of a temperature however.' He coiled his stethoscope. 'Look here, old man, let me send you into Exeter for some tests. Any objections?' He listened to the objections without interest. 'Quite . . . so shall we say an ambulance will pick you up at nine tomorrow?'

'Ambulance!' Berry glared balefully. 'Have you listened to a word I've said?'

'Bit too early? Make it ten.'

Berry expelled a sigh like a trumpet note. 'I will drive myself. How does that sound?'

'Jolly good.' Dr Harris grinned. 'Thought you might prefer that, actually.'

'Crafty old bugger,' Berry commented as soon as the door closed.

'Takes one to know one.' Val took Edwina from Berry's lap. 'Time for her nap. I've got a good chicken soup for lunch. Will you be able to manage it?'

'Of course.' Berry looked up. 'Val, I love you.'

Val nodded. 'I know. I love you too. But after lunch you're going to rest however much you love me. And I'm going out.'

'You're a hard woman.' But he grinned. 'Where are you off to?'

'To see Roly and Co.' She made a face. 'There's trouble at t' mill.'

'Oh God. Not Jannie again?'

'Eve is leaving apparently.' Val sighed. 'I'll tell you all when I come home. What a family!'

But he said soberly, 'We're all one family, Val. Never forget that.'

'I'm never allowed to!' But Val grinned as she spoke; she had never felt bitter and her guilt had been expiated by Berry. She kissed him now. 'Please do as the doctor says, my love. I think you know you are head of this crazy family even if you are the youngest! We all need you.'

He caught her hand, staring at her in wonderment. 'How do you come up with things like that? I'm an obsessive, one-legged painter, mainly supported by his wife's money, estranged from his two brothers because— '

'No!' She could not bear him to refer to Morag and Jannie. 'It's not like that, Berry. You're our candle flame. You might burn us if we're careless but you give light and comfort.' She looked at him seriously. 'That's how it is, darling. So please do as Doc Harris tells you. Please.'

He said, 'Oh my God, Val.' He shook his head helplessly and released her. 'I – I love you. But you're crazy.'

Val was with Jannie for the rest of the day while Eve looked after Edwina downstairs. It was horrifying to look into Jannie's pale marbled blue eyes and see such emptiness. Eve had given up on her already and Jannie's hair was unkempt, her face sticky with sweat. Val almost dragged her to the bathroom and gave her a bath. She tipped her head back and washed the lanky hair, then towelled it vigorously. All this had no effect at all on Jannie. She directed her gaze at Val occasionally but without seeing her. Val had been appalled at her thinness two years before; now Jannie was just skin and bone, her joints sharp and childish.

Val got her back into bed and went downstairs ready to do battle with everyone there. But Dusty, in from burning back the heather out on the moors, was pathetically grateful to her for coming and Eve was completely surrounded by the five demanding children.

Val said, 'She really has had a breakdown this time.' She went to the Aga and looked in the stockpot. 'Some soup I think. And you'd better telephone Dr Harris.' She looked at Dusty. 'Something has happened. I don't want to know what it is, but I think you'd better pull up your socks.'

Dusty stammered his innocence while she made some soup and toast. Eve said nothing. She had Edwina and Roly on her lap and was leaning between them trying to hear what Peggotty was saying. Val thought she looked pretty awful. Her face was devoid of make-up and her over-permed hair was in small separate clumps over her head. Val worked out her age; she must be mid-fifties. It probably was all too much for her.

She went back up and fed the soup to Jannie spoonful by spoonful. She wondered what on earth was going to happen. If Eve left, someone would have to take on the children.

She said urgently, 'Speak to me, Jannie! Say something – anything!'

But she was talking to herself.

Eve spoke behind her. 'Val . . . can I have a word?'

Val wiped Jannie's mouth and picked up the empty bowl. 'Be back in a minute, darling,' she said brightly and followed Eve onto the landing.

Eve said immediately, 'Look, I know you think I'm a rat deserting a sinking ship and all that . . . but I really must leave, Val. I'm sorry.'

Val said, 'But the children . . . can't you hang on until a housekeeper can be found? A nurse for Jannie?'

'She'll have to go to hospital, Val, surely that's obvious?'

Val stared at her. 'Do you mean a mental hospital?'

'Psychiatric. There's no stigma these days.'

'I know that. But . . . she is your daughter, Eve.'

Eve walked to the top of the stairs. Below them Dusty was telling Julie to shut up. He sounded at the end of his tether.

Eve said, 'I am not the best person. It's probably *because* I'm her mother. I think she must have seen something. Something she would prefer not to have seen.'

'I don't understand.'

Eve rounded on her. 'Well, you should do! You've had experience of seeing your husband with other women!'

Val stared uncomprehendingly at first; then she said incredulously, 'You? And Dusty? Oh my good Lord!'

'Quite.' Eve sounded brisk. 'So you see the sooner I'm out of her sight the better.'

For two pins Val could have pushed her down the stairs. She said wildly, 'She always wanted to protect you! D'you know that? She used to talk in her sleep!'

'For God's sake, Val! We're grown women now! She should understand after what she did with your husband!'

Val gasped as if Eve had thrown water at her. 'You – you *cow*!' she shouted. 'You good-for-nothing,' she drew a deep breath and hissed, 'whore!'

Eve started to laugh. And then she switched the laugh off and walked down the stairs. 'I'll stay until Dusty gets another woman,' she said significantly and gathered the weeping Julie to her. 'Is Daddy being horrid, darling?'

Val turned and went back to the bedroom and held Jannie against her shoulder, rocking her like a child. But to no avail. She wept when she told Berry about it.

'She was so pleased about her mother . . . she thought – after all these years – Eve had changed. And even if she hadn't . . . well, she had that Roger Vallender man back home. She went home now and then to see to things . . . Jannie probably thought that was . . . sufficient.'

Berry held her as she had held Jannie, rocking her gently, kissing her forehead.

'Darling . . . we can't judge. Neither of us. Sex is so all-powerful. Would it matter if Jannie had never found out?'

'Yes, it would! It would!' But her protests were without conviction. Morag had been her best friend, yet she had practically seduced Morag's husband. She sobbed helplessly. 'I don't know what to do about Jannie . . . I can't help her again – they'll send her to an institution somewhere. I know it. Dusty is hopeless and Eve . . . Eve is so hard . . . like steel.'

Berry sighed into her curls. 'We'll go there. Lock, stock and barrel.' She jerked away to look at him. 'Just for a time,' he qualified. 'I can keep an eye on the children . . . drive Julie into school . . . that sort of thing. You know you can cope. You can cope with anything.'

She did not deny it. She said, 'What about . . . Darling, what about Jannie? If she knows you're there it could all start again. Her – her – infatuation.'

He put a hand to her cheek. 'It never stopped, Val. You know that.'

She closed her eyes momentarily. 'Yes. I suppose that is part of . . . it.'

He sighed again. 'She'll come round. For me. I don't know what will happen then. But – well – I have to talk to her. That's . . .' he smiled ruefully, '. . . that's my job in all this. Wouldn't you say?'

She said slowly, 'You're a realist, Berry. I'm a pragmatist and you're a realist.'

'What's the difference?'

'When it comes down to it . . . nothing.' She kissed him long and hard. 'I always saw through you, Berry

Reid. Right back to the time you cajoled and bullied us on the potato field.'

'I know.' He smiled again. 'I think you both saw through me . . . Jannie was the only one I fooled. And then you met Hugh. And you all fell for him.'

'You don't think I still love Hugh? How could you? This past year seems to have welded us together . . . I thought you knew that.'

He stared at her for a long time while the smile died. Then he said slowly, 'The trouble with realists, they often don't believe in miracles.'

'But then . . . you are a painter too. So you know miracles happen.'

They held each other again.

They had been three days at the farm when Berry went to Exeter for a barium meal X-ray. His throat was no better and if Val had had time to think she would have been very worried. But life at the farm with five children, a frantically guilty Dusty and a very sick Jannie, left very little time for any kind of thought. Berry did not appear to be ill at all; he managed soup and drinks and drove Julie into Barnstaple each morning, then Ros to Gallenwick and reversed the processes later. Dusty was up before dawn for the milking and saw to the Aga, fetched coal for the sitting room fire, laid the breakfast . . . the organization was tight but it was working. But Jannie remained exactly the same. Dusty brought her downstairs sometime during the morning and they all talked to her as if she were her old self. Occasionally there would be a tiny flicker of life in her eyes when Berry was in her line of vision, but each time it went almost as soon as it appeared. They put Roly on her lap and her arms would automatically hold him for a few minutes, then drop away and he would slide to the floor and crawl off towards his father.

On the fifteenth of October, Berry left early with Julie, intending to drive straight on to Exeter afterwards. Dusty took Ros to Mrs Pargeter as usual; Val settled the three little ones for their morning naps and went into Jannie.

'Bathroom time,' she said brightly just like that awful nurse at the rehab. unit., Murch's sister-in-law. 'Then we'll go down and have a cup of coffee, just the two of us.' She manhandled Jannie across the landing to the bathroom. 'I'm doing an oxtail so that Berry can have the broth – you can share it with him . . .' She pushed Jannie onto the lavatory seat. 'I'll make your bed while you wash.' She left her without much hope. In half an hour Jannie would still be sitting there, staring at the wash-basin.

Val flapped the blankets and sheets about and smoothed the eiderdown, her mind suddenly racing. Murch. What had happened to Murch in the last eighteen months? She would be ideal at the farm if she could ever bring herself to forgive Jannie. Val had her address for forwarding letters. But of course she would have another job by now.

She tore downstairs to the phone and her handbag. The number was in Weymouth: probably Murch was staying with her sister-in-law. The operator put her through and Val introduced herself and ate humble pie.

'I know how you must be feeling, Murch. Me more than anyone else!' She spoke as bracingly as possible. 'But I've forgiven and almost forgotten. Jannie was not herself. And I'm afraid she is still very ill indeed. I don't know of anyone else who could cope with the situation here . . . there are four small children to be considered besides Mr Durston.'

There was a long silence. Then Murch said heavily, 'Are you doing everything as usual?'

'No. Berry is helping me and so is Durston. But Berry is not well and I'd like to get him home . . . you know.'

'Only too well.' Murch was not going to give in without a struggle. 'I blamed him as much as her, Mrs Reid. She was dotty and he let her get away with . . . he should have known better.'

'Murch, if I can forgive him, surely you can?'

'Well . . . I was always fond of him. Of course. Alice had nursed him at Radipole and I felt I was continuing her work.'

'Which you were, Murch! I promise you that!'

'But that Jannie. Mad as a hatter by the sound of it.'

'Well . . . she isn't well, I admit. But she is no trouble. Just very . . . dependent.'

'I am trained for nursing, of course. And it's not the same here, sharing a kitchen and a bathroom . . . a very small house. I'd have the run of the kitchen at the farm?'

'The run of the house, Murch. And it's almost as big as the abbey and twice as convenient. There's a Mrs Skinner who does all the cleaning – and does it well. And Dusty would take on a girl to help with the children.'

'Hmmm.' Mrs Murchison was hooked and landed. 'When were you thinking of me starting?'

'Yesterday!' Val laughed her relief. 'Seriously, Murch. As soon as you can. And I can't thank you enough.'

'We'll have to see how it goes, mind.'

'Of course. But I know you're the right person, Murch.'

She put down the phone and looked up at a faint sound. Jannie was standing at the top of the stairs, naked, dripping water everywhere. She took the stairs two at a time. It had happened before. At least she had got off the lavatory seat and washed herself.

'Well done, darling,' she said, shepherding her back to the bedroom. 'Now let's dry you off and think what you're going to wear today. It's quite chilly . . . a nice jumper and skirt?'

But Jannie was lifting the bedcovers and creeping beneath them and suddenly Val could not cajole her any more. She tucked her in and leaned over her, tears in her eyes.

'Oh, Jannie . . . I've done my best, darling. Murch is

going to come and look after you. Don't worry about anything. Just relax.'

Jannie looked at something inside her own head and after a few more seconds, Val crept away.

Immediately Berry came back Val knew something was terribly wrong. It was mid-afternoon and Dusty had taken all the children off to meet Julie from school. Berry's car drew up amid the honking of the geese, but he did not emerge at once. She pushed the kettle onto the hot plate and fetched cups and saucers from the dresser. Even then the car door remained shut. So she went outside.

It was cold that day; she would never forget how suddenly cold it was. The leaves were gone from the hawthorn hedge and it creeked in the wind like a rusty gate. The geese stalked back to the pond, their feathers only slightly ruffled by it, but their yellow eyes baleful and dangerous. She stopped by the car and Berry opened the door.

'Wind's in the east,' he commented. 'It's bitter on the tops.'

She swallowed. 'What's the verdict?'

He stood, holding the roof of the car, getting his balance. Then he turned and smiled at her, his wide joyous smile.

'I love you, Val,' he said.

'Oh my God. What is it?' she asked again.

'A blockage in the throat. In the oesophagus to be exact.' He put out a hand and she took it. 'They're going to have me in and stretch things a bit. Make it easier for me to swallow.'

'A blockage. Is it – is it – a growth?'

'Cancer? Say it, Val. Don't be afraid of a word.' He squeezed her hand. 'They don't know. They've taken some scrapings. They'll let me know when I go in for the stretch.'

She was paralysed for a moment. Then she gave a

great cry and held him to her and realized, not for the first time, how thin he had become in the past few weeks.

But all she said was, 'If only it were me!'

He ruffled her curls. He did not try to reassure her. He simply said, 'No. Because of Edwina.'

She looked up; saw him through a mist of tears and choked, 'I've got to be strong. Berry – help me to be strong.'

'All right. Let's have some tea.'

By the time Dusty came back it was as if she had lived another lifetime. She told them all about Murch and how wonderful it would be to have her. Dusty asked where Jannie was and she said Jannie was resting.

Berry said, 'I'll go and sit with her a while.'

'I'll take over later, old man.' Dusty took another slice of cake and bounced Roly on his knee. 'So you're leaving us again, Val?'

Val said, 'Berry's not well. The tests show a blockage. It might not be . . . sinister. But then again — '

Dusty was shocked but as optimistic as ever.

'Just because Dad had it, there's no reason to suppose Berry has too.'

'Your father had cancer?'

'Yes. Didn't you know?'

'No.' Val gave Edwina a rusk.

Julie quavered, 'Is Uncle Berry ill?'

'No, of course not!' Dusty swept her on to his other knee. 'The Reids are never ill!'

'Mummy's ill,' Julie reminded him.

'She's not a real Reid.'

Val shook her head at him and said, 'Perhaps that's a good thing. In the circumstances.'

Julie clamoured for explanations then discovered that Ros and Peggotty were going through her school satchel. She leapt on them furiously and there was the usual squabble. Val picked up her own daughter and sat as close to the Aga as she could get. She wondered how she would bear this.

Upstairs, Berry sat close to Jannie's bed and talked quietly as usual.

'Doesn't seem long since Ma and Pa slept in here. Pa was a big man, fairish. Like Hugh. He went to nothing at the end of course.' He smiled into Jannie's unseeing eyes. 'I expect I shall do a spot of wasting away too, Jannie. What will you think of that?'

Jannie was as unresponsive as ever and suddenly Berry grabbed her by the shoulders and shook her.

'Do you hear what I am saying, Jannie Mears? I'm going to die! Quite soon I expect! You said you loved me! You said I'd given you back your self-respect! Well . . . what can you give me now, Jannie? Can't those fish-blue eyes express anything any more?'

He had dragged her half out of the bed and realized her nakedness.

'Look at you! I painted you nude, d'you remember that? All shadows and green water. You weren't ashamed of your body then, Jannie. Now you cower under the clothes . . . you won't wash or feed it. Soon it won't be beautiful. And it will be your own fault.'

She said nothing. Her head hung lifelessly.

He pushed her back into the bed and wrapped her up roughly.

'Christ Almighty, Jannie! You could do something about yourself. I can't do a thing! Not a damned, bloody thing!' He put his hand on her chin and forced her head round to his. 'Do you realize that? I've lost any power I might have had. And you . . . you're throwing yours away!'

He turned and stumped out of the room. Back in the bed, Jannie stared at the door. And began to cry very quietly, very gently.

*   *   *

393

Morag's voice on the telephone started off brightly – 'Val, how nice to hear you,' and then slipped into a very low key indeed. 'Of course we'll come down. Oh Val . . . I'm sure it'll be all right. But of course . . . when?'

'Not too long,' Val said steadily. 'He's had the stretch, so he can take soup and things still. But it is malignant and he won't have an operation or anything, so . . . don't leave it too long.'

'Oh my dear Lord . . .' Morag said. 'Val, I should be encouraging you— '

'Don't be silly. I know what is happening. So does he. We're not afraid.'

'Will you come to Clevedon? To Redley Lodge? I could help you then.'

'I thought of it. But he doesn't want that. This is his place, Mo.'

'Yes. I know.'

'And Mo. Bring Harry with you. I think he and Edwina should know each other.'

Morag said nothing. Unless she intended to cut herself off entirely from Val, it would be impossible to keep Edwina and Harry apart. She had not seen Val now for almost seven months.

Hugh went down that same evening. It was a difficult drive across the dark lanes of the moor and the descent to the abbey was hair-raising. Hugh had always understood Berry's need for isolation; he now understood Val's disinclination to return to this place. The house, silhouetted against the dark sea, looked like something from a Victorian novel. He parked the car and pulled the bell rope and was thankful when the kitchen light jumped on above his head and Val's voice called down reassuringly. Thank God for Val and her practical common sense. Morag wouldn't last a winter in this place.

He was shocked by his brother's appearance. During the autumn as his throat became more and more constricted Berry had been unable to eat solids and his weight had dropped alarmingly.

Hugh said, 'Why didn't you let us know? This hasn't happened overnight. Val – I know Berry is obstinate but you could have phoned Morag.'

She smiled slightly. 'I don't think so.' Her smile deepened as she watched comprehension dawn in his grey eyes. 'Anyway, Hugh, we didn't take it seriously for ages. A sore throat. That's all it was.'

Hugh turned to Berry who was sitting in a chair by the fire. The painting table had been put away; there were at least twenty canvases stacked along the walls. He thought of the comfort of his own sitting room at home.

'Listen, old man. They can operate. Then you can have radium treatment.'

Berry shook his head. 'No operation. No drugs. I like the idea of fading away here. In this room. It will look different. It will change each day.' He nodded towards the television set. 'We've just had a weather forecast. Gales on the way. I'm looking forward to those.'

Hugh looked at Val who was sitting beneath a table lamp with some sewing. Her needle did not pause. She held up a small garment for him to see. It was a pair of dungarees in gingham.

'She's crawling now. You'll see her tomorrow.'

For a moment his mind whirled. He thought that Morag was right and that the further apart they were the better. The situation was . . . ridiculous.

Berry was talking. 'It was good to get back here. The farm is so . . . busy. And poor Jannie looks like a ghost already.'

Hugh's sense of the absurd increased. How on earth had Val coped, looking after the girl who had slept with Berry . . . how had Berry coped?

'No improvement then?' he asked.

'She seemed to respond to Murch. Didn't she, Val?'

Val nodded and continued to sew. 'I think she recognized Murch's disapproval! It must have rung a bell for her from the summer before last or something.'

Berry laughed. 'Poor old Murch. She didn't know

who to blame for all that. Me or Jannie! I think we got equal rating in the end.' He shook his head. 'She'll pull Jannie through if anyone can. Jannie looked after her when she was ill here. They were close. Murch won't forget that.'

'And then she'll come to us,' Val said as if discussing an afternoon tea engagement. 'Just to help me out with Edwina.'

Berry chuckled. 'That will be good for Val's guilt thing. Did I ever tell you about the time she routed Murch's sister-in-law at the hospital? Poor Sister Murchison was determined I shouldn't be let loose with this Shirley Temple look-alike. But . . .' he went on with the story and Hugh listened and managed to smile and tried not to feel as if this was a nightmare.

One by one, sometimes in pairs, people came to say their farewells. Doc Willie and Mrs Maitland; Juliet and her husband with the terrible twins; students who had spent time at the abbey in the past; Morag and Eric. Finally Durston brought Jannie and Mrs Murchison over. Doc Willie, who had never been good at emotion, said briskly, 'I shall look for you out of that window.'

Berry said in his new husky voice, 'I'll be there. Hope I get on with Winnie.'

The doctor looked rueful. 'You will.' She sighed. 'I think – I'm afraid – looking back, my sister was very gullible.'

Berry smiled. 'Well done, Doc. You got there in the end.'

Mrs Maitland wept and held him to her ample chest. 'I know we're all going the same way. But this is just dreadful . . . dreadful.'

Berry kissed her. 'Not unless you make it so.'

He took great pains with the students he considered promising. 'Don't forget the great secret is in the looking. If you can paint a picture that makes the viewer look again with new eyes at the reality, then you've succeeded.'

To Jannie he said, 'Hello, water sprite. You're better.'

She spoke in a shaky whisper. 'I had to get better to come and see you. It's not true, is it, Berry? Tell me it's not true.'

'Everything is true, Jannie. Look at it and believe it, for God's sake. Our ridiculous fling, your ghastly mother, Dusty cracking up and pretending not to. It's all true. It won't go away. Live with the bad bits, cherish the good bits.'

'I don't think I can. Not without you.'

'Bollocks!' he said to make her smile. But she did not. He sighed, dredging up strength to find something that might help. 'You're so damned capable, my girl. The kids . . . cooking . . .' He grinned suddenly, 'Sex. You're wonderful at that.'

She whimpered, 'There's no-one now. Dusty doesn't . . . won't . . .'

Mrs Murchison came into the room and stared in horror at the two of them up to their old tricks again and both of them ill.

'Don't you know any better!' She swept up to Berry's bed and practically lifted Jannie off it. 'Mr Berry has had enough company for this afternoon, thank you very much, miss! And your own husband is waiting to take you home.' She glanced at Berry, her expression softening slightly. 'I'm staying on now. So you've only to ring your bell and I'll be with you.'

'Thanks, Murch.' He was glad for Val's sake. She had been hard put to it dividing her time between Edwina and himself and all the visitors. He looked up at Jannie. 'Keep an eye on Val for me. Won't you? She'll need you.'

Just for a moment it looked as if Jannie might dissolve into tears. Then she disengaged herself gently from Mrs Murchison's iron grip and nodded.

'Of course. You know I will.' And she left the room under her own steam.

* * *

On January the fourth 1958, as the first sputnik finally
burnt itself out in the atmosphere, Berry Reid died.
Dr Harris and Mrs Murchison were both with Val, and
though Berry was in a coma, the doctor assured her that
he could still hear her.

She held him and talked to him steadily until the
faltering pulse in his neck throbbed its last. She never
remembered what she said but she knew it kept the
link between them strong and unbreakable beyond that
moment of death. His response was so strong it was a
physical sensation. Part of Berry came into her own body
that night. She never doubted it for a moment.

And Mrs Murchison said, 'It's snowing . . . look, it's
snowing.'

The flakes looked grey against the window. Val stared at
them knowing that there were colours there somewhere.
And suddenly they became pure white. And then blue.
And then a warm golden shower.

She was not surprised.

CHAPTER TWENTY-FIVE

After the funeral, in the church where Berry and Val had been married twelve years before, they all congregated in the music room at the abbey. Morag was reminded of Margaret McKinley's funeral when she and Val had barely had time to think in between passing sandwiches and making sure everyone had a drink. From her courses with Matthew Arnold she knew that funerals were necessary rituals, but she wished ardently that this one could be over very quickly. She longed with all her heart to be back in the red brick house in Gardens Road at Clevedon, waiting with Harry at the window for the first glimpse of Hugh as he came down from the office. Just as she had waited for her father to return from the infirmary. It was nothing to do with Val . . . surely? There had never been any question somehow of 'forgiving' Val. In fact in some strange way she had not yet worked out, it had not only been her time with Berry that had opened her eyes and heart to her true feelings for Hugh; it had also been discovering that Val loved Hugh. Because she had always known that's how it was. Hugh might have been comforting Val; but Val would never have let it happen if she had not loved Hugh.

Morag had accepted that. In a way, she could have been closer to Val than before . . . because of it. Except for Edwina.

Val, passing her with a tray containing eight cups of tea, said, 'Mo? Are you all right?'

'Of course!' Morag smiled brightly, horrified that her feelings had been so plainly written on her face. 'What about you?'

'I'm fine. I'm enjoying this. Hearing all these lovely

things about Berry.' She smiled over her shoulder. 'Nobody said them when he was around, did they?'

She did not wait for a reply; the question had been rhetorical. Morag looked over a cluster of heads for Hugh and saw him with Eve Mears, obviously trying to keep her from Jannie who was sitting, white-faced and still, by the fire. Morag turned and made for the kitchen and began cutting cake. That too was a mistake because of course Val returned for more tea.

She said, 'Actually, Mo, in reply to your question – seriously now – I am OK.' She poured with a steady hand. 'I must tell you. Probably just an emotional thing of course. But on the night Berry died, the snow changed colour. It was as if he was telling me to keep looking at things. You know how he did that. The snowflakes were just grey in the darkness. Then they changed . . .' She smiled shakily. 'Am I as mad as Jannie?'

'Don't be silly, Val.' Morag swallowed with some determination. She said, 'It's the tears. They refract the light. You remember – science lessons?'

Val laughed. 'I wish you hadn't said that! Anyway, I wasn't crying.'

'A slight film on the surface . . .' Morag was silenced by Val's sudden look. She cleared her throat and went on, 'Colours or no colours, he's with you. You don't need me to tell you that.'

Val finished pouring the tea and put down the pot. It was as if she were waiting for something else from Morag. When it did not come, she said firmly, 'No. I don't.' And then she picked up the tray and left the room. And Morag wanted, more than ever, to go home and pretend none of this had happened.

Dr Harris sipped his tea appreciatively and kept an eye on the clock.

'He was a remarkable man. No-one realized – Vallery excepted of course – that he was in constant pain.'

Mrs Maitland said, 'He drove himself, Doctor.

Didn't he? All that work from twelve years ... it's remarkable.'

Dr Wilkie gave up on Jannie and joined them. She said tentatively, 'It was as if he knew he didn't have long. And he had so much to say through his painting.'

'Yes.' Dr Harris glanced at an abstract in oils entitled 'Life at the sharp end'. He said, 'I'm not the best person to understand exactly what he was saying. But he certainly worked.'

Dr Wilkie said, 'He made me cry. Since Winnie died I've made a point of never weeping.'

Morag overhearing this last remark was suddenly transfixed with her tray of cakes. That was something Berry had done for her too; made her cry. For a moment she could hear his voice saying urgently, 'Mo ... please don't ...'

Mrs Maitland said, 'Shall I take that cake round, Morag dear? You are looking so white and tired.'

Morag passed the tray over without a word and went towards Hugh who was now crouching by Jannie massaging one of her hands between his.

She said without preamble, 'This is too awful. How is Val bearing it?'

Hugh looked up. 'I don't know. I thought you would be with her.' He smiled at Jannie. 'Shall I fetch Val here, Jannie? You'd like to talk to her I expect?'

'No.' Jannie shrank into herself visibly. 'Val is his widow. I can't be his widow.'

Hugh continued to massage the small hand between his own. 'Of course not,' he said gently. 'That's why you might be able to help Val.' He glanced at Morag. 'You go to her, Morrie. Don't let her feel on her own. Not today.'

Morag swallowed. She thought of Harry and Edwina back at the farm being looked after by Mrs Murchison.

She said suddenly, 'Hugh – you should be the one. You go and – and – just be with her. Jannie and I haven't seen each other for ages.'

He stood up slowly. 'Mo . . . this has got to stop.' He spoke in a low voice. 'You have forgiven me. Why can't you forgive Val? She needs you now more than ever.'

'I have forgiven her – of course I have!' She looked at him miserably. 'But you see, there's Edwina.'

He frowned slightly. 'I know. But . . . Berry wanted her so badly. Can't you see that if we let her become a – a problem, we're taking her away from him.' He tried to smile. 'All right, don't look like that, my love. I'll go and talk to Val. Stay with Jannie. She's in a bad way.'

Morag sat on the fender and looked up at Jannie's tiny pinched face.

'Is Mrs Murchison looking after you properly, Jannie?'

'Yes.' Jannie looked into the fire. 'He made me cry. Did you know that?'

Morag almost groaned. Jannie went on, 'When I was ill and didn't do anything he told me he was going to die. He told me I was throwing my life away. He made me cry.'

Morag said slowly, 'I think he made us all cry, Jan.'

'But when I started to cry I got better. Don't you see?'

'Oh yes. I see.'

'And now he's dead. And there's no-one who thinks I'm anything.'

'Don't be ridiculous, Jannie! Dusty isn't good with words, but it's obvious to everyone he adores you!'

Jannie smiled thinly. 'He was making love to Eve. They looked so right together. Like dancers.'

'Oh God . . .'

'In a minute they'll go off. They will make their excuses. And they'll go into one of the monks' cells and they'll do it again. And again. And again.'

'Jannie, stop it! You're torturing yourself quite deliberately. I'm not saying it didn't happen – once perhaps. You know yourself what Eve is like and Dusty is very weak and is so anxious about you . . .' She picked up the hand that Hugh had massaged. It was ice-cold and seemed

402

limp and lifeless. 'Listen, darling. I was thinking. When the better weather comes this spring, will you come to Clevedon? Bring the children. I'd like you to help me with some of my relaxation classes. After all, you've had four children – three naturally and one by Caesarian section, and you've gone through all the horrors of postnatal depression – I'd like you to talk to people realistically about what happens. I think you could help immensely. Will you consider it?'

'Me?' Jannie tried to smile. 'You're trying to find something to take my mind off things, aren't you?'

'I'm trying to think of ways of helping some of my patients, Jannie!'

Jannie succeeded with the smile. But she still looked like a death's head.

'I told you so,' she whispered.

'What?' Morag took her other hand as if pulling her physically out of her living nightmare.

'I told you they would go. Can you see them?'

Morag looked around; then released Jannie's hands and stood up. Dusty and Eve were no longer in the music room.

She said quickly, 'Jannie, they're probably helping Val in the kitchen. Stop imagining things!'

Jannie said, 'Berry would have believed me. I told Berry. Everything. How she shared her boyfriends with me.' The smile widened hideously. 'Now she is sharing my husband. I suppose it's fair and just.'

Morag said, 'I'll go and find them, Jan. Wait here and within five minutes I'll be back with them.' She was suddenly energized by her anger. At that moment she knew that if she found them together she would attack them physically.

Hugh said, 'Val, I'm so sorry. I don't know what to say.'

Val was washing up at the sink overlooking the cliff. She kept glancing out of the window hoping it would snow. It hadn't snowed again since the night Berry died. Of course if it did the cliff track would be impassable. But she still hoped it would. She looked round at her brother-in-law and smiled.

She said, 'You've already said how sorry you were and if there is anything I need you would be only too glad— '

He interrupted. 'Not about Berry. You know how I feel about Berry. I meant about Morag. I thought Berry's death would bring you two close again. It seems not.'

Val put a soapy cup onto the draining board. 'She seems worse if anything.'

'It's Edwina.'

'I can't do anything about that.' Val's smile inverted ruefully. 'I seduced you, Hugh, because I adored your kindness . . . Berry could be unkind. I was a bit in love with you I think. But I didn't reckon on Edwina.' She smiled properly again and patted his arm. 'I don't regret it, Hugh. Because it meant Berry could have a child.' She looked at the dark cliff again; no snow. 'He told me he wanted a child more than anything in the world. It's worth losing Morag for ever to give Berry a baby.' She turned almost fiercely. 'Edwina is going to be Berry's daughter, Hugh. Always. You do understand that?'

'Oh, my dear.' He wanted to hold her. He had wanted to hold Jannie. He laughed shakily, 'You three . . . you must get together somehow.'

'I know. Tell Mo what I've said, will you? It might help.'

'I have . . . pointed that out, actually.' He took the tea towel she was handing him and began drying the cups. 'It needs something . . . to happen. So that Morag realizes how important the three of you are to each other.' He sighed. 'She forgave me so easily, Val. It was almost as if she was glad for me . . . for you.'

Val grinned and butted his shoulder with her forehead. 'No-one could be angry with you for long, Hugh. She is lucky . . . she is very lucky.'

The door opened and Durston came in. He took in the situation and said immediately, 'I haven't seen a thing! Sorry – I'll go elsewhere. I'm hiding from Jannie's frightful ma!'

Hugh exploded. 'For God's sake, Dusty! Why do you always open your mouth and put your foot right in it! Val and I are talking about Morag! As for Eve ... she's gone. That Vallender chap called for her half an hour ago and she slipped off without saying any goodbyes. Thought it would be more tactful.'

Dusty sighed and collapsed into a chair like a deflated balloon.

'Thank God for that! I thought she was after me! One small indiscretion and the female sex imagine you're enslaved for life!' He glanced at Val. 'Sorry, old girl. Tactless again ... I know, I know. Heart's in the right place most of the time though. Which reminds me – how about coming back to the farm with us? You can't stay in this place all on your own – Berry would hate the thought of that.'

Val sat down at the table. 'Daddy, Hugh and Morrie are staying with me tonight, Dusty. And then I want to be here – only for a while. Murch will come back to help me and we'll clear up slowly. Then I'm going to Daddy's.' She glinted at Hugh. 'I know how Mo feels about that, but I can't help it. I want to go back to Redley Lodge.'

'Of course,' he said. Dusty nodded judiciously. 'Best all round,' he said. 'There will be a place for Murch with us. You won't want her in Clevedon, will you?'

Val shook her head at him helplessly. 'No, Dusty. Murch will come back to you. She is devoted to Jannie actually.'

Dusty was making appreciative noises when the door opened and Morag came in. She smiled at Dusty with obvious relief.

'I'm glad to see you. I think you should take Jannie home now before it's completely dark. She's waiting for you.' She bit her lip; she had never been on easy terms with Dusty. 'She needs you. Badly.'

For once in his life Dusty said the right thing. 'And I need her, too.' He stood up. Physically he was like Berry; bigger, more burly. He patted Morag's arm. 'I know you girls worry about Jannie. So do I, of course. But she's getting better. Really. She's getting better. You've both been . . . angels.'

He opened the door and looked down the length of the music room to where Jannie was now standing, gazing towards the windows and the dark sea beyond. People were going in and out of the landing door collecting coats; Jannie was isolated.

Val pushed herself under Dusty's arm and said, 'Jannie!' But Jannie did not hear; she began to move with sudden purpose towards the window-seat. Morag suddenly knew what was in her mind. Winifred Wilkie and her lost love. Jannie Reid and . . . hers. Morag staggered slightly and then started to run towards her; Mrs Maitland was in her way. Jannie was on the window-seat and the casement opened at her touch.

'Jannie!' Morag screamed.

Jannie looked round then. Her eyes were pale sky-blue, wide and despairing. She met Doc Willie's astonished gaze and spoke to her. 'I know how Winnie felt. It's the sensible thing to do. It's not crazy at all. It – it's so obvious.' Then she focused on Morag. 'Don't try to pull me back, Mo. Stay where you are.' She smiled as Morag halted abruptly. 'Golly, you did it! No-one has ever done anything I asked before. Not really. Thank you, Mo.' Now her eyes moved to Val. 'Darling Val. He loved you too, I know. But you see I gave him a son . . . did you know that? Did *you* know, Dusty? Roly is Berry's. And Edwina is Berry's. So . . . look after them well in the future, won't you? They are bound to love each other. Bound to . . .' She sounded dreamy now and her head turned towards the open window. Morag moved slowly towards her.

Val said loudly, 'Jannie – listen to me! Roly is not Berry's child! Neither is Edwina! Berry could not have children. It's a medical fact, darling! Roly is Dusty's son! I promise you I am speaking the truth.'

Jannie turned. Her face was wide open. She looked like a small girl who had been deprived of everything she held dear. She gripped the window-frame and half stood so that her back was wedged into the embrasure. And then she let out a terrible, animal cry.

Morag leapt and as she did so her hair fell from its bun and cascaded around her shoulders. She flung her arms around Jannie's waist and brought her to the ground in a tackle more often seen on the rugby field than the hockey pitch. Her hair was like a screen around them. She held Jannie fiercely, protectively. At the same time Val was there, encircling them both. She was weeping. 'I'm sorry, Jannie . . . so sorry.'

The three girls knelt together, a tight trio, their faces invisible behind Morag's hair. Hugh went to the window and fastened it securely. Dr Wilkie said, 'Maitie dear, I think we should all leave.' Dusty seemed turned to stone, gazing down at the three women, his face working uncontrollably.

Hugh said, 'I think it might be best. Are the lights all on? Eric, shall we see people to their cars?'

Eric indicated the three crouching women. 'Should we leave them?'

Hugh said confidently, 'Dusty is here. He'll keep an eye.' He smiled at Eric. 'I think it might be all right now.'

Everyone drifted out, muttering farewells to Dusty, hesitating by the women then moving away. At last the room, hazy with cigarette smoke, redolent still of paint and brush cleaner, was still. Dusty sat down shakily near the fire. The silence cocooned them.

Morag was breathing fast; she said jerkily in a low voice, 'There's nothing to be sorry for. None of us must be sorry. Not any more. We've got each other. We're together. We forgot that . . . for a time.' She touched Jannie's forehead with her lips and said quietly, 'Hugh is Edwina's natural father, Jannie.'

For a few seconds more Jannie continued to weep; then Morag's words sank in and she stopped, hiccuping on sobs. She leaned back from the tight triangle to look from Val to Morag. Then she whimpered and said, 'Poor Morrie . . . the strong one . . . poor Morrie.' She drew Morag's head to hers again, offering comfort. And then, quite suddenly, she did the same to Val so that both of them rested on Jannie's thin shoulders. It looked incongruous, as if Jannie must collapse beneath their weight. But she did not.

After a while Val said huskily, 'We said no apologies. But I want you to know – both of you – that even though Berry was infertile, I shall always think of him as Edwina's father.'

The silence went on very gently and then the three began to disengage themselves. Morag said, 'Thank you, Val.'

Val said quickly, 'It wasn't an apology.'

Morag managed a small laugh. 'No. To me, it sounded like an absolution.'

Unexpectedly, Jannie said, 'That's how it sounded to me, too.' She released her hold and moved Morag's hair so that it fell in a cascade down her back. 'I didn't realize, Val . . . it was a heavy burden.' She looked up suddenly to where Dusty was watching them. Her voice quavered up and down the scale. 'I – I'm glad Roly is – is – ours, darling. I'm glad.'

For once in his life, Durston was silent. He nodded.

Jannie sat back on her heels. 'I think I can let Berry go now. I have to let him go, don't I, Mo?'

And Morag said, 'Yes.'

That summer, after much consultation, Lyn Abbey was converted into a school of art in memory of Berry Reid. The dark old hall was extended into the side rooms so that it became an enormous gallery lit from all sides; teaching went on in there even as visitors walked around viewing the paintings. The music room was where the master classes were held; the monks' old cells made excellent bedrooms for the students.

Dr Wilkie retired from the Bluebell School that July, and she took over as principal of Berry's – as it soon became known – and lived with Mrs Maitland in the basement flat. Sometimes, during a gale, she would stare out of the small round windows at the flying spray as if she could see people out there. When Val was visiting with Edwina, she would join her.

'It's so exciting,' she commented as the sea hammered to come inside.

Doc Willie nodded. 'Berry was always exciting,' she said. She thought about it. 'So was my sister,' she said as if making a discovery.

Val never saw snow change its colour again. But she knew it had. She told Edwina about it in her stories so that if ever it happened to her, she would know why. And when Edwina was ten years old she told her cousins, Harry and Roly, about it.

Roly laughed uproariously. He thought the Clevedon Reids were 'soppy' anyway because they couldn't skin a rabbit or set a trap for a mouse. But Harry nodded with the air of wisdom which he seemed to have been born with.

'It depends how you look at it,' he said frowning at Roly. 'I bet you think that dandelion is yellow, don't you?'

'Oh no!' Roly made a face. 'I think it's made of pure gold! Eh, Teddy? Eh?'

'Twit,' Harry commented without rancour. 'If you look, each of the yellow bits are actually a different colour. Orange . . . even white.' He picked the dandelion and held it up for them to see. Edwina was entranced but did not want to show it. Harry was younger than she was by a whole month and Roly was older by another month. And Roly could set traps, and skin rabbits and stalk the Exmoor deer.

She said, 'Yes. But *snow* . . .'

'It's just white,' Roly said with finality.

'But white . . . what is white? White isn't a colour. It's there waiting for colour to . . . to . . . come.' Harry waved his hands helplessly. He looked at his much-loved girl cousin. '*You* know,' he said.

And Edwina did know, but she couldn't admit it in front of Roly. So she shook her curls frantically to make both boys laugh and wondered why she got on so well with Harry when they were alone, and with Roly when they were alone, but not with Roly and Harry together.

It was that year – 1968 – in November, that Val heard of a young American artist who had a one-man show in a tiny gallery in Chepstow. She telephoned Jannie immediately.

'Leave the children to Murch for the weekend. I want the three of us to go and see this exhibition together.'

'Why?' It was a long time since Jannie had tried to throw herself out of the music room window, but she was still unwilling to go very far from the farm. Peggy was pressing for them all to go to Australia 'and see what farming is really about', but Jannie felt safe in her corner of Exmoor. She liked shopping in Barnstaple – even Exeter – and she would spend a day at the abbey with Maitie and Doc Willie, but Clevedon was nearly three hours' drive away.

'Well . . . I've got a funny feeling about this artist. He's not thirty years old. He's from the States. And his name is Prosser Stevenson.'

'Typical American name.' Jannie paused. She thought she should know that name. Stevenson. She frowned, concentrating. Through the kitchen window she could see Durston practically wading through the mud. It had rained incessantly for three weeks. She could imagine Redley Lodge with its central heating and

410

thick carpets. And Edwina was no trouble at all. Not like her four.

She said, 'All right. I'll come by train. What a month to be visiting.'

'I don't like November,' Val agreed. 'But maybe this year something good will come of it. Doc Willie needs new blood down at the abbey. This might be the answer.'

She telephoned Morag next. Morag caught on immediately.

'It couldn't be. Could it?' she asked.

'That's what we're going to discover,' Val said with her usual common sense.

The gallery was in Castle Street, small and on three floors. The rain made the windows opaque and the grey November light did not do the exhibition justice. Even so, it was possible to see that this artist loved colour.

Morag said doubtfully, 'Garish, d'you think?'

'Not at all!' Val was definite. 'He's painting light. Sunlight – strong, very strong sunlight. Look at the shadows. That tells you how strong it is.'

Jannie flipped through the catalogue. '"Mexican Pampas",' she murmured.

'There you are.' Val was triumphant. 'And what about number twenty-four?'

Jannie looked again. '"Table Mountain"', she murmured. 'That's South Africa, isn't it? So you're right, Val.'

'What would he make of Exmoor in the winter?' Morag wondered.

'Are you going to offer him a place at Berry's?' Jannie asked.

'I think so. Don't you?'

Val looked towards the stairway. A young man was coming into view in deep conversation with a woman in her twenties. He was dark, broad-shouldered. He could have been Berry.

Val said, 'Caroline Prosser, Jannie. She disappeared rather quickly that autumn term of forty-one – d'you remember? She was being evacuated to America. To get away from the war. And ... perhaps ... from disgrace.'

Morag was smiling almost against her will. 'Berry admired her figure very much if I recall.'

Jannie's face was suddenly open with comprehension. 'My dear Lord,' she breathed. 'He asked her to go dancing with him!' She looked at the other two, incredulous, almost outraged.

Val said quietly, 'How wonderful. Girls ... how wonderful! Berry has a son. As well as a daughter, he has a son.' She took their hands. Her eyes were dark blue and enormous.

The three of them stood very still, watching Prosser Stevenson cross the room and examine one of the catalogues. They could so easily have wept. Instead, they began to laugh. And when he looked up and raised his brows at them, it was Morag who said, 'Could we have a word with you? When you're free of course.'

He grinned and showed beautiful American teeth. He said, 'I'm always free to talk to ladies.'

The four of them stood there for some time, laughing. Together.

THE END

THE KEYS TO THE GARDEN
by Susan Sallis

Widowed Martha Moreton was a devoted mother to her only child, Lucy, and when Lucy married Len on a golden July day, Martha tried hard to make the best of things. Len was a good man who would make Lucy happy. They wouldn't be living far away. And the arrival of grandchildren was something she anticipated eagerly.

Unexpectedly, Len's job took the newly married couple overseas, where their first child was born. But sorrow, not joy, came with Dominic's birth. On their return, Lucy's best friend, Jennifer, as flighty as Lucy was conventional, was anxious to provide her own kind of consolation . . .

Martha, who was experiencing unlooked-for and at first unwelcome changes in own her life, clung fast to the maternal bond that meant so much to herself and Lucy. Everything she had come to depend on was overturned, however, before Martha was able to find her own kind of happiness in a very different existence.

One of Susan Sallis's most poignant and involving novels, *The Keys to the Garden* explores the mother-daughter relationship with a rare insight.

0 552 14671 4

COME RAIN OR SHINE
by Susan Sallis

There were four of them: young women, dressed decorously in black, employed at an exclusive jewellery store in the 1960s. Close friendships were forged as Natasha, Prudence, Rachel and Maisie worked together under the benevolent rule of the two Markham brothers.

Years later Natasha, newly divorced and back from America with a fifteen-year-old daughter, decides there must be a reunion. Pru, always the mysterious one, unexpectedly offers Prospect House, a property she has inherited in the Malvern Hills where they may all forgather. Rachel, married to her former boss, a Liberal MP, gladly leaves a tangled domestic situation to join the friends she hasn't seen for so long. And Maisie . . . Maisie, perhaps the most vulnerable of the four, mother of five children, wife of the unpredictable Edward, fails to arrive at Prospect House. The drama of her disappearance has a far-reaching effect on the lives and destinies of them all.

0 552 14636 6

CHOICES
by Susan Sallis

On an expedition to choose her wedding dress, accompanied by her fiancé Miles and her parents, Helen Wilson's life changed without warning. A devastating car crash left her with only memories for consolation.

As Helen came to terms with her loss, she discovered that Miles had kept something from her which made her see him in a very different light. She moved to Flatners, a cottage overlooking the Bristol Channel, and with her new friends – pretty Peggy and her small daughter Rosie – living next door, Helen settled into an entirely new existence. While encouraging Peggy's relationship with Joshua, a social worker, Helen became aware of her own complex feelings towards Harry Vallender, the previous owner of Flatners.

Harry had a very special reason for wanting to know Helen. In the aftermath of death and lives turned upside down, love tentatively began to flower . . .

0 552 14549 1

A SELECTED LIST OF FINE NOVELS
AVAILABLE FROM CORGI BOOKS

THE PRICES SHOWN BELOW WERE CORRECT AT THE TIME OF GOING TO
PRESS. HOWEVER TRANSWORLD PUBLISHERS RESERVE THE RIGHT TO
SHOW NEW RETAIL PRICES ON COVERS WHICH MAY DIFFER FROM
THOSE PREVIOUSLY ADVERTISED IN THE TEXT OR ELSEWHERE.

☐	14060 0	**MERSEY BLUES**	*Lyn Andrews*	£5.99
☐	14448 7	**DREAM CATCHER**	*Iris Gower*	£5.99
☐	14537 8	**APPLE BLOSSOM TIME**	*Kathryn Haig*	£5.99
☐	14567 X	**THE CORNER HOUSE**	*Ruth Hamilton*	£5.99
☐	14686 2	**CITY OF GEMS**	*Caroline Harvey*	£5.99
☐	14692 7	**THE PARADISE GARDEN**	*Joan Hessayon*	£5.99
☐	14599 8	**FOOTPRINTS ON THE SAND**	*Judith Lennox*	£5.99
☐	14603 X	**THE SHADOW CHILD**	*Judith Lennox*	£5.99
☐	14492 4	**THE CREW**	*Margaret Mayhew*	£5.99
☐	14693 5	**THE LITTLE SHIP**	*Margaret Mayhew*	£5.99
☐	14752 4	**WITHOUT CHARITY**	*Michelle Paver*	£5.99
☐	14753 2	**A PLACE IN THE HILLS**	*Michelle Paver*	£5.99
☐	12375 7	**A SCATTERING OF DAISIES**	*Susan Sallis*	£5.99
☐	12579 2	**THE DAFFODILS OF NEWENT**	*Susan Sallis*	£5.99
☐	12880 5	**BLUEBELL WINDOWS**	*Susan Sallis*	£5.99
☐	13136 9	**ROSEMARY FOR REMEMBRANCE**	*Susan Sallis*	£5.99
☐	13756 1	**AN ORDINARY WOMAN**	*Susan Sallis*	£5.99
☐	13934 3	**DAUGHTERS OF THE MOON**	*Susan Sallis*	£5.99
☐	13346 9	**SUMMER VISITORS**	*Susan Sallis*	£5.99
☐	13545 3	**BY SUN AND CANDLELIGHT**	*Susan Sallis*	£5.99
☐	14162 3	**SWEETER THAN WINE**	*Susan Sallis*	£4.99
☐	14318 9	**WATER UNDER THE BRIDGE**	*Susan Sallis*	£5.99
☐	14549 1	**CHOICES**	*Susan Sallis*	£5.99
☐	14636 6	**COME RAIN OR SHINE**	*Susan Sallis*	£5.99
☐	14671 4	**THE KEYS TO THE GARDEN**	*Susan Sallis*	£5.99
☐	14747 8	**THE APPLE BARREL**	*Susan Sallis*	£5.99
☐	14867 9	**SEA OF DREAMS**	*Susan Sallis*	£5.99
☐	14744 3	**TOMORROW IS ANOTHER DAY**	*Mary Jane Staples*	£5.99
☐	14740 0	**EMILY**	*Valerie Wood*	£5.99

All Transworld titles are available by post from:

Bookpost, P.O. Box 29, Douglas, Isle of Man IM99 1BQ

Credit cards accepted. Please telephone 01624 836000,
fax 01624 837033, Internet http://www.bookpost.co.uk or
e-mail: bookshop@enterprise.net for details.

Free postage and packing in the UK. Overseas customers allow
£1 per book (paperbacks) and £3 per book (hardbacks).